WITH

FEB 0 7 2019

A SUDDEN DEATH IN CYPRUS

A SUDDEN DEATH
IN CYPRUS

Michael Grant

This first world edition published 2018
in Great Britain and 2019 in the USA by
SEVERN HOUSE PUBLISHERS LTD of
Eardley House, 4 Uxbridge Street, London W8 7SY.
Trade paperback edition first published
in Great Britain and the USA 2019 by
SEVERN HOUSE PUBLISHERS LTD.

British Library Cataloguing in Publication Data
A CIP catalogue record for this title is available from the British Library.

ISBN-13: 978-0-7278-8835-8 (cased)
ISBN-13: 978-1-84751-960-3 (trade paper)
ISBN-13: 978-1-4483-0170-6 (e-book)

All Severn House titles are printed on acid-free paper.

Severn House Publishers support the Forest Stewardship Council™ [FSC™],
the leading international forest certification organisation.
All our titles that are printed on FSC certified paper carry the FSC logo.

Typeset by Palimpsest Book Production Ltd.,
Falkirk, Stirlingshire, Scotland.
Printed and bound in Great Britain by
TJ International, Padstow, Cornwall.

For Katherine (K.A.) Applegate, the real girl in the window.

ONE

At any given moment there are about two hundred thousand fugitives from American justice and about forty thousand fugitives from Her Majesty's justice, running free in the world. Two of those fugitives, one from each nation, were within fifty yards of each other on the beach a bit north of Paphos, on the Mediterranean island nation of Cyprus.

One was about to die. The other was not.

I was the 'not.'

I wasn't strictly on the beach, rather I was on a stool beside the tiki bar drinking Keo, the execrable local beer, and wondering if the immediate vicinity was sufficiently sparsely-populated that I could light a cigar without causing a riot. Cypriots probably wouldn't care, but this was not a Cypriot beach, it was a tourist and expat beach. The Paphos region at the extreme western edge of Cyprus is home to thousands of expats, mostly Brits, but with Russians, Germans, Israelis, Lebanese, various Balkan types, Scandinavians and the occasional American thrown in for good measure.

The British fugitive, the one who was about to be subtracted, was a woman, perhaps forty-five, with forgettable brown hair and shoulders that glowed faintly pink, suggesting a failure of sunblock. She lay on a blue-and-white-striped canvas chaise longue, facing the sea, her back to me. Her chaise was tilted at just the right angle to aim her cleavage in my general direction, though I doubt it was intentional, but as I had already seen a fair bit of the Mediterranean, and all of the beach, and there was nothing more compelling presenting itself, I spent some time contemplating those sunburned swells.

She was not on sand – there are precious few sand beaches on Cyprus, and the Turks have the best of them – but on the grass just before the sea wall which left her two or three feet above the narrow, pebbly strand below. Her chaise was in a row of identical chairs and she was reading a book on actual paper. A bottle of local white wine – rather better than the beer – rested in a bucket at her elbow. Like approximately all women over the age of bikini, she wore a broad straw hat and whenever she looked up, the back of her hat came down and blocked my view. When she looked back down at the book, I saw plump pink breasts and a blue one-piece bathing suit and legs that probably looked better without perspective turning them into tapers ending in tiny sandals.

'Peek-a-boob,' I said to Theodoros, the barman, as the hat brim lifted again.

Theodoros – twenty-something, dark bed head, dark bedroom eyes, with competent but accented English and a degree in chemistry – stopped polishing a glass and stared at me.

I grinned at him. 'See, it's peek-a-boob because—'

'I understand, Mr Mitre. I'm just not going to encourage you with a phony laugh.'

I couldn't see the book the woman was reading, but my few needy glimpses of the cover assured me that it was not one of mine. I write. Now. Didn't always write, but now I write and have produced five reasonably well-received, and moderately successful – or perhaps not entirely *un*successful – mystery novels, all set in the city of New Midlands, a fictional locale located almost exactly where you'd find Chicago. New Midlands: Chicago, but with far more rich and attractive people committing far more complex and fascinating crimes than actual criminals have the energy, imagination or resources to pull off.

'I've heard you phony-laugh for customers before, Theo,' I said.

'My contempt for that particular . . . *jape* . . . is evidence of my underlying respect for you, Mr Mitre.'

I liked Theodoros because he spoke English well enough to get a joke. Everyone on Cyprus speaks English, or thinks they do, but Greek to English is a big leap and few manage it. There aren't many bartenders who can drop *jape* into conversation.

'Well, grab me another beer, Theo, and I'll come up with a more sophisticated witticism.'

My name is David Mitre, at present. I've gone through a few names, including the insufferable 'Carter Cannon,' which was ridiculous, like a superhero's alliterative secret identity. I've also been Martin, Alex, Frank, Thomas, Michael and now, David. The David Mitre Wikipedia page uses the word 'reclusive' three times. There's an author headshot but it doesn't take much Google-fu to discover that it's a stock photo. The model looks a bit like me, but not really. For one thing, Mr Stock Photo grows a much more convincing beard than I could ever manage; I stay clean-shaven. Mr Stock Photo also doesn't quite capture the subtle fight-or-flight paranoia that radiates from me.

Here is why I kept focusing on the woman with the cleavage: because of the way she was looking around. People generally do look around a bit when they're on a pleasant green verge beside sparkling water, but there are different ways of doing it. A person waiting on someone will look and then check their watch or phone. A person enjoying scenery will let their gaze wander, left, right, up, right again, maybe whip out that phone for a picture. But she wasn't looking for a waiter – she had barely touched her wine. And she wasn't looking for a toilet, she'd gone ten minutes earlier.

Ms Cleavage – probably not her real name – was looking around in a more methodical way. She would read her book for almost exactly two minutes, then scan left to right. All the way left, all the way right.

If I were a character in my own fiction, I might claim to have pulled a Sherlock and immediately deduced that she was one of the fugitive tribe in which I hold membership. But that would be stretching a point. I was looking at her because something about the way she scanned the world around her bothered me, and I have no better explanation than that. Just something off.

I didn't really sense anything unusual was about to happen until I caught sight of the waiter, entering stage left.

I, too, look around more than strictly necessary. I had discovered Fugitive Vision soon after jumping bail in Reno, Nevada nineteen years ago. How we look at the world – physically, not metaphorically – is very much a matter of culture, and westerners tend to focus about ten to twenty yards out, occasionally widening to take in context, but mostly folks look to recognize a face, a face that is in their immediate vicinity. Fugitive Vision pushes out further so you focus about a hundred yards out, looking for faces the instant they are close enough to be recognized. Like submarine warfare, it's all about seeing before you are seen.

The waiter was a black African, Somali maybe, presumably one of the luckier refugees to come ashore in this refugee-besieged nation, and had caught my eye not because he was anyone who might recognize me but because of the way he moved. Among the many jobs I've held in my forty-something years is waiter. I know how waiters move and it wasn't like this. The waiter had a drinks tray on his left palm – so far so good – but he steadied the wine bottle upon it with his right hand. And the bottle itself was positioned toward the edge. The outer edge. Which, as any half-bright server would know, was madness. Or at least awkwardness.

There are two ways for a waiter to carry a wine bottle: in the center of the tray, or in his hand with the tray folded under his arm.

Then there was the way he walked, loping, swaying a bit, side to side. Watch a waiter move sometime: it's left in front of right in front of left. And there will be a swivel to the hips useful for cutting close to tables and chairs. This guy moved like Jar-Jar Binks, or the guy from the Grateful Dead 'Truckin'' logo. No wonder he couldn't balance a bottle.

An impressive yacht, practically a pocket-sized cruise ship glided by like an iceberg passing by on a conveyor belt. Tan young women in small bathing suits waved at us. Theodoros brought me the beer.

'You've got to start stocking better beer, Theo.'

'I have Peroni.'

'Like I said.'

Ms Cleavage looked up as the vendor's shadow fell over her. I saw her shake her head, 'no, not for me,' and return her gaze to the book.

The waiter knelt, set the tray carefully on the grass and reached into his pocket for his wine opener.

Then I saw the knife.

It was a serious knife with a double-edged, seven-inch, blued blade. This was not a pocketknife or something lifted from the kitchen, this was a professional's tool. The vendor bent over

Ms Cleavage, too close, as though he was speaking to her in a whisper. She looked up again, annoyed now. I caught a glimpse of her face reflected in his mirrored shades.

He slapped his left hand over her mouth. His right hand went behind the chaise longue and stabbed the blade right through the blue-and-white-striped canvas.

The blade entered around what I guessed would be the latissimus dorsi. He worked the knife inside her, pushing down on the leather-wrapped handle to lever the blade upward and slice into her lungs, then pulling upward, muscles straining, to force the tip down toward her liver. Then he twisted the knife in place, widening the entry wound. This all took maybe four seconds.

The woman jerked. Spasmed. And again. And a kick that sent one sandal flying.

But it was over quickly. The African might not be much use as a waiter but he knew his business with a knife.

Despite his twisting, he had to get his body weight into the job of pulling the knife out and when he did blood gushed from the tear in the fabric, splashing red on the grass. Christmas colors, red and green.

I shot a look at Theodoros. He had not seen. No one had, not yet.

I got up from my stool, beer in hand, said, 'Put it on my tab, I have an appointment.'

Theodoros nodded, preoccupied with new customers, and I walked directly away, up toward the resort hotel. I was on the terrace when the first scream rose behind me. I put on a frown and looked around in a perfunctory, befuddled sort of way for the benefit of any possible cameras, shrugged and went on through to the hotel's lower level, up the stairs to the main lobby and out to my car.

I got in and drove away keeping to the speed limit not for fear of traffic cops but because it's hard to concentrate when you're shaking and fighting the urge to vomit.

When the killer had pulled the knife out it was like slicing a wineskin. That was not a memory I wished to savor, but imagination – so very useful in my current profession as writer – now supplied lurid and detailed mental images of internal

organs crudely butchered. I'd been too far away to hear anything
but a slight gasp, but ever-helpful imagination provided sound
effects of cleavers on rump roasts.

I have not lived a sheltered life. I've seen people in the act
of being killed. It's not a good thing to see, but I had more
immediate issues to deal with. There's the old line from
Casablanca. 'Round up the usual suspects.' It doesn't matter
what the crime is, a fugitive is automatically a 'usual suspect'
and my passport, which passed muster at border crossings, could
start raising red flags if cops really started looking.

So, I drove off, congratulating myself on quick thinking,
regretting only the excuse I had given. An *appointment*? That
could come back to haunt me.

When I got back to my rented hillside villa I poured myself
half a tumbler of Talisker and drank it down as my nerves
jumped and twitched.

We all see murders on TV and in movies or read about it in
books; it's a very different thing when you see it in real life.
There is a terrible wrongness to it, something you feel in your
soul – if you believe in such things as souls.

I told myself it was someone else's tragedy, not mine. I
reminded myself that I am not superstitious and that it was in
no way an omen or a warning. I told myself it really didn't
matter and had nothing at all to do with me.

And it didn't. Until it did.

TWO

My rented villa had come with an unexpected nuisance:
the lower floor was rented separately. I had learned
this only upon moving in and my landlady, Dame Stella
Weedon, a Brit expat, tried to la-di-da it away as some sort of
local custom. But the reality was more sinister. There was a
movie shooting on the island, a rom-com of some sort involving
George Selkirk, then fifty-one years old, and an unknown
French actress half his age named Minette. Just Minette.

In the world of clickbait, they were known as Kirkette because the alternatives were Morge, Selette and Georgette.

The downstairs renter was not Minette or George, let alone Kirkette; the downstairs renter was Chante Mokrani. Chante – pronounced 'shont' unless you wanted her to punch you in the neck – was personal assistant to Minette, and Dame Stella would have given her last sleeve of Hobnobs to get either part or all of Kirkette to attend one of her frequent parties.

My first encounter with Chante had come when I marched downstairs to ask her to turn down her music.

'Hi. I'm the guy who lives upstairs,' I said by way of introduction.

My first impression of her was that her first impression of me was unfavorable. It was dislike at first sight. She disliked everything about me, every detail, as she looked me up and down and back up again. It wasn't actual hate, it was more a sort of disappointment, as if I was the birthday present she really did not want or a dish she had not ordered.

This was disturbing to me. I'm a good-looking guy. I'm not George Selkirk, maybe, but women simply do not turn their noses up at me on first sight. Usually they don't actively dislike me until I've emptied one or more of their bank accounts. Sometimes not even then.

'Yes?' Chante Mokrani said.

'The music. I was wondering if you could turn it down.'

'Why?'

'Why?'

'Yes. Why?'

So, right away I knew she wasn't British. A Brit would have apologized and turned it off entirely. He would have called me a wanker as soon as I was out of earshot, but first he'd have turned it off.

Chante was on the elfin side, not tall, with stylishly-cut, vaguely punkish black hair, several piercings, moderate gauges in her ears, angry dark eyes and a thin-lipped mouth which did not raise expectations of warm smiles.

'Because it is very loud,' I explained. I added hand gestures, pointing at my ears with both index fingers.

She shook her head. 'No, it is not very loud. It is fado, not rock music. Fado.'

'Yes, I know it's fado—'

'Tânia Oleiro.'

'I'm just not that crazy about Portuguese blues cranked up to eleven.'

That made her blink. She had not expected me to recognize fado, the mournful Portuguese version of blues, full of lost loves and, presumably, complaints about Spaniards.

'It is not the volume you complain of,' she said with a French accent. 'It is that it makes you sad.'

Normally at that point, confronting a not-yet-charmed woman commenting on my emotional state, I'd have tried still harder to charm her, perhaps charm her into bed. But I had at least fifteen years on her and she was very far from finding me tolerable, let alone charming.

'What if I don't wish to be sad?' I said, adding a *so-there* smile.

'Ah,' Chante said, nodded wisely. And closed the door.

And left the music playing at volume.

The second time I'd run into her had been in my kitchen. I had come stumbling down out of my bedroom at the ungodly hour of ten in the morning wearing nothing but underpants and found her going through my cupboards.

'What the hell?' I had demanded with regrettable lack of originality.

'Birthday candles. Do you have any birthday candles?'

'What in the holy fuck would I be doing with birthday candles?'

'Minette wishes to have a birthday party for Amadou.'

My raised eyebrow elicited the explanation:

'Amadou is her dog.'

'Of course it is. How did you get in?'

'Both doors have the same key,' she explained. Not even a hint of defensiveness mind you, no consciousness of guilt. If I pulled that sort of . . . Well, I *had* pulled that sort of thing many times actually, but not recently.

The third meeting happened the morning after the murder. Once again I stumbled down the stairs from my bedroom, aiming like a wobbly missile toward the coffee maker, when I found her in my kitchen.

'Jesus Christ. What, more candles for your movie star's dog?'

'Only an egg. You have no eggs?'

'I have eggs in the fridge.'

'But why would you put eggs in a refrigerator?'

'It's how we do things in America,' I said and pushed the start button on the coffee machine. 'What do you need an egg for?'

'I am making a piperade.'

This was my chance to once again display my erudition and basically stun her into admiration. 'What are you doing for espelette peppers?'

Oh yeah: that stopped her. She withdrew from the refrigerator holding a carton of six eggs and stared at me with dark, distrustful eyes. 'Aleppo peppers. You can find them in the farmer's markets.'

'Piperade with eggs.' I nodded reluctant approval. It was acceptable. In fact it sounded good, and I suspected would sound even better once I had my coffee. 'Is that for your movie star?'

'Minette has no scenes today. She is spending the day with a friend.'

'Friend, huh? That sounds like juicy Hollywood gossip.'

'Do you like such gossip?' Her English was very good, but still *goh-SEEP* sounded cutely French.

'The very act of telling you how little I care about Hollywood gossip exhausts my entire year's allowance of interest in Hollywood gossip.'

She took that on-board. She had a habit of looking away when she was thinking, like she wasn't looking at you, but at your shadow. It wasn't a stare into emptiness, it was as if she saw someone standing immediately behind you, peeking over your shoulder. She focused on that visual echo.

'Ah,' she said, then nodded, turned and walked off with my eggs.

'Agenda item,' I muttered. 'Chain lock. Or a Rottweiler.'

I poured coffee and carried it and my laptop out onto the patio. The sun was up, the Mediterranean was sparkling and dotted with happy sailboats, the coffee was hot and bitter, and aside from the fact that I'd been thirty feet from a grisly murder the day before, all was right with the world.

I have a morning routine that involves signing onto a VPN, opening an incognito window in my browser and googling my aliases, filtering for the previous twenty-four hours.

Nothing. There never was. Still . . .

I closed the incognito window and went to Goodreads to obsessively read the most recent reviews of my books. This was accompanied by grunts of approval or angry snorts of dismissal.

'Go get eating utensils, hurry while it is hot!'

I spun around, guilty, and closed my laptop like I'd been looking at porn. Chante had three plates balanced on her left arm like a diner waitress, two dishes of spicy red piperade with an egg coddled in the middle, still cooking from the heat. The third plate was toast.

I really saw no alternative to getting silverware. Also napkins, marmalade, butter and salt.

I sat facing the prime view, Chante took the chair to my right and turned it halfway, either to see the water or avoid seeing me.

I pierced the eggs and let the yolk spread creamy goodness. I took a bite. Cocked an eyebrow at her. Took another bite.

'This is actually good.'

'Yes.'

'You cook.'

'*Évidemment*,' she said, which is French for 'duh.'

'No, I mean you *cook*. The dish is perfectly seasoned, the presentation is professional, no dribbles or greasy thumbprints on the plate. The egg isn't off by twenty seconds either way, so you may have actually taken into account how much it would continue cooking as you carried the plates up here.'

She briefly made eye contact before explaining to my shadow, 'I have had some training.'

'You cook for what's her name?'

'I do many things for Minette. I am her assistant.' She betrayed a hint of pride.

I nodded. 'Cool.' We ate and then sat back and relaxed until it was clear that in this relationship I was the busboy. I cleared dishes and brought us both fresh coffees.

'Will you write now?' Chante asked.

I frowned. 'You know who I am?'

'I know that you are a writer. Madame Stella told me. She said you would be quiet.'

'I don't suppose you've read any . . .'

Her look was either pitying or contemptuous, somewhere on that scale. 'I do not read popular books.'

Great. She was a snob. A French snob, no less, and no one can touch a French snob, it goes deep with them, especially as regards food or literature. Or language. Or clothing. Art. Architecture. Philosophy. Almost anything, really.

'Don't worry, I'm not that popular,' I said with acid sarcasm.

'No,' she agreed. Like she had checked my BookScan numbers.

Yeah, well, my latest barely missed the *New York Times* list, I'm outselling most of Elmore Leonard's backlist, and I was shortlisted for an Edgar, so fuck you. I did not say.

She stood up. 'You can leave the plates on the little table beside my door,' she said. 'I must go to the market. Is there anything I can bring you?'

'Eggs,' I said. 'Someone took mine.'

'And the money?'

Had I been the violent as opposed to the nonviolent sort of ex-criminal, that's when I would have strangled her. I fished out a twenty-euro note. 'Bring me the change.'

When she was gone, I spent some time looking up coverage of the murder on the beach on several English language Cyprus news sites, as well as Google-translated Greek language sites.

The consensus was clear: murder was bad. Murdering a foreign tourist was arguably worse (though the Greek language papers were less convinced of that).

Police were releasing no details, but had issued an official statement which read in part, 'Haven't got a fucking clue.' Or words to that effect.

I read the comments sections because they're often a better insight into attitudes and you get information that doesn't quite rise to the publishable level. In this case, the killer was black, therefore obviously an immigrant or refugee and, well, shrug, that's what happened when you let in people who were not

Greek. So sorry for all those refugees, but we can't very well have them stabbing tourists. Some comments pointed to the murder of an expat nine months earlier and suggested that a wave of expat-related murder was sweeping the island nation, which might well lead to a panicked exodus of expats and there goes the real-estate market.

All fine by me, I was in Cyprus but not permanently, I had a one-year lease with eleven months to go. So, if a woman being stabbed to death in Paphos was an excuse to shrug and blame nonwhite outsiders – deplorable, certainly – but all the better for me: the less hue and cry the less likelihood of me being dragged into it.

I opened the travel article I was supposed to be writing for *GQ* magazine, reminded myself of where I'd left off and what I needed to write next, and got down to it, convinced that I was as safe as ever I could be.

THREE

'**M**r Mitre, I am so glad you could come!'
'David, please, and I wouldn't miss it. I was honored to be invited.'

Not true. Left to my own preferences I would not have attended the party, but if I meant to blend in rather than attract attention, I had to curb my misanthropy. If you don't meet people when you move somewhere new, you don't know who to toady, who to ignore, who to keep an eye on and most importantly, who to bribe.

So, when Dame Stella Weedon, along with her dotard husband, Sir Archibald Weedon, had invited me to a soiree at her much larger villa and made it clear in that politely insistent way that the British do so well that I was expected to show up and play the part of the largely obscure visiting author in her cast of partiers, I agreed.

Dame Stella was just the sort of woman I'd have aimed my charm at back in the old days. She had family money of some sort and was not at all bad-looking, a very well-preserved fifty or maybe fifty-two, so not ridiculously older than I. She had expensively blonde hair, a forehead Botoxed to marble, and the tanned and well-displayed legs of a younger woman. She wore an overly-vivid floral pattern dress, which was the second thing I noticed after the white gold-and-diamond necklace that must have made someone at De Beers happy. I ballparked it at about seventy-five grand USD. A fence might get forty, meaning I'd clear a good twenty, twenty-five. And the necklace almost certainly had brothers and sisters in an easily-popped safe.

Not that I was . . . But you have to *look*. Looking is not illegal.

Introductions followed, variations on 'Instantly-forgettable person? I'd like you to meet David Mitre, the mystery novelist you've never heard of but now have to pretend to be a fan of.'

They were happy, they were charmed, they were excited, they were indifferent. I matched one of those emotions, but I'm a capable enough actor to appear interested, so we all got along just fine, chatting about wine and food and whether British Airways would add a flight from Paphos to Gatwick, which led to complaints about air travel, and led me to ponder whether, when (not if) I went to hell, it would just be an eternal cocktail party.

Chante was there, talking to two women. Minette was not. Nor was handsome George Selkirk. But I was pretty sure at least a few of the movie folk had deigned to come and eat Stella's free prawns.

The action took place mostly on the expansive terrace beside the inevitable infinity pool, three dozen people in resort wear holding glasses of wine and snagging hors d'oeuvres from passing waiters. It was a warm night, late May, the dividing line between 'rather warm' and 'too bloody hot.' The moon had either set or not yet risen, and cirrus dimmed the stars. The Mediterranean was black ink, decorated by twinkling ships' lights, distant floating votive candles, full of fat tourists, or fish, or smuggled goods. If I'd been able to swap the wine for Scotch, light a cigar, and get rid of all the people, it would have been a lovely night.

'You are Mr Mitre, I believe?'

I was at the edge of the terrace looking with some longing at my own villa down the hill. I smiled (some might prefer the term 'grimaced') and extended my hand to a short, stocky man with more scalp than hair, densely-black eyebrows that seemed on the verge of becoming an eyebrow, singular, and a missing canine tooth. He was wearing a low-end gray suit with elbows that would need patching soon, a white shirt that had been stained by coffee at least once and never successfully cleaned, tired black leather shoes from the Stolid Footwear catalog, and an air of bone-deep skepticism. That wasn't enough to prove that he was some sort of cop, but it was enough to raise the little hairs on the back of my neck.

'I am Cyril Kiriakou, and may I say that I am a big fan?'

'Oh, thanks,' I said, hoping my heart's skipped beats wouldn't be apparent. 'I didn't even know my books were translated into Greek.'

'Hah! Very true. I read them in English. In your efficient, unflowery prose, which I find so refreshing.'

In the *New York Review of Books*, 'efficient prose' would be an insult. Not one I could deny, frankly, but definitely an insult.

'Thank you again,' I said. Because he was not the *New York Review of Books*.

'I don't wish to take up your time,' Kiriakou said, 'but in my official capacity I do like to meet new members of the expat community.'

'Official capacity?' I asked, as I measured the distance to the door using the great-panicky-leaps unit of measurement.

'Yes, I am the assistant chief of police for the Paphos region.' He waved a hand vaguely, presumably to sketch the extent of his territory, which at very least included the terrace. 'I had hoped to meet you at some point, in both my official capacity, to welcome you to Cyprus, and unofficially as a true fan.'

'Is there a great deal of crime on Cyprus?' At least I think that's what I said. In my head, it sounded like *wa wa wa wa wa wa wa wa wawa?*

Kiriakou shrugged with hands as well as shoulders. He tilted his head side to side. He raised his eyebrows. 'Normally, no. Pickpockets, tourist scams, the usual domestics. In an average year, we get around twenty murders – the lowest rate in the

EU.' He deployed the statistic as a point of pride but he didn't look personally happy about it. 'And of course very few of those would be of any interest to your readers.'

'What, dull murders were they?'

He laughed and nodded. 'Drunken bar fights, revenge kill-ings, domestics, usually cut and dried. That is the phrase? It is an Americanism, I believe.'

'Yes. It is. Though we usually say just cut and dry.'

He glanced around to see who was within hearing, turned a suddenly serious face to me and lowered his voice. 'At the moment, however, we have a murder that does not fit any of those categories.'

'You must mean that poor woman on the beach, yesterday.'

Blink. 'Indeed.'

'It seems I just missed seeing it. At least I must have, I didn't notice anything. I did hear a scream as I was crossing the terrace of the hotel, but I assumed it was just children playing. From what I saw on the news it must have happened right after I left the beach bar. I feel terrible that I . . . Well, this sounds bad, I guess, but I've never been anywhere near an actual murder, and to be a mystery writer and miss an actual murder . . .' I did a self-deprecating laugh that had it lasted another second would have become hysterical. 'Well, it's a bit of a missed opportunity, to say the least.'

Kiriakou was watching me and smiling, nodding as if he understood, though perhaps did not quite share, my bloodthirsty curiosity. He held that smile after I stopped talking. Held the smile and the look, waiting.

I told myself it didn't mean anything. Cops are like that, they're trained in the uncomfortably-extended conversational pause. Also trained to smell fear, and I smelled. I didn't like being near a senior cop. A beat cop, no problem, but an assistant whatever of whatever? But I was not an amateur, so I would not try desperately to fill the silence.

'Of course for me it is just work,' Kiriakou said at last, shooing work away with a flutter of fingers. 'Work for which, to be quite perfectly honest, I have only limited experience and even more limited resources.'

'But you must have suspects?'

'Suspects plural?'

'Well, there you have me, deputy chief, you see, if I were writing the story of the murder I would need suspects, plural. Otherwise it would be a rather short book.'

The policeman looked pained. He had quite an expressive face, unlike American cops who work hard to appear emotionless. What I did not know was how much of it was show. He winced, his fifth or sixth expression in about two minutes.

'I wonder what an American policeman would do?' He made a lopsided smile. 'NYPD? Or your own New Midland police?'

I shrugged. 'Arrest the first black guy they saw and beat a confession out of him?' I paused and added, 'That's a joke, of course. Mostly. I suppose it would be all the usual – fingerprints and . . .'

'No fingerprints were found.'

I stopped myself from saying, *What not on the wine bottle?* The guy wasn't wearing gloves. Instead I said, 'Forensics on the murder weapon?'

'We do not have the murder weapon.'

'Eyewitnesses?'

'Oh, plenty of those,' Kiriakou said, with a roll of his eyes and a wry smirk. 'The suspect was male and black. We questioned twenty-three witnesses and those two points are all they agree on. I have one eyewitness who claims he saw the suspect running with a Kalashnikov and yelling, *"Allahu akbar."*'

'Mmm,' I said. 'Eyewitnesses. Almost as reliable as your daily horoscope.'

He blew out his cheeks. 'No physical evidence, not even footprints since it was on grass. Useless witnesses. And no motive. Yet it was clearly premeditated. The man had carried a bottle of wine on a tray, like a waiter. And he had the presence of mind to wipe both clean.'

I concealed my surprise. The killer had stopped and calmly wiped his prints? 'Who was the woman? The victim? Was there a romantic thing, maybe?'

His eyes dismissed the possibility of romantic entanglement, as well he should – I'd thrown it out there to make myself look a bit thick because I had a bad feeling about where this was going.

'Ah, now there's where it becomes interesting,' Kiriakou said, moving too close. 'She had a British passport, but our routine query to the British Home Office came back with a suggestion that the passport might be a forgery. That is perhaps not too surprising. But then, just this afternoon, the Home Office said it was indeed a valid passport.'

'Bureaucrats,' I said, and got no reaction.

'What caught the eye of my clever assistant – she is much more techno than I – is that the two replies came from different origins. Both emails appear to be official emails, but only the first comes from an internet address associated with the Home Office.'

I said, 'Well, you're asking the wrong guy if you're looking for information on internet-related issues.' More calculated thickness on my part.

'So, I followed up with an acquaintance of mine at Scotland Yard, a fellow I met at a conference in Geneva. I sent him the dead woman's fingerprints. And just before I left to come here for Dame Stella's sparkling and delightful party, I heard back.' The words 'sparkling and delightful' came with a nod toward our hostess across the terrace where she was chatting up a distinguished-looking gent.

I favored Kiriakou with a look of benign, even conspiratorial amusement. 'Are you building suspense, Mr Kiriakou?'

He liked that a lot. 'Ah! Of course, the writer in you looks for literary tropes. Hah hah!'

I was a bit surprised that he knew the word 'trope,' let alone how to use it properly. It's not the sort of word an assistant police chief typically comes across, and it came to me that a few years earlier *Publishers Weekly* had used that word in a review of one of my books. Had Kiriakou researched me? That wasn't good. But my puzzlement was almost immediately replaced by a much starker emotion, because Kiriakou spoke the 'F' word.

'It appears the victim was a fugitive. There are both British and Belgian arrest warrants for Rachel Faber.'

I don't think my squeak was audible. 'A fugitive? Ah, the plot thickens.'

I don't always spout lines of Conan Doyle when I'm startled, but it was the best I could manage.

'Ah, but that much plot is all we have, it has not thickened any further,' Kiriakou said. Then, hesitant – well, hesitant unless he was playing me – he said, 'I don't wish to impose on you in any way, and please you are free to say no, and I will understand. But . . .'

I waited with an expectant but resolutely not guilty look on my face.

'I wonder if you would have an hour free to have lunch with me and perhaps offer me your insights?'

'Of course, I would be happy to,' I lied. 'But I hope you understand that I'm only a writer, I am not a trained investigator. I'm certainly not a murder cop!'

To which he replied with a Cypriot shrug, 'To be quite perfectly honest, neither am I. Normally such cases are handled by the chief inspector of criminal investigation in Nicosia, but poor fellow, he is in hospital for an operation. Hernia. Very painful.'

At that point Dame Stella swept by, gathering me up to glad-hand her other semi-celebrity, the movie's assistant director, as well as various local pooh-bahs and some geezer named Jeremy Berthold, who Dame Stella whispered was 'a very important man in the British expat community.' I stood nodding thoughtfully as Berthold and Stella's loopy hubby and a man who looked far too much like Rowan Atkinson discussed the eternal reunification negotiations.

Suddenly Berthold turned to me. 'So, you write paperback mystery novels, do you?'

And just like that I hated him. 'Actually I write manuscripts which the publisher turns into hardcovers, and a year later releases as paperbacks.'

He was a big man, maybe fifty-five, wide and beefy in the shoulders. He had the look of a man who'd been professionally fit at some point in his life, maybe ex-military, and had let himself go a bit to seed. He was trying the Oxbridge snob act on me.

'But popular novels, yes?'

'Not as popular as I'd like. I mean, sure, I outsell most of your Booker Prize-winning . . . I have that right, don't I? It is the Booker Prize, right? I sometimes confuse Booker and *Bake-Off*. Anyway, I would love to be still more popular.'

I finished that up with a grin I save for snobs. It's a sneering gangsterish grin, openly challenging; the toothy version of *Bring it on, pal, bring it on.*

I love a snob. They always think they have something. They don't understand that the thing they think they have is only as real as I'm willing to make it. Berthold's eyes took on a distant chill and something distinctly not Oxbridge was looking across at me. Credit where it's due, for a posh old snot he quickly parsed the situation, read my cockiness correctly and said, 'Then I must wish you success.'

'Thanks,' I said cheekily. 'And I'm terribly sorry, but your name was . . .'

I left him to mutter about rude, uncultured Americans. It was stupid of me to poke an important guy in the expat community, I was trying to fit in and go unnoticed. I should have ducked my head sheepishly and made some self-deprecating remark. But my blood was up, as the old saying goes: I had an actual cop to worry about and some puffed-up old fart who wanted to score points off me was irrelevant.

Out of the corner of my eye I tracked Kiriakou, who wandered genially around the room shaking hands and working his expressive eyebrows. The threat of panic was past, leaving a sour paranoia in its wake. There's a definite tendency among my people – fugitives, not writers – to sound the alarms. Ten false alarms for every justified one. But a conversation with a cop the day after a murder right where I happened to be drinking beer was, by definition, a justified alarm.

As soon as I could do it without attracting attention I made my farewells, found the door and threaded my way through parked Mercedes and BMWs – and a rather nice old Triumph – to the privacy, if not safety, of my villa and the comfort of the Isle of Skye's best.

FOUR

I committed my first crime at age four.

We were living in southern California in those days. My birth father, sensible fellow, had seen where things were headed and had disappeared. My very young mother and I were living with my maternal grandparents.

And I wanted money. No doubt my need was great, I don't recall the specifics, but I can only assume a desire for candy was involved.

But first, before crossing over to the dark side, I tried entrepreneurship. I had a black plastic toy medical kit from which I dumped the stethoscope and syringe, and that thing you use for looking in ears, and into which (the kit, not the ears) I poured a boxful of vanilla wafers. I set off around the neighborhood as the world's first (and probably last) door-to-door vanilla wafer salesman. Amazingly I was able to sell some to a bemused woman who answered her door. I think she gave me a dollar. But even in those days a dollar didn't go far, so when I got home I noticed some crumpled bills and loose change on my grandfather's mahogany chest of drawers. I took the money and claimed it had come from robust Nilla sales.

Four years old. My first misdemeanor. If only I'd thought to take a commemorative photo.

My second crime came later when, at age twelve, I tapped my mother and stepfather's telephone landline. It was easy enough: a matter of a headphone, a wire stripper, and some black electrical tape. The crime: successful but pointless. Neither parent had anything interesting to say, by which I mean that none of their calls were about me.

By age nineteen, I was a high school dropout working for a major law firm in Washington DC, in the law library as a messenger and obtainer of hard-to-get documents. My boss called me into his office one day, and said, 'I need you to run something over to a fellow at the Government Printing Office.'

'Okay.'

Then he pulled out a sheet of paper. He laid a small stack of greenbacks on the paper, folded it neatly, stuffed it into an envelope, sealed it and held it out to me. 'It's an invitation to my daughter's bat mitzvah. Discreet, right?'

'Discreet,' I agreed and took the envelope.

Not much of a crime, though I imagine bribing a government employee is a criminal offense of sorts, unless you're a campaign donor. The interesting thing to me looking back – as a guy whose current job is creating characters with backstories and motivations and notions of good and evil – is my complete lack of qualms. Steal from grandparents: nothing. Wiretap parents: nothing. Deliver payola: nothing. I had seen Bugs Bunny cartoons, I knew there was supposed to be a devil on one shoulder and an angel on the other, but I was morally one-shouldered.

A year later, despite having dropped out of high school, I had beaten the various tests and been accepted to San Francisco State University. It was my last attempt to reintegrate into normal society, I suppose. God knows what I had in mind. Bong construction wasn't my *declared* major, that would have been philosophy, but getting high and seducing arts majors was much more fun than reading Kant and Husserl. I dropped out and, in one of the inexplicable sudden turns that define my life, ended up working for the Denny's restaurant chain as a graveyard shift manager, eleven p.m. to seven a.m.

Skimming off the register at Denny's was pitifully easy, so long as you didn't go overboard. We all skimmed – management to pay the help off the books and improve their labor cost numbers, and we humbler employees because, well, because fuck it: there it was, all green and foldable. But skimming is too much risk for too little reward. You don't want to end up in general population at Chuckawalla, or God forbid Folsom, having to admit you got popped for a forty-dollar-a-day skim; that's just embarrassing. So, on the theory that I had not yet made a complete hash of my life and needed to get on with it, I pulled my first major felony.

I knew the physical layout of Denny's restaurants, and I knew how lazy managers were about using the awkward safes in their offices. I drove a few towns away to a unit with the identical layout, cut my way through the roof access, then down through the office ceiling where I found what I expected: an open safe stuffed with seven thousand dollars. It was all very *Mission: Impossible The Movie* if the movie had had a props budget of ten dollars. Sure, it would have been great to have a laser to cut through the wallboard, but a box-cutter worked well enough.

Needs must, as the Brits say.

For a while after that I drove around the US in an ancient but lovable green Karmann Ghia convertible with a paper bag of cash in the trunk. Good times. Especially that commune in . . . somewhere hot. Peyote plays hell with memory. Arizona? New Mexico? One of those. I remember fleas, cacti and lots of sand.

Two more Denny's burglaries, one for a solid ten grand, and I'd basically found a way to live as a parasite.

Then I was arrested. Not a good moment. I had walked into an acquaintance's antique shop in Carson City (where no fencing of questionably obtained goods took place, nope,) and I had seen the two detectives sitting there, questioning him about my whereabouts. I had played it cool for fifteen seconds, pretending to shop, then made for the exit. Twenty yards down the street they called my name: Martin DeKuyper, my actual birth name. If I remember correctly.

You might bluff it out and keep walking if a cop calls John Smith, or Joe Anderson, but Martin DeKuyper was too specific to pull off the 'I thought they meant some other . . .'

Handcuffs. Mug shots. Bend over.

That was not a good day. However clever or suave or tough you think you are, it's hard to carry it off in what the cons call a four-by-four: handcuffs, shackled ankles and a chain around the waist of your freshly deloused orange onesie.

Oooh, I'm prisoner number 6732 and 32 is my lucky number!

I spent eleven days inside before I could make bail. The food was lousy, and a constant fear of a beating, a rape or a knifing tends to cast a pall over things. I was a young smartass, a two-bit burglar, chump-change embezzler and failed vanilla-wafer salesman. I wasn't the kind of hard case who hurt people. I didn't go around frightening folks. No one was locking up wives and daughters for fear of Martin DeKuyper. I wasn't one of *those* guys, but there were definitely some of those guys in that cage with me. I was admittedly a bad boy, but some of the men in there were evil.

People who dismiss the idea that you can sense evil have never been to jail. Look for guys with tears tattooed on their faces, or guys who are small and weak yet everyone steers well clear of – even guys with big swastika chest tattoos stretching from nipple to nipple.

That's another sign, the swastika tattoo.

I finally made bail, promptly jumped said bail, and began my life as a fugitive from justice.

Not quite twenty years had passed since then, with half of that time spent expanding my criminal repertoire beyond burglary into the exciting and lucrative world of scams and cons and the occasional high-value theft. I started in the domestic market: the posher reaches of New York, Washington, LA, Houston and points between, before realizing that my work would be so much easier and safer if I took the act overseas. And I enjoy foreign travel: it broadens the mind.

It was crime that made me a writer. No grifter can avoid being a decent storyteller, and you meet very interesting people out there in the world outside the law. I was good at lying, good at inventing legends about myself, good at building narratives that would appeal to widows and divorcees with more money than sense.

In this I had been helped by my appearance, which runs to the Clive Owen, dark hair, blue eyes, impishly flirtatious sort of thing. I can pull off the open-necked white shirt and blue blazer look, and was in fact pulling it off at the moment. Or I can do the worn designer jeans and Tommy Bahama camp shirt. I can even manage not to look ridiculous in a tuxedo. I look like I might be the ne'er-do-well third son of wealthy parents – trouble, but of the fun kind, like that ginger prince, what's-his-name? Harry. The kind of man women like for a few days or a week while hubby is away on business.

In a well-run, successful scam, I could clear a quarter million. A burglary could net from twenty-five large to a hundred grand. I made about as much on my first book, all-in, as I did on a decent burglary, and I suppose I could have gone on doing both, but I was getting older, the universe of lonely women in the one percent demographic is not endless, and I had by then reached the essential insight that all criminals come to if they're bright enough: the game is not fox and hounds with clever fox evading pursuing hounds, tally-ho; the game is tightrope walker and floor.

The police are the floor. I was the guy on the rope. One wrong step, and the floor would be waiting. It would wait forever.

So, about ten years back I sized everything up, and went straight. Well, straight aside from fake ID and the occasional bit of creative accounting. And being a fugitive.

Straight-*ish*.

But the thief and the con were still part of me, probably always would be. I still saw the weakness in security systems and the vulnerabilities in people. I sometimes amused myself figuring out just how one would go about stealing, say, the Mona Lisa from the Louvre. (I have a plan.) Or creating a fake charity, signing a celebrity to attend, throwing a gala and walking away with the contributions while I had teams go through the empty homes of attendees. (I have a plan for that, too.) Or using an office-cleaning service to access computers at a brokerage house and selling the passwords to the Armenian mob.

Okay, that one I actually did. It was quite lucrative, but with several terrifying moments involving guns and threats of castration. Credible threats.

I have a natural repugnance for violence, so I never hurt anyone except in their wallets and pride, and only then if they could afford it – there's no point stealing from anyone who isn't rich. Middle-class people will call the cops over a hundred bucks, but my victims could shrug off a hundred large just because they didn't want to waste an hour talking to dull working-class folks like detectives.

Anyway, the point is that while I was a crook, I was not a bad person. Mostly. And in the early years I held firmly to that belief. I was a gentleman thief, like Cary Grant, more amusing than threatening.

But then Arthur Wilson Janes disagreed with that generous

self-assessment, and did so in convincing style by putting a nine millimeter in his mouth and blowing his brains all over the gorgeous interior of his two million dollar Bugatti.

Not my fault. I told myself.

An unfaithful wife and fifty grand from a man who drove a car that cost almost fifty times that? Kill yourself over *that?* Over a bit of cuckolding? Over chump change? Anyone who would do that was already suicidal, I told myself. Not my fault the guy couldn't take a joke, I told myself.

Not my fault at all, I still told myself on lonely nights as I waited for Ambien and whisky to send me off to dreamland.

And yet, there were the consequences, even the mundane sequelae, the fact that my victims had to fill out insurance forms, and upgrade their security and perhaps be embarrassed or humiliated. Or endure a divorce. Or blow off half their head while destroying a gorgeous leather interior and shattering the moon roof.

I've read that a man's brain does not reach full maturity until he's in his twenties and that this explains a tendency in many males to reckless behavior, to sociopathy. I was a late bloomer. I was in my early thirties when it began to occur to me that I was just possibly a bit of an asshole.

But by that point I'd already long known in that way you can suppress but never quite shake off that I had taken a wrong turn in life. Well, several wrong turns, a couple dozen, but it was one particular point in time that stuck with me, one particular wrong turn, one indelible image that haunted me: the image of a girl in a window.

In a few days, it would be exactly nineteen years since I'd done the stupid thing and rejected that escape. I don't remember the exact date when I learned that Janes had painted his impromptu Rothko in blood and viscera. But I remember the exact goddamned date when I started firmly down the road to making that happen.

FIVE

The morning after Dame Stella's party I went shopping. I'd been putting it off, getting lazy in my old age, getting cocky, but my brush with Kiriakou had lit a fire under me. On my shopping list were useful folks I could bribe efficiently. And then lunch with the cop.

First stop, church.

'I would like to make a contribution,' I said.

'Whakh?' That's how she said it, with a 'kh.'

That stopped me for a second. 'A contribution. To the charity thing, you know. Because I admire your work.'

'Enh?'

'The kids and all. You know, feeding poor kids or whatever it is you people do. The charity thing.'

Every single person on Cyprus speaks English. Every single one of them but this black-clad butterball with the dandruffy bun. I was in what I took to be the office of the more important of the local Greek Orthodox churches, a bit of intelligence I'd picked up at the party by eavesdropping on a rather stunning young Cypriot woman. Marvelous, what the charity did for local poor kids – like the children of the people who cleaned expats' homes, no doubt – and I was here to deliver my bribe.

Contribution.

If you're a stranger in town, and especially if you're a foreigner, and you want an accelerated degree of grudging acceptance from the yokels, you contribute to a prominent charity. In Cyprus, the Greek Orthodox church isn't just a church, it's the single greatest power. They own something like a fifth of the island's economy, a fact testified to by an impressive number of very large and quite new churches, all spotlessly clean, shiny and vibrant in pink and tan, bell tower and dome.

There is a bit of a 'thing' still going on in Cyprus, a thing involving Greek Cypriots and the Greek Orthodox church on one side, and Turkish Cypriots and Turkish immigrants and Islam on the other. Long story short, they don't like each other.

Long story less short, Greek Cypriots are still pissed at the Ottoman Turks who ruled from 1571 to 1878. The Ottomans were fantastically corrupt and not terribly tolerant, and when some Greek Cypriots carried out a bit of Turk-massacring in 1821, the Ottomans responded by hacking up a bunch of Greek Orthodox clergy they'd invited over for lunch.

The Ottomans eventually gave Cyprus to Britain in 1878 and the British swept in and imposed religious tolerance, a legal system, a deep respect for proper queuing etiquette and an insistence on driving on the wrong side of the road.

There followed a period of relative peace, then in 1960 Cyprus declared its independence and chose an archbishop named Makarios to play the George Washington role. They typed up a nice constitution which laid out a peaceful sort of side-by-side, let's-all-get-along, kumbaya arrangement between Greek and Turkish Cypriots and it was as much as several days before the two communities started taking potshots at one another. By 1964, the two sides were getting along so well that the United Nations had to send troops. Who are still there.

In 1974, the Greek Cypriot military launched a coup, attempted to unite with the Greek military junta and the Turks decided, no, that wasn't happening and invaded. They seized the northern third of the island and declared the independent country of the Turkish Federated State of Cyprus which was embraced by a host of nations including Turkey and also Turkey.

Greek Cyprus cleaned up its act, joined the European Union, and the two sides settled down to decades of mutual loathing across a Green Line that split the capital, Nicosia, like John le Carré's Berlin.

Cyprus lives in a rough neighborhood, just about one hundred and fifteen miles from Aya Napa to Beirut, Lebanon, and another fifty miles gets you to Damascus, Syria, and Jerusalem is just two hundred and thirty miles off. This is not a neighborhood for letting bygones be bygones.

Nowadays, Cyprus (the Greek part) has a democratically elected government, but the real power is arguably still the Greek Orthodox church. Which is why I'd decided that it wouldn't hurt to have some element of said church believing I was a swell guy. My plan now delayed by ancient bun-lady.

Fortunately, there was a poster for an NGO named Feed the Forgotten on the wall, so I took out my envelope of euros and held it up under the nose of the boy on the poster – he wasn't starving, but he was thin, and his smile held just enough sadness and just enough hope.

Please, sir, I want some more.

'Contribution. Money. Euros.'

'Euros?'

'Get 'em while they last.'

She took the envelope, peeked inside, closed it, took two breaths, then pulled out the cash and counted it with suspiciously-adept fingers. She said something in Greek that was probably a number.

I nodded, and said, 'Yes, two thousand.'

She made a face like that was just more work for her, showed me a 'stay here' finger and bustled away. A minute later, she was back leading a man wearing overalls and an amazing beard.

'Hello, I am Father Fotos.'

'You're kidding. I mean, sorry, nice to meet you. Father. David Mitre.'

It does not come naturally to me to call people 'father', particularly when they look about nineteen even from behind General Longstreet's beard. He made an apologetic face, wiped grease from his hand and we shook.

'I'm sorry to trouble you, Father . . . um, I just wanted to make a small contribution to your charity work.'

I could not say 'Father Fotos' and keep a straight face.

'Not so small,' he said, grinning. 'May I ask how you heard of our work?'

'At a party, actually, at Dame Stella Weedon's house last night.'

'Ah. Well, we are very happy to take your money and put it to good use.' He tilted his head and looked at me from merry brown eyes narrowed with skepticism but not hostility. 'And is there anything we can do in return?'

Do you mean like put the word out that I'm a good guy who loves him some orphans so you shouldn't believe anything bad you might hear about me? I did not say.

What I did say was, 'Oh, I have, like, no knowledge of the situation. But I had some tough times when I was a kid, so . . .' Abashed smile, humble shrug, and I was heading for the door when he touched my elbow and I let him lead me out of the . . . whatever the official ecclesiastical name is for an entry-way office and out into the . . . whatever the official ecclesiastical name is for the church part. With the seats. The pews.

The church was, in my inexpert opinion, over-decorated, with far too much reliance on gold leaf. Behind the altar were about three dozen icons, painted before the discovery of perspective, many old bearded fellows and the occasional robed woman, all with gold dinner plates hovering behind their heads. They stared down at me. One old guy was definitely not buying my bullshit. Fortunately, Father Fotos was.

'You are the author,' Father Fotos said.

I nodded. 'You are well-informed.'

'I hear many things,' he said with a sort of self-mocking seriousness I liked. 'Also, my wife was at Dame Stella's party. In fact, I would not be at all surprised to learn that you heard of our mission from her.'

I blinked, processing that.

He said, 'Yes, Mr Mitre, we have married priests in our church. Indeed, you cannot be a priest unless you have not only a wife but a child.'

I'm sure the altar boys are relieved is what I did not say, because I was there to make nice. Instead I said, 'Is she a blonde, very Egyptian pyramid-painting eyes, serious and intense but still like she'd probably . . .' And I stopped myself right there.

'Were you about to say that she looks like she'd probably be very good at visiting the sick and comforting the afflicted?'

I had to grin. 'That was exactly what I was about to say.'

Father Fotos shrugged. 'I hear confession, you know. I've heard men confess their attraction to my wife.'

'I assume you penance the shit out of them,' I said. 'She's too young for me, but when I stop noticing women like your wife someone needs to put me out of my misery.'

'Now I have a confession,' he said. 'It's one I'm sure you've heard as often as I've heard a teenager confessing to masturbation. It is this: I have always wanted to be a writer.'

I suppressed the groan, but my eyes did go a bit opaque at that point. Then I saw the profit.

Your honor, I call Father Fotos of the Hot Wife as my character witness.

'Tell you what, father, let's grab a coffee some day when we both have time, and I'll lay my accumulated writing wisdom on you.'

'And for my part I will save your soul,' he said.

'Ambitious.'

All at once the bantering was over. He glanced a bit nervously at a nearby icon. 'My wife tells me you spent some time talking to our assistant chief of police.'

'Kiriakou?'

'Yes. Cyril Kiriakou.'

'I did, yes.' Wait. Now I was the one deploying the old lengthening silence trick. I could see he wanted to tell me something and was working through the doctrinal barriers in his head.

'One hears things,' Father Fotos said at last. 'Not in the confessional, of course, I would never violate the sanctity of the confessional, why you could safely unburden—'

'You don't have that kind of time,' I interrupted.

'Well, one hears things. I can only say that many things are not what they seem. All that is gold does not glitter.'

'Really? Tolkien?'

He did not laugh. 'Do you believe in good and evil, Mr Mitre?'

I shifted a bit uncomfortably. Some of the painted saints were giving me the eye, already not liking my answer. I said, 'Father, Nazis performed medical experiments on children. So, yeah, I believe in evil. I just don't think it involves some horned, hooved, pitchfork-toting Halloween figure.'

'Well, Mr Mitre, there is evil on this island. So very much good, but still, there is evil.'

I waited it out. And he added, 'And you have perhaps already touched the edge of that evil.'

I took from this a warning that Kiriakou was corrupt, which no doubt would seem evil to this bearded adolescent but to me was encouraging news. When you have no money, corruption is evil; when you do have money, corruption is convenient.

My next stop was an environmental group that as best I could figure out wanted us all to bathe in a teacup and eat grass, I didn't really know, but I doubted they could do much damage with a thousand euros. Ditto the centrist coalition party, which rejected a direct contribution with appropriately disapproving looks before directing me to a completely separate group that engaged in 'activism.' Those guys practically snatched the money out of my hand and would have picked my pocket if I'd hung around long enough.

The picture I was painting through the medium of cash-on-palm was of an expat with a social conscience, a well-to-do American (thus assumed to be a braying imbecile), who was trying to do right by the locals. A cynic (no more than ninety percent of the Cypriot population) might suspect I was buying a little influence. And they would suspect that because I was in fact, buying a little influence. For an investment of four grand I now had eco-warriors, local politicians and a priest all ready to say, *No, hold up there, officer: David Mitre is a good man. Why, just look at this orphan he fed. And he never wastes water.*

The only thing better is paying cops and prosecutors directly, and I expected to get to that, but it can be very sketchy business. Bribing cops requires research and planning, and even then it is dangerous as hell because you just never know when you're going to run into an honest cop. I'm told they exist.

I was therefore perversely encouraged by Father Fotos' dire warning and I hoped my lunch with Kiriakou would show me the way. Cyprus wasn't quite squeaky-clean Denmark when it came to corruption, but it wasn't Somalia, either, and I couldn't just stuff money in cops' pockets. Probably.

The discordant note was that if Kiriakou was corrupt he was subtly so. His suit and shoes were not the suit and shoes of a man on the take. I decided to hold off on open bribery attempts during our lunch.

We met at a café off the main drag in lower Paphos.

Paphos has three prominent, distinguishing characteristics aside from the endlessly gorgeous Mediterranean seashore. First, it is actually slightly less Greek than a Greek Town neighborhood in Brighton or Cleveland. The signs are in English. The food on offer is largely British, especially the full English breakfast. And if you bump into someone there's a good chance that *they* will apologize.

Second, it's an oddly haphazard place with no notion of zoning laws, so that three-story, blocky apartment buildings and restaurants – some quite fancifully-built to resemble castles or lumpish approximations of circa 1965 Disney funhouses – stand side by side.

Each building is topped by identical water tanks on rusty platforms, one tank for each apartment in an apartment block, which may go some way to explaining the lack of high rises. Water is an issue on Cyprus. I knew this because the eco-warriors had given me a flyer and I had not yet come across a trash bin to toss it into.

But the most surprising Cypriot feature was the cats. There were cats everywhere. Cats on beach chairs. Cats nestled in banks of succulent ground cover. Cats on pool tables. Cats on bars. It's as if some mad decorator had thrown them around like accent pillows. You couldn't go twenty feet in any direction without seeing a cat. Paphos is a tough place for birds and mice.

There was a tabby winding its way around Kiriakou's corruption-denying shoes as I stepped up to his table. Kiriakou spotted me, half rose to shake my hand then settled back into his rattan chair. He looked tired, but friendly.

'Shall we have some wine?' he proposed.

'Please,' I said.

'Would you like to see the list?'

'I'd much rather leave it to you, Cyril.' Deliberate first-naming. It's expected of Americans – we're allowed.

Kiriakou nodded and said something in Greek to the waiter.

'Still or sparking water?'

'Sparkling, please,' I said.

We chatted about the weather. It had been a dry winter, far less rain than normal and virtually no snow up in the mountains. Global warming, no doubt, we agreed.

We agreed as well to share some olives and a plate of fresh anchovies. For our mains, he went with prawns, and I chose a seafood pasta. The appetizers came quickly as did the wine, which was a not-terrible Ayioklima white.

'What new developments in your investigation, Cyril?'

He made a grunt, emphasized with a shrug. 'Nothing useful, I am afraid. We searched the victim's hotel room.' He lifted a leather document holder from the floor where it had been propped against his chair leg. From it he drew a paper and spread it out for me.

'I'm sorry, but I don't read Greek. Or speak it, I'm afraid.'

'Of course,' he said. 'I will translate. The victim had a camera, but the data card was empty, all photos deleted. She had . . .' He glanced at the list. 'Three dresses, all with UK or French labels. Four blouses. Slacks. A skirt. Bras and underpants.'

'Expensive?' I asked.

'Neither expensive nor cheap, off-the-rack things from John Lewis or Galeries Lafayette.'

'Not helpful,' I opined sagely. 'Books? Laptop?'

'A Lee Child novel . . .'

I resisted a sneer. I liked Child; I did not like the fact that he outsold me ten to one.

'. . . a guidebook to Cyprus. A Greek-English phrase book. And there is a laptop, but it is password protected, as was her mobile.'

'You went through the usual passwords? 1-2-3-4-5-6? Qwerty? Password?'

'And many more.'

'I don't suppose you have friends at the NSA or GCHQ?' I said.

He barked a laugh. 'Ah, but we have all been told modern devices are unhackable.'

'Yes, we have all been told that. And if you believe it, I've got a bridge you can buy cheap.'

He was unfamiliar with that wheeze, so I explained it to him.

'In any event,' he said, 'I don't think the intelligence world is anxious to help a local police officer.'

'No,' I admitted. 'A written diary, perhaps?'

He shook his head.

'Medications?'

That brought up a quirked smile. 'A common fiber laxative, ibuprofen, basic first-aid, bandages and an antibiotic cream.

The only thing even slightly unexpected was a medical-strength cortisone cream.'

'Hmm. Your medical examiner will probably discover a skin disease, dermatitis. Eczema. Psoriasis.'

He agreed that was likely. 'Our coroner will be conducting his examination this afternoon.'

'Was there a prescription label?'

'At one time, but it had been removed.'

'And, how old was the victim?'

'According to her passport, she was thirty-nine.'

Of course. If you were using fake papers why not stop at thirty-nine? My passport said I was forty-one, though I was one or two years older than that.

'And this is the passport about which you have some doubts?'

'Yes.'

'I assume you opened the hotel room safe?'

His eyes twinkled and he gave me a conspiratorial look. 'Indeed, and that is where we found something . . . interesting.'

I stabbed a playful finger at him and said, 'You're building suspense again, Cyril.'

He spread his hands, fingers smeared with whitebait grease. 'I do what I can to make my dull job interesting. Yes, it was in the safe that we found a different passport, also British, but with a different name. That, and five thousand euros, as well as a thousand in British pounds.'

'Ah,' I said. 'Credit cards in her purse?'

'Two. An American Express card and a Visa, both under the name she was using here, Rachel Faber. And in the safe, another American Express and a MasterCard, names matching the second passport.'

I narrowed my eyes. 'There we go. That's better. You pulled the records?'

'Of course. In the second name which was . . .' He pulled out a Moleskine and thumbed pages. 'Hynson. Amanda J. Hynson. Each of those cards had auto-withdrawals. One for a Netflix account, the other for an online subscription to the *Independent*.'

I decided to share some of my professional fictional sleuthing wisdom. 'She'd pay those to keep the accounts active.'

'Precisely.'

'How about the Rachel Faber cards?'

'Numerous charges from here on Cyprus, beginning two days ago. Cafés. Shops. A hired car. A tour guide.'

'A tour guide book, or a tour guide of the human variety?'

'Only books, unfortunately.'

Thus far I approved of Rachel/Amanda's tradecraft. If she was on the run, she was no fool. Of course, there were other sorts of folks who kept fake passports. 'How were these credit card accounts settled?'

'Hah. Now there, we see the mystery writer's mind at work,' Kiriakou said admiringly. 'All four cards, in both names, were paid from a bank account in—'

I held up a hand. 'Let me guess. Zurich? The Caymans? Luxembourg?'

'Conister Bank,' he said. 'The Isle of Man.'

'Interesting choice. Not much to work with, is there?' I said.

Kiriakou looked disconsolate. 'You must excuse me for a moment,' he said making the face you make when your prostate has squeezed your bladder. He slid the paper back in his document holder and placed the holder back on the floor.

Ten seconds to get to the bathroom, thirty seconds at least to do what was necessary. Should I or shouldn't I?

I had a perfect cover story, Kiriakou had asked me to help. On the other hand, he was known in the restaurant and waiters only pretend not to see what's going on in the dining room.

I used my feet to squeeze the document holder and drew it to me. I placed it on my lap as if it was all perfectly natural, and drew out the list while simultaneously opening my iPhone camera. I spread the list on the table and leaned over the paper, frowning in concentration as my hand mostly concealed the phone.

I shook my head as if I was disappointed, slid the paper back in and pushed it back into place.

There were a hell of a lot of items on that list that Kiriakou had not mentioned. I wanted to know why. Why give me the banking information? Was it all deliberate? Was I being played? I couldn't see how or why.

When Kiriakou came back I said, 'Listen, Cyril, have you learned anything about the perp? The killer?'

He grinned. 'Perp! Hah! That is so very American. The perp! Sadly, we have learned very little.'

'No name or address?'

A shake of the head.

Right, you're running a murder investigation and you can't find a black African on Cyprus where the black population amounts to a few refugees, some university students and an occasional tourist? I did not say.

Instead I blew out a frustrated sigh, and said, 'I'm afraid you have badly overestimated my skills, Cyril.' I spread my hands. 'I'm just a writer, not a murder cop. I make things up. It's much easier that way.'

We had coffee. We chatted. And we went our separate ways.

My takeaway from the lunch was not reassuring. I did not like that he dropped the Isle of Man bank into the picture, that felt . . . off. I did not like that he'd left his briefcase behind when he went for a pee.

The other takeaway was this: I had repeatedly called him by his first name. But he had not once referred to me by any name, not Mr Mitre, not David.

SIX

Normally I'd have spread my influence-buying out over several days or weeks, but the faux beach-waiter Jack the Ripper, and the expressive policeman had motivated me. I suspected or perhaps just feared that I had set off an alarm bell in Kiriakou's mind. I would have bet serious money that if I legged it straight to the airport I would be stopped.

I needed an 'exit visa' of my own devising.

I had budgeted fifteen thousand euros for various bribes and gestures of sincere friendship, of which I had thus far dispensed four thousand. The majority of this I hoped would find its way into police hands, one way or another. But I had a very bad feeling about offering Kiriakou an envelope stuffed with currency. A man wearing a ten-year-old Casio watch was either straight . . . or bent but smart.

I drove north to Latchi along the excellent EU-financed highway. I had leased a white Mercedes C-class convertible which I drove at autobahn speeds. There are signs indicating speed cameras all over the Cypriot highways, but fortunately they had never actually installed said cameras, and fast driving on a highway is an excellent way of finding out if you're being tailed.

I wasn't. Probably.

Cyprus is a sere, stony place. The island taken as a whole looks like a massive rock barely covered by lichen. Limestone and sandstone pokes out everywhere, jutting here and there as if determined to mock vegetation's weak efforts at colonization. In low points, in gullies and washes where topsoil pauses on its way to the sea, the Cypriots hacked out little vegetable gardens, and at the right time of year there are flowers everywhere, rather like you'd see in a good year in the Mojave.

People will try and tell you the island is named for the Cyprus tree, which would make sense were it not for the fact that the tree is spelled cypress, and no one seems quite certain of the etymology. But they do have cypress trees on Cyprus, as well as palm trees – the two trees least likely to provide shade on a hot day. Up in the mountains they grow some pines and cedars and such, but in the Paphos area the surprise is that there are still plots of land scattered here and there that feature banana trees, which look like stumpy, shabby palm trees.

Despite the fact that Cyprus seems determined to shed all of its topsoil and become a big, shiny white rock, they grow wine grapes of both familiar and exotic species, along with avocados, oranges, kiwi fruit and pomegranates of the sweet yellow and the bitter red types. The watermelons are excellent.

You also see carob trees everywhere, brown pods hanging and looking like an infestation of chocolate chrysalises. They make a sweet carob syrup which locals sometimes use to dress salads. And of course there are olive trees; you can't get your Mediterranean membership card unless you grow olives.

In the few short weeks I'd been on the island, Cyprus struck me as a place struggling daily to cling to life. Bridges cross what were once rivers, but which are now empty, all the water having been diverted into reservoirs so that local school kids have a reasonable beef with the requirement that they memorize all of the island's no-longer-there rivers. But at the same time Cyprus is undeniably quite alive, and can point all the way back to the tenth century BC – three millennia – and say, *We're still here; and how long exactly have you people been around, Yank?*

Latchi is outside the usual tourist and expat zones, a small fishing village, or at least the modern European iteration of a small fishing village. The harbor is a 'U' lying on its side, open to the east. It's on the north side of the island, nearest to Turkey. Also nearest to Rhodes and other Greek islands. Convenient.

I parked and walked down around the marina, past the usual sleek sailboats and bloated cabin cruisers. I even saw a few legitimate commercial fishing boats, compact little wooden craft with one-man superstructures. Maybe there were others out at sea, working to put cuttlefish and grouper and sea bream on tables, but for the most part it was cabin cruisers for hire, for fishing or sightseeing. It was the captain of such a vessel that I needed, but first I had to find my man. I had a type in mind, and I figured a bar was the first place to look.

It took four hours of nursing beers and striking up conversations at three different bars to find what I was seeking. Four hours of Greek Euro-pop music. There are times when the fugitive life can be tedious.

'I hear you might be looking for a boat.'

I looked him up and down. Aussie by the accent. Late middle-aged, flabby, sunburned, no wedding ring, translucent greasy gray hair cut by an amateur and not a talented one. He wore a mis-buttoned Filipino cotton shirt, khaki shorts and loafers that would not be carrying him much further before they came apart. That was all the Sherlocking I came up with, but all I really needed to see was the pitted red nose, the sheen of sweat, the rheumy eyes and the tremble in his left hand.

'I may be,' I admitted.

'I'm Brisby Wilson. Cap'n Brisby Wilson, though everyone calls me Dabber.'

'Walter Mosely,' I lied.

It was a risk. The use of an alias would put a dangerous light in Kiriakou's eyes if he found out. The flip side was that if cops were looking for me they'd start with the name, David Mitre. You want to confuse the trail wherever and whenever you can.

We shook hands. His grip was strong but damp, trying to convey authority but undercut by boozehound's sweat glands.

'Maybe we should take a table?' I nodded toward a far corner. 'But first, let me get you a drink, you look like a man with a thirst.'

He was. He was a man with a thirst for gin and tonics. Make it a double, if you don't mind, mate. Make it a double in a regular rocks glass so we didn't have too much tonic water fouling the gin, eh?

'I guess you do mostly sport fishing runs, huh?' I asked.

'Yih,' which is the Australian word for 'yeah,' which is the Californian word for 'yes.' 'Last week I took a party of Jappos – sorry, Japanese – out and came back with a tuna that weighed in at just over four hundred kilos, which is one hell of a lot of sushi, right?'

'That's big for a tuna? Want to order some food, by the way?'

'Nah, but should another G and T arrive I wouldn't push it away.'

He was doing the big, bluff, plainspoken Aussie thing. The big, bluff, plainspoken alcoholic Aussie thing. I'm no prude, but large quantities of gin consumed in the absence of solid food does not scream 'social drinker.'

I ordered another round and sipped beer.

'What kind of boat do you have?' I asked.

'Ah, the *Fair Dinkum* is a fine, fine boat. Not much to look at, but I'm not one of those spit-and-polish types, I'm a blue-water sailor.'

The *Fair Dinkum*? Honest to God? Not the *Bounding Kangaroo*? Not the *Shrimp On A Fucking Barbie*? I said none of that.

I adopted the awed face appropriate to a non-sailor upon meeting a real Old Salt, a true Man O' the Sea. We chatted a bit about fishing and about fish. After a few more G and Ts, he started complaining about the harbormaster, the Cypriot authorities, the damned trigger-happy Turkish navy, and every customer who ever demanded a refund over some bullshit complaint like the boat running out of beer, water and gas. Or partially sinking.

I fed in hints that while I was a fine, upstanding fellow, I occasionally walked on the wild side. 'Husbands don't always like me,' I said with a knowing leer that I copied from George Selkirk.

Oh, guffaw, guffaw, he knew just what I was talking about, mate.

'It's not such a problem, usually, in a regular country, rather than a dinky little island,' I explained. 'I mean, if you happen to diddle the wife of a politically-connected man on this island, where the hell do you run?'

Much manly laughter. Did he believe my story about jealous husbands? Not for a millisecond. He wasn't meant to believe it, he was meant to understand that I might need to do a wee bit of smuggling of some sort, possibly some fleeing. Bluff and manly gave way by degrees to crafty and greedy.

'Yeah,' I said. 'I wish I had a boat. You know? I don't want to own one, God forbid, I'm no sailor. But it would be, I don't know, let's say reassuring, if I knew there was a boat. With a captain. Someone I could call. Even on short notice.'

Amazing how fast a man can sober up when the prospect of actual folding money appears. The courtship phase was over, we both knew what we were talking about; we were getting down to hammering out the terms.

'What you want to do is put a captain on retainer, like,' he said, helpfully, and in no way suggesting that he should be that captain, no, that would be unseemly. Still, he was of the opinion that I would want to reach out to a true blue-water sailor, someone who could steer the boat to Rhodes, say, without ending up docking at Gibraltar. Hah. Hah.

'Is that where most people go? Rhodes?'

'It's one place,' he allowed, nodding judiciously. 'There's also Turkey, of course, lots of little fishing villages spread out along the coast. They patrol, though, and that can add to the expenses.' He rubbed thumb and forefinger together, in case I was too dense to grasp that he was talking about bribes. 'And there's the Lebanon.' A shrug. 'Not Israel, they don't fuck around looking for a fistful of euros, bloody Jews just start shooting.'

I did not ask him about Egypt because Egypt was on my mental list as a likely bolthole. It wasn't my favorite country, but it was disintegrating in slow but relentless fashion, a country where literally anything could be had for a low, low price. Instead I steered the conversation to Lebanon, because there was no way in hell I was going to Lebanon. There was a well-connected Lebanese-American gentleman I knew who might welcome me with open arms and also bullets. But if my bluff, blue-water Aussie sailor decided to rat me out, I wanted all eyes looking in the wrong direction.

'Well, I have to tell you,' I said, summing up. 'You're too humble and too generous to say so, captain, but I think I could not possibly do better than to retain you. Would five hundred euros . . . I don't really know . . .'

His tongue darted out to lick his lips. If I ever organized a poker game I'd want this guy in the game, only with more money to lose.

'That would, well . . .' He made a show of considering. He moved his fingers as if ticking off the expenses he would have to cover. He shook his head. 'To be perfectly honest, a thousand would be better.'

'No problem,' I said. 'Obviously that's just a retainer, just so I have a phone number to call. If I end up taking a trip . . . a sea voyage . . . I'd pay your standard fee.'

We both knew if it came down to it I'd be paying multiples of his standard fee. I dug out my wallet, opened it discreetly but not so discreetly that he couldn't see how much more cash I had, and counted out ten hundred-euro notes.'

'Do you need a receipt?'

'Your handshake will be plenty,' I said.

I slapped another hundred on the bar on my way out and said to the barman, 'Whatever Captain Wilson wants, and you keep the change.' Let those two fight it out.

I had various do-gooders on the hook, and a way off the island. Total cost: five thousand euros and the prospect of a tedious session of hearing how Father Fotos thought he should write a novel about a young, Greek Orthodox priest. With a hot wife. And I had survived lunch with Kiriakou.

So, not a bad day's work.

But there was more to be done because the final stop on my high-speed 'please like me for money' tour would have to be a house of ill repute, which I knew would not be nearly as much fun as it sounds. But I was tired and I was hungry and just not in the mood. So, I drove back to Paphos, eyes on the rearview mirror, arranged for a 'thank you for inviting me' bouquet to be delivered to Dame Stella, dined in town on steak and a bottle of Margaux, because what the hell, if I was going down I'd do it with a belly full of excellent Bordeaux. I returned to my villa around 9:30, feeling pretty pleased with myself. The antidote to fear is action and I'd done what I could for now.

And then there was a knock at my door.

SEVEN

Two people stood on my porch, sallow in the dim glow of the low-wattage porch light. One was a thirty-something Asian man. He was a bit shorter than me, struggling to reach five ten, thick, with muscles bulging at the seams of his clothing.

The other was a tall, elegant black woman, with a short natural hairstyle, sleepy eyes and full lips permanently quirked into mild amusement.

He wore green khaki chinos and a pale blue Polo shirt, carefully tucked in, beneath a blue blazer that really did not go with either the shirt or the chinos. Then again, the black brogues didn't go too well, either. He had the look of a man who wore an invisible necktie at all times, stiff, uncomfortable, maybe even a bit defensive, but nevertheless projecting authority and control.

She was late thirties, maybe even extremely well-preserved early forties, wore loose natural linen slacks that made her legs

look nine miles long and a blue silk blouse with one more
loosened button than was strictly necessary. She also wore a
jacket, but hers had not come straight from Brooks Brothers by
way of Men's Wearhouse. She was more J. Jill by way of
Filene's Basement.

I did not see handcuffs, but there was not the slightest doubt
in my mind that they had some.

'Mr Mitre?' the man asked. 'Mr David Mitre?'

Cops. American cops. My least favorite kind.

One question rose screaming up from the paralyzed depths
of my brain: were they here to take me in? Or were they just
here to verify my identity prior to pushing through a warrant
and having the Cypriots pick me up?

I glanced over their shoulders. One car aside from my
Mercedes: a silver Kia Picanto, standard low-budget issue from
Sixt car rental, with the telltale red tourist license plate. There
was no Cypriot police vehicle.

I breathed.

'Yes?'

And out came the leatherette wallets and the blue-and-white
cards with those extremely unwelcome letters, F, B and I, over
an official Justice Department seal.

'Special Agent Delia Delacorte,' the man nodded at the black
woman. 'And I'm Special Agent Frank Kim.'

I frowned, forced a short laugh and said, 'Aren't you two a
bit far from your usual stomping grounds?'

'May we come in?' Kim asked.

I stepped back and swept them in with a stiff swing of my
arm. 'Can I get you something to drink? Coffee? Tea? Wine?'

Hemlock?

Kim did not need any of my beverages, thank you, but Agent
Delacorte did. She would have whatever I was having. My first
thought was that I was going to guzzle most of a bottle of
Talisker, it being likely that I might not see it again for ten
years or so. But I walked on wobbly legs into the kitchen,
ground some beans, measured some coffee and ran though my
options.

Could I turn right around and find Captain Dabber – probably
still at the same bar?

This was all unfair, that was the thing. Absolutely unfair. No one burns more fiercely at injustice than a criminal, and this was just wrong, this was not in the rulebook. I was nowhere near any job I had pulled, I was pretty sure no one had made me, and I'd been clean(ish) for almost a decade, come on! FBI? *Here?*

I brought two coffees on a tray and was rather proud that I delivered all the necessaries without nervous clattering. Little fears make you jump, but real fears, the big fears, well, they do flood the system with adrenalin but unless you're an amateur you use all that hormonal heat to focus on the most ancient of all human dilemmas: fight or flight?

I was extremely focused. I was confident that my Merc would outrun their Kia, but how much support did they have lined up from the locals? Could they shoot me? In a foreign country?

'Here we go,' I said. 'Do you take sugar? Milk?'

Delacorte shook her head slowly, side to side, still with that knowing smirk.

'So, how can I help the FBI?' I asked.

Delacorte sipped and crossed her legs which drew the linen tight over what I guessed would be spectacular thighs. Kim sat with legs apart, balls bulging aggressively against Dockers, weight slightly forward, a badger ready to pounce.

'Mr David Mitre,' Kim said again.

'That's me.'

'The author.'

'Yep.'

'Do you mind telling us why you are here on Cyprus?'

I shrugged. 'I may be setting a book here. I like to spend some time, get the local color. And I'm on deadline to write a piece for *GQ*. You know, all that writerly stuff.'

He waited.

I waited too, with a benignly quizzical expression glued on, pushing my panic down and down to join all the other fears I'd suppressed over the years. I assume all that festering emotion will eventually grow a tumor and kill me, but I had more immediate concerns.

'Is that it?' I asked, finally.

Kim sighed and shook his head with the sincere sympathy law enforcement folks feel for criminals. 'I'm afraid not, Mr Mitre. You see, we have reason to believe that Mitre is not your only name. A David Mitre, born the very same day as you, age seven days at his death, is buried in a cemetery in a little town near Broken Bow, Nebraska.'

'Well,' I said. 'That's an interesting coincidence.'

Kim did not smile. Delacorte did, but she wiped it away quickly.

'This Nebraska town, they never have gotten around to computerizing all their records. Birth records, death records, they're all there, just not cross-referenced. So, it seems they issued a birth certificate for David Mitre nine years ago. It was sent to . . .' He paused and pulled out a notebook, made a show of flipping through the pages before saying, 'Ah, here it is. Yes, the BC was mailed to Cranston, Rhode Island. To a letter drop at a UPS store.'

'Okay,' I said, still doing the puzzled face while Delacorte's half-lidded eyes mocked me.

'Mr Mitre,' Kim said with so very much regret, 'we have evidence that suggests you obtained a passport under false pretenses. And, not just the one. We have linked you with two other identities as well.'

And there it was. Time's up! Game over!

'Okay,' I said again, in a lower register.

'Do you have any way to explain—'

'Oh, for Christ's sake,' I erupted, nerves getting the better of me. 'Can we cut the bullshit? Are you here to arrest me or not?'

Kim started in with, 'I'm just trying to ascertain—' before he was silenced by Delacorte raising a languid hand.

'I think we're all on the same page, Frank,' she said. She had drunk a few sips of her coffee and set the cup back down, slow but very precise. Cup met saucer with hardly a sound.

'Cookie?' I said, nodding at the small plate of Hobnobs. I was caught. I was well and truly screwed. I could afford to be insolent.

That brought a genuine smile from Delacorte, one of those big, wide, inviting smiles, the kind of smile I was absolutely not going to be seeing again until I was a shambling old wreck being dropped off at the nearest bus station after doing my time.

'Mr Mitre,' Delacorte said.

'David, please,' I said. 'It's my favorite of all my names.'

'David,' she said with a gracious dip of her head.

'And I'll call you Agent Delacorte. So, what are we doing here, special agents K. and D.?'

'There was a murder the other day,' Delacorte said.

What?

'Yeah, I heard about it.'

'The victim was a British national also, coincidentally, traveling on a phony passport.'

'Huh.'

'A British national with a couple of warrants out for her.'

'Huh,' I repeated.

'You witnessed the murder.'

'Not quite. I almost did but—'

Delacorte held up her iPhone. 'Would you like to see the video?'

You shouldn't, as a rule, start to like the folks who want to lock you in a cage, but I kind of liked her despite everything. I liked her eyes. I liked the mockery in them. She was a woman I would never have tried to con. I sighed. 'From the yacht, I assume?' Goddamned tourists and their cameras.

'The resolution is quite good given the distance.'

'The miracles of technology,' I said.

'You were there, you saw, and you beat it out of there.'

This was not right. True, but not right. If they had video they knew I didn't do the crime. And anyway, ex-burglars and ex-grifters do not suddenly take up murder late in their careers. Also, I was white and the killer was not, which was the one thing all witnesses agreed, and which should be plainly visible on the video on her phone.

I detected a faint hint of light on the distant horizon. Hope pulled its head out of its hands and looked up through swollen, tear-streaked eyes. I sensed that the two specials had an as yet undisclosed weakness.

'Okay, I was there,' I said. 'And as soon as I saw what was going down, I bailed. So?'

'Well, David, here's our situation. We are what's called legal attachés, "legats." That's the term of art for FBI agents assigned to embassies. We deal in counterterrorism and organized crime, for the most part. That's all public knowledge.'

'For the most part' and 'public knowledge.' Did I catch the implication that they might sometimes involve themselves in things which were neither terrorism nor organized crime? Yes, I did.

'Terrorism?' I laughed. That, at least, I was innocent of.

'We know you're not the number two man for ISIS.'

'I applied for the job,' I said. 'But they went a different direction.'

'A woman is murdered. We recognize one of our own fugitives on the scene. We make a few queries. We're interested in the American witness, *you*, but, no disrespect intended, we are not *very* interested in you.'

'Should I feel insulted?'

'It's not that we don't care about theft or fraud, we do care. And all other things being equal, we would submit an extradition request and have you picked up and flown back to the States.' Then, out of sheer spite she added, 'In coach.'

'But all other things are not equal?'

She shook her head like she was in slow-motion, never taking her eyes off me. 'No, they are not, David. You see, as fascinating as you are, the dead woman is more fascinating still. We are very interested in finding out what happened to her. Very interested in who killed her and why.'

'I'll bite: who killed her? And why?'

Delacorte shrugged, a minuscule gesture, almost a suggestion of a shrug. 'We don't know.'

'Why do you care?' I asked.

'I'm afraid I can't tell you that,' she said. She tilted her head and watched me.

'She's a – what is the current term of art? Do we still say "person of interest," or is that no longer in vogue?' I asked.

'Mmm. Interesting suggestion. Unfortunately, there's only so much I can tell you – the US government is reluctant to grant security clearances to escaped fugitives.'

'That's rather close-minded.'

She liked that. 'So. So, there is only so much we can tell you. And only so much we can do here in a foreign country as legats. We have no power to order a legal search, and we have no power to arrest.'

'That must be very frustrating for you.'

'It can be. But when we operate outside the United States we are required to be circumspect. Indirect. To use whatever, or whomever, is legally available to us.' A sly and slightly terrifying grin appeared. 'Guess who is legally available to us.'

The truth dropped on me like a Road Runner cartoon anvil. 'Jesus H. Christ,' I blurted. 'You . . .' I peered at her, doubting my conclusion, but she nodded encouragingly, like a kindergarten teacher with a kid who had almost recited the whole alphabet and just needed to remember what comes after *elemenopee*. 'You want me to . . .' I couldn't finish it. It was absurd.

'Yes, David,' Delacorte said, coming to my rescue. 'You've got a perfect cover story, the whole visiting author thing. You are quite good at gaining people's trust. Obviously. And you are already connected to the local expat community via your landlady, Stella Weedon.'

'Dame Stella. She really likes people to use the "dame." British, you know. They take that stuff seriously. Well, the ones with the titles do, anyway. You think this is connected to expats?'

'And you are quite intelligent,' Delia Delacorte said, carefully not hearing my question.

'Thanks,' I said.

'And we have you . . .' She let it trail off, as if too delicate to complete the thought.

'By the balls?'

'I'll keep them safe for you,' she said. 'Maybe give them a little squeeze every now and then.' She mimed the squeezing. Far and away the most erotic threat I've ever received.

'What's in it for me?' I asked. Because it's important to pretend that you have a say in things, even when a lovely FBI agent is demonstrating her ball-squeezing technique.

'We have no authority here,' Delacorte said, and she regretted the fact. 'The locals are not big fans of the US of A at the moment.'

'Few people are. Including most Americans.'

'And there are the ongoing reunification negotiations . . .'

'Which will go nowhere,' I commented. Greek Cypriots started from the position that all Turks – and their progeny – who'd come to the island after the 1974 Turkish invasion had to go home. Ethnic cleansing is a nonstarter.

'So, we can't really poke our noses into this case.'

'Certainly not without sending a big, flashing neon message that the dead woman had already caught the eye of the FBI.'

'Mmm.'

'Which brings me back to what's in it for me.'

Delacorte unfolded her legs and leaned forward, elbows on knees. 'We don't want *you*, David. It's like fishing. We went looking for a shark, and we caught, well, not a guppy, but not a shark, either.'

Dissed by the FBI.

'So, to extend the metaphor I'm what, bait?'

The sleepy look disappeared, replaced by predator's eyes. 'Don't sell yourself short. You've pulled off a string of felonies in the US and despite that we could probably only convict you on two counts – at least at the federal level. As to your activities outside the US, well, that's not really our problem. No, you're a clever man, David. You're good at what you do, or at least what you used to do. You have a very healthy balance at a bank in Luxembourg.'

Seriously? They knew about my allegedly secret bank account in Luxembourg? Was nothing sacred? How about my other account in the Caymans?

'I don't suppose you can tell me what this is all about?' I asked.

'Murder's not enough?'

'Murder's too much,' I said, as the memory of a knife being twisted up, down, left, right loomed in my memory. 'But it's a symptom not the cause.'

'See? I said you were clever. You want to know what this is all about?' She took a moment, looking down. Then she glanced over at the long-silent Agent Kim, who was content to sit and give me unblinking cop stare. Finally she said, 'I can't tell you anything, David. But I can make an observation.'

'Observe away,' I said with a generous wave.

'Well, as a general observation, it's my opinion, that a man who would harm a helpless child should be impaled on a fucking telephone pole.'

There was no smirk in that. Agent Delacorte had put teeth into that remark. Unless she was a very good actress, that was pure, distilled, essence of righteous, law-enforcement-grade hate.

'And if I help you, you forget you ever heard of me?'

She shook her head, drawing back, and that flash of fire was gone. 'I never forget, David. However. I do sometimes misplace files. Isn't that right, Agent Kim?'

'She's disorganized sometimes,' Kim agreed. I would not have thought him capable of even minor wit.

Delacorte stood up and Kim followed her lead. Standing closer now I could see that she was very nearly my height.

'Don't run, Mitre,' Kim warned, doing his bad-cop thing. 'We'll catch you.'

'And Luxembourg?' I asked.

Delacorte smiled. 'Is that a country? Never heard of it.'

EIGHT

My first thought, after they had gone, was: *Run!*

My second thought was: *Scotch!* I went with that.

I understood Agent Delacorte's thinking. Someone surreptitiously tied to, or at least of interest to, the US government had been murdered. They wanted to know who done it, but American agents were not at that moment held in high regard anywhere in Europe, certainly not on Cyprus, and in any case the FBI could not get involved without signaling a degree of US interest not yet known to the Cypriots. Which the FBI presumably did not want to do.

What to do, what to do? Delacorte must have wondered. Oh, look! It's a US citizen whose balls I have in my pocket. He's 'clever,' knows at least a little about investigations, and can weasel his way into expat society and achieve a sort of attenuated 'local' status. He won't even cost anything, he'll spend his own funds just to curry favor, so there is the bonus of less paperwork to be filled out. And if it all blows up, we can deny everything with much loud haw-haw-hawing at the notion that we would ever do business with a man wanted for multiple felonies.

She could sell me out and anything I said about our implied deal would be instantly dismissed.

Well, Agents slash legats Kim and Delacorte were no doubt very good at their jobs, but I wasn't a complete mook.

I pulled out my phone, tapped the Nest app, pulled up the living-room camera, and played just enough to be sure the microphone had picked everything up. The video was not on my phone, it was already in the cloud. The NSA would take about two seconds to break in and wipe it – if they knew it existed – but the FBI was not the NSA. The FBI would need to know the video existed, and then they'd need a legal basis for a search warrant, and then they'd be stuck living with it because the FBI does not destroy evidence.

Here's some good, sound advice to aspiring criminals: know the law and the people who enforce it. Cop ≠ cop. Each organization comes with its own limitations and each individual cop comes with a full set of strengths and weaknesses.

And yet, I reminded myself, they knew about my bank account in Luxembourg.

Or did they?

She hadn't named the bank, or the amount in the account. Had it been a bluff? They could have simply traced the movements of my passport, noting a four-day stay in a country which, while lovely in a damp, bucolic way, was better known as an excellent place to hide money.

I tapped another app, muttered one of the several curse words I use for addressing apps, remembered how to do what I wanted to do, and sent a copy of the video to an account owned by my lawyers, one in New York and one in Paris. So now there were three copies. I sent another duplicate to my own secret Gmail account, opened it on my laptop and slid the video onto a memory stick.

Four copies. No, five, because I kept one on my laptop in a password-protected 'invisible' file.

Cloud, lawyer 1, lawyer 2, laptop and memory stick. Try

getting all five of those, Agents K. and D. Delacorte had me by the balls, but she would never be able to deny that she had made a deal, at least a clearly-implied one. If they threw me under the bus I'd drag them under with me, which meant I had at least some leverage. And I had confessed to nothing.

'Small consolation,' I muttered. Then I froze, replaying the moves of the two agents as they entered the door, crossed the room, sat . . . and I went for coffee. Yep, there went Agent Kim, jumping up the instant I was out of the room.

I found the tiny microphone neatly inserted between a standing lamp's plug and the outlet. Power supply and near invisibility: hidden in plain sight. Nice.

Such sneaky people, FBI agents. And playing a bit unfairly, frankly: bugging a private citizen without a warrant? For shame!

I fumbled in my junk drawer until I found a pen-sized voice recorder, set it to record, laid it on the coffee table, and went to take a long, hot shower, and to hell with the water restrictions. Having taken first steps, I decided to go ahead and have my nervous breakdown in the shower, with hot water running over my head.

Was I going to prison?

That question tended to cut through everything else happening in my mind. Was this it? Was it finally happening? Was I well and truly fucked?

I forced my thoughts back to avenues of escape. The best option was to hop aboard my Aussie's boat and head for Egypt. Or, better still, look for a tramp steamer at sea, pull up alongside and wave a fistful of cash. I could just hop aboard Cap'n Wilson's boat and run to Egypt or transfer to a steamer at sea and ride along to Tunis or Marseille or Genoa. Those were my options. No way I'd be able to get a flight out of Larnaca or Paphos.

I had come to Cyprus for a cluster of reasons – plenty of sun, a big English-speaking expat community to disappear into, and enough regional turmoil that authorities would have their eyes peeled for terrorists and refugees, not for retired gentleman thieves.

I could run. But I could not run as David Mitre. I could not still have that life and run, and I had done the thing no fugitive should ever do: I had come to value my present identity.

There was, however, the *other* option. I could actually try to figure out what had resulted in a fellow fugitive taking a knife to the lungs.

'Right,' I muttered into a stream of water, 'because now I'm Hercule fucking Poirot.'

I turned off the water, toweled, dressed, and recovered my voice recorder. I did a bit of light editing then leaned the recorder next to Agent Kim's listening device and hit play in a loop. I arranged throw pillows around the device, muffling any sound not coming from the recorder. Kim and Delacorte could listen all they liked to a twenty-minute loop of ambient noise. I swapped out the SIM card from my phone, not by any means perfect as a way to avoid being tracked, but every little bit . . .

I made a late-night snack of refrigerator antipasto, arranging fresh red peppers, some slices of *lountza*, the Greek version of *cappacola*, olives, *loukaniko*, a local sausage, some crumbled feta on a plate and toasted some bread. I made coffee to counteract the Talisker I'd panic-drunk.

I carried it all out onto the moonlit terrace, set it down, sipped the coffee and decided a sip was enough and I still needed whisky. Got whisky. Sat back down. And asked myself the question I had so often asked myself in my day job as a writer: what the hell is going on? What is the plot?

I typed:

> *Brit fuge (?) connected (?) to US law.*
> *Stabbed in the back.*
> *African. No ID. No knife. No evidence.*
> *Brits say no then yes to vic's passport.*
> *FBI says, 'Aha! We got you!'*
> *FBI says . . .*

What exactly had I gleaned from Agents Delacorte and Kim?

> *Passing yacht.*
> *Security clearance issue.*
> *Bad shit involving kids?*

'This is definitely some deep bullshit, here,' I muttered around a mouthful of salami. Then, 'And how the fuck did they get video that fast? And ID me?'

In what, twenty-four hours, Washington had heard about the murders, reached out to the yachtsman, gotten them to turn over their stills and video? And then dispatched Delacorte and Kim? From where, the Rome or Athens office?

'No, no, no,' I said, shaking my head. Agents K. and D. were already here. In fact, they'd had the victim, poor Rachel/Amanda under surveillance. That's how they knew about the yacht, and how they knew that some dude – me – had practically levitated away from the scene a millisecond after the stabbing.

Poor Rachel/Amanda had been looking for threats, I'd been watching the doomed woman while also looking for threats, and we had both missed the Eff Bee Eyeballs trained on her the whole time.

I resisted the urge to go to the hidden microphone and tell them what I had figured out, and add a 'nyah nyah nyah' or some equally contemptuous remark.

More advice for the aspiring criminal: don't taunt the FBI.

I glanced at my watch and reached a decision. Play the game, at least for now. Play the role Kiriakou, Kim and Delacorte seemed determined to force on me.

Eleven p.m. Now what?

Whorehouse, obviously. Sex workers know useful things like who is and is not bent in the local constabulary, who runs the rackets, who is scarier than who and . . . Well, that was it, unless you wanted advice on how to get a guy with ED off in under ten minutes.

In the old days, I'd have had to do some legwork to find such an establishment. I'd have gone looking for bars and pubs with a large upstairs and few windows. Or I'd have gone to a bar and hung around until some far-too-pretty and far-too-friendly woman with what the Stones called 'Far Away Eyes' sidled up beside me and allowed me to buy her a drink.

But God bless the internet, because it took about fifteen minutes of rooting around on message boards to find what I was looking for. The biggest annoyance was weeding through all the price-driven reviews – everyone wants it, few are willing to pay. But I eventually found what I needed in references to a place that was 'way overpriced,' and 'a little snobby.'

Chante was just walking up the hill as I headed to my car.

I nodded politely. 'Chante.'

'Mitre,' she responded. It came out more *mee-TERR* than MY-tur.

'How's Cypriot Hollywood life?'

She stopped and looked at (well, almost at) me and said, *'L'enfer, c'est les autres.'*

'Hell is other people? Should I take that personally?'

A single eyebrow rise, rather like agent Delacorte. 'You have read Sartre? *A l'université?'*

'Yes, but not at university. I didn't do college for long. I am a graduate of the university of life.'

I think for a second there she was starting not to despise me, but 'university of life' restored her contempt. So, being me and not some wittier person I added, 'School of hard knocks.'

And she moved on by.

The cathouse – I'm sure there's a politically correct word for it, but it did not come to me – wasn't much of a place from the outside, just another private home by the look of it. But it was a villa with seven cars parked outside; seven cars which, I was gratified to note, included more than a reasonable proportion of Mercedes, Jags and BMWs. Music throbbed from the villa as I killed my engine, not club music, more ballad-y stuff. Emo music, if that's still a thing.

I walked up the gravel to the front door where I was met by a large gentleman seated on a folding chair, smoking a small cigar and reading a magazine. He challenged me and I explained who I was and why I was there by handing him a hundred-euro note.

I was met inside by a woman who would be the spitting image of Madonna (the singer, not the mother of Jesus), if she'd gone in for a face-lift. She accentuated the Madonna comparison with an outfit that showed off some cleavage and hinted at BDSM, and sheathed her arms in long sleeves, either to hide track marks or flabby underarms. Possibly both.

'Good evening,' she said with a thick but manageable accent.

'Welcome to my home. I am Madame Meunier. May I get you a drink?'

I introduced myself as Walter Mosely again, and said, 'Perhaps a Scotch? Neat?'

'Will you follow me, please? I would like to show you the many pleasures we have for your enjoyment.'

A Scotch appeared and we sauntered – sauntering is really the only way to walk through a bordello – into the main room. I'll say this: for a Mediterranean cathouse it was not badly decorated. Yes, a bit too much gaudy gold paint and some eye-rolling erotic art, but Madame Meunier had dialed it back from full-on Trumpian gaud. The air was dense with competing perfumes, the lights were pink-tinged giving everyone a nice healthy glow, even the three middle-aged bald guys at the short bar.

I know of few things sadder and funnier than a sex-worker line-up. Six women ranging in age from eighteen to maybe thirty, brunettes, redheads, blondes, big, small, natural and enhanced, and all of them thinking the same thing: Am I going to have to fuck this guy?

Without being too full of myself, I was not the worst-looking fellow they'd ever seen. I'm clean, not a member of the reptile family, and present no danger of crushing. And I like women and women sense it.

I've been to brothels – there, that's the word – as part of setting up a mark or on occasion doing what I was doing now: buying information. But I don't like them. I have nothing against sex workers, they're just working stiffs paying their bills, but having half a dozen women lined up like cakes in a shop window for me to buy has never sat quite right with me.

I walked down the line, offering my hand to each woman in turn, speaking a few words. I wasn't looking for a hair color or a breast size, I was looking for intelligence and boldness. A few words and I can give you a rough assessment of IQ; it's not a Jedi mind trick, it's in the voice, the word choices, the speed of response. As for boldness, that's in the eye and the touch.

After a couple minutes I had it down to two: a gorgeous young Russian and a dreamy-eyed Egyptian. I guessed that the

Russian girl might be connected to people far scarier than me.
I have at times brushed up against Russian mobsters and while
this is not advice that will be necessary to any normal person,
I suggest avoiding them.

I picked the Egyptian girl, ordered a bottle of decent
Champagne at three times retail and retired to her room, which
came complete with a big whirlpool tub and a bed and far more
mirrors than were good for my vanity.

'What you like, honey boy?' she asked in execrable English.

'Well, first, I've forgotten your name.'

'My name Joumana. Is mean "pearl." You like see my pearl?'
Wiggle, wiggle, breast thrust, pouty lips.

'I'm sure it's there, Joumana, and I'm sure it's lovely, but
that's not quite why I'm here.'

Joumana was going for the exotic look, with kohled eyes and
gold glitter. She wore a black-and-gold brocade robe that fell
almost to the floor and would have been quite demure if not
for the fact that it was unbuttoned and open at the front revealing
a complicated net of black straps zigging and zagging to finally
resolve into a bra and garters. It was from the Agent Provocateur
collection. I knew this irrelevant trivia because I had once had
to remove an almost identical outfit using nothing but my teeth
since my hands were tied with silk rope and . . . Well, it wasn't
easy. Or relevant, really.

Joumana was very pretty, in excellent physical condition and
her eyes could melt concrete.

I sat on the edge of the bed – the other choice being the side
of the in-room Jacuzzi tub – and before I said anything I counted
out five hundred euro notes. Not enough to cause her to spon-
taneously combust, but emphatically more than the going rate.

'I no do anal,' she said with charming directness. 'No potty
things. I ask my friend to join us? She is very—'

This is the sex-worker version of 'Would you like fries
with that?' Brothel upselling.

I waved a hand, cutting her off. 'Do you mind putting on
some music?'

She blinked a couple of times, not in any hurry, then pulled
a phone from the pocket of her robe and swiped a few things.
Music swelled from speakers above the tub.

'You are astonishingly sexy, very beautiful, and if I were here for sex you'd be all I needed and more.' That is how you compliment a sex worker. 'But I'm not here for sex.' That is how you worry a sex worker.

My guess about her intelligence was validated by the way she produced a laugh that lasted a half second and carried a world of cynicism within it. She sat down, tugged her robe closed and suddenly learned to speak much better English.

'Information?' she asked.

'I'm afraid so.' I added another hundred and held the cash toward her.

She wanted to reach for it but hesitated, looking up at me with her hand itching to scoop.

'This will not make any trouble for you,' I said.

That was enough. She unburdened me of my euros.

'What is your question?'

'My question is this. Imagine you are the mother of a child here on Cyprus. What are the things you would worry about?'

That caught her off guard. In a brief flicker, I saw the truth in her eyes: she *was* a mother.

'You are worried about children?'

'Sure. Let's go with that.'

She shrugged and blew air out, making her cheeks and lips flap in a not-terribly-courtesanish way. 'There are lots of drugs.'

'Yeah.'

'And I would worry about criminal gangs. We do have them, here.'

I have some passing acquaintance with LA and Chicago street gangs. I doubted the Cypriot version was quite as scary or nearly as well-armed. 'Yes, gangs,' I agreed. 'But gangs are businesses and some of those businesses threaten children, and some do not.'

'Do you mind if I smoke?' She was already tapping out a Turkish cigarette.

'Not if you don't mind.' I drew a Montecristo out of my jacket's inner pocket. As she lit up, I cut the stogie, warmed it a bit over my cigar torch and puffed it to glowing light.

We were both much happier now.

'What is it you want, Mister . . .'

'Walter, please,' I said. 'I'm a writer, doing research. I want to know about the dark underbelly of Cyprus.'

She liked the phrase 'dark underbelly,' and repeated it a few times with various different points of emphasis. 'This is Cyprus. They were masters of smuggling since before Father Abraham.'

'And does that tendency extend to children?'

'Are people smuggling children? Why? There is no great shortage.'

I laid out another hundred and said, 'That's as high as I go for rhetorical answers.'

'And for more?'

'You give me something useful and you walk away with a week's earnings and none of it has to be known to management.'

'Maybe this room is bugged.'

'Of course it's bugged,' I said. 'That's why we're listening to this music. It's also all being videoed, which is why we're sitting here, this way, with my back to the camera inside that bronze of Rodin's eternal angel, and the other camera in the corner up there in the molding.'

Athenian galley eyes narrowed. 'Are you police?'

'Rather far from it.'

'Intelligence?'

I shook my head. 'Just a curious writer.'

'Information can be dangerous to those who possess it and those who give it out.'

'I find the best antidote to fear is cash.'

There followed a period of silence as she worked this out, weighing this and that against what she thought I might give her.

'Ten thousand euros.'

'Jesus!' I erupted. That was way too big an ask. Either she took me for an idiot, or what she knew was scary. 'Two thousand. Tops.'

'Three now. Three more when you see that I'm telling the truth.'

'You're going to trust me to come back with an extra three grand?'

'Yes, Walter, I am.' Which meant not really, but she sort of

wanted to tell me what she knew. I counted out some more
euros and kept them in my hand.

'It's the refugees,' she said. 'A boat arrives at least once a
week, overflowing with desperate people. I . . . I was once one
of those desperate people.'

'Okay.'

'Some of the refugees are girls or boys, not yet . . . I don't
know the English word.'

'Young? Prepubescent?'

'That, yes. When they land, they are interned for evaluation
as terrorists or criminals. Those suspected of crimes are
separated out, which sometimes leaves their children . . .' She
shrugged.

'Children separated. Okay. And?'

'And it just so happens that the pretty ones, the sweet virginal
girls, the innocent young boys, well, their parents are almost
always classified as suspected criminals or terrorists.'

'And deported?'

'And deported, with assurances that their children will follow
soon. Of course they do not. The children are placed in care.'
The words 'in care' came with a heaping helping of cynicism.

'And?'

'And what do you think, Walter? What do you think happens
to them?'

That put a stop to lighthearted banter. I take an extremely
liberal attitude toward property crimes, for obvious reasons, but
that laissez-faire attitude does not extend to murder, torture or
rape. It very definitely does not extend to child rape.

'You have names?'

She shook her head.

'If you were to keep your eyes and ears open, do you suppose
you might overhear something? I'm told all the best people
come here, sooner or later, the connected, the powerful.'

'You need to know this for the book you are writing?'

I didn't answer. She knew better. Instead of lying I asked, 'I
have this theory that in the back of any working person's mind
is a number, expressed in euros or pounds or dollars. A number
that, while it would not make them independently wealthy,
would buy them some freedom of action.'

'Ah?'

'Yes. I think of it as their "happy number." Not a fantasy number, but a number that would make them . . . happy.'

She considered, sizing me up. 'We return then to ten thousand euros,' she said at last.

I sighed. Negotiation has never been my strong suit. 'Okay. That is doable, *if*. If you give me what I need. Get me a solid name and it's worth ten thousand, wired to your secret account.'

'I have a secret account?'

'Of course you do.'

She finished her cigarette, stubbed it out in an ashtray that had been liberated from some distant Ritz-Carlton. She walked across the room, dug her purse out from under a tangle of clothing on a chair and came back with a slip of paper and a pen. She wrote something, folded it and gave it to me, carefully out of view of the cameras.

'Now, we must make it look as if more happened than a conversation,' she said, and opened her robe.

It made sense. The cameras were rolling after all, and vanity demanded I put on a decent show.

'Tempting, but no. Tell the madam I just wanted to talk about how my wife won't give head. You've had those conversations before.'

That earned an actual laugh.

I pumped her for more information and picked up a few tidbits, but nothing of immediate interest.

I didn't look at the paper she'd given me until I was back out in my car. On the paper was a long number. Her bank account.

And, the name Dep. Polis Cheef [sic] Cyril Kiriakou.

NINE

The Portuguese have a word: *saudade*. *Saudade* is a longing for what was, but also for what never was: a time, a place, a fantasy, a hope, a man or woman or an in-between. It's a dreamy, wistful sadness, the essence of their

6

fado. But, because the Portuguese are an old people, old and wise in life, that sadness can also be a pleasure.

Back in the bad old days before cars came with electronic back-seat drivers with clipped English accents forever suggesting turns you've just missed, it was possible to take a wrong turn. And when that happened your natural tendency – at least if you were male – was to plow on ahead, denying that you were lost. But eventually the signs that you'd taken a wrong turn would begin to accumulate.

In Austin, Texas, life had opened its hands and offered me a choice. I could go on as I had been, digging the hole ever deeper. Or I could go with the girl in the window.

Austin was a low point. Not my first or my last, but very low. Low as in sleeping under bridges, low. Low as in checking laundromats for loose change, low. I was in my early twenties, and in the first depressing weeks of my life as a fugitive from justice. To make it all worse I was perversely reading *Crime and Punishment*. A bit on-the-nose as a book choice, but I'd found a paperback copy in the Trailways station, which is where I kept my stuff in a locker and showered in a sink. Good times.

I got a job in a restaurant and started earning money legitimately, performing actual work and being paid in tips. So, no more bridges, and I was able to get a foul, roach-infested apartment, just off the University of Texas campus.

One night as I was coming home I glanced up and saw a girl in a window. In those days, I had not yet become the suave ladies' man I became in order to suavely ingratiate myself with marks. And I certainly did not make a practice of randomly deciding to knock on the doors of women I saw in windows.

But for whatever reason, and I never did come up with a satisfactory motive, I immediately went over, knocked on her screen door and after some hemming and hawing, we went for a beer.

And afterward we kissed.

It was not my first kiss. It was just the best.

The next night we slept together. And that, too, was the best, not because we engaged in theatrical displays of acrobatic lovemaking, but because I was already halfway in love.

I told her everything. Told her I was a thief. That I had jumped bail. I was compelled to be honest, like she was Wonder

Woman and I was wrapped in the Lasso of Truth. There was something different happening, something I had not experienced before. I knew, and she knew, in ways that are hard to describe, that we *worked*.

I have no superstitions. I don't do faith. I don't back sports teams, let alone religions. I am a stand-alone, a guy who takes a position off to the side the better to observe and exploit. But that first night it was as if my head had been turned for me, and my eyes focused for me. Like the great Hand of the God I did not believe in had reached down and said, *'There, you stupid, self-destructive fuck, go meet that girl.'*

We had a three-week affair. We were inseparable. But she was graduating college and had a job offer in Maryland. I had no ties to Austin. There was no reason I couldn't go with her to Maryland. No reason at all.

Faced with a future of love and friendship and all that good stuff people think is so important . . . Well, the God-I-Don't-Believe-In had it right: I was a stupid, self-destructive fuck, and out of habit I had cased the restaurant where I was working. It was a hangout for Texas politicians and lobbyists, and I had seen thick envelopes surreptitiously exchanged. I knew a money-making opportunity when I saw it.

The GPS of Divine Direction was telling me to turn right. I heard it clearly. I knew it spoke the truth. I knew, that's the thing. I knew.

So naturally, I turned left.

As I stood now on my terrace gazing out at the dark Mediterranean and the night lights of Paphos, I heard a voice singing and saw that Chante had walked outside onto her smaller patio, which was below and to the right of mine. She was smoking a joint and singing a melancholy French song with lyrics of loneliness and loss.

'Not helpful,' I muttered under my breath. I stepped back so she wouldn't see me.

I had a feeling not unlike the turning point in Austin, of being on a knife's edge. I had a terribly embarrassing thought: what if I actually did something . . . *good*?

This was followed immediately by the darker voice within

me wondering if I was being spoon-fed by Agents K. and D. Had they sensed some inner core of decency they could exploit by deliberately hinting this was all about kids?

The two voices – Gollum and Sméagol – debated in my head. The Clash had framed my dilemma perfectly: should I stay or should I go? I could call Dabber and we could sail away on the good ship *Aussie Cliché*.

It would mean the end of David Mitre. The end of my made-up city of New Midlands with all its colorful characters. No more Joe Barton, cynical private dick with a heart of gold and the obligatory drinking problem. I would have to rebuild from the ground up, new name, the enormous time-suck of creating a new identity . . .

Even before I started writing I knew that my life was a book, the Martin DeKuyper story, written by Martin DeKuyper. For a long time now the probable ending had been, '. . . so he was sentenced to ten years and served three before taking a shiv to the kidneys.'

A different ending tantalized me now: '. . . so the FBI let him go in recognition of his service, and he lived happily ever after, writing books and marrying the girl in the window.'

Gollum sneered at that.

TEN

I woke early, too early for the day's planned adventure – lunch with Father Fotos. The sun was up but had not yet fully committed to appearing. The air was fresh and cool and salty.

I was frowzy from lack of sleep but decided to work. I had half a manuscript which I had barely touched in days, and if I didn't get some pages down it would fade from memory and I'd have to reread the damn thing from the start – a waste of a day – just to figure out what I was supposed to be writing next. And I had the stupid *GQ* piece, a thing I could interrupt as necessary without losing my place.

I began to assemble my *mise en place*, as Pierre Gagnaire might say, my writing set-up: coffee, two cigars, cigar torch, coffee, two bottles of water, screen cleaner, power cord, sunglasses and coffee.

And without warning I sensed a person behind me, jumped like a cat, spun and settled upon recognizing Chante.

'Jesus, you scared me. You know there's a doorbell, right?'

'I missed the bus. You must drive me to the set.'

'Must I? Some people might think to add a "please."'

Her response was to look at her watch. Pointedly. Like I was the one running late.

'Fucking hell,' I said, filled with righteous indignation and already knowing I'd do it because, as any professional writer will tell you, the excellent excuses for *not* writing encompass pretty much anything.

I put the top down on the car, obscurely hoping the wind would annoy Chante.

'Where are we going?' I asked as we pulled away.

'I will put it in your GPS.'

She did. And I said, 'That's an hour and ten minutes!'

'Yes.'

'You take a bus there?'

'It is not a public bus, it is a coach provided by the producers.'

'Ah.'

I had not yet driven inland, up into the mountains, and once we turned off the A6, I found myself on a scenic road passing through moderately scenic villages. There were actual trees up here, forests even, very different from the Cyprus I had seen in the lowlands. Up here it was suddenly Tuscany, red-tile roofs, villages perched in unlikely spots, even the occasional small vineyard.

We caught up to the bus.

'If you pull in front of it, I will wave to make it stop,' Chante said.

'Nah. Now that I'm up here I want to see the set.'

'I will not introduce you to movie stars.'

That irritated me. I shot her a glance full of that irritation. 'Do you seriously think I give a fuck about movie stars? Let alone some French flavor-of-the-week?'

Chante didn't answer, but she was amused in a straight-faced, French sort of way. She silently mouthed, 'Flavor-of-the-week.'

'Where are you from?' I asked.

'I live downstairs.'

I sighed, and after a while she relented. 'I am from Bayonne. You will not have heard of it.'

'Southwest coast near the Spanish border. Hence the piperade,' I said. 'Basque country.'

She looked at me like I'd sprouted an extra head.

'I know!' I said, mocking her. 'An American who knows geography! I even know a bit of history, believe it or not. France and Algeria, for example. Mokrani isn't a French name, so, let me venture a guess: '61? '62?'

'1962,' Chante admitted. 'My father emigrated as a child. My mother is French.'

We arrived at the tiny village of Lofou. Lofou is the real deal, a village of sandstone walls and red-tile roofs and narrow cobbled streets. It had only a hundred or so actual residents but at the moment looked like it was under siege by tractor trailers, panel trucks, a flatbed and two buses, like tanks lining up to attack. Dozens of men and women of the competent, lanyard-wearing variety were hustling equipment out of the trailers onto golf carts and pickup trucks for the brief shuttle into the town center. I threaded my way through them, suddenly acutely aware that I was in an expensive convertible with the top down and yet was a nobody. You could see it in the speculative glances followed by the frowns followed by the dismissal. Nope: I was not worthy of attention.

A perimeter of sorts had been set up: a guy with a neon yellow safety vest and an especially-impressive lanyard sitting in a canvas folding chair. As we rolled slowly forward he bestirred himself and raised an officious hand.

Then he smiled and said, 'Ah, Chante! With your own chauffeur!'

He waved us on and with hand gestures indicated what had been an open space in the middle of a traffic circle but was now a sort of chaotic camper and RV show.

'Let me off here,' Chante said.

'I need a pee,' I said, and squeezed the car onto churned mud behind the open-sided craft services tent.

The instant I came to a complete stop Chante was out of the car with nary a word of farewell, let alone thanks.

Busy girl, presumably.

I wandered around the camp, found a porta-potty, did the necessary and moseyed back to the craft services layout in search of coffee. The food table was surprisingly attractive, with great mounds of croissants and ice trays coddling yogurt and an omelet station manned by a young chef complete with toque. Half a dozen picnic tables had a middle school cafeteria vibe in that each had the feel of a clique: dudes with tool belts and gaffer tape at one table, extras with swivel heads looking for movie stars at another, people wearing protective robes over costumes at another. I snagged a brioche and a coffee and spotted a smaller table, unoccupied, and plopped myself there.

I was happily tearing off chunks of brioche when a presence loomed and I looked up to see a strikingly beautiful woman who, at first glance, probably qualified under the half-my-age-plus-seven-years rule. Younger but not creepily younger. She had a cup of tea, which was a strike against her, but on the other hand was the utter gorgeousness thing. I was completely prepared to forgive her the tea and propose marriage.

I smiled and motioned for her to have a seat.

'Nothing to eat?' I asked her. Americans are notorious for starting conversations with complete strangers. Europeans sneer, but at the same time they're a bit jealous.

'I am . . . do not . . . *le petit déjeuner*,' she said. '*Je suis toujours au régime.*'

French. I can manage French just well enough that French people don't instantly want to gag me with a sock. *Régime*. She was on a diet.

'*Régime*?' I repeated with a fair approximation of a Gallic shrug. '*Mais pour vous c'est ridicule.*' A diet? For you? Ridiculous.

Which I think was a compliment. Probably. Anyway, she didn't tell me to fuck off, so that was a good thing.

She asked me who I was, which I took to mean what right did I have to be drinking free coffee.

'I'm not with the movie,' I confessed. 'I just drove my neighbor up here. She missed her bus.'

Chante suddenly appeared behind the starlet and it was then that the penny dropped.

'*Madame*!' Chante said to Minette through gritted teeth while glaring at me.

'Ah, Chante,' Minette said. 'I am speaking with your charming driver.'

'Actually, we are neighbors.' I deployed my number six grin, the one that conveys cheeky impertinence. 'And good, good friends.'

Take that . . . *neighbor*.

'Hair and make-up in ten minutes, *madame*,' Chante said.

Minette sighed. She was small, Minette, smaller even than Chante, who was no Amazon. She had wheat-blonde hair which might even be natural, mesmerizing lips that turned down at the corners, a broad forehead and amused eyes. I liked her. I think I'd have liked her even if she wasn't the most beautiful woman I'd seen in a very long time. I'd have liked her less, but I'd have liked her.

'Will you not introduce us?' Minette asked Chante.

'Minette, David Mitre. He is a writer.'

'Of novels, not scripts,' I added hastily.

'Well, we must be certain that Mr Mitre is invited to the fundraiser,' Minette said, *toujours en francais*, as Chante's eyes measured me for a coffin. 'It is for a very good cause.'

The star stood, and so did I. She shook my hand and excused herself to go off and be slathered in entirely superfluous cosmetics.

'I will be with you in one moment,' Chante said to Minette. Which left us alone.

'You must not sleep with her,' Chante said.

'Sleep with her! Jesus, Chante, you're getting ahead of—'

'Read some of that Hollywood gossip you despise,' Chante ordered. And she was gone.

'Who owns the fucking Mercedes?' a harried woman with a clipboard yelled.

I raised my hand, went to the car and drove back down out of the forested mountains with thoughts of Minette on my mind. Chante's warning translated to me as an endorsement of my chances. A brief, torrid affair with a stunning

French actress? At very least it would make a great story for me to tell in the common room of whatever prison I was heading to.

ELEVEN

I intercepted Fotos on his way to our lunch date and fell in beside him. Fotos led us to a little round table beneath the overhang of an unambitious café. He lit a Camel. I lit a Cohiba Esplendido – I usually like a fatter stick, but this had a gorgeous flavor, which started out cedar and evolved into a sort of Mexican chocolate spiciness.

'So,' I said, once I had achieved a centimeter of ash, 'you want to be a writer.'

There followed half an hour of off-point questions like 'what's your inspiration?' and 'where do you get your ideas?' Even my old favorite, 'what software do you use?' This is standard. There's an old saw about amateur warriors talking tactics while professionals talk logistics. In my (current) line of work the equivalent would be 'wannabes talk inspiration, professionals talk rights deals and options.' I've been on book tour, I've spent time in green rooms and dark bars with writers and not once have we ever talked about inspiration. You might get a conversation going about Oxford commas, but mostly we literary *artistes* talk money.

But I plowed through it all with a nuanced blend of encouragement and superior condescension. It's what they expect. Then, as the sun grew hotter and the shadows shorter, it was my turn.

'I have a question for you, Father. I heard something disturbing the other day about refugee kids.'

His emotions, as best I could judge, went: surprise, puzzlement, worry and finally, caution. 'Our charity work has not been primarily involved with refugee issues.'

I don't give a fuck about your charity, dude. I'm not checking up on how you spent my contribution; you could spend it on cocaine and bestiality porn for all I care, is not what I said.

'I guess it's the pictures, you know? You see them on Twitter or wherever, these little kids . . . I mean, I'm not sentimental, but it kind of breaks your heart, doesn't it?'

'Indeed, it is heartbreaking, the very word. Heartbreaking,' he agreed, just bleeding human decency and concern and empathy all over the table.

'What happens to kids who wash up on Cyprus from Syria or Egypt?'

'From more places than that, I'm afraid. Libya, Iraq, Somalia, Sudan, Saudi Arabia, even.'

'And what do the Cypriot authorities do with them?'

He shrugged. 'They are taken to processing centers and from there to a facility in Kofinou.'

'Kofinou. That must be a hell of a place. I mean, it's got to be hundreds, maybe thousands of kids.'

He shook his head. 'Perhaps not that many. You see, Cyprus' laws do not allow for family reunification. You can apply for legal status, but that does not mean you can bring your children. In fact, refugees avoid Cyprus, if they can, because the Greek Islands have more favorable terms.'

'Interesting. And all the refugees know this?'

'The refugees know nothing; but the smugglers know. If you are a Syrian or Lebanese or Egyptian trafficker, you know.'

'So, say I'm a refugee father with two kids.'

'You would perhaps try to reach another destination.'

'I found this picture online.' I pulled out my phone and handed it to him.

'Yes, yes, that is the boat that was driven ashore two weeks ago by high winds.'

'Zoom in. I count seventy-eight people on that dinky boat. Eight or nine look like kids, at least to me.'

'Yes, yes, of course.'

'So, in that case where they came here sort of involuntarily, those kids . . .'

He favored me with a benign, pastoral smile. 'I see. You want to help them?'

Yes, because I am Mother Teresa reborn. I am to the milk of human kindness what Kentucky is to Bourbon. Basically, I am a bit of a saint. Don't you see the gold dinner plate on my head? I also did not say.

'I don't know that there's much I can do . . .' Modest shrug. 'But I'm interested enough to want to know more.'

But then, a troubled shadow crossed his unlined brow. 'I . . . well, there are some men who go looking for . . .'

If you wish to signal outrage without going overboard, you press your lips together, pull back a few inches, and narrow your eyes, just once. 'Father Fotos, I am not a pedophile.'

'No, no, no, of course not, I never for a moment . . .'

And just like that I had the location of the camp in Kofinou, and a contact person who would be very happy to speak with me, at least according to Fotos.

Now I had a different issue. Could I trust Fotos or not? Should I? Was there some better option? I could get someone online to do a job of translation for me, or I could ask Fotos. On the surface the online option would seem safer, but there's a problem with the internet: it's a permanent criminal exhibits storage facility. What I committed to email could be shared endlessly.

'Father, I have a bit of a confession.'

He smiled, sensing a joke. 'Then what a convenience that I am a priest.'

'I . . . uh . . .' Quirky smile, hesitation, long pull on my Esplendido. 'Well, some people – people of the police variety – have the mistaken notion that I have some skill at investigation. I was given a document, an inventory of a certain victim's possessions . . .' I paused for the two seconds it took Fotos to reach the unavoidable conclusion that this involved the Paphos beach knifing. 'And the police officer kindly translated it for me, but I have to confess my aural memory is not all it might be, especially when I'm hearing information while simultaneously distracted by impure thoughts directed at a delicious plate of fish.'

Lying, fiction writing, pretty much the same thing.

'Is that your confession?' He played along. 'Impure thoughts about fish?'

'We still don't have time to go into my sins, not even if we just stick to gluttony.' I paused to produce a wry, abashed smile.

'No, the confession is that I have forgotten half of what this policeman translated. I was wondering . . .'

I opened my iPhone, swept around for a bit and turned a photo of the inventory sheet around so he could see.

Did he believe me? He seemed to. He was a young priest and maybe still a bit naive. I hoped.

Anyway, I got my translation, which I wrote down carefully so as not to forget again, then hurried back to my villa, checking to see whether there were any parked cars with bored police inside. Nope. Not yet.

I spread my notes out on the kitchen island, pausing only to start the coffee maker.

This was the list, minus various items of clothing, dresses, skirts, slacks, tops, bras, panties, and three scarves, with labels from Marks and Spencer, John Lewis, Galeries Lafayette, Anthropologie – all mass-produced and untraceable, and all painstakingly detailed by police officers with no interest in fashion:

> €5,000 – mixed denominations
> UK passport name: Rachel Faber
> UK passport name 2: Amanda J. Hynson
> UK driving license: Rachel Faber
> Cannon digital SLR camera – wiped data card
> Book: Little Town, Big Trouble by Lee Child
> Guide book: DK Eyewitness Travel: Cyprus
> Book: Lonely Planet Greek Phrasebook and Dictionary
> MacBook Air laptop
> iPhone
> MacBook charger
> iPhone charger

All of that, I knew. The electronics were tantalizing, but I was no better than anyone else at breaking into an iPhone or laptop. In lazily-written thrillers there's always a guy in some picturesquely squalid basement room surrounded by glowing lights and Marvel action figures who only needs to grumble and tap a few keys. Those people don't actually exist. Anyway, I wasn't in possession of either the phone or the laptop.

MiraLAX
Ambien (label removed)
Benadryl – over the counter
Ibuprofen – over the counter
Purse-size first-aid kit
Hairbrush
Comb
Portable hair dryer
Mousse
Spirit gum
Artificial nails
Artificial eyelashes
Lipstick – Show Me the Honey (Lancôme)
Lipstick – Berry In Love (Lancôme)
Lipstick – Boom Meringue (Lancôme)

I paused to google the lipstick colors. As I expected, they were quite distinct and different and I smiled: good fugitive tradecraft that. Easy to run to the ladies' room, apply a different lipstick, wrap a scarf over your head, add sunglasses, stuff your sweater or coat in a bin, and walk out a different person.

I travel with two stocking caps in different colors, an extra pair of very noticeable sunglasses, and cotton balls to puff out my cheeks and lips. (I can do a credible Vito Corleone when necessary.) And like poor Rachel/Amanda or Amanda/Rachel, I keep a small bottle of spirit gum. In an emergency, you can fashion a temporarily-plausible mustache out of clipped hair and spirit gum. In fact, I'd had occasion to use it once, though in that case I sliced a few inches off the back of a ponytailed professor and . . . But, long story and not relevant.

Purse
Wallet
Swiss Army knife
Small coil of wire
Six plastic cable ties

That stopped me, as it must have Kiriakou. You might use cable ties to secure loose items in your luggage. Then again, you might use them as effective non-magnetic, airport-travel-safe handcuffs.

And maybe she had pictures to hang with that wire. Unless. Unless she also had . . . I scanned down the list, looking for sticks, rods, something . . . yep, carabiners would do it. Very innocent – carabiners have a dozen valid uses. You wouldn't necessarily be wrapping wire around them to form a garrote.

I stood back and digested the fact that Rachel/Amanda might be a fugitive like me, but was definitely a bit more bloodthirsty. Garrotes are not the weapon of choice for nice people. It is not a weapon of self-defense. The thing about a garrote is that its only use is for committing murder from behind.

I scanned down the list for other weaponry. The Swiss Army knife maybe, under very limited circumstances. The scissors? Meh.

A small refillable spray bottle, empty.

And? And, a small bottle of Tabasco sauce. It was the sort of thing lots of people carried, people who liked spicy foods. But you could also dump it into a spray bottle, maybe dilute it with just enough alcohol, and voila, homemade pepper spray.

'Rachel slash Amanda,' I muttered, 'You were a bad, bad girl.'

I googled her names. Too many hits to be useful.

The list held nothing else of interest, at least nothing I spotted, aside from the credit cards and their possible charges.

Those fictional guys sitting in basements who can instantly hack into the NSA mainframe? They don't exist, but guys who can pull up a credit history? They're a dime a dozen.

I swapped SIM cards in my phone, fiddled around till I got a connection. I opened my WhatsApp, scrolled till I found the guy I was looking for, and typed:

> Me: Hey. It's John Johnson from that conference in Vegas.
> Not me: Sure.
> Me: I have a couple numbers.
> Not me: I have a number, too. It's the number 500. Also the symbol: $
> Me: Routing and account?

He sent me his bank account information. Surprise! A Cayman's bank.

I opened my bank app and did the requisite swiping and tapping, then went back to WhatsApp and typed in the credit card account numbers.

Nine minutes later I had the complete readouts on Rachel and Amanda. It seemed my buddy Cyril Kiriakou was not being entirely forthcoming.

I could ask. It would be risky, though. Kiriakou might be the kind of guy who kept a close eye on credit inquiries involving him. But nothing ventured . . .

> *Me: I also have a name for a deeper dive.*
> *Not me: I also still have room in my bank account.*
> *Me: Cyril Kiriakou. But you might need the Greek spelling.*
>   *Hang on.*

This took some doing, but I was eventually able to Google something I was pretty sure was the policeman's name in Greek script. I cut and pasted it into the app.

> *Me: Location Cyprus. Occupation cop. Age approx. 50.*
>   *Dark hair. 5'8" give or take.*
> *Not me: That's harder and it's the middle of the fucking*
>   *night here. Tomorrow first thing upon seeing deposit*
>   *receipt.*
> *Me: Fair enough.*

I made a list of questions for myself. In no particular order:

> *Who has 2 passable UK passports?*
> *Why?*
> *Who knifed her?*
> *Why?*
> *What warrant's out for her?*
> *Kiriakou. Bent?*
> *WTF is this all about?*
> *Profit?*
> *Run?*

Minette and then run?
WTF was a cop doing at Dame S. party?

That seemed like a swell list, an excellent example of my sleuthing skills as well as my list-making skills. It occurred to me that there was one question I could answer fairly easily.

I hiked up the hill to Dame Stella's house and found her husband, Sir or Lord or whatever he was, Archie Weedon. He was harassing a gardener who appeared to be spreading mulch in a flower bed.

He looked up sharply when I said, 'Good afternoon.'

He was a tall man, early seventies, thinning gray hair combed back over a shiny scalp. He wore very fine fawn wool slacks, a crisp white shirt open at the neck and a navy blazer. No tie, so I suppose he was dressing down for yard work. For a second, I caught sight of the guy he must have been before his brain started to turn to Swiss cheese: stern, steely, arrogant. But then he blinked and the steely look was gone, replaced by benign befuddlement.

'I'm David Mitre, I rent your villa. I was at the party,' I said.

'Party?' he asked, and frowned in confusion.

'Yes, I was just wondering if I might speak with Dame Stella. A matter of no great importance, so if she's busy . . .'

She wasn't, or at least she was willing to have me drop by with a rent check a few days early. She was sitting by the pool and invited me to join her for tea, and in the spirit of comradeship I actually drank some, hiding my shudder of disgust. Dame Stella was wearing an open, thin wrap over a one-piece bathing suit.

You're rich, have great legs and a husband who surely isn't keeping you overly-amused. I could have a hundred large out of your hands and into mine inside of a week. I did not say.

'A little bird tells me you made a substantial contribution to the church's poor box,' she said, smiling approval.

'Well, you'd mentioned the work they do . . .' A modest shrug.

'Are you playing up to me, David?'

'It's a lifelong habit of doing whatever beautiful women tell me to do,' I said.

She liked that just fine. 'And squaring accounts with the Almighty?'

I grinned to hide the suspicion that she knew more about me than she should. 'Why would I need to curry favor with the Almighty?'

She laughed, and it was more snort than she intended, but she said, 'I suspect a man like you has a few . . . indiscretions . . . on his conscience.'

'My . . . indiscretions . . . leave neither party to them requiring or wishing for forgiveness,' I said, playing along. 'Well . . . not usually.'

That apparently exhausted her need for flirtation, because she asked, 'How are you getting along with Chante?'

'Her? Oh we are, oh . . . just bestest friends.'

'She can be abrupt.'

'She can be damn rude,' I countered. 'I want to thank you again for inviting me over.'

'I hope that policeman wasn't a sad bore.'

'Nah. He was fine. Friend of yours?'

'Kiriakou?' She did nothing to hide her distaste. 'Kiriakou is not a friend. An acquaintance of Jez's, they play golf together with my husband sometimes. But it is wise to stay friendly with authorities, so when he asked if he could come . . .'

'He invited himself?'

'He very nearly pleaded. He is a big fan of your writing. And as I said, he is a friend of a friend.'

'Jez? I . . .' I made a confused face.

'Jeremy Berthold. Jez. He's, you might say, the unofficial head of the British expat community. You were introduced.'

Oh, you mean the big old guy gone to seed who likes to play literary critic? The Oxbridge twat with the stoned trophy wife and the fifty thousand dollar Patek Philippe for which I could probably get a good twenty grand? Okay, fifteen grand? I did not say.

'Kind of a beefy guy? Ginger? We just exchanged polite non sequiturs.'

'Yes, that's him,' Dame Stella said, not sure whether I should be reproved for describing him as beefy. 'He's been here for years and years and I suppose struck up a friendship with the policeman.' That last word came with a sauce of distaste.

It was too hot a day for the cold chill that shivered my spine. 'And Kiriakou wanted to come just to meet me? Huh.'

'I do hope he wasn't too taxing.' She reached over to lay her hand on mine on the table.

'Not all,' I said, and put my free hand over hers, giving a brief squeeze and standing up. 'Well, I have to run.'

I wasn't sure if I meant that literally.

TWELVE

I set off toward the divided capital of the divided island with the unpleasant fact that Kiriakou had traded on a friendship just to get in the same room with me. I listed the possible reasons as, 1) Kiriakou really was a fan, 2) he somehow saw me as a concern or even a threat, 3) he had some other reason to want to be at the party and I was just the excuse.

The number 2 selection was what worried me. If the answer was number 2, then the source would have to be the Specials, K. and D. I couldn't see why they'd rat me out and then try to use me.

Or. Or Kiriakou had spotted me at Theo's bar, knew I was an eyewitness, and wondered why I had broken the sound barrier leaving the scene. In which case: why was a Cypriot policeman watching a murder and doing nothing to intervene?

The drive to Kofinou was an hour fifteen along the A6 which follows the south shore before heading north toward Kofinou reception center, refugee camp, whatever they called it. An hour fifteen if you obey the speed limits, but it was a bright, stunning day, so I put the top down and did it in fifty-five minutes.

The initial, successive rushes of terror had faded a bit, weakened from too-long prolongation. Weakened as well by the sense that I was at least *doing* something now. So much of the fugitive lifestyle – sure, it's a *lifestyle* – involves waiting and hoping, waiting and fearing and hoping, unaware of what enemy armies may be forming up to come after you. You live in a constant state of cringe.

Now at least I had the vague outlines of what was happening. Emphasis on vague. I had a scrap of a hint of a promise from Agents Kim and Delacorte. And I had something outside of narrow self-interest to add motivation, something which had some resonance for me. I had never spent serious time in prison, just some incidental jail time, but I shared the criminal brotherhood's moral taxonomy of crime.

At the top of that taxonomy are the bosses, the royalty of hard, smart guys who run gangs or crime families. Below them come all those who successfully crime for cash, your drug dealers, your bank robbers, your embezzlers, your con men, your better class of burglar. Emphasis on *successfully*, because crooks are capitalists and have the same underlying moral code as every CEO ever profiled by *Forbes Magazine*: money is good, money creates its own justification.

Less successful crime-for-cash activities – sticking up liquor stores, street muggings, shoplifting – are treated the way you might treat a child practicing the French horn: that's sweet, honey, now go to your room while I take an Advil. No one *hates* these types, we just don't think they're especially *cool*.

Then there is a connected but separate branch on the crime family tree: the violent criminals. Here, too, success is important. If you pulled off a righteous murder for the honor of your gang: respect. If you did a manslaughter or aggravated battery because of some intolerable insult: okay. Doesn't make you a hero, but okay. If you're just some out-of-control asshole who murders for no good reason, you may be feared, you will certainly be treated with care, but you are not an object of respect.

Down below the successful cash criminals, down below the righteous murderers, below the less successful cash criminals, come the creeps, chief among them the rapists. The only people who like rapists are other rapists. The rest of the criminal world has mothers and sisters and wives and girlfriends and are not fond of the rapist species. There is no rapist's track to achieving respect in the joint.

Then, down there, way, way down there at the very bottom, are guys who prey on children. A stone-cold gangster with three kills on his sheet and five more no one knows about, may also be a father with a couple of kids to his credit. And that man believes the moral gap between himself and a child predator is as vast as the gap between *homo sapiens* and the herpes virus.

I'm not quite ready to elevate murderers to high moral status, no matter their motivation, but I've had nice, long conversations with killers and gangsters when I would never exchange a word with a short-eyes beyond 'get the fuck away from me.'

I suppose the truth is we all need someone to look down on, and being at no great altitude myself, I could still at least despise those people. Now, for the first time since, well, ever, I could just about convince myself that I was doing something decent other than writing stories.

'David Mitre,' I intoned, 'aka Alex Lobach, aka Carter Cannon, aka Frank Mates, etcetera: defender of children.'

Sure. Why not? And if it got Delacorte off my back (or even onto hers) that would be absolutely great. Win-win.

I swiped Bluetooth on my phone and pumped music to the car stereo: Toots and the Maytals singing about the stressful effects of pressure.

You got that right, Toots. You too, Maytals, when the pressure drops on you, you gonna feel it. But music in the car with the top down and a bright sun overhead does take the edge off.

The refugee reception center in Kofinou is conveniently located near absolutely nothing but hills, rocks and the rusting hulk of an abattoir. That is not a metaphor: there used to be a functioning slaughterhouse quite close at hand where the refugees could enjoy the smell of dead pig. Who doesn't enjoy dead pig smell? Especially when it's an animal you consider unclean?

The town center of Kofinou has a neat little stone church and pretty much nothing else. The refugees are well away from town and with minimal bus service, because it's one thing to let a few refugees in, it's a whole 'nother matter having strange people with not-white skin speaking strange languages touching the vegetables down at the local AlphaMega. Above the sign pointing to the refugee center there's still a small sign for the abattoir.

Reception and Accommodation Center for Applicants of International Protection, the big sign reads.

It's rolling hill country, kindling-dry straw interrupted by carob trees. In the distance, the mountains loom, the most prominent being Stavrovouni mountain, which is topped by the Stavrovouni monastery of the Holy Cross. I wondered if the monks up there used telescopes to spy on the Muslim residents of the camp.

From the wide-open gate, I could see most of the original camp, two dozen half-sized shipping containers set in a herringbone pattern on both sides of a paved street. The containers had doors and small windows and air conditioning units resting on the slab foundation. They were painted in pastels now faded by the relentless Cypriot sun.

I knew from the satellite view on Google Maps that there was an addition in the form of another two dozen containers that essentially mirrored the first part but with a single covering tin roof. But not shown on the satellite imagery was the tumorous growth that was the result of what was happening in Egypt. Syria had calmed a bit, but Syria was small beer next to Egypt which acted as a conduit not just for its own explosive population, now approaching one hundred million, but for Libya, Chad, Sudan, Yemen, Somalia . . . It seemed at times as if the entire population of Saharan Africa was trying to push its way up the Nile to the Mediterranean. There were refugees who had walked fifteen hundred miles from Congo, and that is not a Sunday stroll.

Most of the refugee flow had gone to the Greek islands, Italy or Turkey, but thousands had found their way to unwelcoming Cyprus. As a result, the original camp and the first extension were now utterly overshadowed by the white, UN-supplied tents that extended down the gully, then up onto the hills on either side, eighty, maybe even a hundred tents, pitched at inconvenient angles and in no particular order.

There was an incongruous fishing boat resting just before the camp gate, looking like evidence of some Noahanic flood that had left this tiny ark behind. Just in front of the forlorn boat was a green sign announcing that this was an emergency assembly point. A dozen or so cars were parked there, baking in what was turning out to be a beastly hot day. Workers were busy installing wiring and plumbing in the concrete shell of what was presumably to be a three-story administration building. Bulldozers were parked on the hillside to the left, having begun the job of terracing the hill to create flat spaces.

Around this rustic campground sprawl a chain-link fence

snaked. Chain link is only effective when backed up by razor
wire, electrical charges, mines, dogs and/or gun towers, and
Europe still has too many memories to go quite that far. It
looked like a minimum-security prison in New Mexico, but a
noncommittal one.

*We'd kind of like you to stay within the camp and not wander
into the hills, unless you have a pair of wire cutters . . .*

An official SUV in United Nations white moved slowly
through languid gaggles of women in hijabs, some in colorful
saffron robes, and men in salvaged jerseys from American and
British sports franchises.

I pulled up to the gate. The guard, an unarmed civilian, challenged me and I showed my passport and dropped the name
Fotos had given me: Calix Petrides. I had assumed 'Calix' to
be a male name and was surprised to find that the name belonged
to a middle-aged woman dressed in jeans and a tan utility vest.
She had gray hair pulled back hard, matching eyebrows, and
the face of a determined beaver.

'Father Fotos sent you to me? Did he mention that I scarcely
have time to eat lunch, let alone entertain guests?'

It wasn't so much hostile as harried and challenging. She
wasn't dismissing me, she just wanted me to justify my exist-
ence. I held out a small pink cardboard box and lifted the lid
revealing half a dozen little pies filled with spinach and feta,
or cheese and bacon, or something the bakery had listed as
'traditional' meat.

'I brought lunch.'

'Nothing to drink?'

'Not unless you drink whiskey,' I admitted, sliding a flask
from my pocket.

'I'll put a kettle on.'

We went into Calix Petrides' office in the existing administration building, a half-sized container like the others, but overrun
with hurrying bureaucrats and NGO workers. Her office, occu-
pying a partitioned third of the container, was likewise overrun,
the window shaded against the sun, with papers in stacks on
shelves and even on the floor. She lifted a stack of folders off
the one visitor's chair, set my box of pies on the desk, and
hit the switch on the electric kettle.

Waiting for the water to boil we chatted about Cyprus and food and the weather. She made tea and for the second time in just hours I drank the vile stuff, and we got down to the job of murdering some pies. She wolfed in a very un-European way, a busy woman, impatient, wondering who the hell I was and why the hell I was there feeding her.

I drew out my phone. 'This will probably sound crazy, Mrs Petrides, but I have become fixated on this photo. This refugee boat.' I held it so she could see the picture, then swiped to an enlarged still of a boy, maybe six or eight. Then I swiped to a second picture of another boy. And finally, a picture of a girl.

She nodded. 'Yes, the most recent boat from Alex. Sorry, Alexandria, Egypt.'

'I can zoom in enough to see faces on a few.' I tapped and swiped. 'These three kids, are they here?'

'Mr Mitre, we currently have one thousand, eight hundred and five souls here in a facility originally designed for four hundred, expanded to handle a thousand, and nearly double that now. They are mostly men, some women and a few children. I do not believe . . .' She took the phone from me, swiped forward and back, pinched to enlarge, peered carefully. 'I recognize one, this boy.' She showed me. 'The other two may be here, or they may have disappeared into the local population. Or perhaps some have made their way to the Turkish side, looking for passage to mainland Turkey.'

'Of course. It must be impossible to keep track of all of them.' I nodded sympathetically.

But now she was interested. She swiveled to an aged computer and with a meat pie held up and away in one hand tapped on a folder labeled in Greek. She tapped various filters, then started mouse-clicking through file photos of kids.

The door to the office opened abruptly for a thirty-ish man, tall, wearing light-sensitive glasses that were still dark from the sun outside.

'Calix?' he said, voice anxious. A look at me, leery but not surprised: he expected to see me there. 'May I have a moment of your time, love?' Irish. The Irish are always over-represented in NGOs. They have long memories of the potato famine and the Irish diaspora. There but for the grace of God, and all that.

Calix heaved herself up, regretting that she had to set the last of the pie aside, and went after him, closing the door behind her. I was up like a shot, pulling my keychain from my pocket, fiddling quickly to find the thumb drive. I stuck it in an open USB slot, picked the folder up, and dropped it in the drive.

The counter said it would take eight hours and nine minutes. One hour and eighteen minutes. Thirty-seven minutes. Four minutes. And settled down at two minutes. If she came back before that, I was caught. A diversion might be necessary.

I opened my phone, hit video and slowly did a three sixty around the room, recording a map of the camp, various workplace instruction sheets having to do with obscure EU regulations, hanging clipboards and the like.

The counter was down to nineteen seconds when the door opened again, and I, in reaching for the box of savory pastries accidentally knocked a big pile of paper to the floor.

'Oh, my God, I'm so sorry, I was being greedy and now I've made a mess.'

She had chilled toward me. We both picked up files but she took them from my hands as quickly as she could. I stood up, asked her about a poster on the opposite wall and with nimble burglar's fingers retrieved my thumb drive. A surreptitious tap on the space bar and I blinked away the computer's warning of an improperly ejected drive.

All in all I was pretty pleased with myself. I might be fairly pitiful at coping with daily life, but if you give me no time to think, I can be a quick, decisive little bunny.

'Mr Mitre, I have work to do, so thank you for the pies.'

She extended a hand.

'But . . . I'm still wondering—'

'Policy does not allow us to share information with, um . . . people who have not been cleared.' She frowned, not liking her own choice of words.

I protested. I asked whether I couldn't just ask around among the refugees.

'Impossible, I'm afraid.' She glanced toward the door on the word 'afraid.'

So, I shook her hand and went for my car. I was almost to Limassol before I noticed that a Land Rover had been in my rearview mirror for too long. One of the advantages of having a chronically heavy foot is that it forces pursuers to reveal themselves. That's my rationalization, anyway, and I'm sticking with it.

I pulled off into the outskirts of Limassol and crept along narrow streets until I found a bar. I parked illegally and raced inside while displaying body language signaling that I really had to take a pee.

When I came out, the tan ten-year-old Land Rover, was half a block away, parked but with its engine running. A man with dark hair and beard all cut to a uniform half-inch and wearing a black leather jacket stood beside it, smoking. He spotted me and quickly looked away showing sudden interest in a butcher shop's window. Then, making a show of finishing his cigarette, he climbed back into the SUV on the passenger side.

I wondered if this was the part where reality followed the Raymond Chandler rule and a man entered with a gun? I hoped not. I am not a gun person, guns being the way to magically turn three-to-five into life.

I pulled back out onto the A6 heading in the direction of Paphos, taking my time till I was sure the SUV was behind me. He was, and he was being a clever boy trying to keep two cars between us, just like he had no doubt learned from watching American crime shows.

I was doing one hundred twenty kilometers per hour, roughly, oh, seventy-five miles an hour, a pretty normal speed in that context, so I stepped on the pedal and the Mercedes responded with its usual smooth eagerness.

He stayed with me through eighty miles per hour. He stayed with me to eighty-five. At that point, he realized he wasn't so much tailing as chasing, and was not likely to be able to keep pace. So, at ninety I saw the Land Rover shrinking in my rearview mirror. I took the off-ramp that led to the British Sovereign Base Area to the south (a holdover of the empire) and the Kouris Reservoir Dam in the other direction, drove until I saw a convenient gas station, pulled off and waited to see whether the SUV was still with me. It was not.

I drove back to Limassol and googled my way to a DIY store where I bought twelve feet of heavy chain, two heavy hinges, a padlock, some two-inch wood screws, a bolt cutter, a spool of heavy fishing line, and sand paper. At the register, I pretended to be French so as to avoid questions. The only things I wanted were the bolt cutters and the line, the rest was cover, so I'd look like a guy with a broken gate who meant to secure it once and for all. As I was French, I tried to look small and dyspeptic and tossed off a '*Zut, alors!*' for verisimilitude. I paid cash.

Down the street I obtained a bottle of Johnny Walker black, an excellent blended whiskey that's perfectly fine for people you don't want to waste good single malt on. I also picked up a can of butane for my cigar torch and a set of brass knuckles. They were in the display case at the register, half a dozen models under glass, alongside wicked-looking clasp knives. I had no use in mind for the knuckles, but well, they're evidently legal in Cyprus – I'd seen them frequently in gift shops – and I did not like the looks of the gentlemen following me.

In a little newsstand, I found a clipboard that was available. Not strictly 'for sale,' but available. It came with a dozen crinkly pages of computer print-out inventory. Very official-looking.

I drove back to the village of Kofinou and found a pleasant taverna with a nice outdoor patio. It was 'Thai night' at the taverna so I dined on the Cypriot iteration of Thai food – much less sugar and even less spice than the American notion of Thai food. I slurped up Tom Ka and stir-fried vegetables and washed it down with Orangina. I was pulling a job, and there's no drinking when pulling a job. Alcohol is for after, when you need to soothe the shakes.

From my table it was a straight line of sight to the distant Stavrovouni monastery up on its mountain, with the camp hidden by the folds of the hills. The monastery is touted as one of the few places you can see a piece of the True Cross. The monastery was founded something like three hundred years after the True Cross was almost certainly recycled by practical Jerusalemites into support beams or perhaps a rustic mantel. Monasteries were the Hard Rock Cafés of the era, displaying various saints' toes and Mary's bra and Peter's fishing rod and whatnot the way Hard Rock shows off Clapton's guitar and Jimi's shoes and Sid

Vicious' syringe. The historical record is vague on whether monasteries also served fajitas.

After dinner I found an isolated pull-off and caught a quick nap to sleep off the wine. Then, with full dark over the island, I drove back toward the camp, taking the turn-off to the abattoir. This proved to be a depressing spot, rusting, empty and yet, despite years without use, somehow still stinking of dead pig.

The camp was just a few hundred yards up and over a hill, but that would bring me back to the original camp, and that was not my goal. I'd gone over the video of Petrides' office and been able to get a pretty good freeze-frame of her map of the camp. The original two sections were now reserved for women and children, with the far more numerous men pushed out into the tents. I was looking for something specific, a favored location, the presidential suite of the camp. It would have altitude, because altitude would first, translate to better cell phone reception; second, offer an improved possibility of catching the occasional breeze, and three, would signal by virtue of its position that it was dominant. And of course it would be farther from the administration areas and the main entrance.

I walked a good half mile over desperate scrub and rock, ducking beneath carob trees whose pods rattled in the branches and crunched underfoot, and came to a dirt track that passed through a field of trash and debris, the detritus of the camp. Having achieved some altitude of my own, I whipped out my trusty Carl Zeiss Victory compact binoculars and settled in to watch.

There's a lot of watching involved in competent, high-end burglary. The difference between a rushed smash-and-grab and a carefully-planned burglary is a whole lot more loot and a whole lot less pursuit. Young kids just starting out in the business don't always grasp the fact that the essential job of a burglar is to not get caught, followed closely by not stupidly turning a three-to-five-year sentence, where you're out in eighteen months, into a life sentence for murder in the first.

Setting aside the morality of it, as a pure economic proposition risking eighteen months against twenty grand makes a whole lot more sense than risking life against the fifty bucks a fence will give you for a flat-screen TV. But until someone opens a Crime University and invites me as a guest lecturer, that wisdom will never reach the young, starry-eyed aspiring thief.

I watched male refugees coming and going and soon identified the bathroom tents and the kitchen tent in the section of camp I was surveilling. There was what looked like a patrol of some sort, three of the men walking the perimeter, smoking cigarettes, but nothing like armed guards. Which was a bit disappointing – I had prepared for a higher level of difficulty.

Still, just because the opposition is indifferent that's no excuse for poor tradecraft. And oh, I felt it coming back, that perverse pride in my more regrettable skills and accumulated wisdom. It felt good. Life as a fugitive is like living next to the North Korean border, there are no worry-free days. You'll have several levels of alert, but you're never *not* on alert. It's a consuming job, and the really enervating part of it is the lack of control. You're the guy on the tightrope, they're the floor. You're the system, they're entropy. And however stylishly you pull it off – and I like to think I do it as well as anyone – you're still a notch lower on the food chain than the law and in the end, you're going to lose.

But now, this sneaking and hiding, surveilling, plotting, planning, composing the lies I might need, running scenarios, all by myself in the night in a place I had no right to be, this was what a master carpenter must feel like standing before a perfect block of wood, tools in hand. I knew this stuff. This was my craft, and I was good at it. I wasn't just waiting for the voice that would say, 'You're under arrest,' I was doing something. Sure the thing I was doing was probably something stupid, but I've seldom let that stop me. I wondered idly what the Cypriot prison was like and wondered whether each prisoner got his own rooftop cistern and a cat.

The chain-link fence was interrupted by a gate with a chain and padlock. Barbed wire coiled along the top of the gate, but only on the gate, and only an imbecile would have tried to enter there.

I could theoretically pick the padlock if I had twenty minutes to kill. I've picked locks. You can buy excellent lock-picking sets on Amazon and watch YouTube instructionals, but the way they show it being done on TV with a bent hairpin, wiggle, wiggle, all done? That's not the way it works in reality. In reality, it takes a lot longer and requires quite a bit of cursing; rather like assembling an IKEA desk.

I could also theoretically cut the lock with my bolt cutters but that would be a big red flag. So, I walked north along the fence for a hundred yards and cut the chain link, snip, snip, snip.

I squeezed through the gap, turned, unspooled my fishing line and used it to tie the chain link back into place. It would take close examination to see my fishing line sutures. Again, probably not necessary, but it's important to take some pride in your work.

I came through the fence at a high point, up a rise sloping down to the camp and walked quickly through dark, dry grass rasping the legs of my jeans, until I reached the first tents. From there I strode with the obvious impatience of a man on a mission: a man armed with a clipboard.

Snores rattled from some tents, TV sounds from others, intense argument from a few. The air was rich with the aromas of urine, tobacco smoke, cardamom, curry and charcoal from the makeshift braziers set up outside some tents. I saw toys, basketballs, soccer balls and plastic-tubing-framed goals, secured behind still more chain link. There were fold-out clothing racks and clear plastic bags of personal possessions not worth locking up.

Glancing officiously at my clipboard I kept moving like a man with a plan, down haphazard separations between tents, stepping over taut ropes, kicking the occasional can or discarded bottle. The 'streets' were empty but for a few men smoking, or people making a dash to the toilet, none remotely interested in me.

I was on alert, nervous but not scared. No one was really going to call cops all the way out to Kofinou because some writer got into a refugee camp. The worst I risked was probably a roughing up from suspicious camp residents. And, too, there was a strange sort of comfort in the familiarity of my worries and emotions. I knew these worries. I knew these emotions: the adrenalin buzz of doing the forbidden, the sense of smug superiority because I was a predator and all the world was filled with sheep. Senses all tuned up, taking nothing for granted, analyzing every detail for possible threat or opportunity.

The cliché would be to compare it to a drug, but that wasn't it, not really. A drug addict is a victim and I was not a victim. I wasn't addicted to this rush, I wasn't helpless to resist it. I had a valid reason for creeping the camp, but that was irrelevant to the feeling which was all tingle and buzz and instinct. As for fear? I felt more fear doing nothing, living the fugitive life, waiting, cringing, waiting. In the action, whether it's a burglary or the closing acts of a con, you don't feel fear, you can't because you are the invader, the user, the one *bringing* the fear.

The truth was I was having fun, more fun than I'd had in a long time. I suppose it's natural to enjoy doing the things you're good at.

What was the line from *Patton* talking about war? 'God help me, I do love it so?'

I had a half-dozen tents in mind as my targets and I listened carefully as I moved between them. A radio tuned to BBC, David Mitchell making a witty remark. Snores. Laughing conversation. The high-pitched voice of an imam ranting on a tape or maybe on the radio. More snores.

Many of the tents had rolled-up one or more sides to allow the cooling evening breeze. I saw cots and bare feet poking out from beneath thin blankets, often lit by TV light. I saw hard, weary men sitting hunched forward, dark faces emerging as cigarette ends glowed bright on the inhale, darkening on the exhale as ash obscured the tip. A skinny old man with a long, white beard sat naked to the waist on a child's tricycle with a broken rear axle.

Then: sullen, monosyllabic male voices, and that, I suspected, was bingo. I would know in a few seconds.

I flicked the canvas in lieu of knocking, and said, 'Hello? So sorry to trouble you. May I come in?'

What had been a murmur of male voices stopped instantly.

'Who is there?' Heavily-accented English.

I had no good answer for that, so I drew the door flap aside and stepped in, clipboard out like a shield. Someone had been frying fish on a hotplate. And everyone was smoking. It was a tobacco hotbox. The interior was not quite toasty enough to bake brownies, but the sides of the tent had not been raised to admit the cooling night air, suggesting that the population of this particular tent valued privacy over comfort.

At the far end were two cots occupied by two sleeping men. In the center, where I would just barely be able to stand up fully sat a small plastic table and four matching plastic chairs. One tent 'wall' was stacked high with water-stained cardboard boxes. An unsteady-looking bunk bed covered a second side. An ancient television was perched atop a bookshelf, which, naturally, I scanned for evidence of my books. (None.) The TV volume was low, tuned to a soccer match, though not one that held great interest for the three men lounging around the table.

I strode boldly forward and stopped, six eyes and three beards aimed at me.

'Gentlemen,' I said. '*Salam alaikum.*'

No answer. Not even a perfunctory '*alaikum salaam.*' Just guarded looks. An old, bald guy with a thready ZZ Top beard and a skullcap was the boss, that was easy to see. Maybe an imam, maybe just some old tough dude, but definitely the boss.

To his left sprawled one of those men you never have to ask yourself whether you can 'take,' because you just can't. He was roughly the size, weight, and density of an armored personnel carrier, but an armored personnel carrier with long, black hair and a patchy beard that couldn't quite keep up. If I ever had to fight the guy, I calculated my odds would be improved if I just went ahead and choked myself.

The third man I made as the psycho, because there's always one. He was too small, too birdlike to be a brawler, but he had nasty brown eyes and was way too still. Worse, he looked smart, which Muscle did not. This guy was a snake.

It was all reassuringly familiar, a scene from any common room in any jail or prison in the world: a boss, a thug and a crazy.

The boss nodded and finally, after looking me over from hair to shoes, answered: '*Alaikum salaam.*'

'I'm afraid that's all my Arabic.'

'I speak English,' the old guy said with a sniff of arrogance, like I was a jerk for implying otherwise.

'I am Michael O'Shaughnessy,' I said, hoping no one would

ask me how to spell it, 'and I am a researcher for the United Nations Agency For Lost And Abandoned Children. UNAFLAAC. I wonder if I could have a moment of your time.'

'You are English?' the boss asked.

'Ach, begorrah!' I protested in an Irish accent every bit as authentic as the Lucky Charms leprechaun. 'Irish, please.' I knew at least one Irishman from the old days who'd have stabbed me in the neck for that accent.

'I am Sheikh Nawaz. And how may we be of assistance?'

I motioned to an empty seat and he nodded. I sat. I set down my clipboard and swung my shoulder bag forward and drew out the bottle of whiskey. 'I don't suppose . . .' I said, tilting the neck toward them. The Muscle licked his lips, then glanced at Nawaz who jerked his chin, causing the Muscle to levitate out of his chair and reappear in two heartbeats with three glasses of varying cleanliness.

I poured. The sheikh took one, the muscle took one, the reptile gave no indication at all, so I took the third.

'Sláinte,' I said. I knew of no Arabic toasts, Muslims not generally being drinkers. Present company evidently excluded.

We drank.

By this point they were pretty certain I was not from the UN. They knew I was there to wheedle information. They weren't sure yet whether they were going to beat me up or just tell me to fuck off, but if my opening gambit was a bottle of decent Scotch, they wanted to see what else I had.

I pulled out my phone, swiped a bit and held up the first enlargement of a kid, one of the boys from the recent boat. 'I'm looking for this boy.' I watched Muscle's reaction. Blank.

'Also this boy . . . and this girl.'

Muscle recognized the second boy, the same one Calix had recognized. His eyes widened and he overcompensated with a scowl. The tension rose a notch.

'These pictures are all from a boatload of refugees who came ashore—'

The old man cut me off. 'We are well-informed on the comings and goings of our brothers and sisters. But these three I do not recognize. Though my eyesight is not what it once was.'

Bullshit, old man, you see through walls when you want to. I've met guys like you, I know. I did not say.

I poured refills. Reptile was deciding whether to stab me in the heart or slit my throat. I was deciding whether I would have a chance to scream like a little girl. Fear was back because I was decidedly not in control. Humans are by definition apex predators but I was the kind of apex predator who stole your stuff; Reptile was the kind who stole your life.

'I wonder if you could take a closer look. UNAFLAAC has allocated funds for anyone who can help us.' I drew a white envelope from my pocket. 'You could use the funds to help your . . . brothers and sisters.' I kept a straight face.

The boss was amused. He didn't know what I was up to, but he wanted that cash. Sheikh Nawaz was a wily old con, but it's hard to conceal greed's glitter.

'Mustafa, take a closer look,' he told Muscle, who now had a name.

Mustafa took the phone from me, glanced at his boss for guidance, frowned, squinted, and looked again at Nawaz, who gave an imperceptible nod.

'This one. I have seen him.' The second boy.

'Ah, well, that is glorious news, sure it is,' I said, recalling belatedly that I was the Lucky Charms mascot. 'Saints be praised. Might I meet the young laddie?'

Nawaz's eyes moved slowly to the envelope. It wasn't subtle, nor was it intended to be.

'For a chance to speak with the young man, ah, well, I could see that being worth, say, two hundred?' I've never bribed a Syrian refugee crime boss before and did not know where to start the bidding.

Nawaz sighed.

'I might go as high as three hundred,' I allowed.

'The number three is very unlucky in our culture.'

No it's not, you old fraud. I did not say.

'Indeed?'

'Better if we make it a thousand. You see, the concept of the zero, essential to all higher mathematics, is an invention of our Egyptian brothers, almost two millennia before your Christ.'

As a spreader of bullshit myself, I rather admired that. And it calmed my concern about Reptile, since we were now in the bazaar haggling over prices.

'There are two zeroes in the number five hundred,' I pointed out, and he couldn't argue that.

This was getting expensive. Getting to the point where I was going to submit an invoice to Agents K. and D. I sighed and shook my head slightly and counted out the cash. Mustafa Muscle rose and disappeared out the back door of the barracks, which left me to make small talk with Nawaz and the snake. We chatted amiably about the weather, and about the TV show *Homeland*, and about what rotters the British are. (Sykes-Picot, dontcha know.) In the process, I was able to teach them the word 'cunt,' its literal meaning, and its common usage in the UK where it is often substituted for 'asshole.' We passed some time just saying the word.

Then, there was Mustafa again, his massive fist resting paternally on the narrow shoulders of a boy dressed only in a long T-shirt emblazoned with the Hooters logo. His spindly legs ended in bare feet, one of which was clubbed. I looked at the photo. I looked at the boy. I showed the picture to the boy.

'Is that you?'

He was fascinated, a sleepy, shivering but curious kid, maybe ten years old. After a while of scanning faces and reacting, I pressed him and only then realized that of course he did not speak English.

Mustafa translated my question. The boy nodded.

'Would you ask him if he knew these other two?' I swiped to the other enlargements.

His nod did not require translation. Nor did the guarded look or the quick sidelong glance at Nawaz.

'Does he know where they are?'

A long stream of Arabic was translated by Mustafa as, 'No.'

I counted out another two hundred. And I handed the kid himself a fifty. Nawaz must have nodded, because Mustafa suddenly remembered more of what the kid had said. 'He says men took them.'

'Men took them? When?'

More Arabic, the gist of which was apparently, 'When they are on land.'

'You mean as the boat landed?'

'Yes.'

'Who were the men?' I asked. Arabic, Arabic, shrug, shrug.

'Okay,' I said, 'How about this: does he know where they were taken?'

He did not.

'Why those two? Why not this kid?'

That took some back-and-forthing before the boy, shame-faced, looked down at his clubbed foot.

Silence followed, during which Nawaz watched me to see just how clueless I might be.

I don't know anything about the Syrian or Iraqi criminal world, but from the sneer forming in the old man's eyes I guessed their view of short-eyes was roughly the same as ours. He was wondering if I was one.

I poured us all another round and the kid was sent off into the night, clutching his cash.

'A person I know once suggested that those who harm children deserve to be impaled on a telephone pole,' I said. 'I wonder if you would drink to that?'

It was an instinct move. I made these guys for professionals, gangsters, and Nawaz for a boss. No doubt they were involved in smuggling, maybe some weed or khat, maybe protection, the occasional regrettable but necessary beating. Maybe they ran some hookers. But my instincts told me this was a conversation between criminals – not nice people, but not animals.

Nawaz relaxed a bit. 'To telephone poles,' Nawaz said, and kept his eyes on me as he raised his glass and drank. He didn't know why I was chasing after refugee kids, but cons have an analogue to what used to be called 'gaydar.' We know each other. He made me for some species of crook, but not, probably, the kind who went after kids. Which left him intrigued but not willing to question me further. Maybe he had another appointment, or maybe he was just sleepy, but either way he was done with me.

Nawaz exchanged a few words in Arabic with Mustafa and detailed him to escort me out. I left the bottle behind.

'Where did you come in?' Mustafa asked.

I pointed. 'Up the hill. I cut the fence.'

He snorted. 'The fence is already cut in three places. Where did you leave your car?'

'At the abattoir,' I said, and he turned and led me in that direction.

I was mostly sure that Mustafa wouldn't kill me as we walked through the sleeping camp. I lit a cigar with my torch and puffed.

'Are you a good man?' Mustafa asked me suddenly.

'No, not really,' I admitted. I had dropped my Irish brogue. Instinct suggested honesty. It does that every now and again.

'Why do you want these children?'

'It's complicated,' I admitted. 'The short answer is I have no choice.'

He stopped, turned, looked me up and down. 'You are being pressured? Who pressures you?'

I sighed. 'People who wouldn't be squeezing me if they could do this job themselves.'

'And those people?'

I laughed softly. 'They're not people I like. They aren't friends. In fact, they're people I've done my best to avoid during the course of my . . . career. But they don't target children. Most people would say they're the good guys.'

I had misjudged Mustafa by a good twenty IQ points. He wasn't slow.

He asked, 'If you find these children . . .'

I shrugged. 'If I figure out what's going on, I'll be in the clear.' Maybe.

'But the children,' he insisted. He was looking me straight in the eyes, albeit looking down about six inches, and said, 'I had two children. A daughter and a son.' No disguising the quiver in his voice. 'Do you have children?'

It was not the time for a smart-ass remark. I'd registered the past-tense, 'had.' *Had* children.

'No,' I said.

He thought it over. Then he reached inside his coat for a knife! No, not a knife, a pen. With which he wrote a number on a scrap of paper and handed it to me. 'This is my mobile number.'

I raised an eyebrow.

He said, 'If you should need help with . . .'
'Telephone poles?'
White teeth in the darkness.

THIRTEEN

I slept late and was awakened by a blinding ray of light coming through shades I had failed to draw completely. Out on the patio it was both as bright and as hot as the surface of the sun. As soon as the caffeine had revived me, I called up Special Agent Delia.

'Yes?'

'I wonder if you and Almost-as-special Agent Kim could meet me?'

'Your villa?'

'No,' I said, remembering the Land Rover. 'The tiki bar.'

She allowed that she could meet me there but not till evening, and that she would be alone. Agent Kim, it seemed, had gone back to Rome. Or Athens.

Interesting.

Our five o'clock rendezvous left me with plenty of time to get some work done. Dammit. So, I banged out a scene I didn't much like for my latest opus, then thought up a few coy drolleries for the *GQ* piece.

The tiki bar was at a distance that could either be a walk or a drive. I decided to walk. A less-than-professional surveillance team would assume that I was with my car, and thus that I was at home, and thus that they should not ransack the villa. The maid service would not appreciate a ransacking.

The sun was heading for the western horizon and a breeze stirred, slowly lowering the temperature from boil to simmer. The sea was smooth as glass, fading from turquoise and sparkle, to deep blue and mystery. I passed a squat stone church so small it couldn't have held a dozen people, and so old that Babylonians might have built it.

Cyprus has been conquered and occupied by a who's who

of ancient colonialists and exploiters: Egyptian pharaohs, Phoenicians, Mycenaeans, the Assyrians who were the Nazis of the Iron Age, Persians, back to Egypt under Alexander the Great's kid Ptolemy; Rome when it was still arguably ruled by its Senate, though later on Trajan came along to murder all the Jews, as one does; Byzantium, Crusaders led by no less than Richard – best sobriquet ever – Lionheart, who sold it to the Knights Templar, who were essentially a Frankish (French-ish) religio-murder cult. Toss in some Hospitallers, too, because the Templars got the cooler name but the Hospitallers were better at handling money. Then came the non-Roman Italians in the form of Genoese and Venetians, the Turks for quite a spell, and finally the British. Don't forget a couple of random years of Holy Roman Empire in there and you're left with one question: what, no Vikings?

'Back to insult my beer again, Mr Mitre?' Theodoros asked.

'I'm meeting someone,' I said.

'Police?'

I shook my head slowly, as I settled onto the barstool. 'So, you've had police here?'

'Of course I had police here,' he said with some asperity. 'A woman was murdered right there.' He pointed, in case I had forgotten. The relevant spot was now occupied by a pink German woman and a pair of loud, sweaty toddlers.

'Did you happen to mention that I was here?'

He came over, placed both hands on the bar and leaned toward me. 'I don't mind lying, especially for customers who tip generously, as you do. But I don't like being caught in a lie, especially not by police when they are investigating a murder.'

'Fair enough,' I admitted. 'And what did you tell them?'

'That I heard screams. I turned and saw the blood. You had already left. The truth.' His shrug modified the word 'truth.'

'Okay. Your future tips are safe.' He didn't immediately turn away. I said, 'More?'

This was his cue to channel some ancient cowboy movie bartender. He started polishing glasses and avoiding eye contact. 'Rumors,' he said.

The whole world has gone from watching or reading tropes to living them.

'Uh-huh.'

'Some think the police are not trying very hard.'

'Some think that, do they? Why do some think the police would slow-walk a murder?'

Shrug.

'Are you seriously hitting me up for a bribe?'

'I have my eye on a car. A Peugeot 308 GTi. Used. The body needs work, but the engine and transmission are still in excellent condition.'

This was getting ridiculous, I was bleeding cash. I slid a C-note across, and said, 'Here, buy yourself a tire.'

He gave me a long, speculative look. Oh, he took the money, but then he eyeballed me curiously.

'Some day,' he said, 'I would like to know why you are interested.'

'Yeah? I'd like to know why some are dubious of the cops. And I *paid* for that answer.'

'There are rumors in the expat community that MI6 and your FBI have both offered assistance and have been turned down. Turned down and told to fuck off. By the police.'

'Politics?'

'Maybe,' he said. One of those 'maybes' that mean 'no.'

'MI6 and FBI are both very good at their jobs,' I said, struggling to generate a simulacrum of approval. 'They have capabilities Cyprus cops may not.'

'We don't usually like foreigners poking their noses in.'

'Really? I'd think you'd be used to it by now, having had, what, three thousand years to adjust?'

'Many dislike the way the UK still controls parts of the island. Others are upset by the numbers of expats. Cyprus for Cypriots, all that.'

'Cypriot nationalism? That's a thing?' I asked. But Theodoros was distracted and when I followed the direction of his gaze, I saw why. Special Agent Delia Delacorte was approaching. She wore a loose, unbuttoned robe over a bathing suit, a conservatively-cut, navy two piece. She was not quite Halle Berry in the famous orange bikini from the old James Bond movie, but she was in the ballpark: Halle Berry with a darker complexion, natural hair and about twenty percent more predatory swagger.

Not Minette, not Halle Berry, but gorgeous, with far more leg than strictly necessary for locomotion.

No, David.

She took the stool beside me, ordered a beer from Theodoros, who delivered it with shocking speed and then took his time asking her if she'd like anything to snack on? Anything? Anything at all? Crisps? Peanuts? A pushy, young Cypriot bartender?

Her thigh brushed against me.

Seriously: no.

Eventually my white-hot glare convinced Theodoros to go drool at the other end of the bar.

'Hi,' I said, extending my hand. 'My name is David.'

She left my hand hovering. 'You called this meeting.'

'Should you be drinking beer while on duty?'

'I'm not on duty, Mr Mitre—'

'I thought we were first-naming by now. No?'

'I'm not on duty, *David*. In fact, I'm taking some personal vacation time. Just enjoying the beach and the sunshine.'

'So . . . I can call you Delia?'

She carried herself with an air of calm that came with a suggestion of danger. Long ago I'd met a woman who I'd figured for a mark. We chatted, hung out, went to a movie together. But as I was laying out the opening moves of my grift over dinner, she suddenly looked up and our eyes locked and I will never forget the cold chill that went up my spine as she said, 'Don't play me. Bad things happen to clever boys who try and play me.' Turned out she was not just the suspiciously well-heeled owner of a fashionable boutique, she was also the sister of a gentleman of the Salvadoran gangster persuasion.

Delia was kind of like that, but with threats of prison rather than artery cutting.

'Or I could go on calling you Special Agent Delacorte. Ma'am.'

'Delia will do,' she growled. 'For now.'

I was dancing on the line between desire and fear. Like a praying mantis that knows that copulation ends in his head being eaten by the female but is still thinking, *Enh, might be worth it.*

'Well, Delia, here's what I know: refugee kids don't always reach the resettlement camp. Especially not the pretty ones.'

'As a private citizen, a tourist on holiday, I find that interesting.'

'But not surprising.'

'My surprised expression would be like this.' She fractionally raised one eyebrow.

She didn't hold the expression for long and I missed most of it because I was not focusing entirely on her face. 'Maybe, Delia, you should lay out for me just what it is you want. Because so far I've spent—' Quickly calculating a reasonable vig, adjusting for inflation, considering bank exchange fees, rounding up to the nearest five grand – 'fifteen large getting this far. I mean, what's going to make you happy?'

'Evidence always makes me happy. Connect some dots. Get me to where I can push this.'

Here is what I did not say: I want to sleep with you, but you scare me, Delia, and having never fear-fucked a Feeb before, I'm quite frankly not confident of my performance. And yet, I am willing to take on the challenge, just please don't eat my head.

What I did say was, 'Do you have someone following me? And doing a lousy job of it?'

'You've picked up a tail?'

That got her attention.

'Not here,' I said with more confidence than I felt. 'But I went to the refugee camp yesterday, during the day, and when I left I had two new best friends in leather jackets driving a Land Rover.'

I gave her a quick rundown of both my visits to the camp, leaving out Mustafa's kind offer. I also mentioned without naming Theodoros or Joumana that there were doubts about how hard Cypriot police were trying to solve the murder of the woman on the beach.

Delia nodded. 'That was well done, David.'

'Thank you, Delia.'

'Shoot me the stills you showed them.'

'The kid with the foot could give testimony,' I said. 'That's evidence.'

'Connected to no one. I need names.'

'Then I need help.' I fished a thumb drive out of my pocket, took her hand by the wrist, ignoring the way she bridled, and trying to ignore the fact that I could feel her pulse, turned her hand over and put the drive in her palm. 'These are the records of juveniles processed through Kofinou. I assume the port authorities and the Marine Police keep records of how many people are on the refugee boats they intercept. If the Marine Police pick up a boat with x number of kids and something fewer than "x" make it to the camp . . .'

Delia nodded, and said, 'I have software tools. My laptop is back in my room.'

I've heard sexier seduction lines. We finished our beverages and headed up toward her car, leaving a disappointed Theodoros still in need of three more tires.

Delia was staying at a three-star hotel a few miles north of my usual haunt, in a less pricey neighborhood with a rocky beach.

It wasn't a long drive in her little rental Kia, but after only a few minutes driving up the stop-and-go coastal route, Delia said, 'What color was your Land Rover?'

I glanced in the wing mirror on my side. 'The color of that Land Rover behind us. I outran him in my Benz, but you're not going to do it in this hamster-powered sardine can.'

The predator cocked an eyebrow at me and pulled a two-wheel turn that left my internal organs behind. She squashed the clutch, threw the gearshift, hit the accelerator hard and all four hamsters revved to panic speed. Right. Left. *Vroom*! Left. *Vroom*! Right!

We hit a parked bike. We ran oncoming cars onto the sidewalk. We murdered a trash bin. But damned if Delia's FBI training wasn't paying off. The woman could drive.

'I hope you got the extra insurance at the rental counter,' I said.

Delia came to a tight four-way intersection, pulled a U-turn, slammed on the brakes behind a parked car, and yelled, 'Down!'

We both ducked. I was bent over, face-to-face with Agent Delia under the dashboard, hoping I looked braver than I felt.

We waited. The Land Rover roared past.

'You've done this before,' I chattered.

'Never as the rabbit, a few times as the hound.' Not a quiver. Not a stuttered consonant. She could have been talking about golf or her favorite cheese.

Delia's hotel was a cement rectangle of six floors above ground, tall for this end of Cyprus, a bland, anonymous and decent if not showy establishment. It was the kind of place where tourists hung their wet bathing suits off the balcony to dry. I wouldn't have stayed there, but Delia was a civil servant. She would have to submit a reimbursement request.

'They lay out a good breakfast buffet,' Delia said defensively.

'They'd have to,' I muttered. Snobbery came very late in life to me, but I'd paid my dues with time spent sleeping under bridges and in public libraries and jail cells. 'There's the bar. I need a drink.'

I finished the Scotch before the slow, wheezing elevator got us to her top-floor room.

Delia's room was international standard Hilton-lite: two single beds, one chair, and a mountain slash parking-lot view. She got her laptop out of the room safe and sat at the desk. I sat on the edge of the bed leaning forward to shoulder surf, hoping – futilely – to see her password.

'This will take a while. I missed lunch. Call down and order some room service,' she ordered me.

'What would you like?' I asked, obedient.

'Food,' she snapped.

I ordered some Greek specialties and a bottle of local white wine. And fresh strawberries, because I wanted to see her eat a strawberry. I already had a mental image of that but I wanted detail. With luck I'd have a strawberry moment with Minette as well, and I could compare. In the interests of science.

I knew that my sudden and growing carnal interest in Delia was a lame attempt at gaining control, I'm not entirely un-self-aware. I was feeling like I was no longer writing the narrative of my life but was being swept up in someone else's story with potentially disastrous consequences. It wasn't hard to trace the mental chain from Delia to Halle Berry to James Bond to the fantasy that like Bond I was irresistible and that once a woman had slept with me she'd be so taken that she wouldn't even mind dying in the second reel. I'd made a lucrative career out of charming women, and now that I was slipping back into the warm embrace of my bad-boy past I was beginning to shed the restrictions of pretended normality, allowing an attenuated version of the old sense of invulnerability to sneak back in.

And Delia was genuinely sexy. That was real. And here she was, right next to me. Her only real flaw was that she was smart and strong. Also experienced. And cynical. And an FBI agent. All in all nothing like the women who'd fallen for my glib bullshit in the past. But that was a bad line of reasoning to pursue because it led right back to a suspicion that I wasn't so much Bond to her Jinx Johnson in this scenario, as Sancho Panza to her Quixote. Robin to her Batman. Donkey to her Shrek.

No more comforting analogies presented themselves.

Delia was onto some secure site and typing in a query. That didn't work, so she tried another query, then another and finally, 'Hah!' She pointed proudly at a spreadsheet. Then she opened a desktop app and merged the data. The Mac chewed on the ones and zeroes as room service arrived and the sun plunged.

I poured wine and offered her the choice of dishes. She went with the moussaka.

'What the hell is this?' Delia asked after her first bite. 'I thought it was lasagna.'

'Sort of. Lasagna with lamb instead of beef and eggplant instead of tomato sauce and béchamel instead of mozzarella.'

She shoveled big bites and quaffed wine and I was just about to reach across and wipe away an endearing bit of béchamel on her lower lip when the goddamned computer dinged and she was back at the desk.

'A total of two hundred and nine juveniles either picked up on the beach or intercepted at sea,' she said. 'One hundred and eighty-five registered at the camp.'

'That's . . .' I'm not quick with numbers unless expressed in terms of dollars.

'Twenty-four,' Delia said. 'Of course this proves nothing. Could be bookkeeping errors, could be miscounts at sea, adults wrongly labeled as juveniles . . .'

'So, what, maybe half that number? A dozen kids?'

'That's not enough?'

'Delia, what is the market price of a child nowadays?'

'It depends. Could be as low as a grand or as high as ten grand.'

'Let's be generous. Ten grand times twelve kids is a hundred twenty grand,' I said, proudly displaying my mastery of the multiplication table. 'How is a hundred twenty worth the effort and the risk? People are being paid off, so figure half of that net goes to the main operator. It's not enough money to motivate a very public murder.'

'No,' she admitted, deflated.

We both stared disconsolately at the laptop.

'So, there it is,' Delia said, 'But it isn't the it we're looking for.'

'You already knew this much,' I said.

She nodded. 'More or less. But I didn't have specifics, and now I do. Thanks to you.'

'I appreciate your gratitude. And since we're—'

'Oh, for Christ's sake, David,' she said, her tone somewhere on the amused–irritated scale. 'I'm not going to sleep with you.'

'Whoa, I wasn't—' I protested too loudly.

'Oh, shut up.' She stood and stretched her legs by bouncing on her tiptoes a little. While still in a bathing suit, mind you.

I did not intend, consciously, to reach for her, it just happened. The next part, where she grabbed my hand and twisted it backward so hard that I had to drop from the bed to my knees, also just happened.

She let me go and sighed. 'Do you think I'm so clueless I don't feel you looking me over like the last shrimp on the buffet table? Do you have any idea how many times I've been pawed by horny guys – and one girl – as I worked my way up at the FBI? I've had assistant directors offer me promotions for blowjobs and in terms just that direct.'

'I didn't . . .' Yeah, that was all I could come up with.

'I am an FBI special agent, I am not a set of tits, you sociopath.'

I had to laugh. 'Special Agent Delacorte, I'm sorry if I made a clumsy pass. But you've been working on me since our first meeting. I'm dumb, but I'm not that dumb.'

Then she smiled, a full-on, ear-to-ear smile that might make some men weak. Men like me. 'Okay, David, let's cut the shit. It's not happening. Not. N-O-T followed by the word "happening."'

I sighed and produced my rakish smile. 'I had to try.'

And I will again. I did not say.

She crossed to the window and looked out through a slit. 'The Land Rover.'

I joined her and shared her view of the hotel parking lot, surprised that night had fallen hard while we were playing with computers and dipping *tarama*. 'Two men. I can't see the driver, but that guy smoking there, the bristly one? I recognize him from when I made them the first time.'

I fell silent and closed my eyes, scrolling back through places and faces. Had I seen the man anywhere else before? If so I wasn't clicking.

'Hey. Let's get a shot of him.' I aimed my phone out of the window, careful not to be spotted, and took several pictures. To Delia's frown I said, 'You might want to run this photo against the videos you people got from the yacht.'

Slight parting of lips. Intake of breath. A quick cover-up as her face went opaque. 'That kind of thing requires manpower.'

'You're the FBI, what, you're all busy?'

'Manpower means putting in a request, running it up through channels . . . By the time I do all that we can make the guy ourselves.'

I drew back and stared at the lovely Delia and, with a grin tickling my lips, said, 'Oh, my God. You've gone rogue.'

'Don't try to be clever, David, you—'

'That's why Agent Kim isn't here anymore. That's why you're so ostentatiously playing the vacationing sun worshipper. They've pulled you off this case.'

I could see I was close to the mark. Close but not a bull's-eye.

'Oh, wait, no,' I said, 'you're actually here for something bigger, aren't you? Is this all just incidental?'

'Not incidental, but not the whole picture. I don't know the whole picture, and if I did I couldn't tell you.'

That seemed like an invitation for me to guess. 'Terrorism?'

Nothing.

'Drugs?'

Nothing.

The FBI, MI6, a lurid murder, a dangerous fugitive with a garrote in her overnight bag, all on Cyprus. Cyprus. Not known for terrorism. Cyprus. Not a major drug route. Cyprus . . .

And then all the pennies dropped at once and a shiver went right up my spine. 'Please tell me it's not Russian money laundering.'

My insides had gone cold. My nether parts, which had been optimistic a moment ago, now retreated into my body.

'Oh, uncool, Agent Delia, very uncool.'

'You're scared?'

'Of Russian mobsters? Of Russian mobsters inevitably linked to the fucking FSB and the GRU and maybe protecting billions – not millions, billions with a "b" – in untraceable mob cash? Nah, why would that worry me?' I laughed a humor-free laugh. 'Jesus Christ on a pogo stick, Delia! I thought we were playing with some pedos and refugees. I didn't know we were walking into fucking Mordor!'

Goddamn if she didn't look disappointed in me. And goddamn if it didn't bother me. No man wants to look like a coward in the eyes of a woman with those eyes. But while the prospect of impressing a beautiful woman is compelling, sheer terror is more so.

'The two things are not necessarily separate,' Delia lectured. 'Anyway, they have no reason to come after us yet, it would be needlessly risky.'

I gaped. 'No reason? Those guys don't need reasons, all they need is a dirty look. Needlessly risky? These aren't tax accountants, fucking hell, Agent Delia, murder is their go-to, it's their first base!'

And you're not even going to sleep with me, despite the fact that it would probably be the greatest night of our lives. I did not say. But definitely felt, with a surge of righteous indignation.

'Joe Burton wouldn't be scared off,' she said.

That was a low blow. Joe Burton is my detective, my main character, my meal ticket. 'Yeah, well, Joe Burton only has fictional balls, and they don't hurt as much when someone slices them off.'

'I'm going to shower and get dressed,' she said levelly. 'You can be here when I come out, or you can run. Word of honor,

I'll give you a twenty-four-hour head start in recognition of services rendered.'

She turned and glided away to the bathroom, snagging an outfit from the closet as she went. I heard the bathroom door lock, so, sadly this was not to be one of those scenes where I would go in, find her showering and we would have steamy, wet sex. Evidently I am not Bond, James Bond.

No one ever admits to being asleep, lacking a sense of humor, or having no imagination. Everyone thinks they have an imagination, but few do, and fewer still are capable of pro-level imagination, the kind of imagination a clever criminal, or novelist, might need. Without imagination the first cave men would still be in the first cave, because it takes imagination to wonder what's over the next hill, or to conceive of a cure for disease, or to imagine strapping on a rocket and flying to the moon. Many good things come from imagination.

But imagination is to fear as gasoline is to fire.

My professional-level imagination began painting pictures of fists in my face, and knives at my throat and me dragging my neutered, bloody body into an emergency room, holding my testicles in my hand while leafing frantically through a Greek-English phrasebook for, 'Would you please re-attach these and could you also recommend a good seafood restaurant?'

I was just tough enough to face down a refugee thug in a camp with lots of people in earshot. But I knew my limitations. Professional killers were not my thing, not my thing at all.

Twenty-four hours head start? In twenty-four hours I could be halfway to anywhere. Fuck the writing career, I could start over with a new identity, new passport, move my money out of Luxembourg . . .

I'm not proud of what happened next.

I stood up, grabbed my flash drive and bolted as I heard the sound of the shower.

FOURTEEN

The hotel was six stories of rooms, plus the lobby level, plus the lower beach-facing restaurant level, eight floors in all and Delia's room was on the top floor. I had taken the elevator up and since the elevator was at hand, having just disgorged a tourist family with a tumble of luggage, I took the elevator down. Also it seemed better to meet some tatted-up Russian thug in an elevator rather than a stairwell.

The elevator stopped on four and I nodded politely to a woman with a baby in a buggy and held the elevator door for her. I was fleeing but that was no excuse for lack of manners.

The elevator stopped next at the lobby level, where I stood back politely to let baby and buggy get off.

Three tourists, Germans, were waiting impatiently to get on and impeded my exit for just a moment. A moment during which I spotted the man from the Land Rover and a second man with him, the driver. The man I'd first seen had head and face shaved to identical quarter-inch bristle-length, pale unhealthy skin, and wore a too-small blue jacket over a tan Polo shirt with the oversized pony logo.

The second man was bald and more generously bearded, which can sometimes make a fellow look jovial, though not on this occasion. He wore a sports coat over a yellow floral Hawaiian shirt.

They were not especially big men, both stood a few inches shorter than me, but they had zero-fat bodies, lean shapes practically vibrating with pent-up kinetic energy and the sort of eyes you expect to see looking back at you from the alligator tank at the zoo.

They might have been law enforcement, but that was not what my radar was screaming. Cops are all about dominance but they generally do it from a stance of reserved confidence. They are trained to hold back until challenged, they don't go looking for trouble. But these two boys? They were definitely looking for trouble. They scanned the crowd in the lobby, glanced toward the big, red-carpeted main stairway, toward the line of pensioners heading down that staircase to the restaurant, at each of the knots of people reading books in the lobby or sipping cocktails in the lounge.

They were hunting, and no prizes for guessing who they were hunting.

I slipped into self-effacing mode, a slight 'oh, I forgot something' gesture, a stab at the elevator buttons, tilt the head down to conceal the face and try to disappear behind the three Germans, two of them middle-aged men and the third a woman who might have been a daughter of one of the men, or . . . Well, there really wasn't time to spin out the many possibilities.

I had punched the sixth floor which was of course labeled eight. The Germans were going to three.

The elevator door began to shut.

Then Bristle spotted me. Worse yet, he saw that I saw that he saw me. We had one of those electric moments of recognition, rather like a mouse must have with a cat.

Bristle yelled something terse and Slavic and lunged.

The German woman reached to hit the 'open door' button for him but I batted her hand away. The door closed with Bristle's hand three feet from the gap.

The Germans all gave me dirty looks and muttered German disapproval.

'Sorry,' I said as we rose, 'I have Tourette's of the hand.'

I smiled sickly at them. They glared at me and turned their backs and the elevator rose at a leisurely pace and . . . stopped on the second floor.

There he was: Bristle. He wasn't even breathing hard from having raced up the stairs and hit the button.

He got on, bringing the smell of too much cologne with him. There was no way I could get off. Rather than turn toward the door and present his back to me, he stood facing me, eyeballing me right over the German's shoulders as the door closed behind him and we rose again.

The Germans would get off on three. And then he, Bristle, was going to kill me. That realization – not a guess but a certainty – dumped adrenalin into my arteries. He was three inches shorter than I, but ten years younger, far more fit, and a professional at the job of thuggery.

My only hope was to get off on three with the Germans.

'*Wo ist die Orchesterprobe*?' I yelped in German. Which translates as 'Where is the orchestra practice?' Because a million years ago in high school I had taken a year of German, and apparently finding orchestra practice was a central concern of German texts in those days.

'*Wo ist die Toilette*?' I asked and leaned close to the nearest German man, who recoiled from the lunatic American, and huffed in a way that rather undercut my attempt at cross-cultural outreach. Three sides of the elevator car were mirrored and I caught a glimpse of a scared-looking fellow I recognized as the guy in my shaving mirror.

The elevator was slowing.

'*Juden Raus*!' I cried, which is a phrase that would have been familiar to Germans in Nazi Germany, perhaps less today. I also yelled, '*Sheisse*! *Schweinehund*! *Weinerschnitzel*! *Auslese*!'

So, 'Jews out!' followed by shit, pig-dog, breaded veal and a term used to describe a wine made from late-harvested grapes.

It's not often that I regret paying little to no attention in high school.

The door opened, the Germans fled, I fled with them and a fist grabbed the back of my shirt and yanked me back with more force than I'd have thought could be generated by a single human being.

I slammed against the back of the elevator cage, smacked my head against the framed poster advertising spa services, and started to yell, but only started because he hit me with a short jab that caught me on the side of the mouth, snapped my head sideways and caused stars to swirl in my field of vision. My knees wobbled.

The next thing I saw was his knife.

FIFTEEN

I remember the first gun anyone ever pointed at me. More than two decades later, and I could still draw you an accurate picture.

I was pretty sure I would remember this knife as well. If I lived long enough. It was a foldable blade, but the kind that locks in place. A four-inch piece of matte black steel, which doesn't sound very big until you consider that the distance between the carotid artery and open air was about an eighth of an inch.

I remembered that I had bought brass knuckles. I remembered that brass knuckles do not trump knives. I remembered that, in the time it took me to fish the stupid thing out of my pocket, I would be bleeding out.

The Russian yelled something that sounded like, '*Wheesos*!' Probably not a term of endearment.

I lashed out with a wild kick and caught Bristle's knee as the door closed behind him. He swung the knife, side to side, not aiming, just keeping me back as he absorbed the pain in his knee and decided between cutting my throat and burying his blade in my eye socket.

I kicked again and he swung the knife and sliced right through my Zanellas. I felt something cold on the skin of my shin.

I yelled, 'Fuck!' Because that always helps.

He reached behind him fumbling for the emergency stop button, but he missed, shrugged it off and I could see his fatalistic 'oh well,' and knew he was going to do it right here, right now.

'*Tipear tu miraysh*,' he said. Only in Russian.

He didn't grin evilly the way bad guys do in movies. He didn't care about me enough to grin, this was nothing personal, he was just taking out the trash.

He kicked expertly at the inside of my left knee, collapsing me into a lopsided bow, used his left forearm to push my face back and expose my neck and *ding*!

An entire gaggle of giddy Brits, two women and two men, none older than twenty, none remotely sober, piled in, oblivious to the fact that I was about to have my throat cut, oblivious even to the fact that the elevator was going up, not down to the bar.

Bristle folded his knife back against his wrist and made a show of straightening my collar.

'You are too drunk, my friend,' he said.

Ah, the glottal vowels of Russian-accented English.

'He's trying to kill me!' I said in a shrill voice. 'He's got a knife!'

There are few things more awkward than a fart on an elevator, but this was one. The drunk Brits gaped around at me, at the Russian, at each other. And then one of the women giggled, and one of the men said, 'Cheers,' because Brits can't go two minutes without a vacuous 'cheers,' and Bristle and I glared at each other, as I yelled, 'I am not kidding, this is not a joke! He's really trying to fucking kill me!'

Bristle made the universal sign for drinking and grinned and then the bastard threw an arm around my neck, pulling me down to him and said, 'You must eat food when drink, yes, my friend?'

Humans suffer from three related mental quirks: confirmation bias, motivated reasoning and cognitive dissonance. People see what they expect to see, see what they want to see, and have no problem dismissing facts they know to be true but don't like. My career as a con man had relied heavily on all three syndromes. But at the moment, they were keeping my fellow elevator passengers from seeing the screamingly obvious.

The elevator stopped on at the top of its route, Delia's floor, where Special Agent Delia would certainly rush to save me if I could only . . . But if I got off I'd be all alone with Bristle McKnifeski in an empty corridor. The drunks stayed on and we were joined by a Muslim family, a steel-gray-haired man with a Saddam mustache, his hijabed wife and a six-month-old baby in the wife's arms. Counting the baby there were now eight and a half souls crammed cheek to jowl in the stuffy hot elevator, all facing away from me and the python arm around my neck.

But it would be okay, I told myself, because no way even a Russian hitman was going to complicate his boss' life by murdering me with six and a half witnesses present.

Probably.

We began our descent and I suddenly spun in place, banged into Saddam's elbow and twisted free of Bristle's grip.

I wormed my way backward, face to Bristle, shouldering my way to the front of the cage, pushing past legs and shoulders and bellies, ready to jump to light speed the instant the door opened. That tipped the scales for Bristle. Given a choice between six and a half witnesses and me possibly escaping, he chose witnesses.

He thrust his knife between two of the Brits and stabbed at me. I shied away like a New York City tourist seeing his first New York City rat, and the blade rather than burying itself in my heart went through the gap between my arm and chest and sliced skin on both sides. I bellowed like a water buffalo. Then – finally – everyone started screaming and yelling. Including the baby.

Bristle, angry now, used his shoulder to shove the hijabed woman and baby aside, but the elevator was too crammed with bodies, and I was using them as human shields; the only other alternative being to let the bastard stab me.

Chaos! Screams and roars and a terrified whinny (me) and the blade stabbed into the door so hard it left a dent in the steel. We were panicked cattle now, surging, cowering, banging on walls, yelling in three languages.

'*Suka blyad*!' Russian.

'*Kiss ekhtak*!' Arabic.

'*Ah ah ah ah*!' English. Of a sort.

Knife fighters don't like to be reduced to nothing but stabbing, but there would be no razzle-dazzle here, so Bristle stabbed and Saddam took it in the shoulder. Bristle stabbed again and cut the fleshy part of my right palm. He stabbed and one of the British women yelled, 'You cut me, you fucking wanker!'

The elevator car rocked on its cable. The light flickered. There was blood smeared on the door, blood dripping down mirrors. My feet slipped in blood and probably saved my life as the next thrust went right past my nose. But not in slow-motion as it would have done in a movie.

The mother in the hijab wrapped herself around her baby and screamed curses as her husband roared in pain and outrage and punched Bristle, not a great punch, a short, weak punch that caught Bristle on the side of the head. Bristle did what came naturally to him and stabbed the knife into the man's stomach. Buried it to the hilt.

Then as the stabbed man sank to his knees, shocked, tearing at his shirt to get at the wound, Bristle climbed over him, foot planted on shoulder, pushed himself up and over, banged his head against the ceiling and stabbed at me as the bleeding man sank away beneath him. I did the crazy thing and pushed myself right at him, head lowered, a desperate bull trying for a kill as the matador stumbled. My head hit Bristle's chest, harder than he might have expected because I had some leverage pushing off.

Bristle's feet tangled in the fallen man's limbs and he staggered back, slamming one of the British men hard.

The Brit yelled, 'Right then!' and brought a hammer fist down on the crown of Bristle's head.

And *ding*!

The door opened and screaming, raging, blaspheming, blood-smeared people tumbled out onto the marble floor of the lobby. I planted a foot on Bristle's face as I climbed over him, a rat deserting the good ship USS *Elevator* with all deliberate haste. Women and children could take care of themselves, it was jibbering cowards first on this *Titanic*.

I ran, slipping and stumbling, but with great conviction, chased by screams and shouts. Across the lobby, out the glass doors, running through a blur, heading into the night toward the parking lot where . . . goddammit! *Delia had driven!*

Rule Number Fucking One of fugitive life – always have a car! Always have a way out!

Behind me came Russian voices. Bristle had joined up with Baldy and I was running flat-out, downhill, scattering sleeping cats, careening toward the water and the lights of town too far south.

Then, I no longer heard steps behind me, and I spared a

millisecond for a glance. A glance at the tan Land Rover that now plowed through the automated gate guard of the hotel parking lot and veered off the road onto the grass verge.

It would be an exaggeration to describe what I was doing as 'thinking' but my jumbled brain-flashes went something like this:

Lights!
Open cafés!
Won't stop 'em!
Water!

I'm in decent shape but I'm not a great runner, though panic was shaving seconds off my time. But I am a fair swimmer and I figured if I could just get across the rocks that formed the shoreline here and dive into the black waves I could almost certainly outswim the Russians.

For the first time in my life I yelled, 'Police! Police!' And, '*Policia*! *Au secours*!' for the benefit of Spanish and French speakers.

Out of nowhere: Baldy!

He was to my right, charging toward me. *How the hell?* He was coming straight down a row of chaise longues, leaping them like he was running the one-hundred-ten-meter hurdles at the Olympics. He would cut me off before I reached the rocks.

My God, he was fast!

But I was desperate. I reached, grabbed the back skin of a tabby, and threw the cat at Baldy. It was a lucky throw and a quick cat. Tabby had all four paws and however many claws stretched horizontally as flying kitty met bearded Russian face.

Baldy let go a satisfyingly soprano howl and spun away as the cat hissed and slashed and dug stiletto claws into scalp and forehead and eyes.

I topped the low concrete sea wall and hurled myself onto the nearest rock. It was slick and I tripped, landed on my cut shin and caught myself with my cut hand and sprang away like a one-legged frog.

A hand closed around my ankle stopping my momentum dead and bringing me down hard. Any air left in my lungs exploded outward in a sob. I rolled and that loosened Bristle's grip. I fell into a wet crevice not two feet wide, a surge of foam covered me, I sucked water and crawled. Crawled and scraped and slithered and kicked until suddenly, I plunged.

Chilly water closed over my head. My back touched bottom, and I let myself slide further until I could bend my knees and propel myself away though the water.

And then I swam. My form was not all it might have been, but my motivation was strong. I swept my arms and kicked my legs and the goddamn swell pushed me back, but not hard enough, not hard enough to defeat my adrenal glands.

I swam and swam and finally, panting and gasping, looked back. I saw two things. Thing one was the two Russians standing on a rock as foam covered their shoes.

Thing two was flashing police lights on the road, which was just two hundred yards behind them.

Bristle stabbed a finger toward me and yelled something in Russian. Probably not, 'Have a nice day.'

I swam down the beach for a quarter mile. Then finally I dragged my wet, cut-stinging, utterly-exhausted body up and out onto rocks. I lay there breathing up at the moon as the shakes took me.

I managed to stand after a while, but it was a near-run thing. I walked on numb feet, feeling the pain of cuts, feeling battered muscles and twisted tendons, fighting the languidness that even mild Mediterranean water brings. My goal, insofar as I had a coherent thought, was to stagger as far as any open business with lights on. But I didn't make it that far. Instead I made it only as far as the idling Kia pulled onto the grass verge.

Special Agent Delia Delacorte was behind the wheel. I could see her in the dashboard light.

She reached over and pushed open the passenger door.

I collapsed onto the seat, draining seawater and rivulets of blood.

She didn't ask anything, just raised an eyebrow.

'I . . .' Sigh. 'I went out for a smoke.' And then the lights went out and my head fell back and I went bye-bye.

SIXTEEN

pried open an eye and saw we were driving.
And went away again, drifting away on sweet, sweet lethargy.

I pried open an eye again when I heard a female voice insisting, 'I can't carry you, you're going to have to help.'

I caused my arms and legs to sort of move, a random flailing that somehow ended with me standing, leaning back against Delia's car with her hand on my chest keeping me up.

'Blood all over my favorite top,' Delia complained, 'and there aren't a lot of shops selling clothes for six-foot-tall women here.'

My bleary eyes noted with surprise that we were at my villa.

'Give me your keys.'

'They'll follow us,' I gasped.

I did my best, but my hand and arm had disagreements about how to accomplish the retrieval of keys, so she finally fished in my slacks pocket and I swear that despite everything there was a bit of an erotic thrill.

She half dragged me inside and dumped me on my couch where I sat played-out and splayed-out like a drunk, legs wide, arms flopped.

'Locks!' I said forcefully. Or may have whimpered.

I heard the faraway sound of a deadbolt being thrown. Then a puzzling sound, which I took to be furniture dragged over tile. Delia was gone for a minute or two during which time I remembered once being at my great-grandmother's house and sitting on a plastic-covered sofa. I wondered confusedly if that had been to deal with blood, because my sofa was done for.

Then Delia was back holding something to my mouth and the happy, malty aroma of the Isle of Skye rose in my nostrils to give me hope. I swallowed a mouthful of whiskey and it burned. It burned so wonderfully.

I noticed that Delia had stuck a knife in her belt, my chef's knife, very swashbuckling.

By then I was able to stand and say intelligent things like, 'I'm bleeding. Fuck. Maid service will . . .'

She led me upstairs to my bedroom, thence to the master bath, where she sat me on the tile floor of the shower and turned on hot water.

I sat there soaking up life-giving heat, with most of a freshened tumbler of Talisker, watching the blood come out of my hand and leg and armpit. After a long time, I found enough strength to stand up and remove my wet and clinging clothing, wincing at my wounds.

In movies, tough guys just shake off deadly encounters. In real life, those things leave you stunned, scared, shaking and needing to metabolize way too much hormonal go-juice. Add chilly water and sudden desperate exertion and there comes a lethargic state bordering on coma.

I turned off the shower and went to the medicine cabinet in search of my first-aid supplies, which I dropped with a clatter.

Delia came in, snatched up as many towels as she could in one hand, took my wrist and guided me back into the bedroom. She spread a towel over the side of the bed and sat me down.

I'd had hopes of being naked with Delia at some point, but I was not presenting as favorably as I'd have liked. I was a drowned rat, hair in my eyes, shoulders sagging toward vertical, sand in my chest hair, draining out the red red kroovy, and acutely aware that terror and the Mediterranean had left me looking somewhat less than awe-inspiring.

She went to work with my supply of first aid, augmenting where necessary with towels.

'You need a gun,' I said. 'The bastards could try for a do-over.'

'David, I have secured the doors and windows. They aren't going to try again tonight, they've got cops to deal with. Besides,' she said, with a nicely ironic tone, 'you're in the safe embrace of the FBI.'

'Comforting, frightening and a bit erotic,' I said.

'The leg will be OK,' she muttered. 'Raise your arm.'

I did, revealing the two opposite cuts, one on the underside of my bicep, the other on my side, blood running down and making delta patterns on my skin.

'You need stitches,' she said. 'Shall I take you to the hospital?'

Not a firm 'I'm taking you to the hospital,' but a diffident, 'shall I take you?' Question mark.

After terror, pain and lethargy comes anger. 'I fucking told you!'

'Yes.' Our eyes met. 'I saw them out the window. I saw them follow you. I came as fast as I could.'

'Jesus Fucking Christ, I'm on a Russian mob hit list.'

You've been bitten by a deadly viper and there is no antidote.

You've got end-stage pancreatic cancer.

You're on a Russian mob hit list.

Delia nodded. 'Looks like it.'

It's hard to argue when people agree.

'I can sew you up,' Delia said. 'Do you have a sewing kit?'

'I have one of those kits they give you at decent hotels,' I snarled. I told her where to find it.

'Any color preference in thread? We have red, white, blue—'

'Basic black will be fine.'

She borrowed my cigar torch to sterilize the needle, then threaded it. 'This might hurt.'

'It's going to hurt like hell, Delia, and I'm going to be a baby about it.'

'More Scotch?'

Of course more Scotch, you crazy, reckless bitch, who almost got me killed and still may. I'll take a syringe of heroin, if you have any. I did not say.

I confined myself to sarcasm. 'If it's not too much trouble.'

It hurt.

Alcohol doesn't make pain go away, it just makes you care less. You read stories about warriors – Vikings, Huns, Mongols, Marines – who never so much as whimper while they have a leg cut off with a pair of snub-nosed kindergarten craft scissors, but I am none of those things. The best I could manage was a string of curses accompanied by flinches, cringes and sudden intakes of breath.

But at last I was sewed, smeared with antiseptic cream, bandaged and even dressed in underpants and a T-shirt.

Delia filled a baggie with ice and pressed it against my jaw where Bristle had punched me.

The lethargy, much aided by the whiskey, returned, all anger and bitterness had seeped out of me. Along with enough blood to make me woozy.

'You okay?' Delia asked me. Gentle. Concerned. Like she was Mommy.

'Yeah, I'll . . . I'm just going to . . .'

She pushed me back on the bed. Pulled the covers from beneath me then spread them over me. I don't think she really gave me a kiss on the forehead, I probably just imagined that.

I probably also imagined drunkenly slurring the opening lick of 'Bad to the Bone'.

Then I slept.

SEVENTEEN

'**B**lack, right?'

My nose worked, and I smelled that most magical of all aromas. Someone had super glued my eyes shut so it was with difficulty that I pried one open.

Delia sat on the edge of my bed and held a mug toward me.

'Black and bitter, just the way I like my women,' I said, attempting a sexy leer which was perhaps less effective than it might have been had the side of my jaw not been swollen.

'I could just pour this coffee over your head.'

I took the mug. I drank. And the life-giving elixir flowed into me.

'How are you feeling?' Delia asked.

I took stock. Pain. Pain. Pain there, too. And there. Humiliation. Shame. Self-loathing. And a probably false memory of having yelled that I had Tourette's of the hand. That couldn't be right.

'I'll live.'

'Breakfast?'

'I'll have scrambled eggs with chives and crème fraîche.

A well-browned banger, toast, butter and marmalade. And some melon – don't cut too close to the rind.'

'Right,' Delia said and left.

I stumbled to the shower, did an ineffectual keep-the-bandages dry dance as I parboiled myself clean again, sprayed deodorant, replaced my sopping wet bandages, practically weeping at the sight of neat black stitches, and dressed. I found Delia in the living room. There was toast on the kitchen counter.

Just toast.

I snagged the toast, freshened my coffee and sat opposite her. She'd used my guest room shower and dressed in some of my clothes – pale blue dress shirt with French cuffs rolled up to just below the elbows – rather fetching – and black sweat-pants – rather not.

'Did you check your wounds for pus or reddening?' she asked.

'That is a question I've never before been asked. But no, no pus. No sign of infection. And your stitches were fairly even.' I sipped coffee and crunched toast. 'I didn't exactly pull off the role of stoic action hero last night, did I?'

I meant it as a self-deprecating joke and expected a condescending laugh.

'Actually, despite realizing that this will just inflate your oversized ego,' Delia said seriously, 'I have to say you did really well.'

I shook my head. 'Joe Burton would not have whined and whimpered and then cried himself to sleep.'

Damn she had a great smile, lots of teeth beneath amused-yet-skeptical eyes.

You're trying not to like me, Delia, but you do. You can't help yourself. I'm charming, smart, tall, good-looking and a (mostly) reformed sociopath, what's not to like? I did not say.

What I did say was: 'So. You going to tell me why this case is so important to you?'

'So important?'

I nodded. 'Yeah, because here's the thing I realized at some point in the night, in between nightmares of being in a wet coffin full of knives. This is about the kids for you. Emotionally, I mean. Sure, money-laundering Russians, but if that was the main focus Agent Kim would still be here, wouldn't he? Feebs travel in pairs. So, something went wrong with the money-laundering case and the agency called you home to Rome. Kim went. You came up with some bullshit involving vacation time.'

She digested that for a few minutes and I glanced surreptitiously around, noting the chair under the front door with some approval. Noting that she'd driven a nail into the tile to lock it in place, with even stronger approval.

One eyebrow cocked upward for a full second. She shook her head slightly, arguing with herself. Then a slight snort of laughter, not amusement, more the sound you might make on realizing you're screwed and have no choice but to go along.

'You know, David, I've read your books,' she said. 'All of them. You're better at avoiding clichés than real life is.'

'What's the cliché?'

'The one about every cop having a case they can't let go of?'

'The cold case trope. Sure. Michael Connelly does it with Bosch. James Lee Burke. Mosley. Lehane. Fucking Lee Child. Milking the backstory.'

'If you say so. Anyway, a few years ago I was working out of Palermo. Sicily. We were providing technical assistance to the Italian *carabinieri* dealing with the Sicilian mafia.'

Already I was not enjoying this story. Were we adding Sicilian Mafia to the equation, now? What was keeping the Yakuza, Murder Inc., and the goddamned Uruk-hai?

'So, while I was on Sicily, there was a big run of refugees coming from North Africa, and we knew the mob would look to cash in if they could. So we thought: opportunity!'

'Sure,' I said. 'Who doesn't get excited at the prospect of picking a fight with the Mafia? In Sicily, no less.'

'It turned out, unsurprisingly, that they were taxing the smugglers. So much per boat, so much per head. In exchange, the mob made sure the *carabinieri* were never at the landing place.'

'I thought you were working with the *carabinieri*?'

'Come on, David, why do you think the Italian government called us in? They knew the *carabinieri* in Sicily were riddled with mafia informers. Anyway, the old men in Palermo are very good at accounting, and they'd began to realize that the number of refugees arriving and being taxed were fewer than the number departing North Africa. So, they questioned some of the smugglers . . .'

'Politely, I'm sure.'

'Ever hear of a mob enforcer nicknamed "Szell?" He was a loaner from the Philly mob, they wanted someone they could trust but who would absolutely have no ties to the Italian authorities. Treason goes both ways.'

'Doesn't sound very Sicilian, "Szell."'

'Real name is Turturici. He took the name Szell from that old movie, *The Marathon Man*? The one where the Nazi dentist uses a drill to—'

'Ah, ah, ah! Stop, stop, stop! I saw the movie, all right? Jesus Christ.'

'So, as you might guess, the smugglers gave up what they knew, and did it in a hurry. It seems there was another organization with their fingers in the pie. See, a hundred refugees might leave in a boat, but out at sea they would run into a patrol boat mocked up to look like an official Guardia Costiera patrol boat. Uniformed crew, the whole deal.'

I liked the ease with which she trilled the Italian 'r's in Guardia Costiera.

Not important.

'Obviously it was a set-up. The smugglers would take on, say, a hundred people in Libya, charging on average six thousand dollars. They are "intercepted" at sea where the fake coast guardsmen would simply seize whatever children were present under the pretense of saving them from the perils of the sea. Occasionally they would also take a woman. Always a *young* woman.' She made a world-weary smirk that turned sour. 'The smugglers don't mind: they've been paid for a hundred passengers, who cares if only ninety reach the destination? If any of them makes too much of a fuss about the kids, well, smugglers don't have a lot of patience. So, the remaining refugees reach Sicily where Italian authorities are overwhelmed. The refugees ask after their children and are told it will all be cleared up. With families spread around various camps, various countries, some getting in, some not, the lost kids are never quite found.'

'How many in a year?' I asked. 'Follow the money.'

'Over just the last fifty-three months my guess is about five hundred kids.'

'Five million, round numbers, if we use the ten-grand figure.

Realistically maybe half that or a bit over.' That, I thought, just might be enough to justify the risk. Call it three million over not quite five years? Six hundred grand a year? Maybe. But my instincts told me there was more going on. Six hundred large is nice money, but a single successful heroin run would earn much more with lower risk.

'You think it's not enough,' Delia said, reading my expression. 'It takes a thief, as they say.'

'Hey,' I snapped, because I was not having that, not for a second. I risked a finger pointing it at her. She didn't break it off. 'I stole money, Delia. Stole money, past tense. I never fucking sold children. Don't ever equate me to those people.'

She took that in and in what I believe is a first for any FBI agent since J. Edgar Hoover was posing with a tommy gun, she said, 'Sorry.'

'So, what's the rest?'

'What do you think it is?' She challenged me.

My turn to think. It took a minute. Chills went up my spine. 'They ransom them back to the parents. Charge them for passage out, grab them and sell them as sex toys, and when they're used up, they sell them back to the family. For?'

'As low as twenty, as high as fifty grand,' she said.

'And we have bingo,' I said. 'If they got fifty large from just twenty of the kids' families, that's a million. If they got half that from the next hundred or so, add another million. Plus the initial three, that makes it a five-million-dollar racket, divided by five years and someone is grossing a mill per annum. Figure half of that goes out in salaries, bribes and expenses, and you're still putting upwards of half a million a year in an offshore bank. But how the hell do refugee families cough up that kind of cash?'

Delia shrugged. 'Extended family, appeals to their village, overseas relatives and of course NGO money.'

'NGO money?'

'There are a couple charities that buy people out of slavery.'

'Doesn't that just make the whole scam more profitable? Supply and demand?'

'You want to go yell at do-gooders trying to save kids? Anyway, when we had enough information we set up a sting, the real

Guardia Costiera and US Navy. The idea was to catch the phony patrol boat in the act, after they'd taken the kids, and be heroes. I was aboard the USS *Bulkeley*, a destroyer. Guns, missiles . . . you could blow up a good chunk of the Middle East with just that one ship.'

I waited. I waited and a feeling of dread crept over me. I did not want to be the sort of man who could already guess what happened next. I did not want to be the kind of man who thought that way. But something very dark and sad was in Delia's eyes.

'The rendezvous happens. I'm watching it on radar. We close in. Five miles out in very rough seas and the smugglers spot us. So, they force the kids over the side at gunpoint. They figure we'll stop to rescue them, and they can get away. Thirteen kids went in the water. No life jackets. Waves. Rain.' The story stopped for a while as memories played out behind her eyes. Then, with an unsteady sigh, 'The Italian boat raced like crazy to save as many as they could, but on the *Bulkeley*, I tell the captain no, chase that fake patrol boat, *get him!*'

I looked at her. Her face was a twisting grimace of pain. Tears filled her eyes and threatened to spill down her cheek. She made a quick, surreptitious swipe at them. I must have been especially vulnerable from the near-death experience because my own eyes started welling up in empathy with her.

I am not good with tears. I always tried to exit any con before the tears started.

'So, we got 'em. We caught up to the patrol boat. They threw up their hands and we went aboard, three FBI in addition to me, and the sailors of course. We searched . . .'

'And found no refugees,' I said. 'No kids.'

She had lost her words. She nodded, and that did send a tear falling. 'The Italians saved one kid. One. We found the first bodies when the sun came up. At first you know, you think, no, that's not what I'm seeing. I am not seeing a little boy's face . . . I'm FBI, I'm not supposed to . . . I've seen things, you know, I mean I've seen dead bodies, I've seen stuff . . .'

Had I not been a dick earlier and tried to put moves on her, I could have put my arm around her. She needed an arm around her. Hell, so did I.

She sniffed, and blew out a shaky breath. 'Anyway, we locked the assholes up in the brig aboard the destroyer. It's not exactly San Quentin, the sailors have other things to do, so I decided I'd go down and check on the prisoners.' Sly pride peeked out beneath her eyelids.

'With a big stick?'

The slightest of nods. 'Anyway, the Chief Petty Officer saw me and he . . . and he . . . goddammit!' More tears, too many for her to wipe away. '"Ma'am, you can't do this," he said. The sailor, the petty officer. He had kids, he had a little boy and a little girl and we both wanted to go and wipe the bastards out.'

'How did he stop you?'

She made a laugh that was as much a sob. 'Well, David, he pointed out that I was supposed to be the law. This, he said, is not a job for law.'

'Ah.'

'Anyway, I walked away. The next morning, it turned out the guy playing captain, the head man, the one who'd given the order to throw the kids . . . well, he committed suicide by hanging himself with his own belt. Which was odd because he'd been stripped and made to wear overalls.'

'I see. You investigated to see who might have arranged the suicide?'

'One of the sailors, either from outrage or because they knew the Sicilians would not want him to talk and thought it might earn him some points with them. I didn't know and didn't much care. I gave the matter a good five minutes' worth of investigation. Didn't find anything.'

'Yeah.'

'Once we docked back in Palermo the remaining crew lawyered up. Money changed hands. The only evidence we had of the murders were distant sightings through lashing rain, and the kid we'd rescued. The one kid the Italians had saved as I sent the destroyer chasing . . .'

'The kid?'

'Disappeared. One minute the authorities had him, and the next minute, poof. The rest of the crew made bail.'

'And also poofed.'

'There was a crew of five on the smuggler's boat. One Algerian, one Lebanese, three Cypriots, including the dead captain. We ran prints of course and found four hits, the captain, the Lebanese, an Algerian and one of the remaining Cypriots.'

'Ah.'

'Lebanon is no-go for us, and Algeria's not much better, so we chased down the Cypriot's history. His name is Panagopolous. Nestor Panagopolous. His day job was working security.'

'For?'

'For a private security firm.'

'Italian? Cypriot?'

'American.' She stopped talking and again I saw the internal argument.

'Delia. I came very, very close to being dead,' I said. 'I get security protocols and all that, but I think you need to tell me whatever the fuck you know.'

She didn't take much convincing. The moral calculus had changed. I'd gone from useful tool to being a guy she knew, liked, despite herself, and who was sporting multiple bright white bandages which were, arguably, (entirely) her fault. 'It's called ExMil International. They have offices and people every-where, mostly ex-military, as the name implies.'

'And that's your angle? You're after that guy?'

'We got a tip he was back on Cyprus, under a different name. Doing work for the AZX Bank.'

'That's a Russian bank.'

'With a branch in Limassol. A very active branch.'

I closed my eyes. My hand, armpit and leg hurt. My jaw was not quite aligned in a way that would make eating corn on the cob easy. And I wanted something more than toast.

'I'm going to make more coffee.'

She followed me to the kitchen and watched as I got to work on the breakfast I had ordered – with plenty for her as well.

'Oh, by the way,' she said. 'I disabled your Nest cameras. And I got rid of our bug, too. The one you had tuned to ambient noise?'

'Of course you did.' I chopped chives. 'You might have made a good crook.'

'I like having a retirement plan.'

'The dead British fugitive, Rachel/Amanda. She was your source on this Cypriot guy.'

'Kim and I were supposed to meet her.'

'Yeah. Money?'

Delia shook her head. 'Passport. She wanted a valid US passport. She wanted to disappear.'

'She had two passable British passports.'

'Yes.'

'But she couldn't return to the UK. Because?'

Delia winced. 'I'm afraid telling you that would definitely be a felony and you don't really have a need to know. I can't *tell* you anything more without risking my job, and I like my job.' She shrugged. 'But you're pretty good at guessing.'

So, it was going to be like that.

I thought for a moment while I stirred eggs. The bangers were in my impromptu stove-top dutch oven, a sauté pan with a second pan upended and used as a lid.

'Can you slice that melon?' I asked. 'Not really quite up for knife work just yet.'

She cut the melon in half, scooped the seeds into the trash, and peeled us each a quarter.

'Okay,' I said. 'Here's my guess. Rachel had a relationship with someone in intelligence, MI5, 6 or GCHQ, whoever. Probably more than a mere relationship, but she did something that soured that relationship. Was she . . .' I quirked my mouth and realized that hurt. 'I have to go with money. She stole.'

I looked at Delia who said nothing and did not meet my eye but also did not say no.

'They had her in place somewhere, as an asset, and opportunity knocked. A bank? A business? She skimmed a bit, did she? Got caught? And ran?'

'This is excellent melon. Have a piece.' She speared a chunk and held it out for me. I snapped it up like a trout with a worm.

'Okay, so Rachel worked for, let's say, MI6. MI5 are just cops, and cops wouldn't think to have a homemade garrote and DIY pepper spray in their overnight bag.'

'A garrote?'

I told her how I had obtained Kiriakou's evidence inventory and had it translated. It was a struggle to make it all sound off-hand, like I wasn't absurdly proud of myself.

'Interesting,' Delia said, frowning. 'Carabiners and wire. I'm not sure I would have caught that.'

'It's not a defensive weapon.'

'No,' she agreed. 'But, look, the Brits don't arrange to stab unreliable MI6 agents on the beach for a bit of skimming from a target bank.'

Did she realize she had just confirmed that Rachel had been working at a bank? I was pretty sure she had. Accidentally. Delia was enjoying the game.

I pulled out two plates just as fresh toast popped. I assembled scrambled eggs with chives and crème fraiche, a well-browned banger, melon, toast with butter and marmalade. It was yet another glorious morning so I led the way onto my patio. Paphos was below and south, a collection of rooftop cisterns, satellite dishes and laundry lines. The Mediterranean reflected sunlight in semaphore flashes that half-blinded me.

We sat like a couple. Delia on one side of my patio table, me on the other. She was looking out, I was looking at her. We both had lovely views.

'So. Rachel/Amanda. Ramanda. Was not just some casual asset, she was an agent,' I said.

'I like the eggs.'

'Gordon Ramsay on YouTube,' I explained. 'So, MI6 places Rachel in a suspect bank. Probably under the other name, what was it? Amanda something. Ramanda sees an opportunity but she gets caught.'

'By whom, I wonder, in this fictional scenario?' Delia asked.

'By the bad guys or the good guys. Or both. Right? One way she's doing time, the other way she's ending up dead. Either way she has to run. She takes her passports and flies to . . . why the hell come to Cyprus? If you're running from the Brits, this is the wrong damn place. If you're running from bent Russian bankers, even worse.'

Delia stayed silent.

I rapped the table with my knuckles. 'Of course, duh. To see you and Kim. You bring her here to ID Panaglop-um, whatever.'

'Panagopolous. So, this is a banger,' Delia said, slicing sausage. Very precise movements. Make a thin slice, spear it on the fork, pile some eggs on top, and past her teeth.

'The guy, Panagopolous. Ramanda knew he was on the island, and she . . . um . . . No, it was *you*, wasn't it? You made it a condition of the deal. You think like a cop, so you want that in-person ID. You want her to point a finger and say, "That's him." You need that to get a warrant. You were going to take her in front of a magistrate, have her ID your perp so you could file an extradition request. My God, you *are* a cop.'

Delia nodded and did not look happy. 'Yes. I'm the cop who got her killed.'

'You weren't going to bust the guy, the Cypriot, at least not right away, though, because you'd found out he was working for the AZX Bank. You wanted his dick in a wringer and were going to squeeze him for information on Russian money laundering, and Ramanda was going to serve him up for you. That's a two-fer for you, Delia, you nail a money launderer and a child-killer. But when Ramanda takes a knife to the spine, the FBI figures, oh, well, there goes our witness, this isn't working out. They call you home to . . .'

'I am attached to the Rome office.'

'Better food than Athens.'

'Yes, David, that's how Bureau assignments work: by the number of Michelin-starred restaurants.'

'North of three hundred in Rome, five in Athens.'

'You're a very strange man,' Delia said.

'Yeah,' I admitted, though I didn't see what was so strange about knowing the best food cities. 'Anyway, Kim goes back to Rome, and you stay, because you care about whatever it is the bank is up to, sure, because you're FBI and all, but you care a hell of a lot more about taking down Panagopolous. Because you're a decent human being.'

'And the other two, the Algerian and the Lebanese. In time.' That came out in almost dreamy tone. She had long savored that thought.

I bussed the dishes, taking my time about it as Delia sat with her legs stretched out in the sun. When I rejoined her, I asked, 'Tell me how money laundering works.'

'You don't know?' When I didn't answer she said, 'Well, at the most basic level it's pretty simple. You're a Moscow drug dealer, you've got a million dollars in cash, but it's all in rubles and you aren't dumb enough to trust Russian banks for long, you might annoy the wrong oligarch and your account evaporates. There's no such thing as a really private bank in Russia, they're all oligarch-owned and operated with the tacit support of Russian intelligence. You can't keep the money in cash, there being no honor among thieves . . . present company perhaps excepted.'

I made a back-and-forth 'could be' gesture with my hand.

'First, you want a bank that doesn't ask too many questions. Rubles or bitcoin, it doesn't matter, money isn't real until it's in dollars, pounds or euros.'

'Deutsche Bank a few years ago,' I suggested. 'Or let's say the AZX Bank. But you want it in and out fast.'

'Purely as an example, let's say that,' she allowed. 'You form some shell corporations, they each have a bank account, and you start depositing your ill-gotten gains into those accounts. The bank then pushes your money out to, let's call it the ABC company, a shell corporation in the Bahamas or Caymans or wherever. Of course you own that shell corporation, too, by way of various other shell corps. ABC invests in real estate and local politicians, the real estate transactions confuse the picture further because never forget, money laundering is all about Three Card Monte. Where's the money? Not under this cup or that cup. From there on you have apparently legitimate money from this ABC corporation and you can spend that money in Los Angeles or London or Paris. The money started out as dirty rubles and turned into clean dollars in a nice, safe, overseas bank with strict bank privacy laws. If the Russian version of the IRS asks how you paid for that yacht you're driving around the Black Sea, you say 'from the ABC corporation of the Bahamas.' You pay just enough taxes and you're an upstanding citizen. There are dozens of variations. But that's the basic.'

'The banks take a cut.'

'Oh, yes.'

'Whoever is providing protection in Russia gets a cut.'

'Of course.'

'I don't get why we need to drag kids into it,' I said. 'If you're some Russian oligarch or mob guy or both looking to get money out of Russia and into the west, why the human trafficking?'

'That is the question. We have pieces.' She held up a chunk of melon as a visual aid. 'We do not have a whole.'

EIGHTEEN

Delia went back to her hotel to face police questions about the extraordinary elevator ride – the cops were questioning all hotel guests. She would spin them a tale of knowing and seeing nothing. They might bother to run a make on her, but probably wouldn't. If they did, they'd see she was FBI, which would mean she'd lied to them, but then again: FBI. The Cypriots might be mad, but not enough to get into a pissing match with the Bureau.

Did the hotel have video in their lobby and hallways? Would the cops be able to connect Delia to me? And the me on the video to the me currently worrying about it?

I scrolled back through every memory of Delia's hotel. Had there been CCTV? I sure hadn't felt it, and my instincts were generally good. So, maybe it would be nothing but eyewitness testimony – bad enough, but given the confusion that sensible people tend to feel when locked in an elevator with a stabby Russian, perhaps not fatal. At least not fatal in terms of evidence available to a random cop. But to Kiriakou? He would know, and if he was bent he might not care too much about the solidity of his evidence.

I checked my locks and managed a couple hours of actual work, not first draft stuff, that takes more focus than I was capable of. But I can copy-edit in a coma, so I did that and cleaned up a fuzzy sentence here and cut a superfluous paragraph there.

It made me feel good. Normal. I like to work.

The day was getting on toward noon when Chante broke in and snuck up behind me in an attempt to kill me by inducing a heart attack. At least that was a perfectly plausible story I could absolutely tell the cops if I decided to bring charges.

Unlikely.

'Jesus Christ!' I said after spinning the chair and rising into a fighting stance. If by 'fighting stance' you mean feet tangled in the legs of an overturned chair and fists raised like some Victorian-era poster of John L. Sullivan. It was almost a pity it wasn't Bristle, he'd have laughed himself to death.

Chante stared at whatever she saw two inches to the right of my eyes and said, 'I come to you with a problem.'

Oh, you've got a damn problem, all right, you rude, inconsiderate, graceless creature. In fact, I barely know you and yet I could start a top ten-list of your problems. I did not say.

'You realize that just because you have a key . . .' I started, then saw she wasn't listening. So I said, 'I'm getting coffee.'

'I will take one.'

I walked back to the kitchen strangling an invisible neck. I brought back coffee and ice water, reminding myself that I should pour neither over Chante's head.

'Okay. I'll bite. What's the problem? And why are you not at the set? Is that the problem? You've been fired?' I suppressed the urge to smile.

'There is some problem with the sets. No shooting today and Minette gave me the day.'

'You're spending your day off with me, how very generous.' My brutal sarcasm bounced off her like ping-pong balls off a tank. 'The problem?'

'The problem is not mine, but that of my employer.'

'Minette?' My interest rose. Fair damsel in distress, me as the white knight, underplay the heroism thing, amazing gratitude sex with much sympathy for my heroically-banged-up body . . .

'She is being blackmailed.'

'That's what's known as a crime,' I opined sagely. 'Call the cops.'

'The blackmailer has a certain video.'

'Hasn't Minette already done nude scenes?' How was I to know? I certainly had not checked her out on Google images. Nor had I clicked on the subheading 'nude.' That would be wrong, as my moral guide, Richard Nixon, once observed.

'It is nothing so simple. And Minette would never be ashamed of her body. How could she be? She is perfect.'

That took some digesting and I covered by taking a long sip. Had Chante just shown an emotion other than contempt? That word 'perfect' had come out all warm and toasty.

'All right,' I said. 'So, what's the video?'

'It is of Minette enjoying sex. With a woman.'

I frowned. 'Couple thoughts. One, she's from Paris, France not Paris, Texas. Two, she's a movie star not a school teacher.'

Chante said nothing.

I said nothing.

She won that stand-off. 'Who's the other woman?'

Chante drew a deep breath. 'Me.'

I would like to be able to say that I did not immediately form a picture in my mind. And then another. And then in this position. And now reversed. And now with me delivering pizza, and neither of them with any cash to pay for said pizza, oh my, whatever shall we do? Yes, I would like to be the kind of person who did not think that way.

'She's a lesbian?' I asked.

'She is open-minded.'

'Oh, good,' I said before thinking. I could work with bisexual. Keep hope alive! Then, 'And you?'

'I am a lesbian.'

Oh, so that's why you didn't fall for my charm. It's not my fault, it's not that I'm getting old and past my prime, it's you, not me at all, it's you, hah! I did not say.

'So, what's the problem? You're both adults.'

For the first time Chante looked uncomfortable. She shifted in her chair and diverted attention by swirling her drink. 'The problem is that Minette is also sleeping with the director, who is also a woman. She is very jealous and will make Minette's life hell on the set if she finds out about us. Minette also has a close friendship with one of the producers, but he is very sophisticated and will not care. But the blackmailer does care.'

'Wait, you *know* the blackmailer?'

'Of course. He is Chris Temple, the actor. He is in love with Minette. And he is very emotional. Very jealous. She slept with him one time only, but . . .' Gallic shrug. – 'he is an American.'

'American' in Chante's mind is a synonym for 'child.'

'Ah. So, Temple wants her all for himself. If she doesn't go along with that, he shows the video to the director. Maybe put the video online, make her out to be some sex-crazed, bisexual sluuuu . . . um . . . sensual woman. With eclectic tastes. And healthy appetites. Is it at least grainy, badly-lit video?'

'No. Even small cameras can record in HD. Thankfully he was only able to record the first two hours.'

'Two hours?' I'd like to be able to say I did not immediately . . . 'Two hours. Huh. Okay. So, what does this have to do with me?' I asked.

'Minette thought . . .' she shrugged, and her lip curled in disapproval, '. . . that you are not connected to anyone on the set. And she said you must understand the criminal mind to write mystery novels.'

'Mmmm,' I said. 'Indeed. What else did she say about me?'

The day may come when Chante gives birth. That event will be less painful to her than pushing out the words, 'She said you were attractive.'

'Really?' I asked, not sounding at all like a high school freshman.

'You are tall and symmetrical,' Chante said. 'Minette's judgments when it comes to men . . .' A slightly different French shrug. 'But she downloaded one of your books and read it. She believes you are worthy of trust and committed to justice.'

'Okay, fair enough then, she really doesn't have much judgment when it comes to men.' I had not intended to say that aloud.

'She thinks you could come up with a way.'

'What's the tick-tock?'

'Tick-tock?'

'What's the time frame. How long do we have?'

She shrugged. 'Until Chris Temple becomes frustrated.'

'Has he emailed this video to you or Minette?'

'No. He has shown it to me. He says he has made no copies.'

'That's a lie, of course.'

'Yes.'

'Great. So, here's the thing I've learned from my, you know, deep study into the criminal mind and so on. There's the first decision point: pay or don't pay.'

'She will not be his slave.'

'Which brings us to the many ways to stop him. The first is to steal the video. Unfortunately he could have it parked anywhere in the Cloud. The second method is to scare the shit out of him. The third is to kill him. So, really just those three ways. And in case you're in any doubt, number three is a really bad idea.'

'Yes,' she said, with clear regret. 'But how does one "scare the shit" out of a rich movie star?'

'Well . . . I may know a guy.'

'And what would you require in return?'

I looked thoughtful as I drifted briefly into fantasy world. In return? The possibilities were endless and all pretty contemptible, frankly. For a knight in shining armor.

I waved it off with my wounded hand and squelched a whimper of pain. 'Nothing. Come on, what kind of guy do you think I am that I'd try to profit from some asshole's criminal behavior?'

Totally straight face. Delivered with convincing sincerity. Sometimes I amaze myself.

This was Chante's cue to thank me profusely and apologize for her obvious contempt for me. Instead she said, 'You have been injured.'

'Oh, this?' I raised my bandaged hand gingerly. 'I tripped and cut myself. Banged my face up a bit, too.' Rather than wait for her disbelieving sneer, I pushed on. 'When can I get close to this Chris Temple guy?'

Chante leaned forward, pulled a card from her back pocket and pushed it to me. 'Minette mentioned a party, you may remember. She is very generous and has arranged a fund-raising party for several NGOs. Tomorrow night. Everyone will be there.'

At which point, she just stood up and walked away.

The invitation was for David Mitre, plus one. I had a plus-one in mind, if he'd do it. And if I was available, which was very much in doubt at the moment, because I had decided on my next move and it was pretty damn likely to end up with me in handcuffs.

NINETEEN

I t was in a Washington, DC parking garage in 1972 that a source who would come to be known as Deep Throat, but was in reality FBI associate director Mark Felt, spoke the three most useful words in the history of investigation: 'Follow the money.'

Follow. The. Money.

Qui bono? Who benefits?

My WhatsApp dinged.

> *Me: Yeah?*
> *Not Me: Your boy K. has account at Bank of Cyprus. CC: Amex and Visa. Monthly mortgage payment: $1,200. Car payment on Hyundai: $125. Total debt: $3,297 excl: mortg. Credit rating: 744.*
> *Me: And?*
> *Not Me: And fuck all. Groceries and shit. Kids clothing. Meals. Car repair. Normal shit. Googled him, rooted around dark web. Nothing but newspaper clips.*
> *Me: Shoot me some links.*

He did. I spent some time going over the history of Cyril Kiriakou, reading news articles awkwardly translated by Google. He'd busted a couple of local drug rings. He'd solved an extortion case. Seven years ago, he'd solved the murder of a sex worker. Four years ago, he'd arrested an art forger on an Interpol warrant.

All this proved only that Kiriakou was a cop. If he was a bent cop, he was being damn prudent about hiding his money. He was too chubby to be a serious drug addict. Gambling? He didn't read as a gambler to me, not jumpy enough. So. Had Joumanou lied? Made up a name? Settled a score with a cop? Was Father Fotos confused? Was Theo talking rot? Had Kiriakou's interest in me been innocent?

I had followed the money for Kiriakou and it had led me nowhere. But this was still all about money, had to be. My credit bureau source did not have access to Kiriakou's income records, just his credit card expenditures. If Kiriakou was on the take, the cash had to go somewhere, and by somewhere I did not mean a Cypriot bank. The AZX Bank, perhaps? And if I assumed the source of Kiriakou's presumptive bentedness was Russian, the Russian bank might lead back to him. Ditto Panagopolous and ExMil.

Were the streams crossing? I sighed.

Deep, deep sigh, because if I wanted to connect dollar-denominated dots, I needed to get into the AZX Bank's computers. It was a fishing expedition, but with two specific targets, Kiriakou and Panagopolous and who knew, maybe the gods would favor me and hand me a nice, neat connection between the two.

I would be Delia's hero. And then, having solved both of her cases, she would jet off to Rome and I would consider where to run next. Bangkok? Rio? Amsterdam? Each had stunning women, but Amsterdam had better restaurants. I'd had an amazing dinner with superb wine pairings at Vermeer in Amsterdam.

Which was not relevant, really.

I drove to Limassol, an actual city of 175,000, with tallish buildings and traffic jams and street beggars. It faces southeast from the bottom of Cyprus, and were you in one of the water-front office buildings you could look out over the B1, the wide main drag which has a Greek name involving too many syllables, across the promenade, the boulder beach, the water, and if you had exceptional eyesight and perfect weather, you might see Lebanon.

The AZX Bank was deeper toward the center of town. I drove around until I found street parking – paid parking creates evidence in the form of tickets, credit-card receipts and the memories of attendants. And I might need my car in a hurry.

I had scoped the area out ahead of time online and had identified three local places that might be useful watering holes. Two were distinctly Greek. One had a more sophisticated look and a name meant to separate it from the herd: Matryoshka.

Not a Greek name, that. And according to TripAdvisor it was more expensive but had an excellent selection of vodkas. The guy I was looking for would want sophisticated, not working class, and he'd want vodka. Presumably.

I considered a walk-through at the bank, but my only readily-available disguise was a stocking cap and banks are not friendly toward men in stocking caps when the temperature outside is August in Alabama. So, I did the prudent and easy thing and installed myself in a dark side-table in Matryoshka and ordered a glass of Fikardos Shiraz and a bottle of sparkling water. I tasted the wine – quite good – but drank the water. The night promised physical exertion, likely including some fleeing, and wine wasn't going to help.

Cypriot banks close at 2:30. I figured an hour, hour and a half past that, and sure enough around four p.m., the quick-one-before-I-head-home crowd had started to come in. A gratifying number of them were wearing suits and carrying briefcases.

I was looking for a Russian speaker with followers, because when the Big Deal goes for a drink he's generally got at least two toadies in tow. But that was a thin reed, and the potential for error was ridiculous. If I found my Big Deal Russian he might not be from the bank down the block, he might work for Aeroflot or be a vodka salesman, so I had to give close consideration to details of style. Good, expensive tailoring, but nothing flashy. He'd wear a watch, a TAG Heuer maybe, something that said to bank customers, 'money' but not '*your* money.' A white guy. Broad face, distinct cheekbones, and an expression of sullen discontent. Nice suit, expensive watch and shoes, air of resentment. Not exactly a photograph, that, but it gave me the parameters of what to look for.

My first target sat with three men in the table next to mine, where I could overhear and not understand, a conversation in Greek.

My second guess looked the part until I followed him into the restroom and discovered that he was circumcised. (The things I do . . .) Muslims, Jews and most Americans are circumcised, but not Russians.

And then someone did come in trailing not two but three toadies and had, yes, the broad face, the cheekbones, the slightly slanted eyes, the good tailoring and pricey shoes. Pricey high-heeled shoes.

She was perhaps forty with blonde hair pulled back into a graceful shape like a conch shell. She wore a designer knock-off gray wool suit with a knee-length skirt. And yes, she did look sullenly discontented, as did the three younger men who trailed her. Each of the three had an identical briefcase; one was carrying an extra briefcase, a finer model, Versace no less. The woman carried nothing but herself, and she did a pretty fair job of it.

There are times for planning, and there are times for instinct. I stood up, plastered on a big ol' American grin and walked right up to her to say 'Howdy.'

'Hi! Are you Tatiana?'

She stopped dead. Did a double-take, and shook her head. 'No. I am not.'

'Oh! Damn. The description matches . . . are you with Alexander the Great Trucking?' Before she could answer, I took a step back, looked her up and down and snapped my fingers. 'No. Of course not, you are way too classy for a trucking company. What am I thinking? You must be like . . .' I paused. And she let me pause because she sort of wanted to know what she looked like. 'I'd say . . . architect? No, wait. Are you in fashion?'

'Fashion?' She did not smile. That alone did not make her Russian, but the way she pronounced 'feshyon?' hinted at it. Her acolytes stood back, none venturing to play the protective male role, none responding as if she was their *territory*. All three slightly troubled by my effrontery.

'Well, I didn't mean fashion *model*, though you could be that, too. I was thinking more of someone who owned a fashion company. I'm sorry.' I made a self-deprecating face and shrugged. 'I'm really sorry, I amuse myself trying to guess what people do. I should have known right away you weren't Tatiana, or from a trucking company, my God. I mean . . .' I looked appreciative and admiring.

'I am not your Tatiana,' she said. 'I am a banker.'

'Ah,' I said, drawing the syllable out like I was being shown a glimpse of a sacred scroll. 'Again: so sorry.'

I went back to my table and made a show of checking the time. Then scrolling through text messages. Then did a 'dammit' face and went to the bar. 'I'm in the wrong place. Is there a bar called Sousami near here?'

I settled my tab, went outside and found a convenient lurking spot. One of the advantages of smoking cigars – or cigarettes, I suppose, though those things will kill you – is that you can lurk outside any building without looking suspicious so long as you exhale smoke.

An hour later, my banker friend emerged, minus two subordinates. Her remaining helper walked her to the AZX Bank building, carrying her Versace briefcase. At the entrance he gave her back said briefcase. She entered the glass doors, walked to the elevator, punched the 'down' button, and as the doors closed on her I saw she was fishing car keys from her bag.

I raced to my car and drove the block back to the bank arriving just seconds after a green Lexus emerged from underground parking.

I followed on a twenty-minute drive up into the hills. I hung back as we left the A6 and motored down surface roads to an upscale development of cookie-cutter villas crammed cheek by jowl. I looked up the name of the development and yes it was tied to a major Russian developer. Russians are hot to buy property in Cyprus, preferably property that adds up to more than two million euros because then you can get Cypriot citizenship and full access to the EU in just six months. It's like the first-class line at the airport: working folks wait, rich folks jump ahead.

But this was not a two-million-euro property, this was a mere, oh, three-hundred-grand villa nestled in an enclave of same. I turned around and drove some distance away before parking near an apartment block and returning on foot.

It was not hard to find the green Lexus.

I walked slowly past, running scenarios in my head. Getting in should be no problem. She might not even lock her doors. If she did, she still might not lock her windows. And if she locked her ground-floor windows she might not lock the second-floor windows. I did not want to use a crowbar, that would raise all kinds of alarm. Nor did I want to spend long minutes exposed as I squatted before Tatiana's front door fiddling with a lock pick.

She might take a long, hot bath. She might not. She might cook herself a meal. She might not. She might be changing for a night on the town. Or not.

I had used up my innocent strolling time and if I hung around any longer we'd be into 'casing the target' time. For that I would have to wait for full dark.

I walked back to my car, considered driving off, but decided to leave the car and find a restaurant on foot. Yet another First Rule of Sophisticated Burglary: don't leave your car near the target. Why? Because your jobs as a burglar are: 1) Don't get caught, 2) Don't escalate, 3) Make enough profit to justify the risk and, 4) Don't help the cops by providing evidence. Cars have make, model, color, a license plate and a VIN. They are the second most dangerous piece of technology you can own after a smart phone. Make sure any car traceable to you stays outside the likely police canvas zone.

I've thought of putting my accumulated criminal tradecraft in a book, but the people who'd read it would probably steal it and there's no profit in that. Also most burglars are not big readers. Also a low-rent burglar is probably carrying a big-screen TV away, and in that case you don't want a twenty-minute walk to your car.

I had a simple dinner of grilled fish, refused the wine and finished with a coffee, using it to wash down two anticipatory ibuprofen because this was likely to be painful. It was dark when I got back to Tatiana's place, dark but with an annoyingly bright moon.

A narrow pathway separated Tatiana's house from her nearest neighbor. Family sounds were coming from the neighbor, and light spilled from their windows, so I hunched over and scuttled fast, praying no one had a dog.

The neighbors did have a dog and it raised a row only to be angrily hushed by ungrateful humans. Around the back of Tatiana's house, I hugged the wall, inching toward sliding glass doors that opened onto a yard with a small kidney-bean-shaped pool. I leaned out from the wall just enough to allow my left eye to look into sheer curtains. The gauze-obscured living room beyond was dimly lit, just a single low-wattage bulb. Was it enough to counter my moon shadow against the curtains?

This thought had the unfortunate side effect of causing the Cat Stevens song 'Moonshadow' to start playing on a loop in my head. Any lyric including the phrase, 'I'm being followed . . .' is not helpful when you're committing a felony.

I crept forward and tested the sliding door. Locked. And not one of the cheap locks you can get past with a simple shim.

Above was the overhang of a balcony with a cast-iron railing, facing the sea over the roof line of the next block. Five rubles said she left the balcony door open so that when the wind was right she could hear the waves. I had to climb, and do it with multiple injuries, while remaining silent. With extraordinary care I moved a small patio table to beside the privacy wall. It was nine feet from the ground to the bottom horizontal on the railing above. The table gave me maybe eighteen inches. I added an unused planter. Perched precariously with my arms up I could just reach the iron bar that supported the railing.

You're going to pop your stitches and bleed all over.

I cursed under my breath. Then I reversed course, walking all the way back to my car to retrieve my short crowbar and a roll of duct tape. I sat behind the wheel taping the crowbar to my injured arm, with the crowbar hook extending four inches past my fist. I pulled off a sock and slid it over the hook. To call it jury-rigged would be an insult to juries and their riggers. It might give me half my normal lift.

I walked back – which was getting tiring, frankly – and crept back down the pathway, and again the neighbor's dog barked and was again told to knock it off.

I stood atop the table and planter assembly and ever-so-carefully placed my sock-muffled hook over the horizontal railing bar. Then I grabbed said rail with my good hand and, relying as much as I could on the strong side, pulled. In a movie, I'd have simply yanked myself up and over in one swift, graceful move. Not being the Dread Pirate Roberts, I placed my feet on the wall and did my own version of the 1960s' *Batman* TV show, pulling, wall-walking, gasping and slipping until my head rose above the balcony floor.

What followed was even less graceful, as I hauled myself up and over. The crowbar, lubricated by the blood now seeping from my bandage, caused the duct tape to slip and I very nearly fell. But at last I was on the balcony.

I squatted there trying not to weep from the pain of reopened wounds on my hand and my armpit, and trying not to focus on the blood I was leaving behind for even the most careless policeman to find.

The balcony slider was not open but it was unlocked, halle-lujah. The room, a bedroom, was lit and empty. I pushed the slider open an inch and listened. A toilet flushed and I went through the door in a hurry, clutching my crowbar-tape-and-bandage hand against my shirt in hopes it would keep blood from falling into the carpet. That sort of thing might be noticed.

I swiftly crossed the bedroom to the door, went into the hallway beyond, and spotted a man coming up the stairs.

She's married?

She had definitely not worn a wedding ring, I notice things like that.

I ducked into what I hoped was an unoccupied guest room and listened till the footsteps receded. I breathed.

The guest room had an en suite and I used it by iPhone light to rinse off some of the blood and unwrap the crowbar, which I hung from my belt. I appropriated a guest towel – powder blue – and wrapped it around my hand.

Then I hid under the bed until I heard no more sounds. It's times like this, staring up at wooden slats and a muslin dust cover half an inch from the tip of my nose, that I begin to have some doubts about my choices in life.

It was past midnight when I crawled out, stretched, popping my joints, and eased my way out into the hallway. Everything was dark, but my eyes had long-since adjusted. I made my way down the stairs to the living room. No one. And nothing to see.

Off the living room a formal dining room had been repurposed as a home office and there, on a glass-topped table, was an open MacBook. An open MacBook with a Cyrillic keyboard. An open MacBook with Cyrillic keyboard and a password prompt.

I wanted to cry.

So much trouble and pain and bleeding, all for nothing?

Then I spotted the pad of yellow Post-It notes. People with Post-It notes use them to write down passwords. A twenty-minute search of her table and briefcase turned up nothing, but she had left her purse by the front door, and in her wallet, folded away where she thought no one would ever find it: a yellow Post-It with five Cyrillic letters, two numbers and an asterisk. A good, solid, hard-to-break password. Unless someone wrote it down for you on a Post-It note.

I logged in, went to Tatiana's history and found the AZX Bank interface. This, too, was password protected but bless Tatiana's laziness she used the same password. I was in! I had penetrated the AZX Bank's computer system. Not exactly using super-hacker methodology, but it worked. Aside from the fact that tabs and files were all labeled in Russian.

I sighed, opened a translation app and settled in. It was almost dawn by the time I let myself out through the front door, holding a thumb drive loaded with a terabyte of documents I did not remotely understand.

TWENTY

'Do you do numbers?' I asked.

'Do I do numbers?' Delia asked. 'What does that mean?'

'You know, are you a numbers person? Spreadsheets and . . . other things with lots of numbers? *Ah gah gah gah!*'

I called her the morning after my creeping of Tatiana's home and computer and mentioned that some of my stitches had come out. So, in the morning she came over to check on me, armed with sterile sewing needles and clear thread that looked suspiciously like fishing line. I would really, really have really preferred a hospital, which is where they keep lidocaine. With enough lidocaine I probably wouldn't have said things like, *Ah gah gah gah!*

'You know, for a big, strong guy, you are a huge wimp,' Delia said.

'Yeah? Let me stick needles in your *gah*! *Fuck*! In your skin. Jesus! I am not enjoying this!'

'You were asking about numbers before you started crying like a baby.'

'I am not crying, I'm cursing. Like a manly man. And looking away. That is not crying! Just manly cursing.'

'Yeah, you're Rambo. So?'

'So, I came across some . . . Jesus H. Christ in a chicken basket! Goddammit can't you use the old holes?'

'Exhale on the pain,' Delia advised, leaning close and squinting to find just the right place to stab me.

'I came across some files from a bank. Turns out they're from the AZX Bank's Limassol branch.'

For a moment, she left off torturing me. She raised a bare millimeter of brow in curiosity. 'David? What have you done? Why are half your stitches torn out as if you engaged in strenuous physical activity?'

'I told you, I slipped in the shower,' I muttered. 'And there, right next to the shower drain, I came across a thumb drive loaded with bank records.'

She did some stabbing. I did some manly cursing and absolutely no crying.

When she was done torturing me – about sixteen hours later, by my somewhat subjective tally – she bathed my hand in antiseptic cream and wrapped me up in gauze and tape. Then she said, 'Show me.'

'You understand that this data just fell into my hands and that no criminal activity was involved. Right?'

'Oh, clearly. That kind of thing happens all the time. That's how we got Capone – he dropped a thumb drive in his shower.'

I handed her the thumb drive. She opened her briefcase, took out her laptop, plugged the thumb drive in, and opened the file in the Numbers app.

'This is eight hundred and forty-six megabytes of data,' she said.

'Yeah. Can you make sense of it?'

'Of eight hundred and forty-six megabytes of data?'

'I thought maybe something would just jump out at you.'

She shook her head and gave me a look full of suspicion that maybe she had overestimated my intelligence. 'No, David, I am not Rain Man.' She shrugged, then reluctantly added, 'But I may know Rain Man.'

'Dustin Hoffman?'

'A guy I sent up a few years ago, a mob accountant. I got him a reduced sentence and now he's . . . well, he's a bit like you, David, a man living under an alias, but in some state with more cows than people.'

Delia rejected my offer of Wi-Fi, instead insisting on using hard wire and a secure app, typed in an address and a note and began uploading the file.

'It'll take a while to load,' Delia said.

'However shall we spend the time?' I wondered brightly. 'The cleaning lady changed the sheets just this morning. I mention that only in passing.'

She didn't even bother shooting me down. 'While we're uploading, let's do some quick searches.'

'Sure, that'll be much more fun.'

She fiddled till she got a Cyrillic keyboard and typed in 'Nestor Panagopolous.'

'Well, hello there,' she said, predatory eyes on the laptop. Tap. Tap. 'No addresses, unfortunately, but look at this. Cash deposits. Six thousand. Six thousand. Five thousand – must have spent a grand before he could deposit it. And it goes back, like, a year. Basically he's depositing cash at a rate of six grand a week.'

'Three hundred large and change, per year? Damned good pay for a glorified security guard,' I said. 'So, your boy is still on Cyprus, and he gets paid in cash which he dumps in a Russian bank. Huh.' I leaned over her shoulder totally ignoring her graceful neck and her subtle perfume.

'Every deposit is on a Monday.'

'Mmmm. And today's Saturday. Can you do a real FBI stakeout without real American donuts?'

'Do I look like I live on donuts?'

You look like you eat a diet of baby gazelles you bring down after a short, desperate chase. Possibly with a sweet, apricot glaze. I did not say.

'I didn't get a chance to ask you how it went with the cops.'

Slight eye-roll. 'Their interview technique left something to be desired. I got more out of them than they got out of me. The guy who was stabbed in the elevator? He survived. And there were two last-minute passengers aboard the two a.m. Aeroflot flight to Moscow.'

'That's good about the flight. The stabbed guy, too, but especially the flight. They'll have more muscle available, though. Let's not get lazy.'

She nodded agreement.

'You don't have a . . .'

'A gun? No, sorry. That's a lot of paperwork and Kim and I did not anticipate needing weapons. Probably for the best, David, I might well have shot you by now.'

'Cute,' I said. 'Hey, speaking of cute. Want to go to a party tonight? It's the movie people. My downstairs neighbor got me an invite. George Selkirk will be there.'

'George Selkirk? The George Selkirk? As in rugged good looks and easy charm, George Selkirk?'

This was the most animated I'd ever seen Delia. It hurt my feelings, just a bit. 'Yeah, that guy, handsome George. You know he's had work done, right? Eye tuck. Chin tuck. Probably some Botox.'

'I actually met him once.'

'On a case where he was a scumbag you wanted to put away?'

'Not quite. When he did the revival of *A Streetcar Named Desire* on Broadway. My friend Sue and I waited outside the stage door to get his autograph. He was very sweet, and even hotter . . . handsomer . . . in person. Taller than I thought, too.'

'So, you'll come?'

'Heh.' She grinned lasciviously. For another man.

'Really?' I said with genuine disgust. 'I'm disappointed in you making vulgar jokes and leering that way. Not at all what I expect from an FBI special agent. Maybe a regular agent, but not a special one.'

'What's the party for?'

'It's a fundraiser for some NGO. You know, rich people dressing up in ten-thousand-dollar designer dresses, spending a hundred grand on catering and decorating, then squeezing out fifty cents for the charity. They could just write checks, but no, they have to get together to tell each other what swell humans they are. The whole thing is an exercise in hypocrisy and narcissism, facile virtue-signaling, which is all you can expect from guys like Selkirk.'

I said all that, at least I thought I did, but Delia heard none of it, as evidenced by her next statement.

'I need to buy a dress.'

It's a sad day when a reformed burglar slash con man slash fugitive ends up going over evidence while the FBI goes dress shopping. I reviewed carefully everything I knew.

> *Rachel/Amanda (Ramanda?) ex-MI6(?) operative gone bad.*
> *Knows Panagop. who Delia wants.*
> *Kim and Delia to Cyprus to ID him.*
> *R/A knifed.*
> *Refugee kids kidnapped for $$.*
> *Panagop. works for ExMil.*
> *Panagop deposits cash on Mondays.*
> *Russian assholes tail me from camp.*
> *Ditto try to kill me.*

And that was it, those were the facts. Then there was a list of disconnected data points that might or might not be facts.

> *Kiriakou asks to meet me.*
> *Fotos makes vague noises.*
> *Joumana says K's bent.*
> *Theo says slow-walk.*
> *No supporting evidence.*
> *Brit expats tied in?*
> *Irish guy tells Calix to stop talking to me.*

Then, more questions:

Who the fuck did the murder?
Ditto who ordered same?
Why?

Here at least, I had a clue. You kill someone for revenge or to shut them up or because they represent competition or a threat. Fiction loves the idea of revenge killings, but professional killers don't usually do revenge, it represents a big risk for little or no reward. The murder of Ramanda had to have been a threat-abatement killing – she was a threat. Which meant as long as I was looking into it I was also a threat. To someone.

So, why the hell would Kiriakou drag me into this?

Was it because Kiriakou had been there, on the scene, making sure Ramanda ended up nice and dead and just happened to spot me engaging warp drive to get the hell out of there? Or because he'd interviewed Theodoros and knew that visiting American author, David Mitre, was the fast-fleeing witness? The first would be proof that Kiriakou wasn't just a little dirty but was in mud up to his receding hairline.

The second answer, the answer Friar Occam would have preferred for its simplicity, did not implicate Kiriakou. The fact was I had behaved in an atypical manner after witnessing a murder. Hell, Joe Burton would have investigated me, too.

But how about Ramanda? Who did she threaten? The Cypriot Panagopolous? Was he a guy who would arrange a midday beachfront hit? No, if he was with ExMil now and had worked with the boys in Palermo back then, he'd do his own wet work, and not in broad daylight. No professional criminal . . .

I paused to take in the obviousness of the fact that had just occurred to me. It wasn't a cold, calculated hit on Ramanda. Professional killers don't commit crimes in the most attention-grabbing way possible. It was either a panic move by someone with no time to arrange anything better, or it was a deliberate show of force – a threat.

In which case, whoever had ordered the hit was someone who knew he'd be safe from a murder investigation. Like, say, a cop.

Whoever had called Ramanda's lottery number had undoubt-edly killed the African after the hit. There would have been a meeting for the final payment to the African knifer, and someone had probably brought a gun to that meeting. Pop. Drive the body up into the mountains, or better yet wrap him up in heavy chains and take him for a sea voyage.

Something was nagging at me. Something I wasn't quite getting. It's a very frustrating feeling, very much like what I sometimes have while writing. Like some segment of my brain, some not-exactly-verbal section of my brain, was waving its hands, signaling 'problem' but without the ability to explain itself.

The Russians who'd come after me were hardcore pros. Bristle had not wanted to kill me in so public a way, he'd adapted to the situation. I'd spotted him, he'd figured that meant I'd go to ground, so he'd had no choice but to take me down right then and there.

What in God's name motivated someone to send a disposable killer to kill you, Ramanda? Who was that scared? Who was in that much of a hurry? Who was so desperate they would send that kind of bloody public message?

Human trafficking is a business of thousands, maybe a few million dollars. Money laundering is a business of tens of millions, even billions. The two business models did not fit neatly together. It was as if McDonald's, in addition to selling billions of burgers, also ran a street-corner lemonade stand. But an illegal lemonade stand that added little to the bottom line while magnifying risk.

That was part of what bothered me. The disconnect between billions and millions and thousands. Why would a money-laundering operation get involved with a universally-despised side business that brought in relative chump change?

The inchoate, preverbal part of my brain was still waving its hands. I shrugged it off impatiently. It would come to me, it always did, but never when I pushed for it to come. Anyway: there was a gorgeous, bisexual French movie star to save.

I made a call with some trepidation. Mustafa answered on the third ring and said something in Arabic that I took to be a version of, 'Hello?'

'You remember a conversation involving telephone poles?'

A long pause. 'Yes, Mister . . . I'm very sorry, but I have forgotten your name.'

'So much the better. Call me David.'

'David.'

'Look, I'll be blunt. I need some muscle.'

'Is this about telephone poles?'

'No. Not as far as I can tell, anyway. This is about a woman who is being extorted by an asshole.'

Big sigh. 'David,' Mustafa said. 'There are many injustices in the world . . .'

'The woman in question is a movie star. It would mean you'd have to attend a party full of rich, famous Hollywood people and whatever passes for high society on Cyprus.'

Mustafa had stopped listening after 'movie star.' He would be very happy to attend. No, he would have no trouble leaving Kofinou, it wasn't a prison. But what should he wear?

Then I dialed Chante, who answered in a harried snarl. 'Hey. I have a date for you, for the party. Nice guy. Large guy. Large, scary guy.'

'Why is he not your plus-one? Why is he mine?'

'Because my plus-one is an FBI agent.'

Credit where credit is due, Chante immediately put it all together, and said, 'Make sure he knows this is not a romantic date with me,' and hung up.

Which left me facing a vital question all on my own: what was *I* going to wear?

TWENTY-ONE

Because Paphos is a British outpost, not an American one, there are fewer posh designer stores than you might expect to find. Lots of full English breakfasts, lots of places to buy souvenirs, lots of jewelry stores where you can buy loose diamonds to hide inside your toothpaste where customs agents won't find them; not as much Gucci or Versace.

They do however have a mall every bit as boring as a typical mall in Kansas, and there one can, with effort, find decent shoes.

Which is what I was doing when who should I run into but
Cyril Kiriakou.

'Mr Mitre!' he said as I emerged from the Aldo store with
a passable Wiellaford loafer and three pairs of socks. 'I was
shopping for my wife's birthday, and I run into you.'

'Yes. What an amazing coincidence.'

'It is, it is,' he said, nodding along. 'Especially so since I
wished to speak with you.'

'Oh? About your murder case? I imagined that was either
solved or, perhaps, put on the shelf.'

He shook his head very slightly and met my gaze. 'Murder
is never put on the shelf.'

'No, of course not.'

'Nor is attempted murder. Even breaking and entering is
taken seriously. Shall we go to Costa and have a coffee?'

It was a short walk, half a mall's length, to the food court
where I was assaulted by the aromas of my one-time home:
Burger King and Taco Bell. The walk was just long enough for
me to run through the possibilities, which came down to two:
either I was being tailed, and professionally so; or Kiriakou had
a GPS tracker on my car. Which would not be a good thing.

We ordered and took a table 'outside', meaning in the mall.

'So, how is it going?' I asked.

He smiled. 'Perhaps I should ask you.'

'You're the policeman, I'm just a writer.'

'Indeed. Yes. Just a writer. Then, as a writer you may find it
interesting that we have suffered something of a crime wave
lately. There was quite a dramatic scene at the Aphrodite's
Conch hotel. It seems a knife fight broke out in an elevator, if
you can believe it.'

'Huh. Was anyone hurt?'

His eyes went to my bandaged hand. Then to the bruise on
the side of my jaw. Then up to me, eyes merry and sly. 'It
seems someone was. Our forensics team had quite a time
collecting blood samples. The inside of the elevator car was
smeared with blood.'

'DNA?' Eyebrows up in anticipation.

'Eventually. For now we have numerous eyewitnesses,
some of them from the elevator itself. Of course we showed

them . . . what is the term of art? Six packs, yes? Six photos, some of people known to be innocent, some of known criminals.'

'Any luck?' I knew the answer. I knew what was coming next. But I was curious about how he'd lay it out for me, how he would build his case. I'd have been more afraid but he wasn't here to arrest me, he was 'fronting' me, poking me with a stick to see what I said or did.

'Well, a very interesting thing. Purely as a joke, you understand, one I thought might amuse you, I inserted a photo of you.'

'Really? A flattering one, I hope.'

He tilted his head, amused by me. 'Surprisingly there are very few photos of you. The official photo you use, it seems, is a stock photo.'

I shrugged. 'I'm a private person.'

'There are photos of you at book signings, but it is fascinating how few of those are usable shots showing your full face. Nevertheless . . .'

'If you dig deep enough in Google Images . . .'

'. . . I was able to have my little joke and insert a photo of you.'

He waited. I waited. We looked at each other. This was the moment where he expected me to lie. If I lied, he'd know. If I lied, he'd produce his trump card, presumably GPS from my . . . And then I remembered: we'd gone in Delia's car, not mine.

'I hope your witnesses did not pick me out,' I said.

'Oh?'

'Yeah, I mean I hope they ID'd the guy you're looking for.' I managed with Herculean effort to squeeze out a confident smirk.

'Well . . . as it happens no one accidentally identified you. Or any of the other mug shots.'

There were definite quotation marks around that word, accidentally. He'd expected to identify me. He'd been hoping to.

'Huh,' I said, oozing sympathy, 'it's funny how people in a lift with a stabby dude don't recall faces.'

'Indeed. I see that you have injured yourself.'

'Got that right, Cyril, I cut the shit out of my hand.' I held it up as proof that I did indeed have a hand, and that said hand was in fact bandaged. 'I slipped in the shower. Hand went right through the glass door and managed to smack my head on the side of the sink stand as I was going down.'

Go ahead and check, asshole, you'll find the glass shower door is shattered. You'll find traces of my blood on some of the glass, which I swept up and bagged but did not put out for the weekly collection. Because I didn't just fall off the back of a turnip truck, pal, I am a professional and it'll take more than some bent yokel cop to ever catch me out on an alibi. None of which I said.

'I'm sorry to hear it,' he said at last. 'Did you see a doctor?'

I shrugged. 'Nah. No need. I put in a couple stitches myself. Some Neosporin. It'll be fine.'

'You stitched your own hand?' He made a disgusted face and winced, which I sympathized with.

'Painful as hell, too, but I can handle pain – with a bit of help from whisky.'

'I salute you,' he said with all the sincerity of a tobacco company spokesman. 'It is a week for blood, it seems. Blood in a hotel elevator, blood on a second-floor balcony in Limassol. I have ordered DNA testing to see if perhaps there is a match.'

I was almost insulted by that because he said it with an understated but definite leer, a *got-you-now* look. In recent years, technology has come online that allows DNA testing in a few hours. But as a practical matter the turnaround for DNA testing tends to be expressed in days if not weeks, and I was pretty sure Cyprus, a country that bought signs warning of speed cameras but no actual speed cameras, had not invested in the latest DNA tech.

I nodded. 'Maybe you'll catch the guy. That would be pretty definitive, matching blood samples from two locations. Excellent sleuthing, Cyril. But I don't see the connection to your murder.'

'Have you been to Limassol?' he inquired innocently. 'It's very different from Paphos.'

'I was there just yesterday evening,' I said.

That disappointed him. 'Business?'

'Curiosity. I wanted to see it. And as it happened, I met a woman and . . . well, we had a nice time.'

'This woman . . .'

I was morally certain now that he had a GPS tracker on my car and was dying to spring that on me. But of course I had parked a good quarter of a mile from Tatiana's house. He could put me in Limassol – conceded. He could put me in the right neighborhood. But the beautiful thing was that his own GPS data would place me well away from the breaking and entering. He had needed me to lie about being in Limassol.

Nice try.

I leaned forward and lowered my voice. 'We spent some time at her apartment. And the embarrassing thing is I don't even remember her name, let alone where we ended up.' I made the universal sign for drinking. 'I was a bit . . . confused, shall we say?'

'Perhaps you entered the address in your car's guidance?'

'No, she had me follow her. Very twisty-turny.'

He smiled for himself alone, shook his head bemusedly and changed the subject. 'I see you've been shopping.'

'I have. I've been invited to a gala tonight and found I had no proper dress shoes.'

'The Feed the Forgotten gala? I suppose they know you as a famous author.'

I glided over the implication that there might be some other way to know me, and said, 'Actually, someone from the movie is staying downstairs from me and was kind enough to invite me. I'm afraid midlist crime novelists don't rank very high where Hollywood folks are concerned.'

We made some more polite noises and parted with a hand-shake. I had the distinct feeling that my pal Cyril was frustrated. I went into the men's room, hid in a stall for a few minutes and came back out. Then, with my Aldo bag in hand, very much the casual shopper, I spotted Kiriakou and tailed him at a discreet distance. I followed him around Carrefour as he picked up batteries and a pack of mechanical pencils. Then back out into the mall, walking with purpose, presumably heading for his car. He stopped suddenly at Marasil, a kid's clothing store, and I had the terrible sense that he was searching the display window for my reflection. Had he spotted me?

But after a moment's hesitation, he went into the store and

emerged ten minutes later with a shopping bag. And then went
to his car.

I drove home with my new shoes, parked and slithered beneath
the hot engine. It took a couple of minutes to find the Spark
Nano tracker up behind the muffler. It's a good device that
retails for $129.99 but can be found on sale for $79.99. I've
used them on occasion. I decided to leave it in place for now:
evidence jiu-jitsu, using the force of the enemy's attack against
him.

I went inside and found Delia and Chante sitting on my
terrace drinking my wine and chatting amiably, an activity I'd
never imagined Chante to be capable of.

Chante was fetching in a tailored dark gray suit, the sort of
thing you wear to apply for a job, but with a pale-yellow silk
blouse it was not eye-catchingly drab. Delia wore a blue dress
with an enticing slit, and a short matching jacket.

'Well, aren't I the lucky one?' I said. 'I get to escort not one
but two gorgeous women.'

TWENTY-TWO

Mustafa had taken a bus to Paphos and we picked him
up en route at a petrol station.

The Mercedes C-class cabriolet is not a small car
unless you have Sasquatch in the passenger seat. With his knees
practically up under his chin, Mustafa still left Chante with very
little leg room behind him. Delia had her own long legs stuffed
in behind me. Neither woman would allow me to put the top
down because: hair.

'We should discuss the extortion issue,' Delia said, having
been briefed by Chante. 'Obviously I have no powers of
arrest.'

'Not here you don't,' I said. 'But if this Chris Temple asshole
thinks he's looking at FBI trouble when he gets back to the
States . . . And if we get an opportunity, Mustafa can have a
conversation with him.'

'Well, so long as you have a carefully-thought-out plan,' Delia snarked from the back seat.

It was not a long drive, fortunately, just a quick hop to what is called the Paphos Archeological Site. The site is an official, UN-designated, please-don't-fuck-this-up site. I had already toured it a week earlier in preparation for my *GQ* piece. Basically it's a lot of mosaic floors from the Roman era. Most of the mosaics are in what was once, long ago, a single house belonging to the kind of guy who could afford a whole lot of mosaic floors portraying a whole lot of classical allusions. I would expand on that in the article, no doubt, but basically: mosaics.

The unnamed Roman who, for the sake of convenience I'd like to call Spurius Flatulus, picked himself a nice plot, well above both lower and upper Paphos, with sweeping Mediterranean views. He had some neighbors (Tittius Agrippa and Pustulus the Elder) who also had mosaics. I assume that was part of the sales pitch for the original real-estate development: Location, Convenience, Mosaics! In truth, they were excellent mosaics, obviously an upgrade over 'builder grade' mosaics, which I assume were just bathroom tile.

There are also columns here and there, standing stark with nothing to support and had I paid any attention in school I could have said whether they were Ionic, Doric or Corinthian columns. However, I can state categorically that they were columns.

We were not there to see either mosaics or columns, we were there to rescue fair maiden, a notion that would not really become a trope until at least a millennium after Flatulus' day.

Delia, Chante, Mustafa and I walked the long gravel and dirt pathway to the *odeum*, which formed the secondary centerpiece of the archeological site. The night was warm with a bit of breeze and I could smell salt water and history. We were not alone on the path: there were gaggles ahead and behind, women tripping in high heels, men marching with grim fortitude toward forced enjoyment.

'You know,' I said, 'Aphrodite was supposedly born here, in Paphos. Her mother was sea foam and her father was Uranus.'

'Here it comes,' Delia muttered.

Because in my early-forties I had still not achieved total

adulthood, I said, 'Yep, water and Uranus. Basically the goddess of beauty was the product of a divine enema.'

This clearly funny bon mot was met with pained silence, which, on reflection, I deserved.

The party was set for the *odeum*, an outdoor theater dating to the second century – the era of Trajan and Hadrian and Marcus Aurelius. It was a semicircle of stone bleacher seats rising a dozen levels, with an overbearing and much more recent light-house looming up behind. On either end of the bleacher seats were small tumbles of sandstone blocks, presumably remnants of the box office and refreshments stands. The immediate surrounding was mostly bare dirt interrupted by more ancient Roman debris, an air-conditioned silver construction-site office off to the side and very stone-appropriate restrooms. In the middle distance was a rough-hewn rock wall holding weeds and dry shrubbery at bay. Way beyond the wall was upper Paphos, modestly illuminated.

We were confronted by a host checking names against a list on an iPad. I was in a giddy mood, with Delia not quite on my arm but in the general vicinity of it, and the prospect of Minette in my future, and an absence of people trying to stab me, so it was with difficulty that I resisted identifying myself as Biggus Dickus. But I guessed that with this many Brits in attendance that Monty Python reference must already have been trotted out.

Once through, we merged into a crowd of perhaps a hundred people not counting uniformed waiters and bartenders. It was a posh, well-dressed crowd: diamonds were much on display, but not the big stuff, not the necklaces or the pendant earrings, more the tennis bracelets, diamond studs and one carat or smaller rings. A good pickpocket could have strolled through and walked off with a hundred large, but that's never been part of my criminal repertoire.

I did what I could to spot any Russian assassins, but the truth was I was safe. A killing here, tonight, with Hollywood people in attendance, would have the entire law enforcement establishment of planet Earth down on you. And your bosses would kill you just for being stupid.

As we headed toward the nearest of two bars I considered

how I would do it. 'It' in this case meaning how I would fleece this crowd if I were still in the business.

After considering various unlikely dramatic scenarios involving Joker vs. Batman scenes with costumed minions surrounding the place, I settled on the less-dangerous notion of obtaining the invitations list. The guest list would be a map to unoccupied homes and hotel rooms – pick out half a dozen likely targets, grab a drill and a backpack, plot a route, and carry out lightning-quick burglaries, drilling out wall safes and running with the loot. That way the suspects would be anyone who had knowledge of the guest list and that would slow the cops way down.

Not that I was really thinking too hard on the subject. It was more muscle memory than anything else: when I see diamonds I have to at least consider . . . I'd want to fence the goods off-island, for sure, and quickly before the alerts went out. Grab the loot and catch a boat to Beirut, maybe? Cairo? Palermo?

But again, that was not why I was here surrounded by people who were probably fully-insured and would scarcely miss . . . No, I was here to save Minette from a foul extortionist and be hailed as her hero. Minette herself likely had a hell of a wall safe collection of baubles. Which I would never even consider. Probably.

It was a bit like being a recovering alcoholic with his one-year chip wandering into the Old Town Ale House in Chicago. Usually I could push thoughts of grifts and jobs out of my mind, but there was just so much potential in this crowd. It almost seemed wrong that none of these people would be ripped off.

'We should break up and mingle,' Delia said. 'We look like a gang on the prowl.'

'Yeah. Chante and Mustafa, Delia and me. Chante, when you locate Chris Temple, text me. Don't do anything until I get to you. And we need a spot. Somewhere a bit private and dark.'

A white party tent had been set up a discreet distance from the bathrooms, with sides raised to reveal an impressive buffet table, stage left if we were watching an Aeschylus play, or whoever his Roman equivalent might have been.

Right where the second-century versions of Minette and

George Selkirk and Chris Temple would have plied their acting craft there stood a low stage and on that stage a reggae band was doing a rendition of 'No Woman No Cry.'

I led Delia up the bleachers to get a perspective on the crowd. I pointed. 'There's Selkirk if you want to go fling yourself at him, Delia.'

'Let's do our business first. Flinging comes later.'

I spotted Minette easily enough. I don't know what it is about movie stars, but even when objective judgment would suggest there were several equally beautiful women, there was something about Minette that made her stand out as if she was being followed everywhere by a spotlight.

There were beautiful women and beautiful men; rich women and rich men; famous humanitarians with the kinds of resumes that make less saintly folks feel small and inadequate; important business people who were little tin gods in their own worlds; government types who appeared daily in newspapers and news broadcasts; a whole array of people who had every reason to think highly of themselves. But none of that mattered when a Selkirk or a Minette appeared. They were stars, and as much as I hated to admit it, they shone like stars and their gravity wells turned everyone else into satellites.

I spotted Dame Stella and hubby Archie. Stella was chatting away amid a small gaggle of people while Archie stood a little apart, perhaps confused, perhaps just bored.

The band stopped playing and Minette and Selkirk walked on-stage to much applause and hallooing. They shared a standing microphone, like presenters at the Oscars, two stunning freaks of nature reading from cue cards.

'Ladies and gentlemen, if I could have your attention, please,' Selkirk said in the voice behind so many Infiniti, Nespresso and Ralph Lauren commercials. 'As you all know, we aren't just here to eat and drink and enjoy the company. We are here to raise funds for The Least of These and Médecins Sans Frontières and Feed the Forgotten. These are the people who march bravely into some of the most terrible places in this world, bringing food and medicine and comfort to men, women and children who have nowhere else to turn. And of course, more locally, they offer support to war-torn refugees, some of whom are with us here tonight.'

There followed a bashful woman in a hijab speaking broken English, and then an Irish doctor who clearly wanted to be somewhere else, with the usual heartbreaking stories.

Then Minette returned. She was wearing a dress that was at once sexy and serious, form-fitting but with no desperate slits or plunging décolletage. Pity.

'Ow-er arts go out to ze childrens,' Minette said. 'The innocents who may be hungry or lack medical care. Who may be living in alleyways or overcrowded refugee centers, or who may be in bondage, held as slaves in countries where no law protects them.'

It was time to squeeze the wallets.

My first thought was that I should be exempt since I'd given money at Father Fotos' church. I was prepared to pony up a bit more, but this entire Cyprus adventure was eating way too much cash. I was trying to get to a point where I could leave my secret accounts alone and live off current earnings, which was not going to be possible if I kept having to hand out bribes.

Delia was nursing a white wine. I met her gaze and raised one eyebrow. She frowned as if she didn't know why I was looking at her.

'Stupid economics,' I muttered. 'If you ransom people, you create a market. Perpetual motion machine.'

'You don't want to rescue people?' Delia asked.

'Rescue, sure; ransom no. The winning move in a hostage situation is to shoot the hostage yourself and say, 'Now what have you got, asshole?' Shoot the hostage, then shoot the bad guy and you've eliminated the incentive. Sends a message.'

'The clean, simple logic of the psychopath,' Delia said dryly. 'That's not what they teach at the academy.'

'Works though. If you're going to make serious money off kidnapping, you want repeat business. So, you don't kill the hostage, you take your payoff . . .'

'What you don't do if you have any sense is entangle high-risk, low-profit trafficking with high-profit, low-risk money laundering . . .'

We both trailed off because the bleedingly obvious suddenly crashed through the layers of stupid in my brain and Delia, despite practically quivering with excitement at the proximity of George Selkirk, reached the same thought at the same moment.

We looked at each other.

'Duh,' I said.

'Yes.'

'It's not one op, it's two. Text your mob accountant.'

She already had her phone out.

Minette was acknowledging board members of the various NGOs. Greek name. Greek name. English name. Russian name. Greek name. Jeremy 'Jez' Berthold. Greek name.

One by one they walked on-stage, as fine a bunch of do-gooders with too much money as you'll be likely to see at any two-thousand-year-old Roman ruin. Seeing him now I recognized Berthold, the honorary mayor of expats. He gave a cheery wave to the crowd and nodded to their applause.

Minette shook hands with the women and endured hugs from greasy old men while Selkirk reversed that order.

Then Selkirk held up a piece of paper and waved it happily. 'Ladies and gentlemen, we have a small contribution to start us off tonight. I have here a check. From Cyprus Expats Inc., and their chairman, Jeremy Berthold. Ladies and gentlemen . . . I feel like we should have a drumroll . . . this check is in the amount of . . .' Minette did a cute drumroll of her fingers on her mike. '. . . fifty thousand euros!'

'Great, so much for me getting by with a crumpled-up twenty,' I grumbled. 'I have to pony up a grand now. I'm starting to think prison would be good for my retirement plan.'

Delia shook her head. 'Nah, we'd freeze your accounts and eventually recover all the money.'

'You know, you're really a horrible person, Delia. Just a horrible, horrible person.'

She laughed.

My phone pinged. A text from Chante with her usual loquaciousness: 'Toilets.'

I tapped Delia's elbow. 'If you're done with your no-doubt shocking Selkirk-induced sex fantasies . . .' I showed her the message.

We found Mustafa – not hard given his size. He was holding forth before three young women, who, taken all together, did not weigh as much as he did. I gave him a nod and he disengaged, followed by appraising eyes. It would never have occurred to me that the gigantic thug would be attractive to women, but there's no accounting for taste. We meandered toward the toilets.

Chante was there. 'He went in there a minute ago.'

'Number one or number two?' I asked.

Chante made a face. 'Most likely smoking.'

'Cigarettes? Weed?'

'Heroin,' Chante said.

I grinned. 'In that case . . .' I looked around. The toilet area was unpopulated with Minette and Handsome George still onstage. Twenty feet further on, well beyond the light glowing from the craft services table, was the low rock wall, and beyond it nothing but weeds and the rocks that didn't get promoted to fence.

'Mustafa? Shall we invite Mr Temple to join us?'

Mustafa took his own survey of the surrounding area and nodded at me, liking my plan.

Chris Temple – one of the up-and-coming Hollywood Chrises – was seated, pants around his ankles, a paper plate balanced on his knees, a glass pipe in his mouth, a couple of square inches of aluminum foil in one hand, and a cigar torch in the other – when Mustafa removed the door to his stall.

'What the fu—' Temple said, before Mustafa grabbed him by the neck, hauled him out of the stall and threw him against the sinks. The actor yelped and started to cry out, but by rotating his wrist Mustafa tightened his grip on Temple's shirt collar and choked off any sound.

Delia, Chante and I followed like spectators. Temple wasn't a small man but Mustafa literally tucked him under his arm like a baguette, carried him to the stone wall and tossed him over. Only on climbing over the fence myself did I realize it was a five-foot drop on the other side. Mustafa climbed over the fence, grabbed Temple again and hauled him, now kicking and struggling, and kept going further than we might have thought necessary, but his instincts were good for he came upon one of the many old, overgrown archeological trenches and sort of rolled Temple down into it.

Temple managed to pull his pants most of the way up and get his phone out but Mustafa hopped down into the trench and relieved him of it. Keeping Temple in a state of near-asphyxiation, Mustafa handed me the phone. It was password protected but had a facial recognition identifier.

'Give me his face,' I said. Then added, 'I don't mean tear it off, just turn his head.' I pointed the phone at Temple and it opened compliantly.

I gave the unlocked phone to Chante. 'Go through it. See if you can find the video. See if he's forwarded it anywhere.'

I hopped down into the chin-high trench and Delia followed. Chris Temple was sputtering and choking and probably turning red though I couldn't be sure in the minimal illumination.

Delia took over. She brandished her FBI ID in Temple's face. 'See that? I am an FBI special agent. Now, I can't arrest you here, but I know who you are, I know your home address, the address of your beach house, the address of your so-called ranch in Montana. I have your phone number, your agent's number, and the phone numbers of *Variety*, the *Hollywood Reporter* and *Deadline*. I can pick up the phone and have your credit-card numbers. I will find everyone who ever supplied you with an illegal substance, and I will tell them you gave them up. Are you hearing me?'

Mustafa let him breathe just long enough for him to wheeze a 'Yes. But I—' The extenuating circumstance Temple wished to explain were choked off.

'Whatever secrets you think you have? Remember: I am the FBI, and if I want to know just how many times you pleasure yourself in the shower, I can find out. You get all that so far?'

'Let him breathe again,' I suggested to Mustafa, who allowed enough air for Temple to croak, 'Yes.'

'Extortion is a felony in all fifty states,' Delia went on like the avenging angel she was. 'In California, it's two to four years. They say every year inside ages a man five years, so you need to ask yourself how your career will fare if you're away for even two years and come back with all your front teeth gone so you could suck some bull con's dick without biting.'

I was shocked. That was like something I might say, not

something I'd expect to hear from an agent of the law. I was a bit turned on, too, but mostly shocked.

Temple started to say something, to protest, to explain, to excuse. I nodded at Mustafa and he gave the actor a light tap that snapped his head sideways.

My turn, and I got to play 'good cop.' 'Here's how it is, Mr Temple. I don't think you're a bad guy. I'm a big fan. I liked you as Cypher. I felt you really captured the character.'

Bless his needy heart, he managed a raspy, 'Thanks.'

'But look, Mr Temple, if you do anything – anything at all – to annoy Minette or your director or any of your co-stars in any way . . . well, if you're still in Cyprus, Chewbacca here will find you, and come up behind you and wrap a piece of piano wire around your neck and pull until the wire hits spinal cord. Indicate that you hear me by grunting.'

He grunted.

'If a video of Minette ever shows up on the internet and you are no longer on Cyprus, the FBI will land on you like a ton of bricks. They'll put you in jail. They'll destroy your career, everything you worked for. Indicate you hear me by grunting.'

He grunted.

'So, you have two paths you can go by. You can be an asshole and either Mustafa or the FBI or both will fuck you up. Or you can turn your life around, man. Go straight. Discover virtue. Be a good guy instead of a low-rent extortionist. Follow your talent, man, not your worst instincts.'

Delia was looking at me with amused disbelief, so just for her benefit I added, 'A life of crime is no good, dude. Come into the light. Isn't that right, Special Agent?'

'Profoundly true,' she said, with only a slight eye-roll.

'Chante?'

'I deleted the native copy and the cloud copy. He emailed the video to one person, an S. Sheppard.'

I cocked an inquisitive eyebrow at Temple and Mustafa allowed him some air. 'My lawyer,' he said.

Delia said, 'Your lawyer will soon be in receipt of a letter warning him that he will be disbarred if that video ever escapes his inbox. Attorney–client privilege does not apply to criminal conspiracies, and then we will be free to rummage through all his dealings with you.'

'Say yes for the nice FBI lady,' I said.

Temple nodded sullenly.

'Put him on the ground,' I said, and when he was prone and wetting himself I knelt down close to him, face to face. 'Just in case neither Mustafa nor Special Agent Vengeance here doesn't convince you, I want you to look me in the eyes, Mr Temple. I want you to take a good, long look at me and tell me whether, as a professional actor, you think I'm just a sweet guy who'd let it go if you fucked me over.'

I didn't do the dead-eye stare, that's a cliché. I did the opposite, a warm, friendly smile with twinkly eyes.

'Nod your head "yes" if you think I'll let you fuck me in the ass, Hollywood. Go ahead.' Then the sudden eruption of convincing rage. I stuck my face so close to his he was breathing my stale air and I gave it my obscene, spittle-spraying all. 'Do you think I will let you fuck me in the ass? Do you? *Do you, you piece of shit?*'

He shook his head, no, but by then he was shaking in pretty much all of his muscles. Mustafa, playing his part to perfection, had to haul me off him. 'No more killing,' Mustafa lectured me firmly. 'You promised no killing.'

I had so much more material prepared, I mean, I've written this kind of scene many times. But it looked as if we'd made our point.

'Chante? Give Mustafa this gentleman's phone.'

She did and Mustafa snapped it in half with one hand. When it was a bent mess of starred glass and popped seams, he tossed it to Temple.

The four of us walked away in complete silence. The giggling didn't start until we were well clear.

'That was good, David,' Delia said, grinning ear to ear.

'Acting!'

'Satisfying,' Mustafa said.

Chante led us to the green room tent where we found Minette sitting splay-legged and looking exhausted. But she rose on seeing us.

'The matter has been taken care of,' Chante reported.

Minette was very happy, very pleased, wished she could find a way to express her gratitude and gave me a nice, long hug. Then she shook Delia's hand, hugged Chante and finally hugged Mustafa. Hugged him, and said, 'Oh!' as she squeezed his bicep. And ran her hands over his shoulders. And said, 'My God, your hands!'

We chatted and toasted and generally congratulated ourselves on our wonderfulness, but it became increasingly clear that Minette felt Mustafa deserved whatever reward might be in the offing. So, after a while we drove back to my villa with more room in the car since it seemed Mustafa did not need a ride. He would be staying behind for a while.

Delia rode shotgun, and would not wipe the grin from her face.

'Oh, shut up,' I said.

'What is the word in English?' Chante asked from the back seat. 'Something to do with impediments to . . .'

'Cockblock?' Delia suggested with way too much glee.

'Just so. Cockblocked.'

'By a refugee!'

Gosh they had fun laughing at me. Such fun. And, well, what could I do? It was kind of funny.

Then Delia checked her phone and said, 'We have to go to some place called Petra tou Romiou. Right now.'

'Petra? Why?'

'There's a refugee boat that's just come ashore.'

I glanced in the rearview mirror at Chante. 'I can drop you off here and give you money for a taxi.'

'No,' she said. And I had by then learned not to argue.

TWENTY-THREE

P etra tou Romiou is a rock. A collection of rocks, really, dominated by a massive boulder, a big, bleached-tan monolith the size of a four-story office building, and various darker rocks scattered around the vicinity. This was the

place where sea foam and Uranus . . . Or perhaps more appropriately the place where Botticelli had Venus standing with
conveniently-placed blonde hair, rising naked on a scallop
shell. His painting lacked the rock and added nonexistent trees,
but it was the Renaissance and Botticelli was not a news
photographer.

On either side of the rock are pebble beaches, with those
pebbles running from gravel-size, to skipping stones, on up to
smooth-worn, fist-sized stones that make a pleasant crunching
sound underfoot while making it impossible to walk quickly.

Normally Petra tou Romiou is reached from a parking lot
across the road. There's a narrow underground walkway, a
one-person-wide walkway that I was happy to avoid as I pulled
over to the side of the road behind a line of cop cars and ambu-
lances, all with lights flashing, and slid and scrabbled down the
steep embankment in inappropriate shoes.

The boat had not reached either beach but had managed, with
extraordinary bad luck, to smack into the rocks and now sat
rising and falling sluggishly, trapped and being slowly but
relentlessly disassembled.

Even by the standards of refugee boats, this craft was so
astoundingly overloaded with people that even in the spotlight
of a Cypriot Marine Police craft a hundred feet beyond it, it
was not possible to make out the boat's color or shape. It was
a saltine supporting a quarter-pound burger; it was an unfunny
clown car; a twelve-ounce beer poured into a six-ounce glass.
People were packed together, standing, holding onto each other,
stumbling and wailing as the boat surged and smacked into the
rock with an audible sound, splintering by degrees.

The captain of the Marine Police boat must have known
something about shoals because he was unable to get near
enough to help. On the land side, locals mingled with cops who
did a great deal of shouting and waving of flashlights and were
generally ignored. Everyone seemed eager to help, and no one
was actually doing anything useful.

One of the refugees leapt into the water wearing an orange
life jacket, a man, young and strong. He surfaced and rolled
over to swim away from the rock, but the sea wasn't having it.
A wave rolled in, lifted him up, flailing and shouting, to smash

him against rock. It didn't kill him, I saw his arms waving and thought I heard him yell, but then he was submerged by a new wave, and when it was past, I saw no more of him.

A yellow rescue helicopter raced up the coast from the Royal Air Force base, its spotlight speeding along the line of surf, but I had little optimism about the pilot's chances – the wind was up enough to tear the tops from waves, the refugee boat moved like a drunken belly dancer, and the people aboard her were panicking, surging this way and that, falling over each other. What could they do from a helicopter aside from lowering a rope and pulling up a handful of people as the Mediterranean Sea carried out its eternal mission to sink and drown?

'They'll drown,' Chante said. She was taping it all on her iPhone.

We were on the beach, the big rocks to our right, ignored as several among many watching a tragedy play out. 'Yeah,' I said. 'Most of them will.'

The chopper added its deafening noise and downdrafts to the scene and I saw a wet-suited diver jump from a hundred feet up, plunge and resurface, holding a rope end. He bobbed beside the stern of the refugee boat, fighting each surge just to stay in place, searching futilely for a place to attach the rope.

'I'm going for a swim,' Delia said.

She didn't invite me, just informed me that she was going in. She handed her purse to Chante, kicked off her shoes, slithered out of her dress and ran in her underwear.

I was a good enough swimmer to know the difference between me, a beat-up forty-something in resort casual, and the wetsuited RAF diver out there, who was being grappled by a dozen panicky hands. I was a good enough swimmer to know that the space between a frisky sea and several big rocks was not a backyard pool. And I had seen *Jaws* more than once and had definite views on the advisability of swimming at night while bleeding.

But Delia was already splashing into the surf like a kid on holiday and I couldn't very well just stand there looking impotent, so with markedly less enthusiasm I began shedding electronics, jacket and shoes.

Just then the sea took hold of the refugee boat, twisted it and smashed the stern into the monolith that was its main antagonist.

The people screamed and pushed toward the bow. People fell into the water. The RAF diver was grabbing at windmilling bodies, fighting to save lives, very much including his own at that point.

The boat and rock played a tune, more percussion than harmony, bangs and scrapes and watery sighs.

It was time for me to decide whether I was a man or a mouse, so I uttered my heroic battle cry, 'Fucking hell!' and followed Delia into the surf.

The bow of the boat tilted slightly up now, not quite a last-act-of-*Titanic* tilt but on its way, as the splintered stern began taking on water.

Delia swam and I swam behind her. I carefully regulated my breathing, exhaling an angry, bubbling, 'Fuck!' into the water on each downstroke, inhaling salt and foam with each recovery stroke. From shore it was no more than two hundred feet, but I was tiring before we reached the first people. Still, it seemed pointless to swim this far and not do anything useful, so I grabbed the nearest drowning person I saw, a young woman, grabbed her by the hair and drew her to me, twisted her around so that her panicky arms wouldn't brain me, and started back toward the beach in a one-armed, scissor-kicking sideways crawl. Subjective physics being what they are, the two hundred feet now seemed to be about nine miles.

Fortunately the water was not terribly deep and I eventually felt gravel under my feet and manhandled the woman until people on shore could wade out to take her from me.

It is hard to overstate just how quickly even relatively benign Mediterranean water saps your energy. I was bent over, hands on knees, gasping and wondering if I had done enough. Then I had a stupid idea that would involve still more swimming and plunged back in before I could come up with a good excuse not to. I powered through the surf, passing through people bobbing like corks, passing Delia who had a man in tow, passing other people straining just to keep their mouths above the water and crying out in desperate Arabic which I was glad I couldn't translate since there was damned little I could do to help.

The RAF diver was around the stern, joined by a second man in a wetsuit from the Marine Police, the two of them overwhelmed by tumbling, writhing, kicking, screaming refugees. But the diver's rope, thick-braided white-and-blue nylon, floated like a water snake. I took an end, formed a loop with fingers gone numb, put my shoulder through it, belatedly realized I had used the wrong damn arm so that the rope would scrape against my cut armpit, and side-stroked my way to the Marine Police craft, coughing and wallowing in deeper water. Some bright fellow aboard deduced my purpose and proffered a boat hook. I fed the loop over the hook, made eye contact with the young cop, and headed back beneath waves whipped to spray by the hurricane of the helicopter overhead.

I rolled onto my back and waved up at the chopper crewman leaning out of the door with his hand holding the pulley line. I made gestures I hoped conveyed the concept of 'rope.' It was still attached at that end to the helo's hoist, and it took a while, during which I seriously contemplated drowning, but they figured it out finally and cast the rope off the hoist. It landed with a splash. I found a section, not the end, unfortunately, but a section I could hold onto, and with the absolute last of my getting-on-toward-middle-age energy towed the tangled mess to shore.

Hands took hold of me and half-carried, half-dragged me out of the water. Other hands took hold of the rope, unsnarled the mess and formed themselves into a queue – God bless British cultural patrimony – and set about playing tug of war with the Marine Police boat.

Between the boat and the straining civilians, the rope was made taut, running in a line just a few feet shy of the refugee craft's plunging stern. Some of the refugees figured it out and made their way to the rope, either on their own, or assisted by the divers and the apparently tireless FBI Special Agent.

I sat shivering and gasping on the rocks feeling that I had swallowed more salt water than was healthy. Someone laid a blanket over my shoulders, probably mistaking me for a refugee. Then Chante appeared, carrying my neatly-folded clothing and without saying anything got me to stand up long enough to dress myself.

I spotted Delia twenty feet away down the beach, looking like I'd felt minutes before. I nodded at her and she nodded back, both of us tired, cold and a bit shellshocked. Chante and I trudged over to help her dress.

Now I could see the rescue operation more clearly. The helicopter had moved off to cut the turbulence from its rotors and used its spotlight to light up separated refugees in the water. The Marine Police were keeping station as well as could be and the civilians on the other end of the rope moved up and down the beach as needed to keep it taut. And spread out along its length were people clinging and being moved along by the divers.

And there were the bodies. At least two, a man and a child, were face down in the surf. EMTs were dotted here and there, kneeling over traumatized and in some cases injured people. A news crew now had a camera going, adding their klieg lights to the eerie scene. Folks from nearby towns were still arriving in cars parked atop the bluff. Many came down to the beach with blankets and Thermoses of hot tea and bottles of grappa.

'That was smart,' Delia said, damply-dressed and recovered. 'The rope. That was smart thinking.'

I grunted. I wasn't feeling very clever. I wasn't feeling as if I'd accomplished anything. It's hard to congratulate yourself while watching a child's lifeless body reduced to flotsam.

'I'm going to question some of those people,' Delia said.

'The fuck?'

'May have useful info.' She didn't wait for me, which is a good thing because I saw no reason to accompany her. I was done.

Chante, watching her leave, said, 'I have arrived in the middle of the movie.'

'Speaking of which, pan that camera around in a full three sixty, will you?'

She seemed surprised by that, but for once did not argue.

We both watched Delia squatting down to talk to a trio of shivering refugees.

'She is incredible,' Chante said.

I could have objected that I was very nearly as incredible, that I'd also gotten a bit wet, and had come up with the idea of stretching a line and was therefore due some respect myself.

But as I watched Special Agent Delia Delacorte in her damp

and sand-patched dress nodding and offering a comforting touch to frightened people while I sucked the last drops from my flask, I was painfully aware of the gap between us, between the sociopath who would occasionally behave well if pressured to do so and if there was no easy way out, and the servant of the law who spent her life trying to protect people. Maybe it was the weariness or the cold affecting my brain, but I could not help thinking that *homo sapiens* needed people like Delia Delacorte, but could do quite nicely without people like me.

No wonder she wouldn't sleep with me. Who the fuck was I?

'Yeah,' I said, 'she is.'

TWENTY-FOUR

J ust over a week had passed since a British fugitive with fake passports had been knifed on the beach. I now had a pretty good idea of what was going on: money laundering and human trafficking. I knew some of the bad guys: Russians around the AZX Bank, Delia's target, Nestor Panagopolous, likely Kiriakou. But I was no nearer knowing who had ordered the hit. And sooner or later Kiriakou would have DNA evidence placing me in a very bloody elevator and a very burgled apartment.

That was bad. Blood evidence at the scene of a burglary is pretty good evidence to have if you're with the law enforcement community. I doubted he'd ever lift a usable fingerprint – I wasn't an amateur – but DNA was bad enough, all by itself. He could actually charge me and convict me of creeping Tatiana's house, which would be ironic given that I was arguably doing the Lord's work.

I walked out onto my terrace with my first morning coffee and leaned over the side, looking for Chante. Not there. I dialed her and got a snippy, 'Yes? I am at work.'

'How's our boy Chris Temple?'

'Nervous.'

'Good. Nervous is good. Hey, send me the video you took last night on the beach.'

'Why?'

'Because I'm looking for someone.' Not much of an answer, but she let it go.

It took a while for the video to crawl across the various Wi-Fi connections so I used the time to make myself a mushroom omelet and a second round of coffee.

What I should have been doing was writing. The manuscript wasn't going to finish itself, neither was the increasingly uninteresting *GQ* piece. Instead I sat peering closely at video. It was poorly-lit and too-distant, but Chante had at least shot it in landscape. In addition to scanning the crowd at my request, she'd shot lots of other video, so I saw Delia in her underwear bravely leaping into the dark sea, and then two seconds of me following her but prancing more daintily than I'd have liked over the stones before the recording stopped.

She'd caught Delia emerging from the surf, an American, a diverse Aphrodite. Though Aphrodite wouldn't have been my preferred Greek god to represent Delia. No, she was Athena, if anyone. If Botticelli's to be believed, Aphrodite stood on a scallop and played with her hair; Athena popped out of Zeus' head wearing a helmet, carrying a shield and hefting a nice long spear, and looking like she meant to use it.

Surprisingly – surprisingly, I say – Chante had not filmed my own bare-chested manliness arising from the surf. Which was probably best for my ego.

After that, I advanced, rewound, paused and enlarged, rinse and repeat. Mostly I zoomed in on concerned faces, none of which I recognized. Until . . . I froze the shot. Too blurry. Advanced a few seconds. Better.

'Fuck. Me,' I said to no one.

Cyril Kiriakou, not on the beach, but up on the road, illuminated briefly by a lighter flare as he fired up a cigarette. Not unusual that he would be there, he was a policeman, after all, except for the fact that there were Cypriot first responders, EMTs and cops all over the beach already. Kiriakou was a late arrival, and he did not go trotting down to see the action, let alone to help.

It was a five-second pan. Two seconds of which was unblurred Kiriakou, before Chante's camera moved on. But then, Chante must have decided to reverse her first *tour d'horizon*. And when the video swept back, there was Kiriakou rushing to a car that had just pulled up, which sure looked like a Triumph TR6. It was impossible to make out the color, but the silhouette was easily recognizable. It might not be the same TR6 I'd seen parked outside Dame Stella's bash, but I doubted there were many TR6s on Cyprus.

I ran the video forward and back a few more times.

Kiriakou rushing to a TR6. That was it. Nothing else there, just some blur.

Dame Stella would know who owned the TR6. So I could either sit down and do my actual job – writing – or I could walk up the hill to ask Dame Stella herself. Being an experienced, professional writer, I immediately seized on the excuse to not write.

Dame Stella, it turned out, was not at home. But Sir Archie was. He was sitting by the pool, watching something on his laptop.

'Hi,' I said. I could have added, Lord Weedon, but somehow I feel whenever I use inherited titles I'm digging up George Washington just to mock him.

'Mr Mitre,' he said. 'Is there a problem with the villa?'

'No, not at all.' I stood awkwardly beside the retaining wall, several feet lower than him. He was distinctly uninterested in having me join him, and under normal circumstances I would have agreed entirely. But now I was feeling dissed, so damned if I would make it easy for him.

'Then may I ask what business you have with my wife?'

'Well, it isn't strictly to do with your wife.'

That exhausted his capacity for rudeness and he waved me up. I trotted up the steps, let myself in the unlocked front door, and joined him on the terrace.

'Beautiful weather,' I offered.

'Indeed. One finds it often is.'

I had already annoyed him, and that annoyed me, so I sat down in a padded wicker rocker without being asked, and said, 'Whatcha watching?'

His eyes flared and his lip curled and for the second time I had doubts about Weedon as some sort of clueless old duffer. His wife treated him like he was misplaced furniture, but he was sharper than that.

'How may I help you?' he asked icily, adding, 'Mr Mitre?' as a reproach.

'Well, I'm thinking of buying a car, and the other night at your excellent do, I happened to spot a vehicle I've lusted after for many years.'

'Indeed.'

'Yeah, a really cool-looking TR6. Cherry! It was in your driveway.'

He frowned, simultaneously baffled and filled with loathing of my impertinence. 'You speak of Mr Berthold's vehicle?'

'I think I met him. Bit chubby, ginger, glasses?'

'Mr Berthold is a highly-respected person in the expat community. He is often granted the title of Mayor, as a sort of courtesy.'

'Cool. What's he do? Real estate?'

Honest to God, his jaw dropped. I was winning the battle of icy British snobbery versus crude American impertinence. 'Mr Berthold is retired from government.'

My jaw did not drop, but a penny did. I excused myself as quickly as I could, trotted back down the hill and set about the Google hammer and tongs. I also sent a quick query to my WhatsApp friend. Google was quicker and in short order I found half a dozen articles confirming Berthold's semiofficial status as spokesman for British expats.

Sadly he had no Wikipedia page, but digging back through British newspaper archives I found a single small, glancing reference. It was in the caption to a photo of cabinet members going into a meeting.

'Retired from government, my ass,' I muttered. Berthold had gone into that cabinet meeting behind the Foreign Secretary. That certainly did not prove that Berthold was connected to intelligence – the Foreign Office is far more than MI6 – but it began, possibly, to explain why in the matter of Rachel/Amanda, the Foreign Office might have conflicting responses on her nationality.

The narrative in my head now went like this: Rachel/Amanda was an MI6 agent in trouble for a bit of skimming or leaking or leaking and skimming; bottom line, she was in trouble with her own people and possibly the bad guys as well.

She thought she'd found a way to get the Americans to help her out. She spotted Nestor Panagopolous and knew he was important to Delia. Delia, being no fool, insisted Ramanda put up or shut up: show me Nestor.

So, Ramanda used her backup passport hoping to sneak into Cyprus unnoticed by MI6. And soon after her arrival, someone stabbed her in the back.

Someone who knew she'd be there, obviously, but who would know that Rachel/Amanda was on Cyprus waiting to identify Nestor P. to the FBI? The FBI for sure, but possibly MI6 as well. So, probably the leak came from one of those two – assuming Ramanda was as careful as I thought she was and hadn't told her gardener and her grocer and her butcher.

Would MI6 sanction flat-out murder of a British subject? I am always primed to think the worst of people belonging to either law enforcement or intelligence, but no. No. MI6 does not go around murdering their sovereign's subjects. And if they did, they'd do a less-visible job of it.

My phone rang. Delia. 'Hey,' I said. 'I have something.'

'So do I. Your tiki bar in half an hour?'

'You'll make Theo's day.'

Delia arrived, not in a bathing suit this time. Theo shot me a dirty look, like it was my fault, but still fawned over her for a good ten minutes. We drank sparkling water.

'You first,' Delia said, when Theo had finally absented himself.

I told her about Chante's video, the TR6 and its owner, Jeremy 'Jez' Berthold. Halfway through she typed the name into an app. 'Interesting,' she said.

'My guess is he's ex-intelligence, still connected. Heard about Ramanda—'

'Who?'

'Rachel slash Amanda. Ramanda. No?'

She shook her head and seemed to be in some kind of pain. 'No, David. We could call her the victim.'

'The vic?' I grinned. 'How about UNSUB? That's much cooler than saying Unknown Subject.'

Delia had learned by now just to patiently wait out my more irrelevant digressions. 'Here's what I've learned,' she said. 'I heard back from my mob accountant. It's a lot of data, but even so, it's just a small slice of the whole picture.'

'Caveat, caveat,' I muttered while making a 'get on with it' gesture.

'He went through what we gave him and according to him there are just too many questionable transactions going on to even get a handle on it. However, amid the usual Russian oligarchs and Saudi sheikhs looking to move money into more stable countries, what popped out was a certain NGO.'

'An NGO?'

'Feed the Forgotten,' Delia said.

'Well, well.'

'And here's the thing: August 19, October 9, November 4 of last year. January 14, March 6, May 10 and June 12.'

'June 12? That's the day before yesterday.'

'Yes.' She grinned her predatory grin. 'Which would be the day before the boat we saw yesterday landed. And guess what? The other dates roughly match up with refugee boats that later landed here on Cyprus. Boats that came from Alexandria.'

'So wait. How does this work? Traffickers load up some refugees in Egypt and ship them to Cyprus. But either somewhere en route, or after they land, the healthy kids are snatched and sold off.'

'And Feed the Forgotten sends a cash transfer to a Lebanese bank.'

'Is this their redeeming slaves thing?' I asked, frowning.

'That's not what the timing says.'

'Where's Feed the Forgotten's money come from, aside from Hollywood people and my landlady?'

'Charitable donations. Many, you will be shocked to learn, come from shell corporations.'

'So wait, let me get this straight. The dirty money flows from various bad guys to the NGO where it is instantly "clean." Feed the Forgotten uses the money to pay traffickers. The traffickers charge their passengers, steal the kids, then extort money from the parents and relatives and, of course, from Feed the Forgotten. A couple times a year, Feed actually produces a rescued victim and parades him around as a success story. And there is no accounting for the ones they ransom but never see.'

We were working our way back logically, step by step to the sudden realization that had occurred to us when we were standing atop the *odeum*: not one scam, two.

'Someone got the trafficking scam going in Sicily after the most recent Libyan meltdown, then relocated it to Cyprus after you and your fellow Feebs busted up that party. Meanwhile Feed the Forgotten was increasingly being used by Russians to move money. Hah! I think that's the bones of it. We're brilliant, Delia. We're Nick and Nora Charles. Frank and Joe Hardy. Morse and Lewis. Batman and Robin.'

Long pause. 'Are you done?'

'Scooby and Scrappy-Doo. The Russians cannot possibly be happy about attention turning toward Feed the Forgotten, or the AZX Bank, or the general topic of human trafficking. Those guys are all about money and lots of it. Also: Mulder and Scully.'

Delia picked up the burden of thinking aloud. 'You're spotted talking to Calix Petrides at Kofinou, alarm bells go off, a call is made, and someone decides to follow you. You seem to be a busybody, and they may well have made me, which makes you more than a busybody. So, a hit is authorized. And did you just leave off Easy Rawlins and Mouse?'

'Easy and Mouse are not partners. One's a righteous detective and the other is a criminal, who . . . Ah. Okay, I see what you did there.' That hurt my feelings a bit. 'So, who killed Ramanda? The Russians? Whoever is running the trafficking operation?'

Delia leaned back, tented her fingers and thought. I also thought. You could practically hear the gears whirring.

'No wonder it never made sense,' I said. 'We were looking for a grand unifying theory for what was two completely different operations. Apples and oranges and the one maybe not liking the other at all.'

Finally, Delia said, 'Nestor Panagopolous.'

'You think he's the boss?' I asked skeptically.

'No, no,' she snapped. 'But he's our lead. We need to find him.'

'Every Monday,' I said. 'Tomorrow.'

'Have you scoped the bank?'

I put a hand over my heart. 'What are you suggesting? Why, I never!'

Delia sighed. 'OK, look, David, we need new rules of engagement.'

So close to making a dumb joke about not knowing her well enough to get engaged.

'I can't have you confessing felonies to me,' Delia said. 'But. You are a notorious liar, and a fiction writer.'

'The two do go hand in hand.'

'Yes, they also go hand in hand with grift and burglary and a few other things.' She looked at me, very serious. 'David, this isn't just a job for me. Being FBI? That's not just something I do to make a living. I graduated from Georgetown Law School, made law review, clerked for an appellate judge. There are a dozen law firms ready to pay me mid-six figures, which, needless to say, is quite a bit more than the Bureau pays.'

'You're a true believer.' I intended it to come out as a sneer, but it came out sincere.

'I am,' she said. 'I believe in the rule of law. I believe people who break the law should be punished. So, you need to understand something, David. I like you. You're smart, funny and fundamentally decent deep down. Way deep down. And if I may quote Minette by way of Chante, you are both tall and symmetrical, so I'd even go so far as to say somewhat attractive. But you and I are different tribes. There's always going to be a wall between us.'

'A prison wall.'

Delia shook her head. 'I'm not threatening you. I will stick to the terms of our deal. When I eventually write the report on this, you'll be a snitch, a confidential informant. Your name will not appear – any of your names. What I'm trying to do is show you the respect you deserve by telling you how it is.'

That shouldn't have bothered me much. But it did. I had just been put in my place. It was a punch to the gut and I don't think I hid it very well.

'Right,' I said. 'Got it.'

'So, without confessing to any crimes, and bearing in mind that you are a fabulist . . . have you any knowledge of the AZX Bank in Limassol?'

'So, you get to be on your moral high horse and yet profit from my low activities? You've got your mob accountant and me, your pet burglar.'

'It's called police work.'

'Yeah, well, I've done enough,' I said. 'I came close to being killed. I'm stitched up with thread from a hotel courtesy kit. I've got Kiriakou crawling up my ass and one way or the other I have to default on my lease and go somewhere else, because I am burned on Cyprus.'

'Yes. You have done enough. More than enough. If you want to walk away right now our deal will hold.'

'You think I won't?'

'Of course you won't.'

'Why won't I? Why won't I just tell you to take your Russian mob and your traffickers and your idiot NGOs and the rest and shove 'em?'

She leaned forward and actually took my hand. There was some of her usual mockery in her eyes, but something warmer as well. 'You know, I'd have thought you were more self-aware, David. You write about characters like you genuinely understand people, but you don't understand yourself, do you? You're not going to run away, not now, because there's something you want and you don't have it yet.' A second later she rolled her eyes and said, 'No, not that, good lord.'

'What then?'

'Redemption, David. You want redemption.'

TWENTY-FIVE

From time to time, generally when I've had a bit too much to drink, I look her up on Facebook, the girl in the window. She got married. And for a time I had to endure photos of her with her husband who I cordially despised, although, hell I don't know, he was probably a decent enough guy.

They were divorced after five years. No explanation, just a Facebook posting and a change of status.

They had a kid who would now be about nine years old. A boy. Looked like a healthy kid. She posted his drawings from time to time.

I would go through her various likes – movies, music, and especially books. Especially books after I started being published. Drunk and weepy I would go to her Facebook page to see if somehow she had read something of mine. Of course she wouldn't know it was mine, the David Mitre persona came much later than our brief affair. But no luck. She tended to read literary fiction, not genre stuff like mine.

She lived in the San Francisco Bay Area where she worked in some capacity I never quite figured out for the Marin County Arts Board. Her son attended school and was doing fine there. She drove a Volvo.

Her hair was shorter, more stylish and more blonde than it had been. She liked travel, especially Italy. She liked Beyoncé and Bonnie Raitt and Lucinda Williams. On her list of favorite TV shows was *Lost*, which I decided had something to do with me. In my fantasy, I was the thing she'd lost.

I can be a bit pathetic after a few too many.

Sober me, rational me knows she had dodged a bullet when I took off. I'd been what, twenty-three, twenty-four? At that point, I was all arrogance, testosterone, paranoia and free-floating anger. I was out for revenge. Revenge against *the man*, against all the authorities and all their power arrayed so unfairly against me. And what had I done at that point? Just a few burglaries, some unnoticed skimming and a bit of bail-jumping. I was furious at the world for trying to lock me up.

I was not always the coolly rational person I now manage to pass myself off as.

In her pictures, the girl looked happy. I searched for subtle signs of deep loneliness, a sense of loss . . . Did not really find any of that.

I was forty-two years old. I had five published novels. I had a bit more than two million dollars in secret accounts. I was tall, symmetrical and had excellent hair. People liked me, mostly, especially women. And yet I was pining for a woman I'd long ago left, and now for a woman who saw me as a lower life form.

So, I poured myself a drink, and lit a cigar, and carried them both out onto the terrace to remind myself that I was in a nice villa on Cyprus, looking at the sun setting over the water, and not in some prison straining to see a patch of blue through a barred window. But there's only so much pleasure to be gained by successfully avoiding the worst consequences of your own colossal stupidity. Some men scale cliffs, some men fight wars, some men create cures for cancer, and I nimbly avoid the consequences of my own actions.

I changed my bandages. It had been almost three days and the cuts were puffy but not infected. Scabs had tentatively formed crusts beneath neat stitches, though the salt water had softened them. I was no longer seeping much blood, which was a good thing, and the pain was now less distracting than the fire ant itch of healing flesh.

I decided I needed to get out of the house. Anywhere, so long as it was out. I drove down to lower Paphos and got lucky with a parking place. I walked along the shore a bit, hotels on my left, narrow, rocky beach on my right, idly counting cats, which, as usual, were everywhere. Every second chaise longue had its own tabby, legs drawn in, sleepy eyes opening to glance at me. So very much like Delia's eyes and just as dismissive.

I felt the tail before I spotted him. It's a sixth sense, which admittedly, can be mistaken – I once played a game of *French Connection* subway shuffle on the Madrid subway before it occurred to me that the guy I thought was a tail was just flirting with me. But in my line of work, you check out these paranoid flashes, you can't just dismiss them.

Back in the bad old days, you'd check out a tail by pausing in front of a shop window and hoping to catch a glimpse of reflection. But technology is a wonderful thing, so I opened my phone, turned the camera to selfie mode and snapped some quick shots.

And there he was about a hundred feet behind me. Thirty-ish, leather jacket, jeans, running shoes. It wasn't Bristle or Baldy.

Possibly a pal of my Russian friends, but my instinct said 'cop' not crook.

I pushed a cat aside and flopped into a chaise longue, taking more pictures, this time of the blood-red sunset, ostentatiously playing tourist. A glance to my right showed that my tail had also decided this was an excellent time to enjoy the view.

I groaned inwardly. The problem was that I didn't even know for certain whether he was of the 'collecting evidence' or the 'ready to commit murder' variety of tails.

I wandered up into the next hotel lobby, sat at the bar, ordered a Scotch and turned to watch the seaward door. And there he was, wandering across the room carefully avoiding looking at me and taking a seat at a distant table where he could face the sea and still see me out of the corner of his eye.

I was feeling a bit down, and when I'm down there's a tendency to want to reshuffle the deck, so I was just about to walk over and confront the guy when I spotted something else. Another guy. Also thirty-ish and alone. Also wearing a jacket despite the warm night, though his was a dark gray Canali sports coat, if I did not miss my guess. I own the navy version, which is not exactly relevant.

The point was that this second guy also did the room-scan, which sort of carefully slid past me like I wasn't there. He did look at Tail #1, though, and frowned.

Interesting. Tail #2 either recognized Tail #1 as a fellow cop, or as a fellow bad guy, or was a bad guy recognizing a cop . . . or something, but Tail #2 was definitely carefully blind to me and unhappy about Tail #1.

Well, fuck it. I was not in the mood.

I carried my drink over to Tail #1, set it down on his table and plopped into the chair opposite him. I watched his reactions carefully.

Cops and thugs are related on the family tree of *homo sapiens* in that neither is happy about being challenged. But the thug will project a danger warning, like a bull lowering its head to bring its horns to bear, or a gorilla beating its chest. A cop, on the other hand, is all about control. They don't send out 'I can kill you' vibes so much as 'I'm in charge here' vibes.

'Hi. I'm David Mitre. But you already know that.'

He took a good two seconds to eyeball me with a flat, unimpressed look. No fear. No threat. Just that imperturbable cop smugness.

'I no speak English,' he said.

'You're a cop in Paphos, of course you speak English.'

He didn't like that. His jaw muscles clenched. His fingers formed into half-fists. But he couldn't think of anything to say.

So I said, 'Listen, dude, I thought I should mention that you're not the only guy tailing me.'

He was unable to hide either his surprise or his quick, sidelong glances.

'Gray blazer, at your nine o'clock. Posh-looking guy with glasses.'

He glanced, held it a moment, and turned back to me, defiant. 'I don't know what you're talking about.'

'Not one of yours, huh?'

'Go away, you are bothering me.'

I laughed. 'Look, officer, the bullshit doesn't work on me. I know you're tailing me, I know you're a cop, I know that guy is also tailing me, and I know he's not a cop because cops don't wear $1,500 dollar blazers unless they're corrupt and lack all subtlety.'

He wasn't likely to ever make chief of police, this policeman, because he wasn't very bright. He tried a bluff. 'If I am a police officer maybe you should be more careful. I might arrest you.'

'What?' I made an incredulous face. 'Look, dude . . . do you mind if I call you dude? Dude, officer dude, if you could arrest me, you wouldn't be following me. Right? You tail people because you're looking for evidence of a crime. Tailing and arresting are mutually exclusive.'

He was caught flatfooted. I almost felt sorry for him. He was probably just picking up some overtime tailing me, probably had very little notion of why. Now he was trying to find a way to assert dominance, but he couldn't and it frustrated him.

'So, officer dude, here's what I'm going to do. I'm going to go ask the other asshole who he is. I just thought you should know. It's possible he might do something unfortunate. And you'll want to be ready. Right? Yeah.'

I grabbed my drink and made a beeline for Tail #2. I took a

stool beside him and by way of introduction said, 'I can't help
but notice you looking at me. I thought I'd save you some time
and tell you that I'm straight.'

Tail #2 was a cool customer. He had the look of a businessman
on holiday, maybe someone who worked in finance and thought
a gray blazer was giddy informality. He looked like money, like
a man whose wife I could divest of some jewelry. He also
looked like he spent serious time at the gym, with shoulders
and biceps both straining against fine Italian wool.

'Mr Mitre,' he said, and stood to extend his hand. Dry palm,
firm, confident grip. 'My name is Breen, Thorne Breen. Pleased
to meet you.'

'Yeah, *enchanté*. Cool name, by the way.' British accent, too
northern to be truly posh, but with a patina of BBC standard
layered over it like veneer.

We sat. I waited.

'You will be wondering why I am following you.'

'I will be, yes.'

'I was hoping we'd have an opportunity to meet.'

'Indeed? So, you're either a wannabe writer, or you're a
messenger.'

His blue eyes twinkled. 'I'm afraid I have no talent as
a writer. But I suppose I do have a message to deliver.'

'I'm all ears.'

Breen tugged at his shirtsleeves which had ridden up. Then
he straightened the hem of his trousers. When he was convinced
that all hems and seams were in the right place, he said, 'We
British have an unusual position here on the island. You may
be aware that we have a long history together, the UK and
Cyprus.'

'You have a couple of military bases in enclaves with leases
extending to the Second Coming.'

'Exactly. And we have quite a large British expat community.
In general, we have an excellent relationship with the locals,
and of course we very much wish it to remain that way.'

'I want to thank you for taking the time to follow me to
deliver that important news, Mr Breen.'

Frosty smile. He was amused by my impertinence. And that's
what he thought it was: impertinence. *Lèse majesté*, the smug

prick. He wouldn't have tried to come off as upper crust around a fellow Brit, but he figured me for an American who thought all British accents were identically cool.

'Given that we are guests in this country,' Breen continued, all calm reasonableness. He was explaining, like you might to an idiot or a child. 'We feel it is very important to avoid drawing attention to ourselves. We don't like to make waves. We cannot afford to be seen as a problem. So, we do what we can to make sure that no expat becomes a problem.'

I was getting irritated. 'Jeremy Berthold – I call him Jez because we're tight – pulled up to the beach last night minutes after a refugee boat came ashore.'

Oh, the improbably-named Thorne Breen was good, this guy: not a flicker. And he didn't waste time spitting out the bait, instead he swallowed it and chewed the hook. 'Mr Berthold is very concerned for the plight of refugees.'

'Uh-huh. Mr Jeremy Berthold, formerly of MI6 . . .'

The amused smile flickered at that.

'. . . and patron of charities, is very concerned with refugee boats. So concerned he got there at record speed. I checked the times. I found out where Berthold lives, and I checked the first tweets about the boat, and guess what? He couldn't have gotten there from his home, not that fast.' This was all bluff, I had no idea where Berthold lived.

'Mr Berthold's comings and goings are really none of your business.' We were getting from 'message' to 'threat' by degrees.

'I'd counter that my comings and goings are none of Mr Berthold's business. I'm an American tourist, not a Brit expat. And yet, here you are warning me to fuck off.'

'Nonsense, no one is telling you to fuck off, Mr Mitre. Enjoy the island. Enjoy the beaches and the sunshine and the food and wine. Stay as long as you like. But perhaps avoid dipping your toes in troubled waters.'

'You know, Breen, the only reason I give a shit what happens on this little island is that a local cop named Kiriakou dragged me into it.'

I said that to get a reaction. The reaction I got what was not what I expected. 'Really? And nothing to do with a, ah . . . vacationing . . . FBI agent?'

Now it was my turn to gulp and try to look unimpressed. It was also time for me to toss off some quip, some bon mot, some kind of intelligent response. But for once no words came.

Breen leaned forward, invading my space, daring me to back up. In a low voice, he said, 'I don't know why you're helping the FBI, Mr Mitre. I don't know why you're sticking your nose into people's business. Our community has among its number several people who wish only to be left in peace and anonymity, and those people, Mr Mitre, have the power to make life very unpleasant for you, unpleasant even to the point of an early end to same.'

There we go, I thought: now *that's* a threat.

'It's like I'm being threatened by the chamber of commerce,' I said.

'Read between the lines, Mr Mitre. You of all people should be able to do that.' He nodded at the bartender, made a hand gesture indicating that he was paying for my drink as well and walked out.

I was gratified to see Tail #1 follow Breen out toward the street.

TWENTY-SIX

Chante was in my villa, on my couch, feet up on my coffee table, reading one of my books. She barely looked up as I came in.

'Huh. I could have sworn this was my house,' I said, doing a comic mime of confusion.

'My toilet is plugged. Dame Stella says the plumber can't come tonight.'

'So, you took a dump here, then poured yourself a drink?'

She had gone to my little bar and was pouring me a Talisker. What was I going to do? Stop her?

I sat down opposite Chante, fighting the urge to ask her what she thought of my book, which would have been needy. 'So how's Minette?'

'Gone.'

'What? Why?'

'They are done shooting on Cyprus. They are going to California.'

'Minette didn't invite you along?'

Chante sighed. 'I am not welcome in America.'

'Please tell me it's because you're secretly a terrorist.'

She did not smile. Granted, she never smiled, but this non-smile was even less smiley than usual. 'I once dated a woman. A Pakistani woman. After we broke up, she blew herself up in a Karachi marketplace, killing six people.'

'Jesus. You didn't suspect?'

'That the same woman who would do anything to give me pleasure, and from whom I withheld nothing in return, would become a fanatic? No, I did not suspect that.'

'Now you're on the no-fly list.'

'Now I am unemployed,' she said, and poured herself some more of what I had to remind myself was my whiskey. My glass, too.

A thought occurred to me. It was a stupid thought, as my brain kept telling me, nevertheless, I persisted and from my mouth came fateful words. 'I have a one-day gig you could do. If you were up for something . . . unusual.'

Her look eloquently conveyed what she thought of what she thought I was asking her.

'No, no. Christ, Chante, give me some credit. For a start, I don't hit on women young enough to be my daughter. And b) I don't hit on lesbians.' I silently added the caveat, unless they're rich. And I don't even do that anymore. For a moment, I was distracted by a swelling pride in my own virtue. Then I arrived back in reality, and said, 'Can you drive a scooter?'

'I am French.'

'Okay, well, Agent Delia needs a guy followed. I'm helping her, but we could use another person. I want someone on a scooter.'

'This would be for Delia?'

The word 'Delia' came out sounding like 'the Pope' or 'Ghandi' or maybe 'Beyoncé.'

'Yep,' I said. 'But I'd be the one paying you.'

'I will accept no pay for helping Delia.'

'No. Of course not.'

'I am sleeping on this couch tonight,' Chante announced, patting the cushion beside her. 'In case I need the toilet. I require a pillow and a blanket.'

Here's the amazing thing: I fetched her a pillow and a blanket. And put a bottle of water on the coffee table where she could reach it in the night.

In the morning, we had breakfast together. Chante cooked – a frittata with potatoes and spinach and feta cheese. She could cook, and she could make a decent cup of coffee. And she was really good at shutting up until said coffee had osmosed into my brain.

After I cleaned up, because apparently that was *my* job, I went outside and crawled under my car. I removed the GPS tracker, and was just scooting back out from under, when I spotted a second device. Two GPS trackers? I removed the second one as well and placed both devices on my dining room table.

Chante looked up at that. 'Those are GPS devices.'

'So they are. They seem to have become attached to my car. Ready?'

We drove to Delia's hotel – a new place, one where people had not recently engaged in an elevator knife fight. I texted her and she came down. Chante moved to the back seat.

I jerked my head toward Chante. 'An extra body. I got her a scooter. Like Batgirl.'

'Hello, Chante,' Delia said. 'It's very good to see you again.'

'Thank you!' Chante blurted. 'I'm happy to . . . do . . . whatever it is you, we . . .'

'Unbelievable,' I muttered.

Delia and I did not discuss the case, not with Chante still mostly in the dark. She didn't need to know what we were up to, nor did she need to know dangerous facts about me, she just needed to know Delia was involved. But Delia did turn around to explain the basics.

'We are following a man who we expect to arrive at a certain bank. We must find out where he goes when he leaves the bank.'

'I arranged a rented scooter for her,' I repeated.

'Good,' Delia said. 'And you really must put the top up, David, we are too obvious.'

We located the scooter rental place, hooked Chante up with a nice little 125cc scooter, and I put my top up. From there it was a short ride to the AZX Bank.

Chante took up position just in front of the bank in a rank of two dozen nearly identical scooters. She sat astride the bike with earbuds in and occasionally played with her phone, looking like any other random, rude, angry, lock-ignoring, couch-appropriating, toilet-stealing girl on a scooter listening to music and waiting for a date.

Delia and I found a coffee shop half a block west. We stood around until one of the outdoor tables opened up and snatched it out from under a pair of Italian tourists. Delia sat facing the bank – she was the only one who knew the guy we were looking for.

'We look conspicuous,' Delia said.

'You always look conspicuous, Delia, there aren't a lot of women who look like you.' I waited. 'That's a compliment.'

'Oh. Thank you. But you know, David, if this was a workplace, that kind of remark would have you up before Human Resources.'

'One more reason to avoid workplaces.' We sipped coffee in silence in the shadow of tall buildings. Traffic flowed heavier than I expected and I was glad I had thought to get Chante on a scooter. Then, I said, 'OK, I can see where it might get irritating. Me hitting on you, I mean.'

'Welcome to the twenty-first century, David Mitre,' she said, but not unkindly.

'So,' I said, 'we've got time to kill. You know my story, what's yours? Where are you from? What do your folks do? What's your favorite movie? What's your position on putting pineapple on pizza?'

'Unalterably opposed to pineapple on pizza. Favorite movie?' She had to think about that, which took some time. I guessed she was sorting possibilities with an eye toward revealing nothing about herself. Then, finally, 'Okay, I've got three movies. *Mad Max: Fury Road* . . .'

'Because Imperator Furiosa,' I interjected.

'*The Sting*—'

'Because you secretly like grifters?'

'Sure,' she drawled. 'That's it. Not that I like Paul Newman or Robert Redford. And, well, *Moonlight*.'

'Because—'

'No, not because it's a black movie,' she snapped.

'I was going to say because it's beautifully shot, and the score is really original, and the acting is great. And there are a couple of moments where your heart just . . . stops.'

That earned a rare Delia smile. But mockery came on its heels. 'Much better, David, much better way to hit on a woman.'

'Cynic. Are you going to tell me where you're from, or is that Top Secret, Eyes Only?'

'I was born in Muleshoe, Texas.'

I showed happy teeth. 'No. I refuse to believe that. First, I refuse to believe that's a real place, and second, I refuse to believe a place named Muleshoe produces people like you.'

'Muleshoe born, but raised mostly in Austin. I did my under-grad at UT. Poli Sci.' She added her graduation year.

'Austin?'

'Have you been?'

I nodded. Yeah, I'd been to Austin, Texas. And there, Delia, I had a chance to be a better man, and you know what? I wasn't a better man. I was just me, and there were jewels to steal and money to scam and some guy blowing his brains out in a Bugatti still in my future. And because life just enjoys fucking with me, you were there, too, Delia, just a few years behind the girl in the window. You'd have been a high school freshman as she was graduating from college, and as I was busy ignoring flashing warning lights the size of the Death Star and hurtling down the path to prison.

I said none of that. Delia already had a low enough opinion of my judgment.

We'd arrived a few minutes before the bank opened its doors and figured we could hold out for an hour before we'd need to relocate both us and Chante or risk being hard to ignore. But just forty-five minutes into our siege, Delia stiffened.

'Hey.' She nodded and I did a slow, casual, where-did-I-put-my-bag turn. 'White male, five eleven, one seventy to one eighty pounds, approximately thirty-eight years of age, blue sports coat and jeans.'

'That sounded so FBI. Can we do "presumed armed and dangerous," too?'

I watched as Nestor Panagopolous – white male, five eleven, one seventy to one eighty pounds and approximately thirty-eight years – sauntered nonchalantly in the front door of the bank.

I texted Chante, who texted back, *I see him.*

Delia and I left the café and walked slowly toward the car, parked illegally around the corner.

My phone pinged. *Coming out. Walking west.*

'Do we follow?' I asked, as we climbed into the Mercedes.

'Not yet. Let's see if he goes for a car.'

The phone pinged. *Yellow Porsche.*

'Douche,' I muttered. I started the engine and drove around the corner. Two cars were between us and Chante's scooter. Two cars beyond that we saw the Porsche. The *yellow* Porsche, which, first of all, is an ostentatiously obnoxious color to paint an obnoxious car, and second, was definitely not the car to choose if you don't want to be tailed.

Panagopolous drove northeast along the wide ocean front that looked like a down-at-the-heels Nice. But he did not go far, just cleared downtown before heading inland and came to a small, nondescript office building of four floors.

We parked in the lot of the next building over and Chante pulled up beside us.

'There will be a plaque or something listing the occupants,' Delia said to Chante. 'Are you comfortable wandering in and taking a quick pic with your phone?'

'Of course, Delia.'

I said, 'Keep your helmet on. They may have cameras. Make it look like you're a messenger in the wrong building.'

I did not receive an *of course, David*, but Chante did leave her helmet on as she marched off.

'She's got a crush on you,' I said.

'I'm flattered,' Delia said. 'That young woman has depth. Layers.'

Chante came back and climbed in the back seat. She leaned forward to show us her photo.

'Heh,' I said.

'Yes!' Delia hissed. 'ExMil.'

We were parked on the street, half a block away from the office building's parking lot, so I didn't worry too much about cameras, but we still had to be very careful. ExMil was nothing but suspicious guys who noticed details and liked guns.

We waited. And waited. And I really had to pee. Using text we arranged the matter, who would pee first, and where. The only spot was a small grocery store, which would not have a public restroom. It would take some talking and possibly some bribing. And since it was a pretty good bet that the store owner knew about ExMil, and had regular customers from there, we couldn't be too obvious.

We managed the peeing and bought food and coffee. As the day grew hotter Chante and I switched places and I went and straddled her scooter leaving her with Delia running the air conditioning. Is it pathetic that I was jealous? The question answers itself.

Naturally Panagopolous chose that point to emerge. He went quickly to his car and burned rubber out of the parking lot. I cursed, started the scooter, and with one hand on the handlebar and the other on my phone I texted *eating north*, which, fortunately, Delia understood to mean *heading north.*

I manhandled my earbuds into place and told Siri to call Delia. Much better than texting.

'Hey. We need to switch places. Pass me and I'll drop back.'

We did that. And repeated the move again in a few more miles as we left urban areas and headed inland on narrow roads. Narrow was not good if Panagopolous was the wary sort.

Panagopolous slowed to turn onto a barely-paved road. We pulled past and braked into a turn-off. Panagopolous had gone up a private road, not a road we could take, certainly not without being spotted. I hopped in the car – the back seat because Delia was driving and Chante did not seem inclined to make room for me.

'Mapping it,' Delia said tersely. The three of us peered at the satellite view. The road only went on for another few hundred yards before it ended at what looked like a small compound of three buildings.

'What do we do?' Chante asked Delia.

'We'll have to sit here and hope Panagopolous eventually leads us to wherever he's living.'

There followed another two hours of playing games on our phones and chatting. Chante started telling Delia her story, and I learned various useful facts. Chante was twenty-three, had left university before getting an art degree. Had worked for a while in a bookstore where, no, they did not stock my books (the snobs), before a friend hooked her up with Minette, who had just lost her personal assistant to pregnancy.

So, not really useful at all, but it passed the time.

Chante's favorite movies were *Hiroshima Mon Amour*, *Bound* and *Entre Les Murs*, of which I had seen none and Delia had seen all but the last one.

It's cramped in the back seat of a C-Class convertible. It's no place for a six-foot-two man still recovering from serious wounds, that was certain. It's even less comfortable when it's your car, and the other two people in the car are ignoring you.

Finally, the yellow Porsche reappeared. Chante, at Delia's suggestion, took to the scooter again, I took the wheel, and we were off.

'We need to discuss what we should do once we have his location,' Delia said.

I glanced at her, surprised. 'I figured you would arrest him. Isn't that the whole point? He's your guy, your *bête noire*. You're Javert and he's Jean Valjean.'

'Nothing would make me happier than turning the prick over to Italian justice. But Panagopolous is just a piece of the puzzle. He could lead us to whoever is up the chain from him. Normally I'd apply for a search warrant, if this was in the US. Then we could grab his laptop and phone, see what we found.'

'Delia? Am I hearing an ellipsis?'

'Ellipsis?'

'The three little dots that suggest the speaker is waiting for the other person to fill in the blanks? Because, um, what you're thinking but not saying is illegal and you're FBI – that was made very clear to me. And, two, that's not just some middle-aged banker, that's a bad guy who works for a company run by ex-SEALS and ex-SAS and guess who wins a fight between me and some special forces dude?'

'I understand if you're scared.'

'Do you seriously think you can shame me into committing suicide? Have you met me?'

She sighed and suddenly banged the dashboard with her fist. 'Goddammit!'

'If you know where he lives you can reach out to the Italians . . .' That sounded weak, even to me.

We followed Panagopolous to a somewhat-past-its-prime development of twenty or so villas. We stopped well back as he pulled his absurd car to a stop and swaggered inside.

We sat there stewing for a while. Delia was a few hundred feet from her guy, her obsession, and suddenly now she was facing the fact that there might not be much she could do about him. We had his home address – we were *at* his home address – and she could try for extradition, but ExMil could easily transfer him to another office out of the country. I understood her frustration.

Chante was listening to all this byplay and beginning, I suspected, to realize she was in the middle of something more serious than she'd imagined. What exactly she was concluding, I didn't know. I supposed her infatuation with Delia was keeping her here.

'We need to catch him in the act,' Delia said. 'If we can do that, we can flip him. Maybe.'

'Well, yeah, obviously, but we'd need to know when the next boat is coming. If he's even still part of that operation.'

Chante finally had had enough of the cryptic talk. 'What is this?'

'This?' Delia asked.

'Why are we following this man?'

I was not in the mood for equivocation or for Delia's claims of security clearances. 'He's a human trafficker who killed a bunch of refugee kids by tossing them into the sea to avoid being arrested. Delia's got a hate-on for him. And it's all tied into the murder on the beach. And also Russian money laundering. Though goddamned if we know how exactly.'

Chante absorbed that, and said, 'And you?'

Meaning me. 'I'm a retired gentleman thief – like Cary Grant in *It Takes a Thief* and—'

'*To Catch a Thief*,' Chante corrected.

'Whatever,' I said.

'And you are not Cary Grant.'

'The point is,' I insisted doggedly, 'I am being blackmailed by Delia into helping her, and now she seems to want me to go beat a confession out of some guy with very well-trained muscles.'

'I never said any such thing,' Delia snapped.

'And by the way,' I said, because I was on a roll of sorts, 'you're no Grace Kelly, either, Delia, because she was nice and would never send Cary Grant to get his ass kicked.'

'Are you a coward?' Chante asked me, her tone scorching.

For a second, I was too outraged to respond, which turned out to be a good thing, because Delia spoke instead.

'No, Chante,' Delia said quietly. 'He is not a coward. In fact, he is quite brave. Brave and intelligent. If David were not an immature, sociopathic man-child, he could have had a career in law enforcement.'

As a writer I am often overpraised. Goodreads, the book review site, has one of my books more highly-rated than *Hamlet*. Granted this is because *Hamlet* is assigned reading for high school kids who take out their rage on Shakespeare by writing bad reviews, but still, the point is I know I am sometimes overpraised. But only as a writer.

But as *me*? As sad as it may seem, *If David were not an immature, sociopathic man-child he could have had a career in law enforcement* is one of the nicest things anyone's said about me. And Delia actually defending me to Chante gave me a warm glow.

You take your pleasures where you find them.

Your opportunities, too.

'Hey,' I said. 'The house next to his. That's a for-sale sign.'

'Maybe he's a bad neighbor.'

'Or it's a lousy neighborhood, despite the superficial suburban blandness. Doesn't matter, really. The point is no one is home next door.'

'What are you thinking, David?' Delia asked me.

'I'm thinking we could place cameras and know exactly when Panagopolous comes and goes.'

TWENTY-SEVEN

I was already doing as much surveilling, sneaking, lying and breaking and entering in a week on behalf of the FBI as I'd done in any given six months of my old life. But an unoccupied suburban home? That barely qualified as a crime. Nothing's easier than breaking into an unoccupied suburban home.

We drove back to my villa, dropped Chante off and picked up some items I happen to have in my possession: a camera, a router, a cell phone uplink, the usual. I grabbed a screwdriver and wished I had a drill, but this would work for a start.

Delia and I drove back to Panagopolous' house. We parked one street over. I'd gotten rid of my GPS tracking devices, so I was not creating an evidence trail and unless I made a real mess of things this would not result in a police canvass of the neighborhood. Me vs. an unoccupied suburban villa was like asking Gordon Ramsay to cook up some tater tots and I was as relaxed as it's possible to be while preparing to commit a crime. I got out and Delia took the driver's seat.

'Call me if you get into trouble,' Delia said, as I leaned down at her open window.

'You're in my contacts under "cavalry."'

'I meant that, by the way, what I said to Chante. You're a brave man.'

'Brave, sociopathic man-child,' I corrected.

She smiled her sleepy, mocking but still genuine Delia smile. 'Well, that goes without saying.'

'Good luck kiss?'

She kept smiling, closed her eyes slightly, tilted her head and as I leaned in the window closed between us. She made a shooing gesture with her fingers and I toddled off up the dark street with my trusty John Lewis messenger bag over my shoulder loaded with the tools of my erstwhile trade.

Down the side alley, around to the back of the unoccupied

house, and a quick shim and the sliding glass door was open. I do love a cheap lock. I popped in, closed the door behind me, snapped on my flashlight while keeping the beam in my fist to allow only enough light to escape. I took the stairs two at a time, opened the door to the room that would be adjacent to Panagopolous' house and got down to it.

There were two windows facing Panagopolous. The roof eaves were shallow, but, I thought, probably enough. I slid the window open and cantilevered myself out, butt on the sill, free hand gripping a support beam beneath the eaves. I spent a few minutes cursing at screws that would not bite, wishing again that I had a battery-operated drill, wishing my injured hand didn't throb as if it was a bongo being played with a hammer, and finally got the camera mount in place. It was small, not invisible, but a casual glance would not spot it. If Panagopolous happened to look out of his window, he would be very unlikely to see it.

I checked the batteries, and covered the green 'power' light with a snippet of duct tape.

Now for the router. For that I needed power and concealment. This took some work, but down in the kitchen I found they had installed a garbage disposal. Under the kitchen sink I found an electrical socket. I unplugged the garbage disposal and plugged in the router, and even took the time to awkwardly screw the router into place behind the sink. Then, with Wi-Fi established, I checked the app and ran back upstairs to adjust the camera to take in a better angle of Panagopolous' driveway.

I named the Wi-Fi 'Athena' for Delia, checked that everything was clean and evidence-free upstairs, and trotted back down the stairs just as the front door opened. I reversed direction, scampering back up the stairs and squatted where I could see without being seen. Two men entered. One of them was Thorne Breen.

Thorne Breen with a gun in his hand.

My brain raced, throwing out disconnected thoughts. They had Delia or she'd have warned me. Why hadn't I checked this empty house for silent alarms and cameras? Was that even what gave me away? What weapons did I have? Screwdriver and brass knuckles which in no universe trumped two guys with guns.

I withdrew to the bathroom which had one door on the hallway, the other on the bedroom where I'd set up the camera. I lifted the heavy porcelain lid off the back of the toilet, flushed said toilet and whistled the tune from the Old Spice commercials – whistled to signal obliviousness. No idea why the Old Spice ditty. I darted into the bedroom, leaving the connecting bathroom door open while silently shutting and locking the hallway door.

It was all about timing now, timing and luck. Would both guys come upstairs together, or would one scout ahead?

Gritting my teeth so hard they were on the verge of cracking, my heart pounding, I stood flattened against the wall, listening.

Footsteps. Cautious footsteps coming up the stairs. I tried to slow my own breathing because the sounds of my own fear were making it hard to hear.

One set of footsteps. The second guy would stay at the bottom of the stairs because they hadn't had time to clear the lower floor. And they could be pretty sure that a) I didn't know they were there, or why would I be flushing the toilet and whistling the Old Spice tune? And, b) that I did not have a gun, this being Cyprus not Wyoming.

The footsteps reached the top of the stairs.

I leaned through the bedroom connecting door and whistled again, which let me say is damned hard to do when you're shaking, pulled back into the bedroom and heard the quiet effort at opening the bathroom door.

Locked. The kick would be coming in 3, 2 . . .

I moved fast across the bedroom, out the door to the hallway just as *crash*!

The bad guy, not Breen, was just recovering his pose, raising his pistol and noticing that there was no one actually on the toilet. I stepped behind him, fast, and swung the porcelain toilet lid hard and even faster.

Nine times out of ten a panic blow will miss or make only partial contact. But every now and then . . .

A good five pounds of hard white ceramics hit the back of his head with all the precision of a well-rehearsed Bourne movie action scene. He dropped like a beef cow that's reached the end of the slaughtering line. I stepped over him, raised the lid high and brought the edge down with every ounce of my strength on the back of his neck.

And that was the end of things going well, because I caught him only a glancing blow, lost my grip on the porcelain which tumbled away, knocking the man's gun across the floor.

I leapt, but tripped over the downed man and smacked my forehead into the sink cabinet. I saw wild geometric patterns and stars and knew I was stunned, knew I had to move fast despite it, started crawling, made it maybe three feet before a hand grabbed the back of my collar and I felt something cold pressed against my medulla.

'Live or die, Mr Mitre. Live or die?' Thorne Breen said.

I was still somewhat preverbal at that moment and gave no answer. Nor did I resist as he dragged me out of the bathroom and kicked me down the stairs.

I tried standing but he was there in front of me and pushed me back with barely a shove. I landed on my rear and decided to stay there until the world stopped spinning.

Breen moved behind me, shoved me onto my side, squatted behind me and tightened a zip tie around my wrists. Then he took my bicep, hauled me partly erect and threw me against a wall where, once again, I decided to just sit down for a while.

Breen did a quick, professional body search, producing my wallet, passport, cigar torch, a Montecristo Petit tubo, my flask, my phone and my useless brass knuckles. He dropped it all negligently on the floor and swept them all away with the side of his shoe.

'Well, then, Mr Mitre. It seems I have you at a disadvantage.'

Lacking bon mots, I stayed quiet, feeling a sick worry for Delia.

'Stay put, eh?' Breen said, and kicked me in the kidneys. The pain was extraordinary and I nearly passed out. Breen then took the stairs two at a time. He was upstairs for a good minute which I used to what advantage I could, by kicking at my meager belongings and scattering wallet, phone, flask, tubo and brass knuckles, and squirming about a bit.

Breen came down more slowly than he'd gone up and he did not look cheerful. He was wearing what I imagine was his 'work' clothing: a black Hugo Boss blazer over a black T-shirt, with sneakers and black jeans – the essential items for the stylish, well-dressed thug.

'You bloody killed the stupid twat,' Breen said. 'You cracked the fucker's skull. His brain is leaking out, and he had little enough to spare. Well done that, it's a neat trick taking down an armed man with a toilet lid.'

Breen had the second gun shoved into the waistband on his right hip. Looking around he said, 'Now where the hell did the knuckledusters go, they would be very useful right about . . . ah, there!' He retrieved the brass knuckles, laid his own gun on the windowsill and slipped them on.

'Nice,' Breen said. 'Much better than using a pistol butt. With the crosshatched grip it would take me an hour to get all the blood and hair and tissue cleaned off. Shall we test these out?'

He swung a short, sharp, well-aimed blow that caught be just below the not-yet-healed previous wound on my jaw. I didn't feel pain, that would come later, what I did feel was shock.

He raised his hand, knuckles out to show me my own blood. 'See? I can throw brass knuckles in the dishwasher, can't do that with a gun. Thank you!'

I sat splay-legged against the wall, fattening lip dribbling red, the front door to my right, the window and the pistol to my left, none of which mattered much since I was too woozy to try a run, and my hands were zip-tied behind me.

'All right then, Mr Mitre, it is time for a conversation.' He squatted between me and the window, reached over, took my bruised and bloodied face, and turned me to face him. 'This can be quick and easy and end in apologies and a ride back to your villa. Or it can end with you permanently, irreversibly brain-damaged, left here to explain to the police in garbled grunts why there's a dead man upstairs and how you came to be here.'

'What, no death threat?' I think that was intelligible, it's hard to know when your jaw is numb and your ears are ringing.

'No, no, Mr Mitre, I'm not a murderer, I'm just a bloke who wants answers. Besides, I've learned from long experience that more people are prepared to face death than are prepared for a lifetime of drooling and shitting in diapers.'

He had a point there, I thought.

'Now, let's chat, shall we? Let's start with who you really are and why you are poking your nose in business that ain't yours.'

'You know who I am, I'm David M—' And *bam*! More stars. Pain, this time, too.

'Let's try again. Who are you, really?'

'Tony Stark,' I said. 'Secretly Iron Man.'

'Now, now, we both know that Tony Stark is not a secret identity, he's quite openly Iron Man.'

I had to get a thug who watched Marvel movies.

'Peter Parker?'

The next blow was a quick toe to the solar plexus, which knocked the wind from my lungs and sent spasms like cramps through my torso.

'All right, all right, I gasped. 'My real name is Carter Cannon.'

He frowned, searched his memory for cultural reference points, and said, 'Well, I rather doubt that, it seems improbable, but let's not get hung up on names. What is it you are doing?'

'I'm installing a surveillance camera to watch the house next door.'

'And why?'

'Want to see where the asshole next door is going.'

'Which brings us right back to "why?"'

'He got a friend of mine pregnant. I'm trying to get him to pay child support.'

That puzzled him and he forgot to punch me. He sighed and even smiled. 'You know, Mr Mitre . . . or whatever your name is . . . everyone thinks they can withstand torture. But it's nonsense. Rumour has it the cousins waterboarded Khalid Sheikh Mohammed for ten days. Ten days! You know how long it took for KSM to break? On his second waterboarding. Day One. The rest was just to flesh out details, and of course for the enjoyment of the agents. Everyone cracks.'

'What is it you want to know?' I asked in a slurred, low whisper.

He leaned closer. His left foot was planted between my knees. His right boot rested so that it was touching my left hip as he loomed over me, all alpha male dominance.

I had a plan. Unfortunately I'm right-handed and the plan required the use of my left hand, which was already growing numb from the zip tie.

'I'll ask you one more time. Why are you poking your nose in other people's business?'

I coughed and made it last, spitting out blood and generally making noise. I recovered slowly, shook my head as though trying to clear it, and said, 'I'm not sure about the black Boss with black jeans, it seems a bit nineties to me, honestly. Should have gone with a nice pair of medium gray Zanellas.'

And that's when he felt it.

You know what hurts worse than a beating? Burning. There's just something about the pain of burning flesh . . .

Breen leapt back like a cat spotting a cucumber. The flame licked up the back of his right leg. He yelled, 'Fuck!' and danced in a circle, trying to turn his head far enough to see what was causing him such pain.

I leveraged myself to my feet and poor Breen was at something of a loss. He was a professional, disciplined, very situation-aware. But at the same time his cotton jeans were burning as a result of my flicking my surreptitiously recovered cigar torch and holding it under the hem of his trousers.

Good wool will not burn, denim will. It's one of the drawbacks of dressing down.

I ran straight at him, hit him with my chest against his left shoulder and knocked him back. He expected me to lunge for the gun on the sill, but no, that was not the move. Anyone who has ever heckled a teen horror movie knows that you never just knock Freddy Krueger down, you have to finish him off.

So, I kicked Breen in his knee, dropping him, then kicked him and stomped on him, all the while him writhing and then screaming as the flames burned deep. I kicked him in the side of the head and in the back of the neck. Then I relieved him of the pistol in his waistband and took the gun from the sill and shoved it in my back pocket.

I was still zip-tied and, not being a real action hero, I was not prepared to incinerate my wrists in the hopes of melting nylon.

'Jesus Christ, help me!' Breen roared. 'I'm burning!'

'Yeah, I noticed,' I said. 'Give me your knife.'

Credit where credit is due, despite excruciating pain, Breen fished out a pocket knife, as he writhed and cried out in pain and panic.

It took a few seconds for me to manage to cut the zip tie. It's very awkward work when you can't see what you're cutting. 'Thanks,' I said and tossed the knife back to him. He failed to catch it probably because he was bellowing in pain and crawling like a fatally-wounded animal toward the kitchen with merry little flames marching up the back of his jeans.

I grabbed his collar, much as he'd done to me, and dragged him into the kitchen where I turned on the water in the sink and used the stylish goose-neck faucet to spray his leg as he cursed and whimpered.

He was in unendurable pain and not able to put up a fight when I searched his pockets and found more zip ties. I locked his wrists together, with a second tie to bind his thumbs. Then two interlocking ties around his healthy ankle and the other ankle which was an angry red horror beneath black scraps of extinguished denim. The smell . . . well, they say burning human flesh smells like a backyard barbecue. Close enough.

I kicked and shoved and manhandled Breen until he was leaned against the kitchen cabinetry. His faux-posh face was all tears and sweat and strained muscles now. The fire was out, but the pain of second-degree burns from his ankle to the back of his knee would be hard to ignore. Still and all, he was a pro and had been well trained, so he made an effort to focus.

I squatted beside him, just as he'd done, consciously, deliberately just as he'd done. I held my cigar torch in front of his face and flicked it. The three nozzles sprayed burning butane upward in a three-inch blue flame.

'Now, here's what I'm going to do, Breen. I'm going to turn this flame and point it at your eye. Your left for a start. And I will hold it until your eyeball bubbles like a fucking marshmallow.'

He shook his head violently.

'You're so right about people sometimes being more prepared to die than to live life trapped in a permanently mangled body.

Do you read Braille? How are you with a white cane? Do you like guide dogs? Very well-trained animals, they are, won't let you stumble into traffic.'

And . . . he was done. He didn't have to say it; his silence, and the character of his silence, spoke volumes.

'Now, Breen, who do you work for?'

Hesitation. So, I lit the torch again and let him feel the flame on his squeezed-shut eyelid.

'All right, all right, you fucking bastard!'

'Talk. Talk or fry.'

'Berthold. I work for Berthold.'

I blinked. Not quite the answer I was expecting, though I should have guessed.

'Not the Russians?'

'No, you fucking goddamn amateur.'

'ExMil?'

'ExMil *are* the Russians, you blithering idiot! Now call an ambulance! Fucking hell!'

'Hah!' The laugh was for the idea that I'd be calling an ambulance. But I was puzzled. If Panagopolous worked for ExMil and banked at AZX Bank, it made sense that ExMil was entwined with the Russians. It was not shocking to imagine that Bristle and Baldy were ExMil as well. 'What has Berthold got to do with the Russians?'

'Nothing, you cunt!'

'Mmmm, that doesn't feel quite truthful. Stay here. Don't run off.' I trotted back to the living room, found my flask, took a quick sip myself to steady my nerves and brought it back to Breen. I held it to his lips and poured a healthy shot into him. 'There you go, that'll dial the pain down by a percent or two.'

I was playing both roles: good cop and bad cop.

'In a hundred words or less, what is the connection between Russians and ExMil on the one hand, and Berthold and you on the other?'

'Just trying to keep a fucking lid on,' he spat.

'Yeah, that's still not—' I froze. I'd heard the sound of the front door opening cautiously. I pointed a warning finger at Breen and crept to where I could peek into the living room.

There stood Special Agent Delia Delacorte. She had a piece of torn duct tape hanging from the side of her head. Another piece trailed from her ankle like toilet paper stuck to a heel.

In her hand, she had the tire iron from my car.

'Hey, Delia,' I said, stepping into view. 'What's up?'

I'd have given anything to have my camera open. No need for video, a still shot would have done it, because Delia stood dead still, mouth open, staring for a good three seconds.

'David,' she said finally, in a patient, school-teacher's voice, like she was trying to find out why a rambunctious toddler had knocked over little Emily's blocks. 'What are you doing?'

'Me? Oh, I killed a guy with a toilet, and I'm questioning the other one in the kitchen. Want to see?'

I don't think her expression was hatred, not really, because she did actually sort of like me. More a combination of rage, confusion, the effects of adrenalin, and perfectly understandable irritation with my smart-ass welcome.

I led the way to the kitchen and performed introductions. 'Delia, this is Thorne Breen, ex-British intelligence—' I stopped on hearing a denial-grunt from Breen. 'Don't bother, Breen; the "cousins?" Who calls the CIA "cousins?" You may be ex-MI5 or you may be ex-MI6, what's a digit one way or the other, right? Anyway, Delia, Breen; Breen, my good friend Delia.'

'I nearly died trying to get in here and rescue you,' Delia said. 'I assumed you needed rescuing.'

'It's the thought that counts, Delia.' Then I spotted the blood coming from her nose. She seemed to notice the blood at the same time and wiped it with the back of her hand. 'Where's the guy who jumped you?'

'The three of them jumped me,' Delia said. 'The third one is now in the trunk of your car.'

'You got a full-grown man into that little trunk?'

'It wasn't easy. I had to push up that plastic thing.'

'The curved plastic . . . You realize that means I can't put the top down and nothing's better than driving with the top down on a warm night under the stars.' I was babbling some, jacked up on the relief of survival and full of my own wonderfulness at having managed to do that.

Breen groaned and cursed us both as a pair of fucking cunts.

Delia went to him and carefully inspected the zip ties. Satisfied that he wasn't going anywhere, she took my arm and led me back to the living room. 'David, are you torturing that man?' She pitched it low not to be overheard.

I shrugged. 'He tortured me first.'

'David, you cannot do that.'

'What? Has the "he started it" rule been revoked?'

She held my arm with more force than necessary and looked me in the eyes. 'You. Can. Not. Do. That.'

'But . . . he's totally ready to . . .'

'I can't let you. It's wrong.'

'Wrong?' I was pretty sure that word meant something, I'd even used it once or twice in a sentence, but it felt weak.

'Yes, David, it's wrong. It's morally depraved. It's against the law everywhere. Almost everywhere. Just: wrong, David.'

I gaped in astonishment. Once again I was conscious of a gulf opening between us. And once again, a faint, far-off voice was whispering that I might be on the wrong side of that gulf.

'But . . . But he's about to . . .'

Delia shook her head. 'I am what I am,' she said, then more stiffly, 'And what I am is a law enforcement professional. I can't let you. Full stop.'

Wrong, I sneered silently. Jesus H., who takes that kind of thing seriously when you're in the middle of a war?

Special Agent Delia Delacorte, that's who.

I retrieved all my gear, even unscrewing the camera I'd so painstakingly installed, just in case Breen didn't clean the scene up as well as he should.

We left Breen, went out and dragged the third man out of the trunk, unconscious from whatever Delia had done to him. We left the dead man and Breen in the house, and thug number three in Panagopolous' driveway on the theory that it would drag him into whatever police inquiry followed. And then we just . . . drove away.

Wrong?

TWENTY-EIGHT

We drove in silence for a long time, both staring straight ahead, like an old married couple leaving a party where hubby groped the hostess.

'Are you angry at me?' Delia asked, finally.

'No,' I snapped. Angrily.

More driving. This time I broke the silence. 'I didn't even think about it.'

'About what?'

'About *wrong*.' I stretched that last word out into a single-word, sarcasm-laden rant. Then I shrugged. 'I literally did not think about it. I never do.'

'You'd been beaten up. And you'd just killed a man.'

We drove. I saw a lay-by, swerved into it, stomped on the brakes and sat there arms on the wheel, bent over.

'Are you in pain?' Delia asked.

I shook my head because of course I was in pain, but that wasn't why I had pulled over. And damn me if tears didn't well up. Jesus. 'Did you check? That the guy upstairs was dead?'

'Yes.'

I had never before taken a human life.

I had never before killed a man.

Completely justified, even absolutely necessary to my own survival. I hadn't been wrong to do that. But my logic did not entirely convince my stomach, which wanted to throw up. I felt the shakiness of metabolizing adrenalin.

'I didn't mean to. I thought . . .' But then I remembered after he'd fallen, after I'd seen the bloody mess of his head, raising high my porcelain shield and bringing it down as hard as I could. He was already down. I was already safe from him. I couldn't know whether it was that first necessary blow that had killed him, or my awkward follow-up ceramic pile driver.

It didn't feel good. Surviving felt great, but even a confirmed

sociopath has to take a pause and take note that he's just joined
the Clan of Cain.

Delia put her hand on my arm and left it there. 'You reacted
in the moment, like a normal person. You're not trained in how
to deal with that.'

I wiped my eyes and laughed that pitiful laugh you produce
when you're absolutely fucking crying like some huge baby.
'I'm self-taught.'

'In the Bureau, if you ever take a life, no matter how justified, there's a whole procedure. Counseling, time off. And we're
trained for it.'

'His fucking head . . .' I turned away, looking out the side
window at my own faint reflection. 'I just react. I do whatever
I need to do. You know?'

She squeezed my arm in response.

'Oh, goddammit,' I said wearily.

'How did you get Breen?' she asked.

'I set his pants on fire.'

She laughed and so did I. It was funny. In a horrible way,
probably. I admit I was confused by the addition of moral
considerations to my thought processes.

'He had me zip tied but I got my cigar torch . . .'

'That was smart and resourceful. And not in the FBI training
manual.' My God, she was pitying me.

'I'm told I'm also tall and symmetrical.'

'Let's go to your place. We'll have a drink.'

I sensed her about to add, *just a drink*, so I beat her to it.
'Relax. Even I know when I'm beat.'

Arriving back at the villa we walked straight through the
kitchen, filled a baggie with ice for my face, snagged a bottle of
Talisker and two glasses and went out onto the terrace. We flopped
in chairs, I poured, she offered a toast. 'To narrow escapes.'

'Mmm,' I agreed. 'Speaking of which . . .'

Delia pulled a wry face. 'Okay, you are never going to
mention this again. I was, you know, peeing. Behind a bush.
The sound of, um, I didn't hear him and all of a sudden there
was a hand over my mouth and a knife at my throat. Then
they duct-taped me.'

'Did they search you?'

'Yeah. But my ID was in my purse in the car and they never looked for it. They didn't ask me anything, just trussed me up and left me in the shrubbery.'

'Breen already knew you're a Feeb. How'd you get away?'

'People think because the bad guys on TV use duct tape that it's impossible to escape. Sorry it took me so long, but I had to mess with the tape and that took some time. Then I had to search in the dark for a weapon. One of the neighbors is missing a decorative paving stone.'

'Yeah, you didn't kill yours at least.'

'Luck, David. I could easily have done so.'

We both sipped whiskey and after a while Delia said, 'This smells like iodine.'

'Peat,' I corrected. 'I've got other—'

'Didn't say I didn't like it.'

I sighed. 'All right, Agent Delia, what is your position on evidence obtained by illegal means?'

'It's not admissible in court. Nor is anything subsequently learned as a result of any such illegal means.'

'You'd have used the surveillance video if we'd gotten that far.'

'Not in court,' Delia said carefully.

'Ah. So, you stopped me questioning Breen because . . .'

'Because it's wrong, David. Look, in my mind, I need to be able to see you as a CI, a confidential informant. I can overlook small crimes. Breaking and entering. Illegal surveillance. I can't rationalize turning a blind eye to crimes against humanity.'

I nodded. 'The whole "wrong" thing. Still working on that.'

'I'm not a court,' Delia said, slightly impatient now, waiting for me to get the message.

'Oh, you want to know what Breen told me. Well, as your CI, I can tell you that he is not involved with the Russians. Or ExMil, which he says *are* working for the Russians.' I told her everything Breen had told me – less than he might have.

Was I actually going to burn his eyes out?

Surely not. The mental picture which that summoned was not one I could quite take on board. Did I really have that in me? To torture a helpless man, however much I had cause to be mad at him?

'So, who is he?' Delia pressed when she realized I'd drifted into a reverie.

'Ex-something, Brit, works for Berthold. The guy in the TR6 chatting with Kiriakou while you were running in slow motion through the waves wearing nothing but a Baywatch suit. At least that's how it is in my memory, but I have taken a blow to the head.'

'Money and kids,' Delia said. 'So, we're right and it's two operations, not one.'

I nodded. 'Berthold, Breen and his boys on one side, probably with Kiriakou. Bristle, Baldy and the banker on the other. Not sure where your guy Panagopolous comes into it, but Breen thinks he's with the Russkis.'

'And still no idea who killed Ramanda.'

I smiled because she'd said 'Ramanda.' 'Two ops. The trafficking thing, worth maybe a few million and very high-risk. The money laundering thing worth maybe billions and relatively low risk. If I'm the boss running both ops, what do I do? I shut down the low-pay, high-risk operation. Minimize risk, maximize income.'

'Maybe money isn't the only motivation,' Delia said.

Sometimes it just takes a single, small, even tangential thought. Like 'maybe money isn't the only motivation.' I closed my eyes. I didn't like that it had taken me so long to get to the answer. And I didn't like the answer I'd come to. 'Who in the criminal world is not all about money? Fucking short-eyes.'

Delia nodded. 'The Russians are about money. The trafficking operation is about money, but also about raping children. That's why they don't just fold it up like any smart businessperson would, because it's not just far-off Saudis or whatever exploiting these children; it's happening here, on Cyprus too.'

'The Russians want it closed down because they're afraid it'll draw focus to them, make them vulnerable.'

'What's the connective tissue between the two ops?' Delia wondered aloud. And answered her own question. 'Feed the Forgotten. They do their banking through AZX Bank. The Russians catch on to Feed the Forgotten's slaves-for-cash scam and recognize the advantage in using a corrupted NGO for their own purposes.'

'And?'

'They won't want to disrupt the system, they want to keep it largely intact and exploit it. They just want the trafficking to stop.'

'If Ramanda gives you Nestor Panagopolous, then . . . what?' I wondered aloud. 'Why does she have to be killed? Is it traffickers or Russians who need her dead? Pedos or money launderers?'

'It has to be the pedos,' Delia said. 'Agent Kim and I were here to ID Panagopolous so we could take him down on the Sicily trafficking thing and use it as leverage to squeeze him for information on Russian money laundering. It was supposed to be a two-fer.'

'Wait,' I said. 'The primary beneficiary of a dead Ramanda is Panagopolous, right? He's the guy she was giving up.'

'But he seems to have a foot in both camps, the pedos and the Russians. He works for ExMil and banks at AZX. But we also know he's a trafficker, or at least was.'

'Maybe he's the go-between, the guy negotiating a separation between the two operations. Like a Wall Street lawyer working out a divestiture deal. The Russians don't want to burn the pedos, they don't give a damn about kids, they just want that whole thing as far away from them as possible. Which means getting the pedos off Feed the Forgotten's cash flow. The pedos don't want war with the Russian mob, but that whole NGO scam has been working pretty well for them.'

I think we reached the same conclusion at the same time. I let her say it first.

'The pedos killed Ramanda,' Delia said. 'They were most directly threatened if Panagopolous was busted and flipped. And they wanted to send a message to the Russians: we can play rough, too. And we will take risks . . .'

She frowned, sensing that last bit wasn't quite right. 'Worse than that,' I said. 'They were signaling that on Cyprus they can do anything they like, as publicly as they like, because at least at this end of the country, the Paphos end, the British expat end, they had nothing to fear from public displays of ruthlessness.'

'Kiriakou.'

'Kiriakou,' I agreed. 'When can you arrange a very public murder and use it to send a message? When you're the cops.' I had my phone and opened my WhatsApp. 'I'm texting my credit bureau guy.'

'Applying for a mortgage?'

'Finding out if Kiriakou has kids,' I said. 'After he confronted me at the mall, he bought a few things, including something from a kid's clothing store. And I remember kids' clothes on his credit card. My sex-worker friend fingered him as a danger to kids and like an idiot I assumed she meant he was just on the take. But Kiriakou shows up at Petra Romiou and is followed too soon by Berthold who just happens to be a board member of Feed the Forgotten. Berthold, who employs Breen and evidently has a desperate desire to stop us from poking our noses into things. And Kiriakou, according to Dame Stella, asked to attend the party and meet me. Why? Because he's protecting the Russians? No, because Kiriakou is all about keeping the murder investigation from going anywhere, and I'm a wild card they weren't expecting.'

Delia nodded. 'If I were here in an official capacity, I'd contact local authorities and get a warrant to search both Kiriakou and Berthold's homes and offices.'

I cocked an eyebrow at her. 'You know I can still hear the ellipses, right? The dot-dot-dot?'

'I would certainly never advise you to do anything illegal,' Delia said without the slightest conviction.

'Right. You draw the line at torture, but not at a bit of second-story work.' I was about to call her a hypocrite, but the truth was we were pretty much on the same page. In fact, we were both in compliance with the prison code: property crime was one thing, child rape was a whole different monster. If Delia wanted to slice the cake that way, fine by me: it left me on her side, and, to my own surprise, I wanted that. I nodded. 'Yeah, okay, I can live with that.'

My credit bureau guy was up, it being just four p.m. on the west coast of the US. My app dinged. Two words: *No kids*.

I smiled and showed my phone to Delia.

'Kiriakou wears cheap clothes and shoes, shows no sign of corrupt money. But he's childless and buys kids' clothing,' Delia said. 'And can't locate one of the few Africans on this all-white island.'

I thought it over for a while and Delia let me do it. She was watching the hatching of a crime. I knew Kiriakou's address in Tala, a large suburb of Paphos best known for being the ancestral home of Cat Stevens. Well, best known by Cat Stevens fans, anyway. Cyprus, unfortunately, does not have Google Street View, but I pulled up both the grid view and the satellite view on my laptop and I did not like the look of it.

I sighed and said, 'He's a cop, living in a tight cluster of homes. He'll have neighbors with eyes out for him, and he's married so his wife may be home during the day. And he's careful, it's not like he'll leave a signed confession lying out on the kitchen counter. But you know what? Just realized something. It's not his house we want, it's where he goes. It's his car.'

'You're going to tail a cop in a Mercedes? Or even in my rental car?'

'Nope. We're going to track him. I have the two GPS trackers I took off my car. I'll download the apps and see if I can get one or both working. Failing that we can just plant an iPhone and use the find-a-phone feature.'

'You still need to get it on his car,' Delia said, 'And neither of us is inconspicuous or unknown to Kiriakou.'

'I will do it.'

Delia and I jumped and spun around and one of us yelped in surprise.

Chante stepped out onto the patio wearing men's boxers and a tank top emblazoned with a faded Ramones logo. She was cute enough, if you didn't know she was evil, and she was acutely aware of being semi-clothed. Not because of me, of course, but because of Delia whom Chante favored with a shy smile.

There followed the inevitable protests from me, demanding to know what the hell she was doing sneaking up on us at two in the morning, followed by the equally inevitable bland explanation that the plumber had not come, so of course she was on my couch, it was hardly her fault that I was so unobservant as to not have seen her.

For the life of me I could not explain how it happened, but somehow I was the jerk. Again.

'How much did your hear?' Delia asked her.

'Everything since I heard your voice, Delia.' She leaned over my laptop, aiming her drooping neckline in Delia's direction, and swiped around the maps application, looking for police headquarters. 'There it is.'

I annoyed my credit-bureau guy again and it cost me another five bills to find out the make and model of Kiriakou's car. A five-year-old, tan VW Golf. There was only really one obvious route from Kiriakou's home to his place of work. We could position Chante at an intersection on a scooter and she could track Kiriakou the last few blocks and see exactly where he parked his car.

Delia said, 'Chante, I have to tell you that this may be dangerous. There are some bad people involved, possibly a bad policeman.'

'It is nothing.'

Delia put her hand over Chante's on the table. 'Listen to me, I'm not joking. I can't have you getting into trouble on my account.'

'It would not be for you, Delia,' Chante lied huskily. 'But for the refugees. My family, too, were once refugees.'

And damned if Chante didn't pull it off, because by nine a.m. the next day, we had a tracker on Kiriakou's car.

And oh, the places he went.

TWENTY-NINE

While my uninvited semi-roommate was crawling under Kiriakou's car for love of Delia, I drove up to the gate at Kofinou Refugee Funhouse and demanded to see Calix Petrides. I was not waved through, rather Calix came to see me. She was nervous about it and as we talked she shook her head no again and again, emphatically, for the benefit of anyone watching.

'Mr Mitre,' she said.

'Ms Petrides.'

'I have nothing to say to you.' Big head shake. 'If you had called, I would have saved you the trip.'

'I'll make this quick. The boat that came ashore the other night. My partner counted nine children on that boat. I want to know how many made it here.'

'As I explained the other day—'

'Yeah, I don't have time for the bullshit, and neither do you because I'm guessing you want this over as soon as possible. See, Ms Petrides, there is trafficking in underage refugee kids going on and you don't strike me as a woman who would have any part in that kind of thing. Am I wrong about that?'

Old trick: put them on the back foot then create common ground that gives them a sense of safety. You wouldn't be involved in this bad thing, would you? Come, join me on Team Righteous.

'Of course not,' Petrides protested forcefully. 'If I knew of any such thing—' Another emphatic head shake for any observer's benefit.

'Yeah, yeah, but whoever warned you off me the other day either knew about it, or knew just enough to know he didn't want anyone looking into it. That Irish guy. He's with Feed the Forgotten, isn't he?'

I took silence as confirmation. Her face was troubled, not just nervous, but troubled. The way decent people look when they hear of something heinous. I made a mental note to log that facial expression and try it out myself. It might come in handy.

'When the shit blows up, Ms Petrides, and boy is it going to blow up, it splatters all over the place. If you don't want to be one of the splattered, the time is now.'

She shook her head no and backed away. Even as she said, 'Only six children were taken in from that boat.'

I had Chante's video on my phone. 'See that girl? Beautiful little girl, isn't she? Have you seen her here?'

This time her negative head shake was for me.

I showed her a boy. No, she hadn't seen him, either.

I let her go, drove a few hundred yards away and texted Mustafa.

Telephone pole time.
Where are you?
Out the front gate, walk a quarter mile.
Fifteen minutes.

He made it in ten. The car actually bounced from the weight of him.

'Thanks for coming,' I said.

'No, it is I who must thank you,' he said moistly. 'The other night was . . . it was . . . it had been a long time, you understand. And to meet Minette . . . A wonderful night.'

'How did you get home that night?'

'Oh, Minette drove me in the morning at first light. The sunrise was very beautiful.' He smiled. 'Very beautiful.'

I hated him pretty hard right then, but we had business to conduct, and anyway it was no business of mine if Minette wanted the big lummox instead of someone more refined and sophisticated.

'I came a bit too close to being dead the other night and I could use someone watching my back.'

'Anything,' he said, as grateful as a dog with a T-bone. 'I can never repay you for the many hours of pleasure . . .'

I considered choking him but recognized that my two hands would not go around his water buffalo neck. 'How do you feel about guns?'

That knocked the starry memories of Minette from his head. 'Guns?'

I produced a SIG Sauer that had been Breen's. Delia had the other pistol. 'I'm not a gun person, but some of the people we're dealing with are, and I was able to obtain this one.' Manly understatement, you see. Ruined a bit when I added, 'He was ex-MI6. And there were two of them. Three if you count the one Delia took down.'

But he was no longer listening. He'd taken the pistol, popped the clip, checked the chamber, looked down the barrel, and slid it under his coat. Almost as if he was a guy who was really familiar with guns.

Just then I got a ping from Delia informing me that Chante's GPS was live. Sure enough, when I opened the app there was a bright blue dot where the police station lot was.

We met Delia outside a do-it-yourself store. She'd gathered a few useful things – bottled water, snack food, a couple of half-meter lengths of lead pipe and electrical tape, some thick zip ties, a pair of bolt cutters, a short crowbar, flashlights and two black canvas gym bags.

'Lousy tradecraft,' I chided her. 'You always want to buy some extra stuff to throw off the . . . you know, to confuse people like *you*. And a potential jury.'

We decided on separate cars, that way if we were spotted we'd have a backup vehicle. Chante drove with Delia, I got Mustafa.

Kiriakou was on the move. We followed from a distance, and when he stopped we sent Chante to reconnoiter.

'There was a robbery,' Chante reported back. 'He was called to the scene.'

After that we tracked him back to headquarters, and then to lunch, and then to an apartment building where he entered accompanied by a uniformed officer, and then to a coffee shop.

And then home.

I had spent the entire day with Mustafa and it was enlightening. His view of Middle East history diverged somewhat from the usual narrative. His version was much more exciting and involved overlapping conspiracies dating back to the Knights Templar. But aside from the impromptu history lesson, we had accomplished nothing. The four of us assembled for dinner at a seafood restaurant just out of town and ate fish and drank wine and discussed Minette's movie career with insights from Chante and Mustafa.

Having not seen her movies, having in fact only seen photos on the internet which had only tangentially to do with movies, I sat glumly watching Kiriakou's blue dot as it refused to do anything but sit in his driveway.

Until just after ten p.m., when the dot moved.

'Probably called to a crime scene,' Delia said, but we piled into our cars and went after him. Out of Tala, the suburb where he lived, up into the hill country.

It was full dark with a half-moon obscured by heavy clouds that had been rolling in all evening. The air carried the chill of impending rain. We stayed well back, well out of sight as

Kiriakou drove on and up, on and up. But the maps left little doubt where he was going.

The dot stopped. The satellite view showed us a small cluster of buildings, a farmhouse with a barn and another outbuilding at the end of a half-mile of dirt road. It was the place Panagopolous had stopped off the day before. Checking on the location's security, maybe? Looking for someone, perhaps?

I pulled off before the dirt road and Delia drove up beside me and rolled down her window.

'This is it,' I said.

'There's no way we can drive up that road.'

'Nope.'

We left the cars in the lay-by, as far back from passing head-lights as we could get and started to hike. The possibility of cameras kept us off the dirt and gravel road, so we stumbled over endless rocks, picked our way around bramble patches, avoided stands of cactus and generally took far longer than a half-mile hike should take.

We saw a vehicle's lights coming up the road, strobing through the tree trunks. And ten minutes later, a second vehicle. Delia and I locked eyes and nodded: yes, this was feeling more and more like the place. The place for what, I wasn't sure. I had some ideas, but I didn't like them much and hoped it was just my overactive imagination at work.

Like the world's most mismatched special forces squad, we crept the last hundred yards in total silence, an FBI agent, a giant cockblocking Arab, a mean French lesbian, and a retired gentleman grifter and thief. And there it was: a farmhouse. And a barn. And a shed. And parked in front of the farmhouse, five cars, a BMW, a Citroën, a Toyota RAV, Kiriakou's Golf and a cherry TR6.

'This is when I would normally call for backup,' Delia observed dryly.

'Nah,' I said, playing along, 'and spoil the fun?'

Mustafa had one bag, I had the other. Chante was to be our videographer. Delia and Mustafa had our two guns. I wrapped electrical tape around one of the pipes to form a grip.

I'd felt right, in control, comfortable, with my little data theft from Petrides, and my nocturnal surveillance of the refugee

center, and even creeping Tatiana the banker's house. All of
that was familiar territory, I could regress back into that life
with the ease of sliding my toes into well-worn slippers. But
things had taken a bad turn with Thorne Breen, a bad turn into
danger of the violent kind.

And he represented a threat even now, my friend Breen. He
was Berthold's tool, which meant he'd have briefed Berthold
on our set-to. This could quite easily be a trap we were walking
into. But I thought not. Berthold had all the arrogance in the
world and a high-ranking cop in his pocket, he wouldn't expect
us to go over to the attack, certainly not this soon. He knew
Delia was FBI and would reasonably expect her to make contact
with local authorities, which would be blocked by Kiriakou.

I was holding a lead pipe in my sweaty fist and asking myself
with some seriousness exactly how one would use such a thing.
Wondering how you know when a blow is hard enough but not
too hard. Lead pipes and guns in the night are not part of my
métier – though evidently toilet lids were – and the fear climbing
up my spine was different in kind, not just degree. I could be
killed right here. Tonight. Thirty seconds from now.

I worried, too, that I might run. It had been nice of Delia to
call me brave, but I'm the calculated kind of brave, the cost-
benefits-analysis kind of brave. What I was feeling now wasn't
the hyper-alert, mind-racing-to-analyze-every-bit-of-data kind
of fear that I knew well; that fear was a rush. This was not a
rush, this was dread. I didn't want to be doing this. I didn't
want to be here.

I did not want to be around people with guns. I'm a sneak,
a grifter, a glib bullshit artist with solid brass balls, but bullshit
doesn't work against bullets. A couple of pounds of pressure
on a trigger . . . an explosion of gunpowder . . . a lead slug
flying at a speed measured in feet per second. I'd written that
scene too many times, it was vivid and real in my head.

But what was I going to do, run away and leave Delia and
Mustafa and Chante? The funny thing was that I was too much
of a coward to do that. Not funny 'hah hah,' more funny 'isn't
it ironic, Mr Master Criminal gets his brass balls shot off
following an FBI agent.'

I sucked air and tried not to sob on the exhale.

We decided to start with the shed, which was nearest to the edge of the trees and farthest from the light spilling from the farmhouse windows and peeking through the seams of the barn's timbers.

The shed was padlocked. Delia whispered, 'If we cut it, there's no way to hide the fact.'

'I got this,' I said, pretty smug, and set to work with my picks and just like the movies had it open in three seconds . . . or possibly twenty minutes of whispered cursing and searching for dropped picks in the dirt, all without managing to inhale completely because my heart was beating the air out of my lungs.

Mustafa stayed outside, Delia, Chante and I crowded into a space stuffed to the rafters with the implements of farm life: a wheelbarrow, various shovels, rakes, hoes and post diggers, a weed whacker, bags of fertilizer, horse tack, bags of oats, and various implements whose use I could not guess.

'What do you think, Delia?'

'I think this is the kind of stuff you might keep in the barn,' she said.

'Unless the barn is being used for something else. Stay here, I'll go peek in the house.'

Delia didn't argue. Of the four of us, I was the go-to guy if creeping around like a burglar was called for.

I plotted a path that kept as much as possible to shadow and hoped to God no one was sitting watching infrared camera feeds.

I ran, stopped, sidled, stopped, ran a bit and flattened myself against the stone wall of the house. I heard nothing inside. The windows were open so I peeked in one and saw an empty kitchen. Peeked in another and saw an empty living room.

I texted Delia: *Barn. Ten minutes.*

I'd thought to bring a knife – the one Breen had thoughtfully provided. If the house was empty, then the parked cars might not be guarded. I crawled in a very undignified way from car to car, slicing tire nozzles as I went. If we had to run, we wanted the bad guys to try and follow in their cars, and that would stall them by five minutes, by which point, if we hightailed down the road, we could be back at our own cars.

I met the other three at the side of the barn nearest the shed.

'Noises inside,' Delia mouthed.

There were two doors, a wide one meant to allow tractors or horses to pass, and a smaller side door on the far side of the building. The large door was locked with a padlocked chain. I peeked around the corner and saw a large fellow of the sort you position beside a door to stop people coming in. We had Mustafa who I'd have bet a few euros on in a throwdown, but a loud fist fight was not the opening move we were looking for. We also had guns, but the guard might as well, and a shoot-out was also not what we were looking for.

I sidled back around to the big padlocked door and nodded at Delia who drew bolt cutters from her pack. Mustafa took them from her and snipped the chain, catching it before it could rattle down and make noise.

He drew the door back and revealed a dark, dusty-smelling chamber that housed three stalls containing two horses, both of whom looked us over and went back to ignoring *homo sapiens*.

The barn had been cut in half by a sheetrock wall tacked up over a lattice work of exposed lumber. There was no door connecting the two halves of the barn, which was unfortunate. I heard music coming through the partition, and the murmur of voices. Then a sharp sound that sounded like a slap, followed by a child's whimper and men's laughter.

'OK,' I said, pretending to have a confidence I did not feel. 'We go in the door past the guard. Mustafa, around the barn, if you would. And we need a diversion that won't look like a diversion.'

'I've got that,' Delia said. 'Chante, will you help me?' Delia pulled a folding map from her handy backpack, and we waited until Mustafa had had time to circle around. Then Delia and Chante stepped out into plain view, both peering at the map by flashlight, two lost hikers who were somehow wandering around in the dark in the middle of nowhere at night.

'Oh, hi!' Delia said to the guard, adding a low, baffled laugh not audible beyond a few feet. 'Do you speak English? We appear to be lost.'

The muscle stiffened, relaxed, took a step and then decided to kneel down in the dirt right after Mustafa hit him in the head with a lead pipe.

Mustafa did a quick search, drew out a pistol, looked at me, and said, 'Do you want it?'

The alternative was giving it to Chante, so I took it. A burglar or confidence man who carries a gun is a damned fool but I had at least handled guns and I was pretty sure (hoped) that Chante had not. In preparing to write Joe Barton's adventures in New Midlands, I'd gone to Las Vegas and fired a wide range of weapons. Research! So I knew to draw the slide and check to see if I had a round in the chamber. And I knew to look for the safety. After that, it was mostly down to pointing and squeezing and being shocked at the noise, as I understood it. I stuck the scary thing in my pocket and kept a tight grip on my lead pipe.

I looked to Delia. We were past the stealthy spying and breaking-and-entering phase now and coming to the door-kicking, for which she'd been trained.

'Chante pulls the door,' Delia whispered. 'I go in left. Mustafa? Right behind me, and go right. David? Don't accidentally shoot me in the rear end. No shooting, we want control, not mayhem.'

I took a deep breath while my mind replayed every cop door-kicking scene in every TV show or movie I'd ever seen as well as the ones I'd written. Most were reassuring. But I focused much harder on the ones that were not.

'Three . . . two . . .' Delia nodded at Chante.

THIRTY

Chante pulled open the door, Delia rushed past her, Mustafa a split second behind.

'Freeze!' Delia yelled, and it was so authoritative that for a second I froze. 'No one moves! You, on the ground!'

I went through, pipe hanging limply by my side.

The layout of the room was not the first thing I noticed. But it's the safe place to start. The stalls on the partitioned side of the barn had been continued on this side, four of them, but improved by extending sheetrock to a false ceiling, making what looked like little offices in an unfinished building. Each had a door and each door was closed. The cubicles were roughly half of the total space, the rest was a sort of parlor, a faux Victorian pastiche with an upholstered love seat, and two leather easy chairs. An oak mantel had been nailed to the wall and a little electric heater glowed red where a fire should have been. Light came from three mismatched lamps.

But before I noted all of that, I saw the framed photographs on the walls.

I am not now, nor ever, going to describe what was in those photos. If I knew where those memories resided in my brain, I would take an icepick . . .

I moved without intention, just moved toward the door of the first stall. It was not locked. I pulled the door open and saw a naked man just getting to his feet, and a naked little girl who was bleeding, and I smashed my pipe into Kiriakou's face and pushed him down and kicked him and straddled him and laid the pipe into his face again and again as he shouted and cried and I didn't give the slightest fuck what he had to say because I wasn't really there, some other person, thing, force had control of my body.

It was Chante who pulled me off. She must be stronger than she looks because I didn't make it easy; I was still aiming for a solid kick to land with pointed toe in just the right place, but Chante pulled me back, out of the room and pushed me into one of the chairs.

I sat there stunned for a moment, stunned not just by what I'd seen, what I was still seeing, but by my own reaction. I do not lose control. I do not ever lose control. Ever. There is no secret David Mitre, who gets a few drinks in him and loses control.

I looked at the pipe in my hand. The business end was covered in blood and bits of tissue and hair, and I was glad I'd forgotten the pistol in my pocket because guns put an end to things and I had not wanted things to end. I had wanted to beat Kiriakou until he was crippled, disfigured, mutilated. I had wanted to beat him till he was paste. A red stain.

I blinked and realized that I'd been gone for a few minutes. Not participating in reality, you might say. In a fugue state.

Mustafa and Delia had been busy doing useful things like dragging naked and semi-naked men off terrified children, whipping on zip ties and settling them on the floor after only the minimum necessary roughness. Although one man who'd resisted Mustafa had an arm at an angle you don't see in a medical diagram.

Four naked or mostly naked men lay face down on the frayed oriental carpet, all with hands held tight behind them with zip ties. Kiriakou was bleeding from every part of his face. His nose was barely discernible. His lips were shredded, gushing blood. A tooth knocked out by its roots poked through his left cheek.

I wondered if I should feel ashamed. But honestly the phrase that came to mind was from the Old Testament: *And God saw everything that he had made, and, behold, it was good.*

Kiriakou forced open one eye, the other being covered in blood, and glared at me.

'Yeah, you go ahead and eyeball me, asshole. I'll pop that fucking eyeball out with my thumb and mail it to your wife.'

Pretty sure that amounted to a threat of torture and was, therefore, *wrong*. And yet it felt just fine and Delia did not leap to intervene.

The girl who'd been Kiriakou's victim, another girl and a boy of maybe six clung to Mustafa. I don't know how those children knew to trust the giant, scary man, but some instinct led them to him and they weren't wrong. He was an oak tree and they clung to his trunk. Mustafa's eyes blazed with rage and pain and tears rolled down his cheeks. I suppose it was a good thing that we didn't have any telephone poles handy.

Chante was holding a girl, a toddler, a little kid who should just be learning her letters.

No children looked to me for comfort. I'm not that guy, I guess. And they may have been put off by Kiriakou's blood spattered all over my face.

Berthold was one of the men face down. He was yelling, outraged, furious, demanding to know who the hell we thought we were and I just . . . went away again for a moment and snapped back to reality only when I felt Delia's hand on my shoulder, restraining not comforting.

'David, no. No.'

I stepped back. Twice now I'd lost it. This was not me, this was not Martin or Carter or Alex or any of the me's I'd ever been. 'Take these,' I said through gritted teeth, and handed the pistol and the pipe to Delia.

They had a sideboard, our gentleman child rapists, and three crystal decanters. The brown one looked like whiskey and I poured myself three fingers and gulped it down.

I sat down again and locked eyes with Berthold. 'Give me a fucking excuse, you piece of shit.'

Weird, I guess, but in a gang consisting of an FBI agent, a giant Arab and an exceptionally rude Frenchwoman, I was somehow in the role of 'bad cop.' As a professional writer, I had good command of language, so I said, 'I won't kill you, motherfucker, I will slice off your cock and make you eat it and as you're chewing, I will put a fucking bullet in your fucking spine and you can spend the rest of your evil fucking life as a dickless old man in a wheelchair pissing through a tube.'

It was the specificity that sold it. That plus the absolute conviction in my voice, because I meant it, I absolutely meant it. And, again, the face dripping Kiriakou's blood must have looked a bit grim.

Chante said, 'I have video, and by now it is in the cloud and in Mr Mitre's lawyer's inbox.'

That calmed everyone down, including me. That was the nail in the coffins of all four men, and they knew it.

Delia said, 'Chante, Mustafa, would you take the children outside? Leave your phone on that table, leave it taping, but the children need to be out of here.'

When they had all gone, Delia looked at me. 'Are you okay?'

Okay? I was sick through and through, shocked at the creature I'd turned into, every muscle fiber in my body twitching, and still on a hair trigger. 'Never better.'

Kiriakou was moaning in pain and spit out another tooth. We found their clothing and pulled out wallets and phones. Both of the unknown men were British expats, UK passports, local driving licenses.

We dragged Berthold into one chair and Kiriakou in another. Kiriakou looked like a balloon a week after the birthday party.

He was drained, emptied out. He was a cop: he knew just how hopeless his life was now.

Berthold was a different story. He still thought he had juice. He still thought he was somebody.

'Mr Berthold,' Delia said, pulling the table closer so she could perch on the edge and look into his face, 'we are going to have a conversation.'

'Call my lawyer, nigger.'

And I was up, because whatever had happened to my self-control, it was not yet repaired. Delia said, 'No, David,' again. So, I sat back down but drew out my never-used – well, not by me – brass knuckles and put my fingers through the holes. All to one side where Berthold could see and Delia could not. Just in case.

'Let's start again,' Delia said patiently. 'Your life as you've known it is over, Mr Berthold. Whoever you thought you were, that's over. As of now, there is not a single person in the expat community, or in the wider world, who will speak so much as a single syllable in your defense.'

She paused to let that sink in, and I could see that it did. Disbelief, denial, and the slow, sickening dawn of realization that it was the truth. I fed on his dread, I reveled in it.

'You are going to spend the rest of your life in a prison cell. But there are bad prison cells, and then there are infinitely worse prison cells. Isn't that right, Mr Kiriakou?'

Kiriakou said nothing, just turned blood-rimmed eyes toward me. I gave him a cheeky wink.

'There are places where a child rapist like you, Mr Berthold, becomes nothing but an object to be passed around by bigger, stronger men,' Delia went on in a serious, measured voice. 'There are prisons where the guards train up new recruits by having them beat short-eyes half to death. Prisons where you'll be in your cell and someone will throw a cup of sulfuric acid in your face and the guards will take their sweet time about intervening.'

I showed teeth stained with Kiriakou's blood.

'Ever hear of rectal prolapse?' Delia asked, as if she was genuinely concerned. 'As a person devoted to the rule of law, I absolutely deplore it, but . . . well, sometimes a prison gang rape can go on for hours. Twenty or thirty cons, one right after the other. The rectum comes loose. It basically . . . falls out.'

Give Berthold credit, he'd managed to look tough for a few minutes there, but 'prolapse' did it. He knew he was hearing the truth. I watched as the fear grew inside him.

'See, what you want right now, Berthold, what you need desperately,' Delia explained patiently, 'is a criminal charge that will get you extradited back to the UK. Cyprus only has the one prison, so you'll be in with general population if you stay here. Now, in the UK, they have places for people like you. You're a British citizen, you'd have the advantage of speaking the language. You no doubt have money stashed away . . . you could have a life in a British prison. So, what you want to do is tell me all about the trafficking scam, but be sure to include everything you know about money laundering as well.'

'I want a lawyer,' Berthold snarled.

'So, you want me to call the Cypriot police. Because, see, the two go hand in hand. Once they take you in, it will be days before the embassy sends anyone to check on you. You're going to want that embassy lawyer to come marching in with an extradition request. Otherwise he's going to give you the number of a local defense attorney and that will be the last you hear from the British government.'

Much of this was a lie. No one was ever going to put a good word in for Berthold. But it was a clever lie with just enough elements of truth for a desperate man to grab for. Berthold was at the low point of his life, a point he never expected to reach, and at moments like that you think, *Home.* And if you're Berthold you start to think of friends you may have in government who may have their own peccadillos to conceal. You start to think maybe, just maybe, I can save myself.

If I get home.

'I'll tell you some things,' Berthold said, and damned if he hadn't regained just a bit of his natural arrogance.

'You two will want some privacy,' I said. I stood up, my body still vibrating weirdly, something beyond the familiar adrenalin burn-off. I grabbed Kiriakou by the neck and dragged and pushed him out the door. Mustafa went back for the other two. We dumped the three partially-clothed men against the barn wall, their asses in the dirt.

Chante had all four children dressed and huddled together in the back rows of the Toyota RAV with the engine running the heater. I don't suppose Chante would have been my first choice to comfort traumatized children, but she was willing.

'I had to change the tire,' Mustafa said to me, raising a suspicious brow. 'Someone slashed one tire on each car.'

I nodded. 'Must be a tough neighborhood.'

I called Father Fotos and woke him up, because atheist hypocrite that I am, his big, gloomy church seemed like a safe place. He would know the right social services. Poor man, I'm sure he'd taken some tough calls in his time as a priest, but none worse than that one.

When I was done, I noticed Mustafa eyeing me curiously. 'I had not guessed that you were a violent man.'

I shook my head. 'I'm not. Maybe a couple of fistfights in my whole life. It was just . . .' I didn't have a word for what it was just. Finally, I said, 'Like it wasn't me. What a cliché. "I was a bystander, Your Honor. It was like someone else just rose up and . . ."' God, I wanted to cry. But I'm a big, strong, manly man and we're not supposed to do that.

'Ah, then you lied, Mr Mitre. Do you recall me asking you whether you were a good man? And you said, "Not really." What you should have said was yes, because there is good and evil in us all, but *Inshallah*, when the moment of crisis comes, it is the good that takes over.'

I sighed. 'The "good" almost beat a man to death.'

Mustafa laughed and did a shoulder hug thing that did not quite snap my collarbones. 'Almost, David. *Almost.* You had a gun in your pocket, you could have killed him.' Then he sort of lifted me to where he could look me in the eyes. 'What did you do with the gun?'

'I gave it to Delia.'

He nodded and patted my back. 'Yes, good idea.'

I couldn't look at the children. I don't even like children; hell, I don't like people, period, let alone children. I couldn't explain to my own satisfaction why I had lost my mind. Stress. Too many close calls. A visceral need to draw a sharp, clear line between me and them? Guilt over what I'd almost done to Thorne Breen? And maybe, I suppose, some things from my own childhood. Best not to dwell, I told myself.

Best not to indulge in analysis when there was work to be done.

We called the Cypriot police. Chante had already emailed them video of the scene, including video of Kiriakou blowing red snot bubbles as he slumped naked. I had checked that none of the footage showed my face, then suggested she forward a copy to the local newspapers as well.

We dragged Kiriakou and the other two back inside their little barn of horror and slipped a zip tie through the latch so even if they somehow got their hands free they wouldn't be getting out.

'I guess it'd be wrong to set the place on fire,' I said to Delia as we settled into my car.

'Listen, David, we have agents who work on tracking kiddie porn. They get therapy, a lot of it. No one can stand it for long. It touches something deep.'

'They're just little kids, that's the . . .' But I didn't know what it was, so I finished with a lame, 'You know?'

'I know.'

Silence for quite a while as I drove through the night. I pulled into the curved driveway of Delia's hotel. I caught sight of myself in the rearview mirror, illuminated by the ghastly neon of the hotel's entry. I looked like a survivor of a slasher movie.

I was goddam proud of that blood on my face.

Police lights came blazing up the road and passed us, heading toward the barn. They would question the men, ask them who had done this to them. My name would come up. Which meant one way or another I was leaving Cyprus.

'I suppose beating Kiriakou was wrong,' I said.

'Illegal, certainly,' Delia said. 'If this were the US and I had authority, I would arrest you even though no jury I've ever heard of would convict you and few prosecutors would be foolish enough to try. But wrong? Beating an officer of the law who used his office to rape children?' She actually ruffled my hair. Like I was her kid and I'd scored a goal. 'I suspect, David, aka Martin, that you've never done anything more right in your life.'

THIRTY-ONE

Berthold had told Delia everything. Once he'd started, she almost couldn't shut him up. The names of three more Brits, a Swede, a Frenchman and two Cypriots, all involved in the trafficking ring. He wasn't the kind of guy who would take the rap by himself, he was the kind of man who thought he'd get better treatment by giving up subordinates.

Berthold had bought Delia's logic *in toto* and he bent over backward to construct a case for extradition. He had profited personally from the trafficking and had paid no taxes on it. He had used classified information from his time at MI6 and from contacts there to blackmail and extort, first in Sicily and then, when that operation came apart, on Cyprus. He had also used his position to subvert Feed the Forgotten, a British-registered NGO, and enrich himself.

And yes, he had ordered the murder of a British national, another corrupt former agent. He'd had her murdered on the beach because Ramanda had brought FBI to the island in pursuit of the very man who was the connective tissue between the traffickers and the money launderers. It had been a dual message to the Russians that he was in control and they had no reason to be concerned, and that he would not be easily intimidated because he was a protected man who owned a highly-placed cop and could do whatever he liked on Cyprus.

Deep down, Berthold believed that once passions cooled we'd see that he was an important man, a man who had once worked in a senior position in government, a man who would be shown some consideration if he cooperated.

Amateur.

He might be an ex-spy and an evil bastard, but he did not know how police and prosecutors think. The Cypriots, the Italians and the British all had stacks of felony charges to play with now, and they would between them conspire to ensure that wherever he ended up, it would be the place most likely to destroy him.

Which left Panagopolous and the Russians. And there, too, Berthold had been very helpful.

I made a two a.m. call to my blue-water sailor, Dabber.

'Unh?' he said.

'We met in a bar a few days ago. You remember?'

That woke/sobered him a bit. 'Yeah?'

'If you have your boat at the Paphos dock before nine a.m., I will hand you an envelope with five thousand euros. We will take a short sea voyage and return to Paphos, where I will hand you another five thousand.'

Had he been alert, he might have tried to bargain, but he was too slow and I hung up on him.

I showered off Kiriakou's blood and decided to just sort of sit down in the bottom of the shower for a while. I suppose that's my safe place. It must have been quite a while because I was interrupted by a soft knock on the bathroom door.

'It's me,' Chante said. 'Delia requested I check on you.'

I toweled off and slipped on a robe and headed straight for the whisky. 'Want one?'

'I have one,' Chante said.

It was chilly out on the terrace. Rain had fallen while I was showering and the chairs were wet, but it felt clean and fresh. Chante sat opposite me.

'How about you, Chante?' I asked. 'You okay?'

She'd been crying. So had I, but I could blame the shower.

Chante's mouth twisted. She jabbed a rigid index finger against her forehead and I understood. Neither of us had a visible wound, but we'd been hurt just the same. There was a poison in our minds and it would take a long time to flush out.

I nodded. I raised a glass and said, 'To Delia.'

Chante raised hers and growled, 'Not just to Delia.'

I said, 'You're right. To the big man. And to you, Chante.'

'Not just,' she said again, and damned near made eye contact with me.

It was by far the nicest thing Chante had ever said to me. Granted it was just two words and I wasn't actually named, but still . . .

She held up her phone. 'I've uploaded everything again, for certainty. Now I am going to sleep,' she said and walked into the living room without another word.

It took me longer. In fact, I ended up drinking myself to sleep right there on the terrace. At some point in the night, I must have regained consciousness for long enough to fetch a blanket, because when I woke to my insistent phone alarm at seven thirty, my bedroom duvet was spread over me.

I made coffee and toast while Chante fried eggs and sausage and mushrooms and grilled a tomato – everything but the beans and the blood pudding – to make a full English.

Delia arrived just as we were sitting down and only then did I notice that Chante had made breakfast for three.

We could have all used some sunlight, but the clouds gave us only glimpses, and the breeze was stiff enough to tear the tops off waves out in the Mediterranean. We didn't say anything more than 'pass the salt,' for a while.

'Mustafa?' I asked after a while.

'He speaks Arabic, Father Fotos does not, so he will stay with them for a while.'

'Underneath all that big and scary, Mustafa's a dad,' I said, and thought, *Or at least he was.*

'Thanks for breakfast, Chante,' Delia said, giving her number one killer smile. Then, to me, 'Will your man be there?'

'I think so. If he's sober.'

Dabber was not sober, but he was there with his boat tied off to the mole, looking sweaty and anxious, but still playing the part.

'I didn't know you'd be bringing two such lovely ladies aboard,' he said, doing a sort of bow as we hopped onto the deck. 'G'day, miss,' he said to Chante. 'G'day, miss,' he said as well to Delia, but I could see that she set off alarm bells. He shot me a panicky look.

I laughed. 'Yeah, she's a cop, Dabber. But she's cool.'

'Yes,' Delia agreed drolly, 'I'm one of those cool cops.'

We set off to sea and as we bounced along Chante did some throwing up so Dabber tossed her a blister pack of Dramamine. Then Dabber pulled me aside to ask, 'What's all this, then, mate? What are we about?'

'Not what I ever expected to be doing,' I said. I showed him map coordinates on my phone.

'That's just open water,' he protested.

'It won't be tonight,' I reassured him. Unless of course Berthold had misled us. The refugee pressure was growing and he'd had high hopes for increased profit and more children to rape.

Why was it that the photos on the wall of that barn were what came to mind? Because I'd been unprepared for them? Because they were sickening trophies that testified to minds so dark there was no place for them in the human race? Because the actual children . . .

Bingo, that was it. I could recall the photos and just feel disgust. I could keep a handle on that. The actual kids . . . that was going to be hard to think about. Forever.

Delia was standing in the bow despite the spray and the wind, which pushed fitfully at her windbreaker, outlining arms and chest. Her face was wet and I was sure her lips would be pillowy soft and taste of salt, and equally sure that I would never know. I went to stand beside her. It felt not-wrong being with Delia as she closed in at last on her *bête noire,* her cliché unfinished case.

But I'd begun to have my doubts about Nestor Panagopolous. I'd been trying to make sense of his role in all this, and the answer that had come was both logical and improbable.

The *Kute Koala* or whatever the hell the boat was called was no speedboat, but it managed a respectable ten knots and the sun was just dipping toward the western horizon when we reached our spot.

'Now what?' Dabber asked, a can of beer in hand.

'Now we wait,' I said.

'And what are we waiting for, exactly?'

'Well, Dabber, we are pretending to be fishing, and we are waiting on two boats set to rendezvous about two miles east of here.

'I don't suppose you know where these two boats are coming from?'

'One is coming from Alexandria,' I said. 'The other will be coming from Limassol.'

Dabber might be a broken-down old drunk, but he was not stupid. He liked zero parts of that story.

'You're either smuggling hashish or refugees, mate,' he said darkly. 'I didn't sign on for neither.'

'Well, captain, it isn't hash. And if this goes well, you will have another five on top of what I've already promised. Fifteen large for a day's ride is good pay.'

'Not if I end up in prison with my boat seized.'

'No prison,' I assured him. 'Possibly death, but no prison.'

'Bloody hell,' he said. 'And, I'll add, a hearty fuck-you. We are heading back and you can keep the money.'

Delia had joined us in time to hear that last bit and I knew that she had a gun, and that no power on earth was going to stop her from getting Panagopolous. But before we reached the point of threats, I said, 'Dabber, I don't know you, but I know you've done some things you're not proud of. Me too. But if this works out, you'll be the man who saved some lives.'

He snorted derisively. 'That and a fiver will buy me a pint.'

'You're right, it won't buy you a damned thing, though the money will. But it will give you something better.'

'What's better than money?'

I did not wink at Delia, that would have been too much. But I felt her listening, as I said, 'It will buy you redemption, Dabber. You're a drunk, and a bit of a cheat, a bullshit artist, a hustler. We both know you've broken some laws, right?' He did not rush to deny it. 'And we both know that's not the worst of it, because it never is. You've done things that don't set right with you. Things you wish you could take back.'

He tried to bluster. 'You don't know anything about—' But I waved that away.

'Don't try to con a con. Sin and redemption, Dabber. Sin and redemption. Do this one good thing. Just this one good thing.' He gaped at me, confused, glanced at Delia, more confused. So I said, 'It doesn't mean you enter a monastery, captain. Jesus, I'm not here to save your soul; if there's a hell, I imagine we'll meet up there eventually, you and me. You can go right on being a drunken hustler and smuggler and general reprobate. But you'll have this one good thing you did.' I patted his heart, showing him where he could store his 'one good thing.'

He opened his mouth but nothing came out. Tried again and again, nothing. Then, with an expression containing bewilderment at himself bordering on panic, he said, 'Well, I'm not sitting here all bloody afternoon, doing nothing. If we're meant to look like we're fishing, then we'd best get the gear out.'

We did, and for hours as the sun sank toward the horizon and the clouds went from gray to mauve to blazing orange, we fished. I'd never been deep-sea fishing before and I honestly cannot recommend it. It's hard on the shoulder and arm muscles holding a great long fiberglass pole while dragging a baited hook around a mile above the bones of a thousand lost ships. No matter what anyone tells you, there's no real skill involved, as evidenced by the fact that the one serious bite I had managed to escape, while Chante landed a twenty-pound grouper.

I hadn't actually seen 'my' fish, but I'm pretty sure it was two or three times bigger than Chante's.

Chante's grouper was tasty, though. Chante cleaned and filleted and fried it up in the galley and we ate hot, crumbling chunks of it with our fingers. Grouper not ten minutes out of the sea, and cans of cold beer – that part of fishing is excellent.

'I may have your boat on radar,' Dabber reported after dinner. He showed us a green dot amid, many other green dots.'

'How can you tell?' Delia asked.

'Direction of travel and speed,' Dabber said, cocky in his sailing knowledge. 'It's making five knots. You could row faster. It must have set out last night.'

'Anything coming from Limassol?'

'Lots of things,' Dabber grumbled. 'But this one here,' he tapped the screen, 'That's on an intercept course, and it's doing maybe fifteen knots.'

'When it gets here, it will look like Cypriot Marine Police.'

'Bloody hell. And then what's the plan?'

I shrugged. 'They'll go for the refugee boat. We will wait and watch. Then, we will interfere.'

'That's not a plan,' Dabber protested.

'Here's the thing, Dabber: as you know, I'm a writer . . .'

'Uh-huh.' There was a bit of skepticism in the man's tone.

'. . . and there are two schools of writing. There are writers who plan it all out in advance, plan every detail. And then there are what we flatteringly refer to as 'discovery' writers. Those are writers who start something and figure it out as they go along.'

'Sounds like a bullshit artist, mate.'

'Yeah,' I admitted. 'Kind of does, doesn't it.'

THIRTY-TWO

R ain came in a thin drizzle, enough to reduce visibility to a few dozen yards, not enough to provide an excuse to turn around.

We followed the refugee boat on radar, Dabber using all his skill to make it look to anyone watching us as if we were just a fishing boat heading back toward land after a long day of battling tuna. Delia, Chante and I all watched the glowing screen over Dabber's shoulder, two bright dots converging as we chugged in a straight line toward Ayia Napa, a course that would look entirely innocent and yet would bring us close to the rendezvous.

We calculated that it would take the phony Marine Police boat a good ten minutes to separate out the children they meant to seize. After all, they were maintaining a pretense of legality, they would need to take their time.

Delia was not confident of success. She didn't say anything, kept a brave face all the while, said all the right things, but I knew her a bit by now and she was nervous. I understood why. We were re-enacting the scene from Sicily, but this time with the *Fair Dinkum* in the role previously played by a US Navy destroyer, and with supporting roles played by a drunk, an irritant and a semi-retired felon.

I was if anything even less optimistic. The outcome might rest on how well the enemy – enemies, plural – communicated, how quickly they reacted. I was worried about the refugees but more about Delia. They were general, she was specific. They were 'humanity' about which one is supposed to feel concern;

Delia was a friend. I liked her. We'd had adventures. Someday when we were both old and wearing adult diapers we could sit side-by-side in wheelchairs at the Cops N' Cons retirement home, pass a bootleg flask and talk about the crazy stuff we'd done together back in the day.

I have a friend who is an FBI agent.

What irony-loving god of fate had set that up?

Then Dabber said, 'That shonky police boat is still making speed.'

Delia frowned. 'Could we be wrong? Maybe it's the wrong boat, just someone heading out to sea.'

The hairs on the back of my neck stood up, because I suddenly knew what would happen next.

'Dabber, full speed. Now!'

'Now, hold on a—'

'Goddammit, *now*!'

Delia was looking at me like she suspected I'd slipped a gear, but then her eyes widened.

'They're shutting it down,' I said. 'The Russians are shutting it all down right now.'

I've said it before: there is a difference between a cop brain and the brain of a successful criminal. Cops think in organized channels, in lines that wind their way through law and training and morality, with secondary thoughts of public perception and even career advancement. A smart criminal sees straight lines, bright clear lines that go from what he wants to how he'll get it.

'The Russians know about Berthold,' I explained tersely. 'It's Panagopolous on that boat. He'll have orders to cauterize the wound.'

'Jesus, no,' Delia whispered, eyes searching the dark ahead. *Not again.* She didn't say that, but it was there. *Not again.*

If Panagopolous was watching us on his radar he did not seem to be deterred. But then, this same ploy had worked once before for him, and all he saw in the vicinity was a day cruiser.

I said, 'Chante, get every life jacket Dabber has and look for blankets below. And put on the kettle.' Amazingly, she obeyed instantly.

'You're assuming I'll do the right thing this time,' Delia said and she wasn't at all sure of it. The predator had leapt, she was in the air her claws outstretched and her prey was right there, right there in front of her. She wanted blood.

On the radar screen the two dots converged, one wallowing slowly, the other moving at flank speed.

'Got a spotlight, Dabber?'

He did. I left the bridge and climbed up to the roof, which has an official nautical name which I'd forgotten. I gripped the radio mast with my left hand – the ups and downs and sideways lurches were worse up there – and switched the searchlight on with my right. It stabbed into spray and mist as I swept it up and then left and right.

'I see them. There! At two o'clock.' I yelled down.

The Marine Police boat's wake fluoresced drawing a dim green line in the water that arced past the refugee craft, sloshing gallons of water over the side. Then I saw twinkles of orange light and a second later heard the distant gunshots. *Pop. Pop. Pop.* Six shots. Eight shots. I wondered if they were shooting at the refugees or us, and had that question answered promptly when a lead slug blew out the *Fair Dinkum*'s windshield.

'They've spotted us!' Dabber yelled quite unnecessarily and the engine slowed. Five seconds later the engine accelerated again and I suspect Delia had showed Dabber her pistol.

The phony Marine Police boat had been painted gray, and a plausible logo had been stenciled on the side. It moved on, a hundred, two hundred yards as we closed the gap at agonizingly inadequate speed.

I swept the light right onto what looked like a ship's lifeboat wallowing so low there wasn't six inches of freeboard. Impossible to tell how many people were crammed on that boat. Impossible to know what had happened to these people to motivate them to flee their homes and take to the sea. Impossible to guess what fragile hopes they'd had, hopes they now knew to be doomed.

Panagopolous was not slowing or veering away.

There was not a single damned thing to do but watch.

The faux Marine Police craft aimed, gunned its engine, picked up speed till it was throwing a bow wave, and smashed into the refugee boat with a glancing blow, port bow against starboard bow. We were close enough now to hear the impact. The screams, too.

I glanced at Delia. She was expressionless, standing rigid, fists clenched. I looked back and up at Dabber and saw the old crook cross himself. Chante was in the bow, drenched by each wave the *Fair Dinkum* cleaved, holding a boathook at the ready.

Panagopolous' boat was coming toward us now, but veered away, leaning far over to make a sharp turn. For just a moment I saw him in profile, the Cypriot killer who Delia had chased to this place and time.

He gave us a jaunty wave and sped off north, heading back toward Limassol, job done.

I heard screams, but that word does not do justice to the reality. To my ears those screams were made of terror, but carried also a demand for an answer: why? Why must we suffer? Why must we die? Why was the world doing this to us? For God's sake, all they wanted to do was reach a place where they could clean hotel rooms and haul trash and drive taxis and not be starved or raped or butchered. For that they were to be punished by watching their spouses, their children, drown before their eyes?

A jaunty wave and their killer was off to a nightcap in some Limassol bar?

Delia was beside me. I couldn't breathe for the heaviness of my own heart beating. What we did next was Delia's call and I could not be part of it.

'Which way, miss?' Dabber called. 'I can stop or I can chase, but I can't do both.'

Delia hesitated. For long seconds. We could not catch Panagopolous' boat but we could follow it in, track it, identify it, call the local cops, probably have Panagopolous and his crew arrested. And dozens of people would sink below the waves.

Long seconds grew longer, until Dabber must have been just about to repeat the question.

'Pick up survivors,' Delia said dully, too low for Dabber to hear.

'Rescue survivors,' I repeated at higher volume. It was the right thing. We all knew it. But this was not a rerun for me or Chante or Dabber, we had not vowed to get the bastards

responsible for the atrocity in Sicily. We were not Special
Agent Delia Delacorte watching her prey motor away.

'I'm losing the bastard. Again!' Delia raged. I'd seen Delia
in lots of moods by now, but this was the closest she'd come
to seeming out of control. She drew her pistol and I think would
have started shooting at Panagopolous' boat but for fear of
hitting people in the water.

'Goddammit!' she shouted, unable to stand still, moving like
she was looking for something to kick. 'I will get you, you
motherfucker! I'll get you!'

I was with her on that, and if she needed help from a toilet-
lid-wielding minion, I was ready. But at the same time, the
chilly little reptile that still occupies a part of my brain was
beginning to guess at an alternative ending. I wasn't sure, not
by a long shot, but I was beginning to suspect that Panagopolous
might not make it to that end-of-shift drink in Limassol. Like
I said: cop minds, even smart FBI cop minds, are not criminal
minds.

I put a hand on Delia's shoulder, which she furiously shrugged
off.

'Hey, Inspector Javert—'

'What? What what what?' she yelled, eyes blazing.

'Not entirely sure he's getting away.'

She stabbed a hand toward the boat now fading from view
in the mist. 'Are you blind? We'll never catch him!'

'I'm not sure we need to,' I said. 'The Russians are shutting
this thing down.'

'Fuck the Russians, I want Panagopolous!'

I was pretty sure J. Edgar Hoover would not have approved
of her language. Then again he was a racist old troll so Delia's
language might not have been his first concern.

'Yeah, I got that, Delia. But right now we've got to rescue
these people. Right?'

She nodded tightly, jaw muscles working, nostrils flared,
every bit the frustrated predator.

I told Dabber to call the real Marine Police. And I used
Delia's sat phone to call the RAF rescue group.

We reached the first of the refugees, Dabber slowing the boat
to a coughing, shuddery crawl, Chante extending the boat hook

toward the nearest half-drowned survivor. I joined her and then, after taking another minute to calm down, so did Delia.

We were just hauling the third person over the side when I saw the distant flash of light, way too big to be a gun's muzzle flash. I gripped Delia's bicep and pointed. The light flared orange for a few seconds and then guttered out.

The sound reached us, a flat report, like someone dropping a sheet of plywood. A smack without bass notes or echo.

I yelled up to Dabber on the bridge. 'You still have them on radar?'

He was silent for a minute. Then, 'I did. Now I can't see them.' Then, after another moment, 'Huh. Bloody strange, that.'

I met Delia's eye, brow cocked suspiciously at me. 'I thought, maybe,' I said, shrugging, 'the Russians know Berthold's done, they know Kiriakou's done, and Panagopolous is the connective tissue. They're bringing a big meat cleaver down on the chain of evidence. It was the smart move.'

'Smart.' It came out as a contemptuous snort. It wasn't aimed at me, but it drew some blood just the same. I'd guessed what the Russian bosses would do because it's what I would have done in their place. If I were a killer. If I were one of them.

I drew the mental curtain between them and me, between evil and . . . whatever shade of gray I was. It was a worn, moth-eaten thing, that curtain, but I needed it.

I raised my voice to be heard by Dabber. 'Captain, see anything at all?'

'What might be debris. And it's not moving.'

The RAF chopper got there before the legitimate Marine Police, but by then we had already taken on sixty-two people, men, women and children. Dabber's boat was as crammed and top-heavy as the refugee boat had been. Chante pushed between huddled, terrified people handing out cups of tea, shuttling Dabber's six chipped mugs back and forth to the galley like a waiter working a busy Saturday night shift.

The RAF dropped divers into the sea and saved more people, loading them onto a rich man's yacht and a working man's fishing boat that had both responded to our Mayday call. We found out later that eighty-four people were rescued altogether. The best estimate was that nine had died. Of them, seven had drowned.

The other two had been shot full of holes. They were the traffickers and the Russians would have insisted on them being very dead with no possibility of them washing up alive somewhere to give evidence.

Smart. That word again.

I wondered how it had been done. Surely Panagopolous must have been nervous, must have at least suspected. When he got the order to make damned sure the traffickers were dead, did he not realize what it meant for him? Had he not searched the boat for the bomb he must have feared would be aboard? Or was he such a fool that he believed himself indispensable? Indispensable to guys dealing in billions of dollars?

He would have radioed in to let his bosses know he'd taken out the traffickers and sunk the boat. And they'd have sent the signal, most likely a simple call placed to a satellite phone wired to dynamite or plastique, or whichever explosive was fashionable among the Russians.

And *boom*.

The floor of the Mediterranean is littered with the bones of men and women of many nations and races, some who should have lived, and others who needed to die. Panagopolous and his crew would float and bloat, then rot and sink, and add more femurs and skulls to the Mediterranean's vast underwater collection.

But aboard the *Fair Dinkum* were sixty-two people whose bones would not be added to that grim exhibit. They were alive. And they were alive in part thanks to me.

I didn't know quite what to do with that realization. So, I found Dabber on the bridge necking a bottle of gin and bummed a swig off him.

'One good thing then, eh?' he said with a curious sidelong glance.

'Looks like. How do you feel?'

'A bit off,' he admitted, and made a worried face of the sort one makes when feeling strange and unfamiliar emotions.

'Yeah,' I agreed. We sighed simultaneously. 'I don't think either of us needs to make a habit of this kind of thing, though.'

'Nah, once is more than enough. I do like your woman, though,' Dabber admitted, nodding down at Delia who was passing through the huddled masses taking information down in a notebook, offering smiles to children, kind words to their fathers and a comforting touch to their mothers.

'She's not my woman,' I said.

'Nah? All copper then? All, strong arm of the law, is she?'

'I suppose someone has to be.'

We drank to that. And drank again to the fact that it sure as hell wasn't either of us.

THIRTY-THREE

S pecial Agent Delia Delacorte had failed in her mission to arrest, try and imprison Panagopolous, but he would no longer be a problem. He was currently providing affordable new homes for crabs.

We met up at the tiki bar, Delia, Chante, Mustafa and me. And Theodoros who would have paid me back every tip I'd ever given him if I would just tell him what it was all about. I didn't, but he lurked at the edge of hearing and polished rocks glasses until they were shot glasses, so I imagine he caught the gist.

Kiriakou and the others we'd caught – very much including Berthold – were now in Cypriot custody. The cops were not happy that a gaggle of foreigners had broken up a pedophile trafficking ring and would, I suspected, take that embarrassment out on Kiriakou. I almost felt sorry for him.

Nah. Not really.

We had not arrested the Russian money launderers, never even put a name to any of them. But Delia had more than enough to shut down the use of Feed the Forgotten as a front. The AZX bank records I had, um . . . found on a thumb drive in my shower . . . made their way to Cypriot and British police and prosecutors. That, too, would not stop the money laundering, but it would sting.

Thorne Breen was arrested at the hospital – his burned leg had become infected. The blood infection had gotten so bad he was raving to nurses about some American who'd tried to burn out his eyeball.

Crazy bastard. Like anyone would believe that.

Bristle and Baldy were never heard from again. A reasonable guess is that they were back in Moscow or wherever, explaining to some hard men how they'd managed not to kill a guy they had trapped in an elevator.

And according to Deadline Hollywood, Chris Temple had checked into Promises, a lovely rehab center in Malibu where he would join such distinguished alumni as Robert Downey Jr and Ben Affleck, Iron Man and Batman respectively. Also he had tweeted something vaguely Buddhist. So, there was that.

I debated long and hard with myself on whether or not to make good my promise to Joumana, but in the end I just could not be a guy who stiffed sex workers.

The Cypriot authorities had questioned me until someone from the embassy showed up and spoke some discreet words, presumably at Delia's urging. I was solemnly informed that it would be best for all concerned if I went somewhere else, somewhere that was not Cyprus. Like, soon.

I was flying out the next morning.

'Thanks for everything, Mustafa,' I said and clinked my beer against his properly-observant fruit juice. 'Sorry there were no telephone poles.'

'Something even better,' he said and raised his glass to Delia. 'Justice. Also, I have an offer of employment.'

'No kidding. What's the gig?'

'I am to be an Arabic interpreter. For the police in Nicosia.'

Delia barked a surprised laugh at that. 'Well done, Mustafa. And well done, David, you've now contributed in multiple ways to truth, justice and the law.'

'And got Mustafa laid,' I said without too much bitterness.

'What now for you?' Delia asked me. I liked the way she asked me because it wasn't tinged with suspicion.

I shrugged and blew out my cheeks. 'Damned if I know. I've been invited to fuck off out of Cyprus at my earliest opportunity.'

'So . . .?'

'So, I'll find another nice, sunny place where I can write and eat and drink and chase women. Try to write faster and make up for the piles of cash I've been bleeding for the FBI. But I'm not telling you where, Special Agent Delacorte, I don't make a habit of updating the FBI on my travels.'

I didn't ask her if she would be true to her word and leave my name out of all official reports, it would have been insulting. I thought about making one more pass at her, but we were beyond that. Dammit.

'That's okay, David,' Delia said, her sleepy, mocking smile back again. 'You don't have to tell me where you're going. I'll know.'

'Oh, you're that good, are you?' I teased.

Delia laughed and said, 'I am, actually, Mister quote Mitre unquote. But I doubt I'll need to be. I plan to stay in touch with your assistant.'

'Assistant? I don't have an assistant, I've never had a . . .' I felt the hairs on my arms stand up as the awful truth began to dawn. 'No, no, no, Delia. No.'

'You need adult supervision,' Delia said.

'She's not an adult, she's a harpy! She's the untamable shrew. She hates me!'

'I wouldn't say "hates,"' Delia said, with a wink at Chante. 'There's a certain degree of contempt, maybe . . .' She glanced at her watch. 'I have to go. The rental car counter is slow and I don't want to miss my flight.'

She gave Chante a long hug and they whispered to each other for a few seconds before Chante broke away, wiping at her eyes.

And suddenly there we were, me and Agent Delia, standing before the sparkling Mediterranean, just feet from where a woman had died and brought us together. We looked at each other, not knowing quite what to say.

'Delia, it's been . . .'

'Yes, David, it has been.'

I thought maybe a goodbye hug. Maybe even a brief but tantalizing kiss. But she stuck out her hand and I shook it.

You know, Delia Delacorte, I like the hell out of you. I admire you. I wish I'd grown up to be you instead of me, though if you ever fuck me over, I have plenty of video that will be hard for you to explain. But, that aside, damned if you didn't budge the trajectory of my life and not in a bad way.

I said none of that, of course.

'Take care of yourself, Delia.'

'You too, David,' she said and headed toward the hotel and the parking lot beyond. She stopped on the terrace, turned, hit me with that dazzling smile and said, 'Stay out of trouble, huh?'

'Me? Trouble? I'm redeemed!'

'Not yet you aren't. We'll see.'

And that warning made me happy.

Chante was weeping and for a millisecond I thought of comforting her, but that wasn't ever going to be a good idea. So, I contented myself with softening some of my sullen resentment when I said, 'So. You're working for me.'

'For you?' She blinked and looked past me. 'I work for myself, you only pay me.'

I thought seriously of choking her but I was pretty sure Delia would say that was *wrong*.

'Pay you? I'll feed you, how about that? And let's get this settled right up front: I fly first class, you fly coach.'

There was, I was certain, nothing Chante could say to that, it was only right, only fair.

And yet, by the time I boarded my flight, damned if the creature wasn't in the seat next to mine.